Mariscal Canyon

Dead

by

W. Phil Hewitt

OcotilloPress®

The Mariscal Canyon Dead
By
W. Phil Hewitt

For information address:
Ocotillo Press
8812 Mosquero Circle
Austin, Texas 78748
ocotillopress@yahoo.com

Any resemblance to actual people, events and places is purely
coincidental.
This is a work of fiction.

Cover Design and Art: triuneimage.com
Author photo: Robert Burns, Memphis
Typesetting: Amy Winn

For orders other than by individual buyers, Ocotillo Press grants a
discount on the purchase of 10 or more copies, single titles, for special
markets or premium use. For details, write Ocotillo Press, 8812
Mosquero Cr., Austin, Texas 78748, Attn: Premiums. Or email:
ocotillopress@yahoo.com

For orders by individual consumers, write or email Ocotillo Press,
Attn: Sales, 8812 Mosquero Cr., Austin, Texas 78748

ISBN: 978-0-9823182-0-1
Library of Congress Control Number: 2009911134
Printed in the United States of America

DEDICATION

This one is for Linda. I love you.

FOR EVERYBODY ELSE

I have traveled, rafted or camped the Big Bend country since the 1970s. Its stark beauty, its sunrises and sunsets will change the way you think about light, color and space. It will change your life. I've done Santa Elena in a raft and traveled over much of the national park and Big Bend Ranch State Park. Those 1,200 foot Santa Elena walls will make you rethink your place in the universe. Big Bend is some of the most compelling, awe-inspiring, drop-dead beautiful country on the planet. If there is something else on your "Bucket List," strike it. Go to the Big Bend Country before you die.

THANK YOU, THANK YOU, THANK YOU

I offer eternal gratitude, first, to Linda Gravatti, for putting up with this seemingly endless novel-writing and publishing process. Next, to my co-workers at "one of the largest state park systems in North America," for doing the same. All of them have been unbelievably tolerant. Thanks to all of them.

I thank those who I wrangled or coerced into reading various parts of the manuscript—Robert Burns of Memphis who read this thing in several iterations while on vacation on the Alabama Gulf Coast. He should have been out walking on the beach or kayaking. He is a true friend. Bob Rosenbaum, my friend of over (oh, my God!, 40 years), whose comment, "not enough action ain't your problem," was an inspiration. And most importantly, I wish to thank my friend and expert editor Amy Winn. The book is immensely better for her work.

To David Riskind, co-worker, lunch companion, friend, naturalist, occasional intellectual sparring partner and author who read the manuscript and provided pithy commentary and suggestions—some of which I actually took.

And to the memory of my dear friend Ann Fears Crawford of Beaumont who taught me more about writing than she will ever know. Ann, here's to the next "Great Adventure." I miss you.

And last I want to mention Miss Reilly of Snowden Junior High School in Memphis. She was my English teacher in the eighth grade. She taught all of us, the bright, medium and dim-witted, how to diagram and appreciate a sentence written in the English language. I pity those who have followed, who have not had the opportunity to learn the language as we did—even if we did not like it at the time.

It has been a great ride! (There, that's my exclamation point for this book. We now have that out of the way.)

phil

CHAPTER 1: THE MARISCAL CANYON DEAD

Five bodies lay sprawled in the chalk dust around a campfire circle in those awkward, vaguely obscene positions the suddenly dead assume. Blood splattered everywhere. The desert dust and the walls of the little side canyon were peppered with blood. The turkey vultures didn't even move when I rounded the canyon wall. Bits of flesh hung from more than twenty beaks. They had no interest in sharing. "Beat it. Scram. Go," didn't work. I fired five rounds from the .45 auto that I carry. I nailed three of them that were snacking on the good stuff—eyeballs, cheek meat, forearms, fingers and hands. Life is tough even for vultures in this rough, high desert south Big Bend country. There was enough protein in this small box canyon for several days' fine dining. I must be losing my touch, though. Time was I'da got at least four.

The horses—Pepper, my small white mustang gelding with black specks, and Star, my brown mare packhorse—didn't want anything to do with all that blood and all those strange smells. Neither did Rusty, my Irish Setter–colored, red German shepherd hearing dog.

"Rusty, come." There was no sense in him getting in the middle of what looked like a multiple murder scene. We backtracked to the large canyon turnoff about fifty yards north. I gave Rusty the reins and the packhorse rope and told him to stay. I left him holding the packhorse rope in his mouth and lying in Star's shadow on Pepper's reins.

I reloaded the .45 and pulled the 7x35 binoculars and digital camera out of their pack on Star.

"OK, Rusty, what you think? I'm gonna see what we have here. You stay." He was the one that actually found them, well maybe heard them first. For two days he'd been a pain. He kept nudging Pepper's front legs and finally stood in the way, facing me in that "If you're going anywhere, you gotta go through me" attack stance that shepherds are known for. He saw it as his job to be between me, the horses and whatever was out there. He even growled loud enough for me to hear. I never heard them, the vultures. But then I don't hear much anyway; that's what Rusty gets paid to do.

When I looked back he was lying in the gelding's shadow. It was hot in this canyon. Even in October the Chihuahuan Desert gets warm early in the morning. It felt like ninety degrees already and it wasn't even ten o'clock. The bodies lay in a little box canyon near a pour off. It didn't rain much in this part of the Chihuahuan Desert, but when it did rain here, it RAINED. The runoff poured from the canyon wall fifty feet above us into a series of five- or six- foot diameter stone depressions called *tinajas*. These depressions, sort of like large stone bowls, saved the lives of lots of Comanches, Apaches, Spanish explorers, Mexican vaqueros, and American military surveyors traveling this bitterly beautiful and unforgiving land of the Big Bend. Some *tinajas* are large enough and deep enough to swim in. These weren't, but they still usually held water when everything else was dry. Yesterday I'd talked with two vaqueros who were looking for some stray cattle. They said that these *tinajas* held water almost all year. But five years of drought had left them dry. These guys lying in their own dried blood might have come here for the same reason that I had detoured south of my route—water. I was just disappointed; they were disappointed and dead.

Where you have five vulture-eaten, blood-soaked dead guys, you have somebody who shot them. I climbed up a slight rise just north of the site. Using the little binocs, I scanned the wall across from the camp. Nothing. Then from another angle, I did a 360 and panned the horizon. Nobody; ninguno. I did a second circle (well, as much as I could do on foot in these broken canyonlands) recon around the site to see if whoever did this might still be hanging around. Nothing, nobody, not a track, human or otherwise—well, except for the vulture tracks, a lot of those. A day later and we'd have had coyotes, mountain lions, and God only knows what else picking at the corpses.

It looked like there was nobody here except me, my animals and these five dead guys. Well . . . , there were also the

2

turkey vultures with their six-foot wingspread and those distinctive red heads. A large number of them resumed their lazy circling, riding the thermals a few hundred feet or so above the canyon floor. Three of them lay dead on the canyon floor, their blood soaking into the sand. The live ones were pretty sure that eventually the intruders would leave and they could resume dining on all that tender meat in the little box canyon.

I didn't have much time. I had almost no water. Some son of a bitch had stolen mine from my cache about twenty miles northwest of here. My animals and I had traveled two days over some very rough, broken canyonlands to get to the river for a re-supply. I had about a half-gallon left for the animals and myself and about ten more miles to go. We'd need that half to get us to the Rio Grande near an abandoned homestead called Talley.

It was still early, a little after ten. But by noon this place would be hotter than the hinges of hell. We had an hour, maybe two, to do whatever we were going to do here.

I called Rusty. As he trotted up I reminded him, "Come on, Rusty. Let's get to work. Heel."

I'm mostly deaf and Rusty is a hearing dog. He is my ears. And he's really good at it. We've been together for three years. Hearing dogs don't bark much; at least Rusty doesn't. It wouldn't help much anyway. It would be like barking to himself. I do enough of that for the both of us, talking to myself, not barking, unless you ask my wife Lisa. But Rusty stays close and can get my attention pretty quick when he hears something I should know about. He listens for sounds that don't belong. So Rusty listened intently as we surveyed the murder scene. Me, I was trying to figure out what I could do here.

Before trampling through the site I shot some frames with the digital camera—panorama shots as well as close-ups of the camp using the short telephoto—stuff to set the scene for when I had to explain all this stuff to the state cops, or Border Patrol or park police. Maybe someone could make sense of this later.

I'd seen a few dead people, mostly from car accidents. But walking into the camp still seemed a violation of these men, not that it much mattered now.

3

I shot some close ups first. Rusty stayed near me and thumped his tail against my calf as I thought out loud. I've always talked out loud to myself. Dogs, and horses too, seem to like the sound of the human voice. Parents, wives, children and even co-workers frequently find it annoying. Some even accuse me of muttering all the time.

"That's weird Rusty. These guys have no camping gear, no guns, no packs, no nothing. They're just five dead guys with multiple gunshot wounds." It was like these guys had dropped out of the sky.

Four of them were in uniform. One wore the distinctive U.S. Border Patrol patch. One was Policía de la Frontera, the Mexican counterpart of the U.S. Border Patrol. Another was a National Park Ranger, at least that is what his shoulder patch said. The fourth body in uniform wore the insignia and garb of a Texas Parks and Wildlife Department Wildlife Management Agent. All of them had multiple gunshot wounds, lots of holes, lots of blood. Brass was scattered everywhere; must have been 200 cartridge casings on the ground. From my days of competitive team shooting it looked like these were 7.62mm x 39mm, the most popular ammo in the world.

We sure couldn't take these guys with us and there was no place and no time to bury them. I decided to record the scene, check for IDs, pile the bodies together close to one of the canyon walls, spread my nylon tent over them and pile as many rocks as possible over the tent. I knew that would not preserve much of anything. But I had to give it a try.

Whoever did this wasn't afraid of wasting bullets. I photographed close-ups of cartridge brass, a bunch of pant legs ripped open by both bullets and buzzards. I didn't count hits, but multiple torso hits will kill you even if the first hit doesn't. Probably AK–47s had done this work.

After searching the shirt and pants pockets of the first two, I kind of expected that nobody would have an ID. I searched all of them anyway, leaving the pockets turned inside out and recording that with the digi-cam. The fifth body was a real mess. A shotgun blast at close range will pretty well destroy a face and head. At least that is what it looked like. What remained of his brain matter was splattered and dried on the canyon wall near where he lay. What the blast didn't destroy, the vultures had worked on pretty well. At least one shotgun round had taken off the man's left arm about eight inches below the shoulder. Fired at close range, it had ripped off much of his shirt sleeve and took off almost his entire left arm. What was still there hung by sinew and a few bloody muscle strings. There was so much blood that at first I couldn't tell whether he was wearing a uniform or not. I finally decided that he wasn't. I couldn't even tell what color he was until I ripped open his shirt. He was white, or what we would call white in Memphis where I grew up. Again, no ID. I shot two or three frames of him. Damn, the camera's memory card was full.

I went back to the other guys. Most of the hand flesh was in some vulture's craw. But all of them had at least partial prints on at least one hand.

"OK, Rusty, how do we do fingerprints without fingerprinting kits? You stay."

Rusty sat.

Rummaging through the packsaddle yielded a possibility, my red leather–bound King James Bible. I've always liked the literary, poetic and lyrical qualities of the King James version. It just sounds right; this is how God ought to talk. Another pleasant surprise: in the bottom of the saddlebag was a throwaway 35mm camera with thirty-six available frames. I brought it, the Bible and my army surplus WWII government-issue canteen back to the site.

Using the King James version as a blotter, my bandana moistened with canteen water and dead guy's blood, I did what I hoped was a creditable job of taking fingerprints. I chose Exodus as the place to record them; it seemed appropriate. Dipping the wet bandana in blood, wiping the mixture on a finger and rolling the digit like I'd seen in the movies, I hoped that this would do the trick. Rusty didn't seem to care. He was panting, clearly hot. It was time to go.

5

"Me too chief. A few more pics and we're out of here." Rusty acknowledged with a thump, thump of his tail.

I shot about fifteen frames on the throwaway, put it in my expanding pants pocket and took a last look at the dead guys.

I dragged each of them to the side of the box canyon; pulled the camera from my pocket, took a couple of shots of the arrangement; covered the bodies with my tent; then climbed to the top of the small bluff and shoved rock and gravel down on them until I thought they were sort of safe from the usual hungry critters. It was mostly wasted motion. Unless the bodies were buried deep, the coyotes and other critters would uncover the corpses and get first call. Vultures would dine on the remains. Desert insects would find the microclimate of decaying flesh, and soon there would be nothing left except scattered bones bleaching in the sun.

I read a passage from Ecclesiastes, Chapter 3, the one about a time to live, time to plant, time to die, etc. I read another verse, my favorite, John 8:32—"You shall know the truth and the truth shall make you free." I bowed my head for a moment and said aloud, "Amen."

#

I took some compass bearings to pinpoint the site, just in case. My animals and I were thirsty, and all of us wanted to be away from this place. Anyplace on the Rio Grande was really looking good compared to this.

"Rusty, OK, let's go to the river." Thump, thump against my calf.

I knew that I had to report this. That would be a slick trick. We were in the heart of the Middle of Nowhere, albeit with pretty good directions as to location. I had digital pics of the murder scene, fingerprints of the dead guys, . . . and about two day's horseback travel to the nearest "authorities."

Mexico is out. I could see it: The little village of San Elizario was the closest, about ten miles up river, once we got to the river. My mental version of the scene was not a pretty one. I

6

go into the village, after making an illegal border crossing, and find the alcalde, or the policía, or the jefe and then:

"Buenos Tardes, Jefe. Me llamo es Lee. Es posible usar su teléfono?" That was assuming that there was a phone and that it actually operated.

"Por qué?" he says. And then I say in Spanish, "To report a multiple murder on the American side." The rest is no fun even to imagine.

"Rusty, let's get some water to drink, have a bath in the Rio Grande, and figure out what we're going to do about the mess these dead guys have gotten us into."

By sundown we were close to Talley, a deserted farmstead on the Rio Grande plain. Maybe we'd get lucky. On the American side the river shore was flat and broad. There was easy access. When the Rio Grande flowed, the river excursion outfitters sometimes put in or took out here. Pepper and Star smelled the water first. Their ears perked up; their gait stretched out, and pretty soon we were there. Everybody got what they wanted. I pulled the packs, saddles and bridles off the horses. Pepper and Star bolted into the river and drank their fill. They rolled in the wet grass along the river before grazing. Rusty, dogs are so cool! They run; they play; they splash; they lick themselves; they drink. And Rusty did just that. Me, I stripped off my boots, my sweat-stained chaps, jeans and shirt. I washed the salt-sweat clothes; spread them out on the Rio Grande rocks to dry. Then I plopped my happy ass in the river. I sat there naked in the afternoon sunshine, drank my luke-warm next-to-last Negra Modelo and generally felt great about being much more alive than those five guys in Mariscal Canyon just south of Elephant Mountain.

And had it not been for those digital pics in my camera and those bloody fingerprints in my Bible, the world would have been just about perfect that late October afternoon—a man, his dog and horses, one more beer and enough food to get through the night. The setting sun reminded us that this was, after all, the Big Bend. We were in the mountains and pretty soon that spectacular mango-orange, purple/mauve sunset would be

7

followed by a damn cold night. It was time for a reality check and the usual chores. I fed the horses the last of the oats and tethered them nearby. Close to the river, at least Talley had green grass. I gave Rusty a double handful of dry dog food. He gobbled it down and he did his usual recon, then curled up on the saddle blanket next to the little one-burner Coleman stove and began bagging zzzzzzs. I pulled out my sleeping bag, spread it over the ground cloth and watched the Rio Grande roll through Mariscal Canyon on its journey to the Gulf.

My supper was a simple affair. The guy or girl who invented Top Ramen was a genius. Mix it with water and anything and you could survive quite nicely. I added a little jalapeno beef jerky, some chili powder and a touch of garlic salt. Dessert was a little almond butter on crackers and my last apple.

Now, sitting on a river boulder in the failing light in my newly washed and air-dried clothes, sipping the last can of my sixpack, I tried to begin making sense of this really weird day. First things first: Who do we report this to? Mexico is out; too many complications. If we had been on the eastern side of Mariscal Mountain, I'd head to Glen Spring, Hot Spring or Rio Grande Village, the National Park campground and ranger station on the eastern edge of the park. But we were on the western side of the mountain. Castolon Ranger Station, about twenty-five miles west, seemed the best place to go. I pulled out my topo map and checked. Sure nuff, you can't get there from here. The canyons along the river here are impassable, unless we were in a raft, and even then we'd be headed in the wrong direction. So, we'd need to head overland in a northerly loop, take the tourist hiking trail or the primitive River Road around Mariscal and turn toward Johnson Ranch about ten miles west as the crow flew, but about fifteen the way Pepper, Star, me and Rusty journeyed. Meanwhile those bodies in that box canyon west of Mariscal Mountain were getting pretty ripe.

#

In about 1902 Elmo Johnson must have searched far and wide to find the most remote spot in the United States. He succeeded. There he established Johnson Ranch. Until the early 1940s, the Johnson family managed a ranching operation, trading post and general store in the deepest part of the "bend" in the Big Bend. The trade was both sides of the river. The border, then and now, was something Washington, Austin, and Mexico City cooked up. To the locals on both sides of the Rio Grande, the river was simply a giver of life. You got your feet wet going north or south. In those days, the fur trappers and animal bounty hunters, Mexicans, Indios and Anglos, could bring their pelts and skins to Mr. Johnson. According to the locals; "He would treat you fair." The Johnsons sold cheese, crackers, coffee, dried beans, flour, work pants, cloth and calico dresses, ammunition, rifles, assorted canned goods and coal oil, in addition to other staples. It was an oasis, but it was still a long way from anywhere.

The only thing that Johnson Ranch had going for it, as far as I was concerned, was easy access to the river. The grass along the shore and the gravel airstrip originally put in by the U.S. Army Air Corps in the 1920s was just the ticket for me and my critters. In the 1930s the United State–Mexican Boundary Commission installed a river gauging station about 500 yards upriver from the ranch site. It was maintained by the International Boundary Commission, and at one time there was an emergency radio phone there. I might be able to use it; then wait until the cops showed up. Or maybe somebody would come by and check the readings and make my life easier. When we reached the gauging station, sure enough, the emergency radio phone was broken. And the solar panels and the antenna told me that technology had fully automated the river readings. So much for that. And there were no river rafters, nobody. So, Castolon it was. And it was at least another half-day to Castolon, near the mouth of Santa Elena Canyon.

#

9

Castolon, Texas, in the southern end of Big Bend National Park is a tourist destination. It's an NPS ranger station. The U.S. Border Patrol and La Policía de la Frontera maintain a helicopter pad with a windsock that hovers behind the Castolon Store and across the compound from the ranger cabins. The fifty-yard-square gravel and dirt compound provides ample parking for the tourists. You can see the mouth of Santa Elena Canyon as it opens into the Rio Grande plain. With vertical walls of about 1,000 feet, Santa Elena is maybe the most spectacular vista in the Lower 48, aside from the Grand Canyon in Arizona. Motor coaches with seniors, minibuses with fewer seniors, small SUVs with couples and with Girl and Boy Scouts, French tourists from Normandy and German tourists from Hamburg, tired-looking hippies from Austin driving ragged out old VW Microbuses, Canadians, New Yorkers, and urban Texans all make it a destination. There is no gas or diesel, but you can buy beer, sodas, bread, peanut butter, snacks, a select group of sandwiches, chips, and the all important restroom.

From the reactions on the day I showed up you'd have thought I dropped off of Mars. I'm sure I was quite a sight. I made the classic western dramatic entrance. A cowboy complete with dog, two horses, leather chaps and black hat rides into town. His chaps are worn; his jeans and denim shirt faded and covered with trail dust. But the horseman sits tall in the saddle and rides into the town like he owns it. Many John Wayne movies come to mind. This particular cowboy from out of nowhere even has a gun on his hip, a big one. The digital cameras pop out. The video cams whirr. For the next fifty years, in many parts of the Midwest as well as in Germany and Japan, me, Star, Pepper and Rusty will be immortalized in prints, slides, videos, and PowerPoint presentations of "My American Vacation."

I howdy howdied a few of them, tipping my really dusty black Stetson to the ladies. I saw Mary Lou Gomez and her son sitting on the veranda of the Castolon Store. Mary Lou was telling some sort of tall Big Bend tale to the tourists. She was the one I was looking for. Her son, Carlito, recognized me and Rusty. He ran to us and introduced himself.

"Señor Doctor, I am Carlito Gomez. You spoke to our school in September. I remember you and Rusty. Come, please allow me to introduce my mother, Maria."

"Thank you, Carlito. I remember you. And I've met your mother several times."

Carlito waited until his mother completed the story.

"Mama, this is Dr. Phillips of the university. He is the man who talked to our school. This is his hearing dog, Rusty. You remember him."

"Dr. Phillips, it is my pleasure. It is good to see you again. Carlito has spoken highly of you and the talk you gave at his school."

"Señora Gomez, Maria, it is good to see you and Carlito again as well. Can I use a phone? It's an emergency. I have a credit card."

Maria was a fireball. She was all of five-two, about forty, weighed maybe 120, and had that curvy look that Hispanic women are famous for. When working she wore her jet-black hair in a bun or in one or two braids that reached down to the middle of her back. Most of the locals knew her as Señora Maria. To them she was the firm but caring concessionaire who ran the National Park Service store that catered to tourists at Castolon. Carlito was fourteen. I had talked to his school class in Marathon a couple of times.

"Carlito, can you give Pepper and Star some water and some oats from the pack? Rusty could sure use some dog food or a can of Spam from the store. I'll pay your mom."

"Sí, Doctor. But where do you come from?"

"Can we talk about it later? Rusty and the horses would be very grateful for the food and water. Gracias."

"Sí, Doctor."

"Señora Gomez, Maria, I really do need that phone. It's really important."

"Señor, I hear you are writing a book at your lonely casa at the end of the road at Big Bend Ranch. I hope your writing is going well."

"Señora Maria, I'm flattered that you remember. And even more flattered that Carlito and his friends remember me. He's really a great kid. I'm sorry; I hate to be rude, but I really, *really* have to make a phone call to park headquarters at Panther Junction. This phone call is kind of important and private. Can I make it in your office or someplace where the tourists won't hear? And please call me Lee."

"Sí, Señor Lee. My cubbyhole is over there at the far end of the store. Turn left when you go inside. Shut the door and you have privacy. Dial 9 for outside. Do you require anything else Señor Lee?

"A beer—no, two—sure would go down good! Negra Modelo, if you have it. Got any limes? If you do, my life will be almost complete, particularly if you have any of those cabrito tacos. One of those would be great too. Thanks."

"Señor, Negra Modelo is no problema. Pero, no tengo limas. Favor usar mi oficina allí. Vale?"

"Gracias."

I fished my AAA battery-powered phone amplifier out of its little leather sleeve in my shirt pocket, gratefully accepted the two frosty bottles of Negra Modelo from Maria and shut the door to her office.

I'd been out of touch with anybody for almost two weeks, and you never really know who is doing what to whom. I really should have called Robert Potter, the chief law enforcement ranger at Big Bend National Park at park HQ in Panther Junction about seventy miles north of Castolon. It was his jurisdiction, but I thought I'd get some "lay of the land."

So, instead of calling Robert, my first call was to Luís. That's Luís Carbajal Galvan, superintendent at Big Bend Ranch State Park, where I was the first and so far only Writer in Residence. The title came with a small university stipend paid in cash in monthly installments, a Texas Parks and Wildlife Department dark green ten-year-old four-wheel-drive Chevy pickup. There was a two-bedroom adobe house that was literally at the end of the road in the largest state park in North America—300,000 acres of some of the most remote, rocky and mountainous desert rangeland in the world. It was quiet. It had incredible sunrises and sunsets, satellite TV that I paid for, electricity most of the time, a generator that I also paid for and a corral and a shed for Pepper and Star. There was even a lean-to carport for my SUV and the pickup. Mercifully, there was an air conditioner, well, actually two. One was an evaporative cooler; we called them "swamp coolers" in the South where I grew up. It worked mainly by adding humidity to the atmosphere and blowing it through the house with a fan. The other was the regular, normal air conditioner unit.

Another perk was that nobody, but nobody, bothered you. It was so quiet that my occasional visitors frequently commented that the silence was deafening. My book on the borderland myths about the New World hiding place of the Ark of the Covenant was going great, until my three-week horseback traverse of Big Bend Ranch State Park and Big Bend National Park had sort of come unglued two days ago near Mariscal Mountain. Finding five vulture-eaten dead bodies will tend to do that.

"Luís? You alone? Good. Close the door. Grab a pencil and paper. I have my amp, so don't talk loud."

I gave him the short version.

"Luís, getting untangled from this is gonna take a little while."

I asked him to come move the horses to a corral at Big Bend Ranch where they could be cared for. He said he'd send Tomás, his head wrangler, to get Pepper and Star.

"Jesus, Lee, what do you think is going on?"

"Not a clue, man. But I'll tell you this, nobody whacks five guys in the middle of the Chihuahuan Desert, removes all their camp gear, brushes out all their footprints, and disappears into thin air for nickel and dime stuff. So, do me a favor. Call Juan Barrera at the Border Patrol office in Presidio. Ask him to call me here. I'm gonna call Bob Potter at park HQ Panther Junction."

"You haven't called him?"

"No."

"Crap. Don't talk to anybody else until you call Bob."

"OK. Alright. I'll do it."

"Lee, tell Bob everything you've told me. Don't screw around. OK?"

"Get your double horse trailer hooked up. Come get Pepper and Star for me. They're pretty tuckered out. Some oats and a little rest at the Sauceda Ranch corral would really help."

"No problema, amigo. Oh, Lee, Tomás, my lead wrangler has the dos caballos slant-load trailer over at Study Butte. He was going to pick up some feed, but I'll send him your way. He can come through the Old Maverick Road down to Santa Elena and Castolon. Shouldn't take him more than two hours. Watch your back!"

"Hell, Luís, I just found these guys; I didn't kill 'em."

"Watch your back, jefe!"

"Sí, amigo. Gracias."

"Lee, you want me to call Lisa in Austin? This thing is going to hit the fan; it will be big news. She'll be worried."

"No, Luís, thanks. I'll take care of that."

"You be careful Lee. We'll come get the horses."

"Bueno."

"Lee, before you go, Lisa called me the other day, wanting to make sure you're OK. She says, and I agree, that you're getting kind of long in the tooth to be making these isolato trips, all alone and out there in the middle of nothing with only a couple of horses and a dog. She and I agree that you can really die out there."

"I know, Luís. And the problem with that would be?. . . Oh, hell, never mind. Thanks for the concern. I'll call Lisa as soon as I can. Can you call Juan, like right now? Oh, Luís, any unusual or weird radio traffic? BP, TPWD, NPS— they looking for anybody? Any staff come up missing or lost or not reporting in?"

"No. Why? Never mind. I'll make the calls. Is this something I should alert Austin about? You know the admin pukes get really weird about this kind of thing."

"Luís, I'm just the writer in residence at the Ranch, so that's your call. My guess is that Austin is gonna want to know about that Wildlife Management Agent. This is really NPS turf. I'm gonna start with NPS at park HQ. Bob will call the Border Patrol, OK? On the other hand, you work for the great State of Texas, right? Do what you need to do."

"10-4, Lee. I'll make the calls."

I called Robert Potter, Law Enforcement Chief Ranger for Big Bend National Park at Panther Junction Park Headquarters. I'd known Bob for over fifteen years. Aside from his membership and the ultra-right-wing faction of the Church of Jesus Christ of Latter Day Saints, he was a great friend. I gave him the short version of the whole thing. He had a lot of questions, but was savvy enough not to ask them on the phone. Hell, I was too. But I wasn't in charge of security in one of the largest parks in the Lower 48.

"Don't you move, Lee; you sit tight. Do not do anything stupid and stay right where you are. Got it? You will take us to the bodies, and I mean right now, as soon as possible. My crew and I will be there as soon as we can get on the road."

"Not a problem, Bob. I'm sitting here looking at a pretty incredible vista of Santa Elena and wishing that sumbitch hadn't swiped my water cache. If I'd had enough water to complete my horseback ride across your park, I'd be at Boquillas del Carmen. I'd be in that small cantina dining on homemade tacos, and drinking my favorite beer with a lime stuffed down the long neck. Don't worry; I'll be here. But I am gonna borrow a shower from one of the rangers here, OK?"

"Lee, be the guest of your National Park Service."

#

I called Lisa in Austin.

"Lee, it's really good to hear from you. Are you at Rio Grande Village? La Linda? Where? I love you. Where the hell in that desert are you?"

"I love you too. You talking from the balcony overlooking Town Lake or where?"

"Yeah, lover. Nine million joggers; about half of them women. All of them have those great tushes and great tits that you like, no cellulite."

"Damn, if I weren't here, I'd rather be there. But only with you and Rusty on the balcony looking at all of that. . . ."

"Lisa, sit down; I've got some bad news. You ready?"

"Yes, what the hell is going on? You don't like phones; Rusty doesn't like phones. This is bad, right?"

"Yep, it is. I found five dead bodies in a remote side canyon near Mariscal a few days ago. They are dead men from two countries, several federal and state agencies, and they have been shot with a lot of bullets by more than one person."

"My God, Lee! Are you OK?"

"Well, kinda."

"You know I told you. You're too old for this shit. You don't need to be doing those crazy-ass 'isolato' adventures any longer. I worry every minute you're gone. You remember me? I'm the one who worried when you sailed across the Gulf of Mexico in that boat twenty years ago, the first of several of your crazy trips."

"And I came home, right?"

"Yes, you did. But that was over twenty years ago. Now, at least you don't sail any longer. But the desert will kill you; you know that. You can die out there and it would take us forever to find your corpse. . . . Wait a minute."

"What?"

"I'm looking at CNN. This thing is all over the news. When did you report it?"

"Hell, I don't know Lisa; thirty minutes ago, maybe forty-five, why?"

"You didn't tell me that one of those bodies was Border Patrol and another was National Park Service. Everybody on

God's green earth will be showing up at Castolon. Don't try to do this by yourself. You might give Susan a call in New Orleans. Having legal advice is not going to hurt you. This thing looks like a major international incident. You are probably going to need a legal ear. Do it, give her a call. I'll give her a call to warn her. You ever thought about getting a simple, safe job?"

"Hell Lisa, I've got a simple, safe job. I just want to write a book; spend a few nights looking at some pretty fantastic sunsets with you; maybe split a bottle of that Hill Country Claret and roll around naked in the West Texas twilight with you. Not a bad idea; huh?"

"Lee, you're in a lot of shit. I love you. I'm calling Susan and you should too."

Phone traffic in West Texas picked up big time. Bob made his phone calls; Luís made his phone calls; Lisa made hers. I borrowed a shower, clean towel, some soap and shampoo and soon felt more like a human being. The phone calls and shower took less than thirty minutes. Maria gave me a carne guisada taco, beans and a beer, and life looked pretty damned good for me and Rusty—for about an hour and 15 minutes.

Rusty heard them coming well before I did. The wail of a police siren is actually more painful to dogs than to people. He jumped upright; yelped; stood on hind legs and pawed my lap! Then I saw them pop over the rise with light bars flashing, and presumably with sirens cranking out that awful, irritating, high pitched squealing sound. The cavalry had arrived. Bob's Crown Vic and the two Border Patrol SUVs complete with wailing sirens and red/blue light bars, skidded to a stop in front of the store, swallowing Maria, Carlito, me, Rusty and assorted tourists in a cloud of dust—so much for good manners. A drive that normally took two hours from Panther Junction, took these guys less than forty-five minutes. Those guys, all of them, boiled out of those vehicles like they were going to a fire, . . . or maybe to a murder. Somehow I didn't feel a whole lot safer. In fact, on later reflection, that's when everything started turning to shit.

CHAPTER 2: "I'M FROM THE GOVERNMENT AND I'M HERE TO HELP YOU."

"Hi, Bob. Qué tal?"

"Lee, I wish we had time to chat, but from what you said, we have a really, really serious problem, right? This is BP Agent Smith and Agent Roberts. They're normally at the check point at Study Butte. We tried calling our guy and their guy here, but no answer. Probably the damned mountains; we'll catch them later."

I thought I might be able to tell them where those guys were, but also thought it might be useful to keep my mouth shut for now.

"I'm with you Bob. I'm pretty sure that you have a real serious problem. Where do you want to do this?"

"I've already asked one of the rangers to loan us his house. His family is in Dallas for the week so we'll have a quiet place to talk. Let's go. . . . What's that?"—pointing to my right hip and my military style holster?

"My .45 auto, why?"

"You're carrying a semi-auto on a Federal reservation Dr. Phillips," said either Smith or Roberts. "That's illegal; you ought to know that."

"If it bothers you guys I'll go put it with the rest of my stuff, O.K.?"

"No can do Lee; gimme the gun."

"Sure Bob, but I want a receipt." I pulled the big Colt out of its holster, ejected the magazine, racked it, and handed both to Bob.

"You don't trust us to give it back?" He racked it again to make sure it was empty. "Still seven rounds in the magazine, right, Lee?"

"Yes to the rounds, Bob, and no I don't trust you guys. You're from the government, remember? If you're going to take it for evidence, you have to give me a receipt."

"Lee, we go back a long way."

"And you're still a cop, right?"

"OK, point made. Here's the damn receipt; let's go talk. You don't mind these guys being with us, do you? They lost some people there, at least according to you."

"No, no problem. Let's do it."

We were headed toward the ranger residence when I saw Tomás drive up with the trailer. Bob and the BP guys gave me some time. Tomás, Rusty and I loaded Star and Pepper in the trailer. I tossed my saddles and camp gear in the back of the pickup and Tomás started to mount up. One of the BP guys noticed that I tossed in a long gun.

"What's that?"

"Shotgun."

"You have it with you on the trip?"

"Yes, why?

"Just what the hell were you doing out there? You have a .45 auto; you have a shotgun. What are you doing with those things?"

"Agent Smith, or Roberts, whichever; I have a carry permit for the .45. I have an NPS ranger permit from Panther for the 12 gauge to hunt feral pigs and javelina. What's your problem?"

"The problem, Doc, is five dead guys on a federal reservation, no eyewitnesses, and the guy who finds the dead guys is carrying a .45 auto and a 12 gauge pump shotgun capable of killing an awful lot of stuff including the five guys he is now reporting. That's the problem."

They wanted to confiscate the Browning 12 gauge. After a little negotiation, I passed the pump over to them and got a second receipt. They did have a point; some of those guys died from shotgun pellets. The feds were happy. I was a bit closer to getting back to my book.

We talked for about four hours; nobody in the room except me, Rusty, Bob and the two BP guys. It seemed to go well. We went through the pics on the digital camera; used a USB port on the BP laptop and enlarged them to fit the 15 inch screen.

"Lee, the digital pics suck."

"Yup, Bob, they do. But that's what we have. I'm an historian and a writer, not a digital camera expert. I'm sure that you federal guys have access to software that will make those babies shine, right?"

"Those black/red blobs in the middle of the crime scene are the dead vultures, right?"

"Yes."

"Doc, there are three of them. You shoot all of them?" asked Agent Smith, or Agent Roberts.

"Yep. Not as good as I was; happens that way when you get older."

"You popped three with how many rounds?"

"Five."

"Damn, I couldn't do that!"

"Well, I could'a killed more. Wouldn't have mattered, though. There are more vultures than people, at least in this part of the world."

Somebody brought in sandwiches and Cokes. I showed them the fingerprints; told them that they were done left to right to match the photos, with the guy with no face last. I asked for, and they gave me, a receipt for my red leather-bound King James Bible with the fingerprints at the book of Exodus. I didn't believe that I'd ever see it again, or at least I wouldn't see Exodus again. And I told the story again.

"Bob, I've told this thing several times. I'm tired of it. Near as I can tell it's coming out the same way every time, right? Right?"

"It is. But what I don't get is how five dead guys, you, and the folks who whacked them, all wind up in the same place at the same time in one of the most remote parts of the park. I just can't get my head around that. I don't believe in coincidences. This whole thing stinks. What do you agents think?"

"I think the Doctor here is not telling us all he knows," said Smith.

Roberts added, "That's what I think too. And I'm still not happy with you having that .45 auto and that 12 gauge on a trip through the public park. Somebody could get hurt. That's why we don't allow people to carry pistols and long guns in the park."

"Either of you guys ever been in the middle of Big Bend National Park? You got any idea how many of the public I ran into during my two-week trek? Zero, well, until I met the two vaqueros two days before I found the bodies. Guys, you either don't believe me or you think I had something to do with it. I'm tired of talking. I've already agreed to stick around and take you folks to the bodies as soon as your choppers and other people get here, which is beginning to look like tomorrow morning. Right, Bob?"

"Yeah. We're borrowing four choppers from the Army. First light is about the earliest they can get them to us out of Fort Bliss in El Paso."

"I've told you everything I know. I want to take you to the bodies and I've agreed to testify in court about what I found and how I found it. All I want to do right now is to get back to my house at Los Alamos in the Ranch. I want to see my wife in two weeks, and write my book. That's all. I'm done here. OK?"

"I still have some questions," said Smith.

The door opened and we were joined by yet another cop, at least that is what he looked like to me.

"Lee, let me introduce Agent Carl Marks, FBI, Agent in Charge, El Paso District."

"My pleasure, Agent Marks. And you want me to tell this story again, right?"

"Yes sir. Do you have a problem with that?"

"Not today, man. I am tired and I don't much like Smith or Roberts. I don't even know you and already I don't like you at all. But probably that's because your colleagues have seriously tried my patience. So, you cannot imagine how little interest I have in staying in the same room with any of you another minute. Rusty needs to take a leak and so do I. Besides, assuming that one of you has the smallest clue about the layout of a computer keyboard, you guys have it all anyway. And I assume that the cute little digital recorder in Smith or Robert's shirt pocket is working, so you have it all anyway, right? Agent Marks, check with your associates. I am out of here!"

"You're not leaving Castolon, are you Lee?"

"Would if I could Bob, but I don't have any wheels and you're not going to let me do that anyway are you?"

"No, Lee, I'm afraid not. If I didn't know you, I'd have to place you in custody as a material witness. But you've already given me your word. Where are you staying?"

"Maria and Carlito offered me the couch in their living room. It comes with dinner for me and Rusty. And I'm late for it now. Bye." As Rusty and I walked out the door I could hear Smith or Roberts muttering, loud enough for even me to hear, something about "uppity historians who are too smart for their own good." Which of course was true.

Dinner was incredible: chiles rellenos, frijoles, arroz moreno, y ensalada from Maria's garden. After two weeks of trail food, this was heavenly. Carlito and I hand-cranked homemade vanilla ice cream on the front porch and ladled chocolate syrup on it. Rusty had another can of Spam; from the way his tail was waging it was clear Carlito had made the right choice.

Halfway through dessert Maria's phone rang. It was Lisa in Austin.

"Lee, you have to call Susan, right now. Don't wait! I don't think you know what you're involved in. Do it, O.K."

"I'll call her in a while."

Rusty heard them first, just about the time Maria, Carlito and I were slurping up the last of the ice cream with chocolate syrup. Then Maria and Carlito, and finally I actually heard the whine of vans, SUVs and RVs pulling that last set of hills on the Castolon road. We walked outside and only then could see the headlight beams cutting through the desert darkness. It looked like the world had discovered Castolon and they were all showing up at the same time.

Nobody was going to get much sleep tonight, what with all the RV generators, klieg lights, satellite antennas going up and down, "testing, testing, one, two," and the red-and-blue law enforcement light bars bouncing light off all the buildings and the other cars, trucks, RVs and communication vans. I stayed for a while, but Rusty was agitated. So was I. It was time to make phone calls.

In short order most of the law enforcement capacity in Texas west of the Pecos was either at Castolon or on the way. Not to mention God-knows-how-many television, radio, and Internet news outlets. Boy, were they surprised to learn that cell phones didn't work too well on the border, and that gas in Panther Junction and Study (pronounced "Stewdy") Butte was twenty cents higher than in Midland, a mere 150 miles away. For the locals this was the opportunity of a lifetime. Maria opened the store and soon sold out of every beer and soda in the place, all the peanut butter crackers, the Spam, the potted meat, the tortillas and even the fiery Big Bend Jalapeno Jerky. That stuff was made by Maria's cousin in Presidio. They sold it for five dollars a stick. A bite would, the locals said, change the way you thought about heat. God help the poor bastards who took a bite without a beer chaser already in hand.

Three other families showed up from the Mexican village of Santa Elena across the river. They hawked tacos, burritos and ice-cold cans of Tecate with lime. The media and the law guys/girls didn't see five dead guys gunned down in the desert in this part of the world in a decade, let alone in one day. There were NPS Park Police; TPWD law enforcement and internal affairs; Border Patrol, West Texas District; Texas Rangers, two of them; and La Policía de la Frontera from the Mexican states of Chihuahua and Coahuila, including a bird colonel who was somehow related to Maria. There was a Brewster County Sheriff's Department deputy, an FBI guy, and some trim, athletic guys in dark suits and ties who kept muttering about homeland security. The dark-suited guys had cute patriotic lapel pins, square-looking bulges around their waists, and earplugs. Most of us figured they were the Gestapo, but they were only Homeland Security and Secret Service. They kept whispering into their coat sleeves.

23

The whole thing looked like the proverbial Chinese fire drill with vehicles backing and turning, stopping and starting; people looking and posturing, yelling and cursing and nobody sleeping—a lot of adrenaline and testosterone. Rusty and I figured it would take a few hours to get sorted out.

I headed to the store to call Susan and was sitting in Maria's cubbyhole with Rusty, with my amplifier attached to her phone when the thing rang, rang so loud even I could hear it.

It was Luís at the Sauceda unit at Big Bend Ranch.

"Lee, as you academics would say, the shit has definitely hit the fan. You can't believe the calls coming in. My bosses in Austin are going nuts over this. The law enforcement guys are flying down additional jefes in the agency jet tonight. We've got to go out and light the runway and then transport them over to Castolon. This is crazy!"

"Luís, I'm sorry. Thanks for sending Tomás. Are the horses OK?"

"Sí, jefe. I'm getting a lot of calls. What can I tell them?"

"Damned if I know, Luís. You know everything I do. One thing though, don't tell them where I'm staying, and don't give anybody our home number or Lisa's cell number. OK?"

"Gotta go, another call. Stay safe hombre."

I was trying to dial Susan when the damned phone rang again.

"Lee, this is Juan in Presidio. Sorry to take so long; was on a multi-agency ops at Del Rio. What the hell is going on? My boss in DC is raising hell, and I'm missing an agent. I'll be there by dawn. You met any of my guys yet?"

"You mean your two asshole agents Roberts and Smith? Yeah, met 'em, don't like 'em, but then the feeling is mutual. They and NPS have my statement and they should have sent the digital photos to you by now. Did you get them?"

There was this dead silence on the other end.

"Juan, you there?"

"Lee, what pics, what statement and, what transcript?"

"Juan, listen to me; understand this. Smith and Roberts were busy typing on their laptop. One of them had a digital

24

recorder in his pocket. I watched them download the pics through their USB port from my camera. Bob has the camera and my Bible with the dead guys' finger prints in it. I figured that your boys would transmit all that stuff, about four hours worth, to you guys at district or wherever-the-hell you wanted it sent. You're their boss, right? Hell, don't you people have wi-fi or satellite or something really cute and up-to-date down here that you transmit data, photos and info over? You're the government, right?"

All I heard was, "Gotta go Lee, see you tomorrow at dawn."

#

"OK, Rusty, lets talk to Susan; we need to get squared away. Hope she answers; it's almost nine-thirty in N.O."

One and a half rings later: "Susan? Lee. I'm calling from Castolon, Texas. What's going on in New Orleans?"

"Busy day whacking bad guys in court. Fortunately for people like me we have no dearth of targets in this country. Lisa said you'd call."

There were some clicks and some dead air on the line.

"Susan, you there? My amplifier is sort of working, been giving me some reception problems. Lisa suggested I call."

"Yes, she did. And you know, she's right about those 'isolato' adventures of yours. A lot of people, including me, Lisa, your kids and grandchildren and maybe even one or two friends worry that you'll die out there, if not in the desert, then some damn ocean or mountain far away and close to someplace none of us can pronounce."

"Come on Susan, we've been down this road before. Rusty and I always come home. Even Lisa can't argue with that. Neither can you."

"Lee, shut up and listen. Between the time Lisa called and now, I've kicked my staff in gear and guess what? This thing you're involved in is a major deal. You are really in deep shit.

25

Every law enforcement agency west of the Mississippi is either there or headed there, right?"

"How do you know that? Never mind. Christ, Susan, all I did was find a bunch of dead guys and I am trying to report it to the authorities, which here would be the NPS cops. Have your people already pulled this thing up on the Web, checked NPS intranet, various police departments, FBI, and all that stuff?

"Lee, surfing those various intranets, especially their internal emails, and most particularly the Border Patrol, FBI and Homeland Security intranets is a federal crime, you know that, right? "

"Yeah, whatever."

"OK, Lee, tell me the story. I have a recorder going and two witnesses to verify what you're saying. You OK with that?"

I relayed the story, now old to me, but seemingly magic to everybody I told it to.

"OK, Lee, listen to me. Shut up. Don't talk to anybody else, not even Luís or Lisa by phone. Stay off cell phones and computers until I get there. Where the hell is this place anyway? My staff can't even find it on a chart. You got a Global Positioning System destination on it? Never mind, we'll find it. Now listen really carefully. Do you formally choose me as your attorney of record as of right now? Say yes."

"Yes."

"OK, shut up and listen, no more smart-ass remarks, got it?"

"Sure, Susan, but all I did was . . . ."

"Dammit, Lee!"

"OK."

"No reason you would know down there in the center of nowhere. This thing is major news. Don't they have hotels there? My staff says they can't find anything. Got your amp turned up? Listen. Keep quiet about everything until I get there. My staff tells me that I can get there in six hours."

"Susan, the feds won't be ready to go to the crime scene until daybreak at the earliest; that's nine hours from now. You really think you can get here in six?"

"That's what the best legal and logistical staff east of the Mississippi says, so I'm assuming it's true. Stick to the story you've told them; you can't get into too much trouble by doing that. I'll be there by daybreak."

"Susan, if they ask, do I tell them that you're on the way?"

"Lee, are you crazy? Don't you dare! Don't you dare! I like surprises—giving them, not getting them. Don't drink; go to sleep; keep Rusty with you. He'll keep you out of trouble. I love you; be safe. Nothing will happen 'til daybreak. I should be there by then."

I gave it one more shot. "Susan, look, this is not a big deal. I'll take them to the site; they will do a look–see; examine and transport the bodies, and I can go back to writing my book."

"Listen, this line is not secure. I'll see you in six. Hang up; stay put."

And, damned if she didn't. About daybreak a ten passenger commercial chopper sat down in the dusty Castolon turnaround. Susan Steele and these two really BIG guys with bulky sports coats erupted from the chopper-guys first. Susan, about 120 pounds, 5′4″ with this incredibly Cajun-black kinky hair cut really short, equally incredibly milk-white skin, was wearing khakis, desert hiking boots, a wide brimmed hat, with a small canvas shoulder bag—sort of like the Israeli Defense Force uses—and a feminine version of RayBans, and it wasn't even full sunrise yet. The two guys don't smile, don't talk and, for all I know, don't even speak English. I do know that when I trotted toward Susan one of them stopped me like a brick wall, with a really BIG gun in his shoulder holster. He patted me down and nodded. Only after their boss nodded OK was it that I get through to my second- or third-most-favorite female on the planet, after Lisa and my granddaughter.

"I thought you carried, Lee?"

"Normally do, Susan. The feds have it; it's evidence. Remember, I shot three vultures with it. So, the NPS cops have it. Actually my friend Robert Potter, Chief of Law Enforcement for Big Bend National Park, has it. I do have a receipt though."

"That should be comforting."

27

"Not really; but there wasn't much I could do about it. Susan, 5 hours and 45 minutes! I am impressed! There are damned few governments that could pull off a trip from New Orleans to Big Bend National Park in that time. Where the hell did you fly from and to? Never mind. Maria Gomez has made coffee. It's in the store."

"Got time for beignets? We brought some."

"You brought beignets to this part of the world? You are an angel. These bodyguard guys have names? Never mind, I think we'll use Bubba and Bubba; that way they'll fit right in."

A chopper at dawn brings out everybody. Bob was there, his uniform rumpled from being slept in, rubbing sleep from his eyes. Agents Smith and Roberts were there, looking a little rumpled but ready to pick a fight.

"Guys, Maria has coffee and my attorney here has four thermoses of Cafe du Monde coffee. She even brought a couple of bags of beignets and two shakers of powdered sugar. Anybody want some? Follow us."

"Lee, has anyone attempted to interrogate you without me being there?"

"No, nobody has asked me anything since last night. What's with the bodyguards? You used to not like all that hardware. Something change that I don't know about?"

"Lee, this is Derek and his twin brother Derek. Don't fuck with them; they will shoot you. Remember that Continental Drilling explosion in the Gulf two years ago? Killed sixteen; twelve missing and five survivors? I represent the dead, the missing, the survivors and the widows and orphans. There is a lot of money at stake, upper eight figures. There is also the probability of lengthy jail sentences for a half dozen corporate big-wigs. I've been targeted twice. The two Dereks are in charge of security and they do a pretty good job at it. After all, I'm still alive."

"Damn, things have gotten a little rough in New Orleans since Lisa and I saw you last."

"Lee, we need to talk. Who is in charge here at the headquarters of the End of Nowhere?

"Susan, this is Castolon, Texas. The sun rises over Mule Ear Peaks and sets in Santa Elena Canyon. That's pretty hard to beat. A day here will change the way you think about light. And they have pretty damn good beer, well, usually they do. Maria got an emergency shipment from the distributor in Midland. Came in about 3:00 a.m. she says. About half of it is gone and it's not even full daylight. She likes me and has set aside a couple of six-packs. But first, let's get some coffee and beignets. Come on Rusty."

"Who is this, Lee?" A gentleman strode up dressed in khakis and the traditional dark blue windbreaker with "FBI" stenciled above the left breast pocket.

"This is Susan Steele, Carl."

"Ms. Steele, I'm Carl Marks, FBI, Agent in Charge, El Paso District. The National Parks Service, as a Federal agency, has turned this investigation over to us"

"Mr. Marks, I'd like to talk to my client privately; then maybe you could fill me in. You've met my client Dr. Harry Lee Phillips?"

"Yes, Ma'am. I've seen the transcripts. I've heard of you. No one told me you were coming to Castolon. Welcome to Big Bend. Dr. Phillips, what would you need a lawyer for?"

"Shut up Lee!"

"Susan, all I'm trying to do is tell these guys what I...."

"Lee, if you don't do what I tell you, I'm getting back on that chopper and I'm flying back to my law practice. So, do you want to talk or do I?"

"Susan; you, please."

She smiled. Mr. Marks are you the agent in charge?"

"Yes ma'am."

"Then you and I can chat after I talk with my client. Meanwhile, I'm going into that store over there and telling my folks to serve your people coffee with chicory and beignets on the front porch. As I've heard my client say about that coffee a number of times, 'It'll put lead in your pencil.' And while y'all enjoy the food, I'm going to talk with Lee. OK? Say yes ma'am." He did.

"Great, let's get to it." Even the FBI and the NPS guys joined in. Maria's coffee is good, but it can't stand up to Community Coffee, or Cafe du Monde Coffee with chicory. This is coffee you can float a spoon in. The only way to survive drinking it is to use huge dollops of half and half cream or hot milk. The two Dereks served the milk, with one eye on their charge and the other malevolent eye on the rest of us, also known as potential targets. After about two cups of the chicory coffee, most of these cops would have sold their grandmothers into white slavery for a third hit. Beignets were a no brainer; everybody loves them.

One of the Dereks brought his boss a cup. It was that dark Mocha color, like caramel that had been left just a tad too long on the stove. When I order the stuff, I ask them to make it "the color of me." I'm pretty dark, with a complexion of a deep mocha tan. Or what clothiers call "tobacco." Well, coffee the color of me is what Susan, Maria and I drank out of those marvelous light blue-and-white speckled tin cups, sitting on the Castolon store veranda about 7:30 a.m. watching the sun pop up just south of Mule Ear Peaks. As usual, it was those nine million colors of orange, yellow and gold. Big Bend sunrises have never failed to take my breath away. It is pretty hard to beat that kind of wakeup.

Sure enough, someone else showed up. Robert Potter. We all referred to him as "General" Potter, although in real life he was only a captain and a pretty decent guy. Bob was one of the few locals who showed any interest in my book. I think he actually hoped that those stories were true. He was a leader in the more traditional wing of the Mormon church and on more than one occasion he indicated that it would be wonderful if the Ark was indeed in North America. According to Bob, Salt Lake, the homeland of Mormon Central, would be the perfect place for a holy relic such as the Ark.

"Ma'am, the beignets were great; coffee with chicory was incredible too! Who brewed it?"

"One of the Dereks, Captain Potter."

"Bob, I thought you Mormon folk didn't use caffeine."

30

"Lee, everybody has a sin; coffee is mine. Ma'am, Lee and I go back a long ways. I would rather do this informally. But, given that you're here, I really have to talk to your client before we get in those choppers and head out to find those bodies. You can be there if you want. I want the FBI agent in charge to be there too. Are you OK with that?"

"Captain Potter, I absolutely insist that I be at the interview and at all subsequent interviews. Dr. Phillips is my client and I will ask that you respect that relationship. I understand that yesterday afternoon, voluntarily, he spent over four hours discussing this event with you and the Border Patrol officers. I also understand that you have seized two of his lawfully possessed firearms. He has a Texas carry permit for the .45 auto and federal permits issued by your office for his use in this park. That is for both weapons and I request that they both be returned immediately. I also insist that since my client has not been charged with any crime, and, indeed, has voluntarily come forward to report one, that he be released from any custody whatsoever immediately."

"Ma'am, I'm afraid I can't allow that."

"Ah, Agent Carl Marks."

"Can't allow what gentlemen; the guns or the custody?"

"Both ma'am."

"In that case, Agent Marks, Captain Potter—my client and I and our associates and Rusty will reboard our chopper, and we'll get out of your life. You can go find your dead bodies any damn way you want. And I am deadly serious."

"Ma'am, I don't think I can allow that."

"Yes, you can. But frankly, Agent Marks, I don't really care what you wish to allow. I have a writ of habeas corpus signed by a judge in this county that requires you to release my client, unconditionally, unless you charge him with a specific crime. Would you like me to serve you now, or would you like me to serve you later? Doesn't matter to me, though I would rather we work this out another way."

"And that would be, ma'am?"

31

"You return my client's weapons to him; he is released from custody, and we will aid you and the federal government in the discovery and recovery of the deceased. He has already told you that he will be happy to voluntarily testify in court as to the circumstances, the scene and what followed."

"Ms. Steele, you know that I can't release the weapons. The Colt .45 auto was used at the scene. We have photos of dead vultures and statements from your client supporting that fact. The 12 gauge was possibly used at the scene, though I doubt it. But until we run it and the Colt through ballistics, I can't be sure. So, until those tests are done, we really must retain possession of the pistol and the shotgun. And, finally, let me assure you Ms. Steele and you Dr. Phillips, that we have no evidence or indication that you were in any way involved in this crime. If you thought you were in custody, we apologize. Of course you are free to go as you wish, though we would hope that you take us to the bodies."

"I understand that because the Colt was used at the scene you really must keep possession of it—chain of evidence, ongoing investigation. Fine. But the shotgun is another story. Will you release it to me or my client after the ballistics tests reveal that it was in no way involved?"

"Yes Ma'am."

"I'd like it in writing. Fortunately my staff has prepared a copy for all our signatures. Please, sign here, and for you Mr. Marks, here. Thank you."

"Lee," Robert Potter broke in, "we really need to get to those bodies. And I assume that you're coming along Counselor?"

"I wouldn't miss it. Normally I'd insist that my client ride with me. But we all know that he should be in the first chopper. Good Luck everybody! Let's get this done."

"Uh, Ma'am."

"Yes Agent Marks."

"The body guards, Derek and Derek; they can't go. Well at least they can't go with the weapons."

"Yes they can and they will, Agent Marks. I thought that might be an issue, so I made some arrangements and a couple of phone calls. Here, call this number. I think that should get you the answer you need.

"Ma'am, that's the number for the director's office."

"Yes it is Agent Marks; please, feel free. You have a satellite phone."

Damned if he didn't. It was a short call, filled with a bunch of "yessir," "yessir," yessir," and "of course sirs."

Marks, a little more red in the face than a couple of minutes ago, hung up. "Let's roll. Captain Potter, get 'em loaded. Derek and Derek are coming too—armed."

CHAPTER 3: BODIES AND MORE BODIES

We choppered into Talley in an Army Blackhawk—big, mean, loud and ugly, but efficient. Susan and her entourage, including Derek and Derek, flew in the second chopper. Everybody else, NPS, BP, FBI and the others including the two pool reporters, rode in the last three Blackhawks. The guys with horses, Jeeps, 4WD Suburbans and four-wheelers had left at midnight. They met us at Talley, where I'd spent the night after finding the bodies. The rough terrain is a lot easier to negotiate, quicker, too, in a four-wheeler or Jeep than it is on horseback. I gave them the compass points. We flew up the west side of Mariscal Mountain and circled the spot. Even they could see the blood spatters on the canyon walls. We landed at Talley and mounted up.

I rode with Carl, Bob, Susan and Rusty in an NPS 4x4 Suburban, complete with a roaring a.c. I did a brief recap for Bob, most of which he already knew. How my three-week traverse of the park had turned sour when I discovered that some SOB had stolen my water cache. That unhappy event necessitated my turn south toward Mariscal Canyon and a surefire water supply at the Rio Grande. He asked a couple of questions about the location of the bodies and observed again that civilians are prohibited from carrying firearms in the park. We had a short discussion about the permit process but Marks let it go. Susan listened; Rusty napped.

"Hell, Bob, I thought I was doing you guys a favor, whacking those javelinas."

"You know, Lee, you were and you did. But you know as well as I do that there are folks out there who oppose killing those, as they call them, "cute little wild pigs." I expect that any day now we'll have a directive telling us to do something really stupid like relocate them."

"Lee, is there any reason you don't use a GPS? It would have given us a much tighter location."

"Bob, I don't like them, GPS. They use batteries. Ever wondered what happens when a battery dies in the middle of nowhere? Guess what: Your ass is lost. Compasses don't need batteries. Neither does dead reckoning."

I picked up the walkie-talkie and assumed the job of guiding the lead chopper driver the last few miles. We were at the turn off. I instructed the driver of the lead Suburban to turn left at the next canyon, explaining that it was about 500 yards on the left. And I also suggested that he slather on some sunscreen and wear a wide brim hat. The religious use of both would keep his brains from getting crispy fried. He didn't much like it, but at least he told me so in polite, 'cop' lingo.

I think all of them were surprised that we found them where I said we would. You'd be amazed at how much manpower the feds can muster when you tell them that they have five dead guys from at least two countries and several state and federal agencies. There was nothing but 'assholes and elbows.' Even those guys with the suits and cool-looking earpieces pitched in. Rusty, Susan, Derek and Derek and I stood out of the way.

"Jesus, Lee, colder than hell at night; hot as New Orleans without the humidity in the day; no water! Christ! How do you people do it?"

"Susan , you get used to it."

"No fucking way! You people are really crazy!"

The agent in charge of the recovery, a six foot tall, shapely thirtyish-looking blond, stylishly dressed in rough outdoor wear—and with a very large Glock .40cal slung low-rise on one hip cowboy style approached. She introduced herself as Carol, Agent Something-or-other, all of which I missed.

"I need to talk to your client Ms. Steele?"

"That depends agent. May I ask the nature of the questions?"

"Yes, Ma'am. We need to know again the direction Dr. Phillips was traveling, where he first saw the bodies. You know, the usual stuff. OK?"

"You OK with that Lee?"

"Yup, let's do it. I'd kinda like to get back to the Ranch. Shit, I actually can hardly believe I said that."

So she asked and I answered: time, direction, how long, when I discovered the bodies, why I was there—that sort of thing. Some of it was repetitive fact checking for the investigation. Almost none of it was new, until . . . .

"Dr. Phillips, did you hear anything unusual in the day or days before you found the bodies?"

I smiled, rubbed my ears, shook my head, "no".

I'll give her credit; she was quick.

"I apologize; that was insensitive. You don't hear well. So, you heard nothing?"

"The short answer is; no I didn't. But, you know Agent Carol, about a day and a half before, Rusty began acting weird: skittish, agitated, being a regular pain in the ass. Occasionally he would get in the horses' way, like he was blocking Pepper, Star and me, maybe even shielding us from harm. He's done that before, but that was for snakes and such. Looking back, I think he must have heard either the chopper or whatever it was took the killers out of here; or he heard the gunfire. But he can't testify. And all I know for sure is that I heard nothing. And, I didn't see anything, well, anything that pertains to your problem until I ran onto these bodies."

"Sir, how did you move the bodies? Pardon and I do not wish to offend, but you're not a linebacker or a weightlifter. You are what about 50, weigh about 175 or so and are about five-ten. How did you do that by yourself?"

"I used my ground cloth, rolled each body in turn on it and dragged it over to the wall. Then I just rolled it off onto the ground. It wasn't particularly difficult, after I figured out from trying to drag the first body. You ever tried moving two hundred pounds of dead weight with no help Agent Carol?"

"No sir."

"Lee, as your attorney, I will advise you to answer just the questions that are asked, not the ones you want to answer."

"Yes, OK"

Sure enough, the coyotes and something else had been there. Despite my efforts, some parts of the bodies were uncovered. But mostly they were where Rusty and I left them. The feds shot stills, about nine million of them; used their digital cameras to shoot moving pics; fingerprinted everybody again and loaded all of them into black KIA body bags—the bags we all see on CNN from war zones.

"Do I need to send you guys a bill for my tent? I have this awful feeling that I'm not going to get it back, right, Agent Carol?"

"No sir, no way you'll get it back at least until after the trial. That's assuming that we actually find out who did this. Send the bill; we'll process it. Excuse me."

She turned and walked away. I heard snippets of phrases.

"No! Impossible! Where? Yessir, he's still here. Sir, she's still here too. Sorry, but I think she's staying. Yessir, I'll make sure they wait. Yessir."

"Dr. Phillips, Ms. Steele; my boss Agent Marks would like to speak with both of you in a bit. There are new developments. I think he has some questions. He'll be here in a few minutes."

The roar of that Blackhawk turbine engine and the heavy thump-thump-thump of its huge rotors was unmistakable. The pilot put it down at the low end of the mesa; an agent fetched their leader.

"What is the deal, Marks? I thought I'd be free to go as soon as I lead you folks to the bodies?"

"Normally Dr. Phillips, that would be true. But we've just found two more bodies. They look like cowboys—boots, jeans, spurs—the usual stuff. Well, actually they look like Mexicans, you know, Mexican cowboys. The vaqueros who told you about the tinajas: what did they look like? Can you remember what they were wearing—shirts, hats, gear, whatever?"

"Lee, be careful; you may not want to answer these questions. I'll stop you if I think we're in trouble, got it?"

"Yes, Susan, but I can describe these guys for the feds. Two more bodies; what the hell is going on here? OK, Marks, let me think. Both had straws, you know straw hats, American style, not sombreros. One had on a blue denim shirt. I don't remember the other one's shirt, but he was wearing one of those Mexican leather vests and riding a big sorrel. He had what was probably a lever-action .30x30 or something similar tucked in a saddle scabbard slung on the right side. Both wore leather chaps, well used. Both wore gloves and both removed only their right glove to shake hands with the strange gringo, but that's the local custom. Both had well-worn lariats slung over those big Mexican saddle pommels. The vaquero without the rifle did the talking; he spoke border English, but we wound up talking mostly in Spanish. He was the one who told me that they were hunting some strays, cattle. Cows, horses and lions, bears and other critters don't recognize the international border. They just cross from one side of the river to the other looking for grass or a meal. He told me about the tinajas. Funny thing though; the other guy was leading a packhorse with a packsaddle. It was slack; almost empty. But, these guys travel light; I figured they'd used up most of their rations and were making a last day or so search before heading back south of the river."

"Lee, you don't mind if I call you Lee, do you?

"Not if I can call you Carl."

"They ask for any coffee, water, beans, anything?"

"No they didn't; they did ask for a smoke, but I don't, so I couldn't help them there. Nothing unusual really. We didn't talk long; Rusty's presence made their horses skittish. So they went their way and I went mine, south toward these tinajas they'd told me about and the river."

"Which way was that?"

"Where did they head? East and north, back around toward the north side of the mountain. Why?"

"What's up there?"

So I explained. Big Bend is not downtown Austin or Dallas or even El Paso. It is really big, a lot of country between people. If you go far enough north from where we stood, you reach Marathon on U.S. 90. The Gage Hotel is the hot spot. If you have enough dinero and you can have a pretty damn good meal at the Gage and some pretty good tequila at the White Buffalo Bar. You go east from where we stood and you will run into Glen Spring or Hot Spring or Rio Grande Village Campground or, on the Mexican side, the town of Boquillas del Carmen. And of course there's the mine—Mariscal Mine. The gringos, early in the 20th century mined cinnabar there. The whole country has cinnabar deposits under it. Anyway, they'd dig it out of the ground, refine and process it into that silver liquid mercury, haul it on muleback or wagons, and ship it out in these seventy-six-pound lead flasks on the Southern Pacific at Marathon. But the mine has been deserted. The mine shafts are boarded up and sealed. The smelter is nothing but a few concrete buildings stripped of everything that is movable. There is a superintendent house, a bunch of shells of outbuildings—the usual ghost town stuff. Almost nothing grows there; probably too much pollution. Mercury smelting kills everything—grass, water table, animals and people.

"Anything else Lee?"

"Nope."

"So, these guys were alive when you last saw them and they were heading east and north?

"Don't answer that Lee. Shut up! I mean it! Agent Carol, Agent Marks, until we get some more information I'm advising my client to stay quiet. So, now what? Your turn."

Agent Marks spoke first.

"Dr. Phillips, Ms. Steele; we choppered up there, scouting the territory; made a big circle and everything was quiet, nothing moving until we got close to the mine. That's when we saw them, dozens of vultures, circling, and circling. We scattered them with the Blackhawk, but all we saw was a hole in the ground, and some vultures sitting on the roof of one of those houses. So, the pilot puts her down about 500 yards away. The closer we got, the worse it smelled—two horses in a hole in the ground, probably a mine airshaft or something. They were about 10–15 feet down on the lip of a really black hole. A few more feet over and those horses, one of them a sorrel, would have been at the bottom of that shaft and nobody would ever have smelled them or found them.

"We called for backup, set up a perimeter and worked out from the horses. That's when we found the cowboys in what looks like a residence. The ones you say you saw a couple of days ago? We're pretty sure it is them; same shirt, vest, chaps. Somebody did a pretty good job on them with a 12 gauge; not much left of faces, blood everywhere in that little room. We'd like to show them to you; get your positive ID."

"My client doesn't think at all; you stay quiet Lee until we get a little clarification here. Got it? Just nod yes; good. OK, Agent Marks, what now?"

"Ma'am; we just want to fly you and your client up there. We need some kind of positive ID on those horses and those bodies. Dr. Phillips here is our first hope in starting the identification process. Neither you nor he is compelled to go; we just think that if these are the vaqueros that he met that would help us. OK?"

After a few minutes more negotiation, Marks and Potter agreed that Susan could follow them up there in her chopper, if we were accompanied by Agent Carol. That meant that one of the Dereks had to be left behind. One Blackhawk led and another followed. Even to me, the most dunderheaded of all people, it looked like we were not so much escorted as boxed in.

We saw the vultures first, circling and huddled on the ground just out of range of the agents' sticks, which turned out to be 12 gauge pump Brownings. There must have been a hundred of them, vultures not FBI. I guess from the vultures' point of view, this was lunch, breakfast and dinner all rolled into one— for days—Turkey Vulture nirvana! The agents turned out to be Border Patrol and FBI guys and probably felt outnumbered. When we landed and the pilots cut the rotors, the smell hit all of us, not as intense as that in the little box canyon where the five decomposing bodies lay; but still something that compelled the use of Vick's Vapo-Rub—the universal antidote to bad smells. Its pungent odor blocks all but the most stubborn foul smells— rotting garbage, decaying flesh, whatever. There was a lot of dead horseflesh and a couple of dead vaqueros close by and the Vick's was just not up to the task.

The horses were first; they were closer, and there were only two. Saddles, bridles, blanket rolls intact. The rifle scabbard was empty. Aside from the fact that they were dead they looked complete to me. The stench was retching; vultures had been at work, despite the food being in that hole.

Bob Potter spoke first: "Those the animals you saw Lee?"

I told him all I knew. I especially remembered the sorrel. The tack and gear, down to the bedrolls look like the stuff I remembered. It sure looked like the stuff that the vaqueros carried. The rifle was missing; the sorrel was a positive. Those were fine animals. Those guys were much better mounted than most of the vaqueros along the border.

"What the hell killed them?"

"We don't know and we're still looking for the packhorse; could be at the bottom of that damn shaft there. Let's hope we find her wandering around this complex. I'm not looking forward to bringing in a crew of climbers to go into that hole. God Dammit, its hot here! How did these people stand it when they were digging that cinnabar ore out of the ground. In the summer this place must make Hell look like The Garden of Eden. How in God's name did they stand it? Never mind, the horses aren't the main reason we brought you here. The main event is this way," as we walked single file up the dusty crooked path to the first small concrete house.

The way I calculated it; these guys couldn't have been dead for more than about three days, but the putrefying intestines and seeping body fluids really impacted the senses. It was all I could do to keep from throwing up. As we stepped inside the low door opening, the evidence on the dirt floor indicated that I wasn't the only one having trouble keeping those breakfast tacos down.

The guy in the vest lay propped against the corner; no face, none at all. He looked like the fifth guy back in the canyon; probably a 12 gauge at close range. The other one, the guy who did the talking had been shot twice, one blast in the gut

41

and a second in the face. His hands were a bloody pulp; they probably took a lot of the blast. The poor bastard was trying to ward off lead pellets with his flesh. It doesn't work. It takes a special kind of cold blooded son of a bitch, a real stone killer, to shoot a man in the face at close range with a large bore shotgun.

Marks spoke first, "Recognize them?"

"Hell, Marks; there's nothing to recognize. There're no faces; looks like one of them has no fingers or hands either. I do recognize the vest on the one guy and the shirt on the other. When I saw them there wasn't any blood, gore and guts splattered all over their clothes. Where are their chaps and hats? They weren't on the horses."

"Got any idea what they were shot with Dr. Phillips?"

"Shotgun, Marks; at close range."

"What about the shell size; any idea?"

"Don't have a clue. Why?"

"Dr. Phillips, we picked up several 12 gauge shell casings from the floor. Any ideas? You carrying any buckshot, Ts, BBs or anything like that?"

"Sure, why?"

 Susan stopped the discussion. "Look, Marks: All I can say is that my client and his attorney are standing in a stifling hot, piss-stench-filled room with two very dead and decaying Mexican vaqueros who look like the guys he says he met on the trail several days ago. From the look of the bodies they were killed by shotgun blasts at very close range, maybe by someone who didn't want you government boys to identify them too quickly— hence no faces and one guy without any fingerprints. Aside from that, I don't think my client can help you; you guys are the forensic experts."

Marks opened his mouth to answer and uttered something that was drowned out by Susan: "Where the hell is this going Marks? What are you insinuating? Are you thinking that my client's shotgun did this? He's the one who told you about meeting these Mexican cowboys in the first place. He even gave you the descriptions that he just verified. Are you accusing him of something? I'm beginning to think so! He's made the positive ID you needed. Unless you have something else directly related to the identification of these men, I'm taking my client and my bodyguard and I'm telling my pilot to crank up my chopper and take all of us back to some semblance of civilization as soon as we can. Any more questions, Marks?"

"No, ma'am. But I may have a few more questions after we collect these guys and do a thorough search of the immediate area for any other evidence that might tell us what happened here. I'm sure you're uncomfortable. Agent Carol and one of the Blackhawks will escort you folks back to Castolon. If you'll wait for us there, I'm pretty sure we can cut you folks loose pretty quickly after I get all your client's bodies corralled. I'm just kidding, ma'am."

"Goddamn, Susan, what the hell is going on?"

"Damned if I know. But this is really a major problem for you. I don't think you're gonna get back to that book really soon. I hope you don't have an advance on it."

"Actually, Susan, I do—a pretty good one too."

"Too damn bad, Lee."

#

Waiting is something neither I nor Susan Steele do well. Rusty was cool. He played with Carlito. He scarfed down another can of Spam and took a nap. We, meanwhile, sipped iced tea and rocked about two hours away in Maria's handmade oak rockers. Maria was gracious as always and did her best not to ask too many questions about the bodies. She did talk about the Mariscal Mine buildings. She remembered some of them. She remembered the layout of the compound, having been taken there several times by an uncle, Tío Gasparito. From what I could tell, Gasparito, or little Gaspar was because his grandfather was also named Gaspar, and he was still living when Maria's uncle was born. According to Maria the family was originally from the little Mexican village and presidio of San Vicente, across the river and slightly downstream from the mine. Tío Gasparito worked at the mine as a teenager. According to Maria the wages were good; the gringo jefes were not harsh. They allowed the workers to return to their villages once a month for visits to their families. They could also take their wages, which were paid in American silver dollars, back to their villages, their wives, girlfriends and families. As Maria recalled, her uncle's most vivid memories were not of the mine work, but of the early deaths of many of his coworkers, most of strange wasting diseases.

Rusty heard them first, the choppers. Everybody ducked; covered their eyes as the swirling dust clouds blanketed the compound.

Marks and Potter slid out of the first Blackhawk; chatted a minute with Agent Carol, and all three headed our way.

Susan stood up. "Something's not right Lee. Their stride is different. You keep quiet unless I tell you to talk. Look at me, smile and nod your head."

I did it.

"Lee, we need to ask you some more questions."

Susan spoke. "Agents, you talk with me first; got it? You understand, Agent Carol, Agent Marks, Captain Potter?"

"Yes, ma'am, but we really need to get some clarification from your client."

"Lee, unless I tell you to talk you will be very quiet, right." Susan could be really assertive when she needed to be.

"Yes Ma'am. You bet."

Even my idiot self had begun to figure out that these guys were beginning to suspect ME of committing at least some of these crimes. So I shut up.

Agent Marks asked first: "You had a 12 gauge semi auto. You had a javelina permit, yes?"

Susan nodded to answer.

"Yes, for the 12 gauge."

Again, yes answer.

"What kind of shells—Buckshot, Ts, BBs? What?"

"Carl, I had slugs for the javelina; Number 4 Buck and Ts for everything else. That's it."

"And you fired exactly how many?"

"That's enough, Marks!" said Susan.

"Ma'am, we think the vaqueros were killed with either buckshot or Ts. That makes your client a suspect or at least a material witness."

"Agent Marks, did you find any evidence that my client was at Mariscal Mine during the last several days? Answer yes or no."

"No, ma'am, we didn't. But as far as we know Dr. Phillips is the last known person to see the vaqueros alive and there are several 12 gauge shells at that scene, not to mention 12 gauge shells at the scene of the other murder down the canyon. So you can see our problem."

"Actually, Agent, I don't see a damn bit of it, but I don't suppose that will make much difference, will it? I have a suggestion. You have a multiple murder scene to investigate. My client perhaps has additional information that might be useful. His life has not been threatened; he is no flight risk. Hell, Marks, everybody in the country has known Lee Phillips for almost twenty years. I think you're leaning toward taking Dr. Phillips into custody as a material witness. Right?"

"Yes ma'am, that's where I was headed, for his own protection. My primary concern is this: Whoever did these killings is out there somewhere. Dr. Phillips was the first person to find five of the bodies and as far as we know is the last person, except the killer or killers, to see the two dead vaqueros. I have a very large investigation that is only beginning. It is a pretty big deal. We have more dead people in three or four days that we get in these counties in a year. The investigators include representatives of every law enforcement agency in West Texas and the Mexicans will send their people as well. So, you bet it is a big deal; witness a very high-dollar New Orleans attorney spending several days out here."

"Marks, can you get Captain Barrera and Captain Potter on that phone?"

"Yes, ma'am."

"If I can get Potter and Barrera, both of whom are longtime friends of my client, to guarantee his safety and his presence in the area for at least two more days, you could live with that, right?"

"He'll be available to review his statement and perhaps to fill in any gaps in what he remembers?"

"Can you do that Lee?"

"Yes. If I can offer a suggestion: Maybe I could spend a day or two with Bob up at Panther Junction? Bob and Mary Lou have the room; Rusty and I have visited before. You can't get much safer than hanging out with the chief of Big Bend National Park Law Enforcement."

So, Marks, Susan, Juan and Bob struck a deal.

On the speakerphone Bob said: "Lee, the FBI will fly you and Rusty to Panther. I have two law enforcement rangers who will meet you. I'll call my bride and she will have your room ready. The kids will be happy to see Rusty. Hang tight until I get there this evening. The rangers have orders not to let you out of their sight. So, they'll be a little bit of a bother."

"Thanks, Bob. Rusty and I will enjoy the stay."

"Hey Lee, think we can talk about that book of yours while you're at Panther?"

"You bet. See you this evening."

I have to admit that spending the evening with Potter and his family was much more fun than an overnight in the Brewster County Jail. Bob was one of the few locals with any interest in the subject of my book. Many were curious in a polite way, but when I told them that I was writing a book about the legends of the Ark of the Covenant in the borderlands, I could see their eyes begin to glaze. Bob was one of the few with more than a passing interest.

His branch of the LDS church was more militant, and I truly believe that Bob thought the Ark would be a great addition to the Temple in Salt Lake. That evening, after supper and after the five kids were in bed, Bob and I took snifters and a carafe of hundred-year-old Napoleon Brandy to the back porch of his casa at Panther Junction. We warmed the brandy over one of those little metal camper lanterns, the kind powered by one candle enclosed in a glass cylinder. I never cared for them; the light is no damned good. I will say that they're great for warming brandy. Mary Lou never joined us in these brandy-enhanced discussions. I think mainly because Bob usually took the opportunity to smoke a Cuban cigar.

"Where do you get those things Bob?"

"Ciudad Chihuahua; Mary Lou has relatives there. You know there's a large LDS population there."

I'm not comfortable discussing a work in progress. Bob knows this, but it was fun to trade stories about the borderlands. In the process we danced around the topic.

I can attest that hundred-year-old Napoleon Brandy is better than about anything else you can drink. After about an hour both he and I had what I like to call a warm glow. Time to turn in.

"Lee, I think Susan will be here early tomorrow. Marks and Texas Ranger Hays have a few more questions. She'll haul you to Alpine. I think you two have an appointment at noon. You're a lucky guy to know her. What do you figure that chopper costs to operate on an hourly basis?"

"Not a clue, Bob. Thanks for the hospitality and please thank Mary Lou for me. If Susan runs true to form, she'll be here at the crack of dawn."

About 6:30, the Whisper Jet landed in the parking lot..

"Hi, tough guy."

Susan, in a new, citified outfit, was there bright and early with a briefcase full of legal shit. It is amazing what high-powered, and high-priced lawyers can do with the levers of the justice system, or as I call it, the due process system. She'd found a judge who agreed that I was a cooperative witness and that neither the feds, nor the local county mounties could hold me as a material witness. He signed the writ, which suited me fine. Nobody gave me back my shotgun; I figured that my heirs would see the .45—maybe. I sure as hell wouldn't. In fifteen minutes we landed in Alpine.

"We're clear until noon. Wha'dya want for breakfast chief—huevos y chorizo, McDonalds, what?"

"How about me, you and Rusty have a regular eggs, bacon, grits, biscuits and two side orders of ham for Rusty in Fort Davis? That OK?"

"You bet, Lee. Derek and Derek will drive. I think Joanne's Café on the Alpine Road in Ft. Davis will work, don't you? You, me, Derek and Derek and all the guys in the local pickups?"

"Hit it; it's only twenty-two miles."

"Hell, Susan, what's next?"

"I don't know Lee, but right now I think the bastards will leave you alone. But you absolutely, positively, really real, must keep your nose clean. Got it?"

"Yup, can I go back to the Ranch? You think the bastards will leave me alone?"

"I doubt it, but give it a shot. When is Lisa supposed to be coming?"

"Now that you've got the fuzz off my ass for a bit she'll be here on the regular timeframe, two weeks."

"Lee, I don't think you're gonna have a problem with the feds or Texas Rangers. You should be out of there in an hour. I called Luís. The pilot will sit you down at the landing strip at the Ranch. Luís or Tomás will be there to haul your ass back to Sauceda or Los Alamos."

Joanne's was great as usual. Susan and the Dereks drove me back to Alpine. She and I did the Q&A thing with Marks and Hays. She was right. We were done in an hour. Then she and the Dereks waited while I picked up some groceries at Garza's Super Mercado.

"Lee, I really have to get back to the Big Easy. I'm due in court tomorrow. You have all my numbers; call if you need me. I love you."

Then Susan's chopper hauled us back to Big Bend Ranch and deposited me and Rusty on the 7,000–foot runway, about ten minutes east of Sauceda and about thirty minutes by 4x4 from my house. She and her keepers high tailed it for New Orleans, or rather Midland, where they would pick up her jet for home. Tomás and Luís were there with Pepper, a cool one (beer for me, water for Rusty) and an offer to ride back to Los Alamos with me.

"Señor Lee, your truck and SUV are at Los Alamos. Star is there too, in the corral. Luís turned on the air conditioner. We thought the horseback ride would be welcome."

"Gracias, Tomás. Muchas gracias. Let's go."

We rode about an hour from the airfield to Los Alamos in silence. Tomás stayed a few minutes; he and I had a beer on the north porch steps. He mounted up and headed west, back to Sauceda.

If you liked quiet, Los Alamos (Spanish for Cottonwoods) was perfect. It had a yard surrounded mostly by a five foot high adobe wall, with a corral and lean-to shed for the horses and a carport attached to the house where the TPWD 4x4 and my little SUV were parked. The 1600 square foot, two-bedroom adobe former ranch house with windows on all sides faced the mountains to the north. It had wide covered porches on the north, west and south sides. All were fully equipped with benches and at least two rockers per side. The cottonwoods, all four of them, the smallest with a diameter of three feet, were in the "backyard," the part of the compound facing Mexico to the south. It was perfect for a ranch house and for someone like me. The bedrooms were small. I actually used the one on the east as a bedroom. The other, facing south, I transformed into an office, with my pc and printer on my rough plank work table that faced the mountains to the south. I had filled the bookshelves covering two walls with a jumble of research volumes, DVDs, notes and office supplies. Most of the "living" occurred in the big central L shaped combination kitchen, living room and dining room. The furniture was worn but comfortable: the usual sleeper couch; three overstuffed chairs; some 1930s-era end tables with generations of coffee cup rings, assorted dried goo, and cigarette burns on their finish; and two World War II wooden U.S. Army packing crates that had found an extended use as coffee tables, the kind that nobody told you to "Get your boots off the furniture." I had added a heavy Spanish-style oak dining table that would seat ten, which was a little strange since there were

49

not ten people within twenty miles in any direction. An assortment of wooden straight-back and ladder-back dining room chairs completed the layout and claimed most of the alcove next to the kitchen. Because it was close to the door nearest the carport, the table was usually cluttered with stuff from outside. It had a good view of the mountains to the north, so I regularly worked there, usually on my laptop.

There were a few amenities devoted to Rusty and my hearing issues. The Ranch staff had installed three doggie doors that Rusty could use 24/7, which was fine with me. One opened to the front porch, one to the carport, the other out the back toward the corral. I paid for them to be installed. Lisa had insisted that I install a lights–On/Off switch in every room with a hanging cord so Rusty could pull on them. So we did, install them that is—one in the bedroom, another on two sides of the porch, one in the kitchen, and the last in the bath. They all had loud awful, siren noises and incredibly bright blinking lights. I hated all of them.

The only other furniture was a large-screen TV hooked up to a satellite dish which also delivered the frequencies for my DSL connection. Luís and the park staff had hung slide curtains with, as they said, "a Southwest motif." They even framed some prints and hung them. There was even the obligatory poster of the Mexican revolutionary populist hero Emiliano Zapata. My contribution was an enlarged print of General Francisco "Pancho" Villa in Ciudad Juárez around 1915, accompanied by a number of gringo soldiers of fortune, most of whom I had identified as part of my research.

The kitchen was basic but spacious: a four burner propane gas stove with oven, a gas refrigerator, the usual cluttered counters, and scarred double tub porcelain sink. My major complaint was that to use the washing machine I had to go outside around the corner to the storage room. The plus was this: the storeroom had been added later. When they built it, the contractors left the old window on the west side. Fortunately for me, it still worked and I used it as my dirty clothes chute. Just strip, open window, throw clothes directly into the washer—the perfect guy solution to a niggling housekeeping problem. Los Alamos had no drier, didn't need one. An old fashioned clothesline was hung on 16d nails strung between two porch posts on the west side. With ten percent humidity, virtually everything dried in about twenty minutes. Sometimes I could start hanging stuff and by the time I reached the other end, a distance of about fifteen feet, the first stuff would be dry.

Luís and the staff had cranked up the swamp cooler. In this country, adding just a small amount of humidity and moving some air was a blessing. I was always amazed at the simplicity of a swamp cooler, basically a fan that blew air over a series of water-soaked coils. Rusty was quiet, really tuckered out; he dozed in the shade of the front porch. The solar power array on the roof combined with my generator and battery set did wonders, keeping all the electronics agreeably working at full throttle. The computer worked fine; despite my efforts to derail it. It was time to get back to the purpose of my stay at the Ranch, my book.

But first, unpack, sort and store. Tomás had piled everything from the packhorse inside the front door: tack, clothes, personal gear, all jumbled together. I split out the saddle tack, bridles, and camp gear and stowed it in the adobe-walled shed next to the corral and lean-to. Next were the clothes; everything was dirty, even I knew that. That's when I found it, the throwaway camera.

"Damn, Rusty, I forgot all about this thing. I'll call 'em tomorrow. They'll send somebody for it." The phone blinked, showing fifteen messages. Tomorrow would be soon enough to deal with technology.

I slept the sleep of the just. No bad dreams for me, no erotic dreams, no dreams of any kind; no falling or those other signals of a life less than perfectly lived. Nine hours in my own bed. Rusty slept on the floor at the foot of the double bed as usual. And, as usual, I woke at five; it was still dark, very dark, black. In October, daylight comes late on the far western edge of the Central Time Zone. Brewing coffee awaited me— Community Dark Roast which told me that, first, we still had electricity and, second, I had remembered to load the pot last night.

CHAPTER 4: REVELATIONS

I sleep in the nude, but if you're at the end of the road you don't have to worry too much about what the neighbors will think. Besides, if it's before daylight, you and the dog can piss off the porch if you want. I didn't and he didn't, but the corral was close and available for the both of us. I fed the horses their oats and hay in that false grey/orange light before dawn, about an hour before that very pale pink light that actually heralds the arrival of another day. Rusty did his recon; I did mine.

"Rusty, ever thought that a naked guy wearing only Rough-out Wellingtons might look a little foolish walking around in the very cool West Texas dawn in the middle of the largest state park in the Lower 48?" No answer of course; he just looked at me like I was King of the Universe. He thumped his very authoritative tail against my naked left calf, and off we went.

No need to go to the curb to check if the paperboy has delivered the local rag, a religious exercise for me in Austin. Here, no curb, no local rag, and the paperboy has no turnaround. Coffee ready; I filled a cup and laced it with evaporated milk. I cranked up the satellite link for my trusty computer. The email total was something like 245, way too much stuff to tackle at 5:30 a.m. The phone messages were less daunting.

"Rusty, look. There are three from your buddy Lisa." Thump, thump!

They were dated before the murders, wondering if I was still alive; the next ten were from Charly Burnside, actually Charlotte Burnside, my longtime friend and incredibly gifted multilingual researcher from the King William District in downtown San Antonio. She knew half a dozen languages; was at home in Spanish and Mexican archives on several continents. She is one of those four or five degrees of separation geniuses. She knows virtually all of the state, local, national, city and private archives and research libraries in the western hemisphere north of the Equator—backwards, forwards and upside down. She knows all the archivists, many of them intimately, the curators, and even some of the receptionists in virtually every repository in Texas, Mexico and most of those in Spain. I was spending a big chunk of my $40,000 advance from the University of Texas Press to buy her time. By call number eight Charly was frantic: "Lee, call me; right now. You're not going to believe what I've found in the Bexar Archives in downtown San Antonio."

Charly said it was important. I quit counting at fifteen. "Lee, this is really important, really, really important!"

Then the last: "Lee, you absolutely have to call me tonight!"

So I did, except it was three days after her last imperative and 6:00 in the morning, now six days since I found the dead guys. Charly answered on the second ring

"Lee, you're all over the newspapers, CNN, FOX, everywhere. You're a celeb. But that's not why I called; I've found something. I can't talk about it on the phone."

"Charly, your messages said call. That's what I'm doing. What have you found? Tell me now."

"Can't, Lee; I found something that will change your book and your life. I'm coming out. I have an open ticket on Southwest. Can you pick me up at the Midland airport?"

"No, Charly, I can't. I'm at Los Alamos; you'll be in Midland before I get off the Ranch. Take Southwest to Midland; rent a four-wheel-drive high clearance truck. I'm paying for it anyway. Come out to the Ranch. Luís and the crew will love to see you again—La Chica Giganta. OK? We'll have incredible steaks; they'll cook 'em. See you soon."

"Lee; no! Remember me? I'm 6 feet 3 inches, a tall girl. I'll fly to Midland and rent something big. Besides, I've been to the desert and I don't like it. Meet me in Alpine. Can I bring you anything?"

"I think I'm good; besides, I have your cell and if I think of something I'll call. You can stop at a Big Box store in

Odessa, Midland or Pecos and pick it up. Deal? OK, see you this afternoon in Alpine. Where?"

"Railroad Blues; I'm bringing the Les Paul. You don't think I'm coming all this way just to see you. Their RRB legendary jam should be good after 4:00 p.m. See you then at RRB, Alpine. OK?"

"Charly, there can't be anybody jamming at four in the afternoon, even at Railroad Blues. Who the hell gets off work that early?"

She just laughed. "Lee, you need to get out more. Where the hell have you been, you academic ding-dong? Short answer is yes, there will be a jam. And you know that Railroad serves beer and anything else you want that's legal all the time! Where the hell have you been boy? You're not going to believe this stuff I found. You and I are going to be famous and maybe rich. The trick is for you to live long enough to finish writing the book. See you later today. Bye."

Click.

"Well, hell, Rusty, back to Alpine; we'll stop to see Juan on the way."

Juan, Captain Juan Barrera, was one of the very few people, aside from Charly, Lisa, Susan and folks like Maria at Castolon and her son Carlito, who were officially allowed to feed Rusty treats. Rusty is a big shepherd and large dogs shouldn't be heavy. If he ate everything everybody offered he'd be a whale.

I showered; blended and wolfed down a grapefruit juice, soy powder and frozen blueberry smoothie and the requisite vitamins. I gave Rusty his dry food; checked Pepper and Star for food and water. They'd be fine for two days. Rusty and I headed out in the TPWD 4x4. Although the truck had AC that actually worked, Rusty loved sticking his head out the passenger window and reveling in all those smells. The trip from Los Alamos to Alpine is a good three hours, most of that getting off the Ranch.

On the way to Alpine I stopped to check in with the Border Patrol District office in Presidio. Juan, the Border Patrol District Director, met us at the office door.

"Lee, I am glad to see you. Rusty! Come, tuna treats today. Sorry I missed the trip to Talley and the mine. Seven bodies in two days! You are not good to be around; people turn up dead. What the hell is going on, Lee?"

"Juan, my lawyer has told me not to talk about this to any of you official guys."

"Lee, it's me, Juan! I've known you for over twenty years. You, me, Lisa and even that Cajun chick Susan have spent much time in the mountains and desert. Amigo y amigo!"

"Juan, you just said it; seven bodies in a couple of days. Hell, man, it freaks me out just to think about it. Besides, I really have to get to Alpine to see a friend of mine. I might stay over. I'll catch you on the comeback, OK?"

"Sure, Lee; anything I can do, you let me know."

"Juan, I'll see you either late this evening or tomorrow; I promise. Maybe we can go to Ojinaga if you're off duty; have a couple of beers and enjoy some great food and conversation."

"OK, gringo; see you on the comeback."

Presidio to Alpine—a long lonesome ride. The land and the vistas get prettier—well, depending on your definition of beauty—as you go north past Shafter, the old silver and mercury mining ghost town. Presidio, Texas is the place the TV weatherman pointed to in the 1950s and 1960s. It had the hottest temperatures in the Lower 48. I always thought it was a good place to be *FROM*. But the locals loved it. To me, the Mexican city of Ojinaga across the river was far more interesting.

I arrived early in Alpine, just time enough to drop the film off at Nowatney's Drug Store; do some shopping at Garza's Super Mercado and truck over to Railroad Blues—the world-famous juke joint, biker bar, grill, local hang out and pillar of the community located right next to the Union Pacific tracks in downtown Alpine. Rusty didn't really like loud places like this; but he knew everybody in this part of Texas—lots of pats on the head, rubs under the chin and offers to feed him, all answered in the negative. Nevertheless, the music at RRB confused him, and me, and even he couldn't hear well enough to protect me. Frankly, I have problems with the volume also. Besides, I don't hear most of the tones.

Sure enough, there were folks on stage with vintage instruments, playing vintage rock 'n' roll, Charly among them. She was the tall chick with the Les Paul. The audience was the usual: assorted bikers, aging boomers, stoned out hippies from Austin or Terlingua, and folks who had accidentally stumbled into the joint off U.S. 90. The band sounded pretty good, even for a semi-deaf guy like me. And even I can tell the difference between musicians who are good and those who are gifted, who are masters at their craft. Charly and all of those on stage with her were masters. I waved; she waved.

"Go say Hi, Rusty."

Rusty bounded up to the stage; got his tongue into Charly's strings and generally t-thump, thumped his way to a set that came to a dead solid halt. She said "Sit"; he Sat. She played two more tunes and bowed out. She put the Les Paul in its case but left it on stage, said her good-byes and leaped off the stage in my direction.

"Rusty, you sure look good; taking care of the boss man? Here, want a burger? Shut up Lee; he'll enjoy it. Come on, let's take a walk."

Rusty munched the hamburger; we walked. There's a little city roadside park, really just a couple of benches under some live oaks a short distance down U.S. 90 to the east. We sat. Charly pulled two beers in brown bags out of her satchel; handed one to me.

"What you got, music chick? It must be good to get you out of San Antonio and me off the Ranch."

"Lee, you run it together like a native—Sanantonio—all one word. You been doing that long? Never mind. You know you're not my only contract. I've been doing some work in the Bexar Archives on the Spanish revolutionary Bernardo Gutierrez de Lara—you know, the Green Flag Republic of 1813, the co-leader of the Gutierrez-Magee Expedition .I ran across a reference to another set of documents, late seventeenth century, early eighteenth. The reference relates to papers of two distant relatives of Gutierrez de Lara—two women on the Spanish frontier, sisters.

"Here's the short version of what I found. First, the stuff I got when I requested it was only one small, slim folder and a small box. The box was tied closed with a string. It contained a diary written in a distinctly feminine hand. The only name on it, an octavo piece, was someone named Maria de S. Arredondo, neatly written on the first page. I checked the request list and as far as I, and the archivist can tell, nobody had ever checked out the folder. I was the first. There was no note as to who donated the papers to the archives, nothing as to provenance. I'm close, very close if you get my drift, to the principal archivist. He checked their records and there is no record of these things ever being donated. However, they were accessioned properly over fifty years ago; but that is all that is known."

"Charly, let's cut to the chase, here."

"Lee, these sisters lived in Santa Fe in the late 1670s. In an age when most women in that culture were not literate, these two women could write and, given some of their literary allusions, were probably classically educated, more than likely privately by priests. Anyhow, they witnessed some of the most vicious struggles of the New Mexico Pueblo Revolt of 1680, you know the time when the Pueblo tribes in Northern New Mexico booted out the Spaniards, including these two women and their families. In the folder there is a manuscript diary. There are eleven letters, seven from one sister and four from the other. I think those four are copies. Because of the name on the archive listing, it appears that the collection comes from the estate or heirs of the sister who eventually settled in Ysleta, near present El Paso. Are you following so far?"

"Yeah. But so far this is not enough for an airline ticket and to get you away from your beloved downtown San Antonio, even for a Railroad Blues jam session. C'mon."

"Lee, give me a break; this is really dramatic. Allow me the drama, OK?"

"Only if me and Rusty don't starve to death between now and the time you finish the tale."

"In that case, let's keep on walking. There's a Mexican restaurant down here somewhere. To continue, Lee: A couple of the diary entries describe the Pueblo Revolt of 1680; the Spaniards' retreat south to what we now consider to be the Texas-Mexican border. They tell of the atrocities—the deaths of one woman's husband and the other's two young children, all occurring on the infamous Jornada del Muerto, the Journey of Death. You've been there. The route goes through the desert south of Albuquerque, through White Sands, and ends at El Paso, which then didn't exist. One sister stopped at Ysleta, a small pueblo of Indians loyal to the Spaniards. The other, the newly widowed one, finds a protector in one Captain Jose Arredondo of the Spanish army. She, and he, trek on to Ciudad Chihuahua, then a major military post on the northern frontier of New Spain. In that part of the journey they are in the company of a handful of soldiers and a two-wheel wagon driven by a priest. Does that name Arredondo ring any bells in your historian head?"

"Nope."

"It should. General Arredondo, a Spanish royalist officer, led an army north from south of the Rio Grande and defeated the revolutionary army led by our boy Bernardo Gutierrez de Lara in 1813 at the Battle of the Medina, just south of San Antonio. The Green Flag Republic troops lost over 1,000 dead—the bloodiest battle ever fought on Texas soil. The Alamo and San Jacinto in 1836 are not even in the same league. The royalist retribution was brutal and barbaric—torture, brutal executions, severed heads displayed on pikes on Military Plaza in San Antonio, the whole nine yards. Anyway, the names Arredondo and Gutierrez are inexorably linked."

"Charly, give me the bottom line here, OK?"

"OK, here goes: The bottom line, Lee, is that given the writings of these two sisters and other archival sources in Mexico and Spain, I, no you, in your book can demonstrate that the Ark of the Covenant was at least for a time resident in the

New World. More important, it may have been housed in a little-known presidio, San Vicente, on what is now the Texas-Mexico border, just south of Mariscal Canyon in Big Bend. And for all I know, it is still here, someplace in the Southwest."

"Holy Shit, Charly; you're kidding, right?"

"Charly, you mean to tell me that the holiest object in both Jewish and Christian history, perhaps the keystone of Western Civilization, was, and maybe still is, hidden in the New World, possibly in one of the most remote parts of the American Southwest, or the Mexican borderlands?"

"Lee, stay with me now! I've had a little time to adjust to these possibilities; you haven't. I'm not kidding! No! Absolutely not; and here is why. The diary and at least two of the letters reference some strange, vaguely understood, and more than likely non-Roman Catholic rites. Maria even copied some of the lettering on one of the crates or boxes that the soldiers and the priest were guarding and that were taken to San Vicente. I brought my sketch and my translation with me. There's one other thing, a strange symbol that Señora Arredondo sketched, but did not explain. It's this."

Using condensation from the Negra Modelo in the brown bag, with her index finger she drew, on the wooden plank of the dusty picnic table, a small Star of David with the numeral seven, written the Spanish way with the cross-slash on it. The numeral was centered in the star.

"Lee, have you ever seen this written anywhere before; run across it anywhere in your research?"

"Never saw it; read about it, or heard of it. You have any ideas?"

"I'm afraid not, Lee, but maybe you will after you read the material."

Charly, if what you tell me is true; do you realize what this does?"

"Sure Lee. It turns "Raiders of the Lost Ark" on its ear. The Ark of the Covenant did not wind up in some wooden crate stored in a vast U.S. Government warehouse. Instead, it is HERE! Get it! HERE, in the Southwest, maybe in Big Bend or

Northern Mexico! I'm not kidding, but you will be more famous than Steven Spielberg or Harrison Ford, the guy with the really cool hat and damn good .38 Special. Come on Rusty, let's go to La Tapatía down the street and get some Mexican food. The mole is to die for. You game? Bring the Doctor too."

Thump, thump! We walked. I thought; Charly talked; Rusty thumped his tail on both Charly's calf and mine and made sure I did not stumble across the next traffic signal.

Charly summarized it all before we got to La Tapatía. How in her work on another project she found a small folder, totally by happenstance. Inside were some letters and a diary. They were related to two obscure women on the Spanish frontier, sisters. According to the documents the two were born in Spain, and both, when the correspondence and the diary began, were living on the northern frontier of New Spain in the same town, Santa Fe. They were there because they were both married to Spanish army officers.

In the Pueblo Revolt of 1680, the locals decided that they've had enough of Spanish Christianity. In one of those rare occasions when they were both organized and united. They attacked their oppressors. They killed every Spaniard they could get their hands on including the husband of one sister, Maria. The entire Spanish community fled south. Eventually one sister settled down in Ysleta; the other in an outpost called Presidio de San Vicente.

"Charly, is this the San Vicente I think it is?"

"Hell, Lee, I don't know. If it is, I wish to add that we think of it as incredibly remote, but then it was on one part of what was known as the Comanche War Trail which was well-traveled and well-known. Most of the material in this folder is in the handwriting of the sister in San Vicente. In this manuscript there is a description of the retreat through southern New Mexico, and it includes her journey to the final settlement in San Vicente. Some of the subsequent letters appear to be answers responding to her sister's letters. Some are not."

"And?"

"It seems that when the large group reached Ysleta, some determined, were driven almost, to continue south across the Rio Grande to the larger outpost of Ciudad Chihuahua. Maria and her soon-to-be new husband, Captain Arredondo were in that group."

"What was her name?"

"Arredondo, Lee: I've already told you. Why?"

"No, what was her other name or names?"

"Her full name, Lee, was Señora Maria de Sosa y Arredondo. Her family name was de Sosa.

"Charly, you know that the de Sosa family has, in recent scholarship, been considered Jewish?"

"Yes, but I'm still not sure about that. Anyway, as the story reads she, her captain, eight Spanish soldados, and an unnamed padre continued south to Chihuahua. That is when the first letter was written to the sister at the Ysleta, pueblo where the Spaniards were hanging on to their New Mexico territory by their fingernails. In that letter, she tells her sister that she and her new Captain husband are going to the newly founded Presidio of San Vicente where he will be the Comandante."

"What was the full name of the sister who stayed in Ysleta?"

"Her name was Señora Josefa de Sosa y Barbo Gutiérrez. The last name is probably why the letters and the diary were assigned to the Bernardo Gutierrez file. I thought you would want to read the entire folder so here it is, on a flash drive and a CD. I've kept a copy, too, just in case you screw it up, given your ineptitude with computers. I don't think I can offer much more until you've had a chance to read the entire folder. You do that, then call or email. No, check that; don't email. Call me on a landline—security. You and Rusty be careful going home."

"Charly, what is the deal? This stuff about security is not like you."

She gave me a quizzical look, like parents sometimes give to a slightly slow child, or relatives give a slightly demented aunt.

"You keep thinking like that and you're going to be really dead and I'll have to take care of Rusty. Lee, look at me. Watch my mouth and lips. You got any idea about what information about the Ark is worth? If that doesn't snap your chain, think about this: What do you think the people who hid it in the first place would do and pay to keep it secret and hidden? You're a bright guy; go from there. There are about a zillion permutations. In this story there is an ample supply of good guys and bad guys. . . . But, let's eat; come on Rusty. Bring him too; he has the credit card."

And indeed we did and I did.

Charly ate some sort of chicken thing with mole sauce; Rusty had an order of fajita meat; hold the sauce and hold the tortillas. I had two crispy tacos with beef. We agreed that I would call after I had read the documents in the flash drive and on the CD.

"So, what now, Charly?"

"I'm going back to Railroad Blues. You're welcome to come too, if you want."

"What's playing?"

"A band called the West Texas Switchyard."

"OK, Charly, I'll bite. Who or what is the West Texas Switchyard?"

"Never heard of them, huh?"

"Nope, should I?"

"'Fraid not; it's a pickup band."

"Sooooo?"

"OK, here it is: the line up: There's this fiftyish biker who plays the harmonica, well, actually several harmonicas. He also plays the flute—don't ask. They must pack well on a Harley. His name is Clarence Darius Smith; call him C.D.— almost nobody walks away standing upright with no broken bones after calling him Clarence. He's 6 feet 3 inches and is really a great guy. But he does wear a Harley chain as a belt. Then there's this really tall blond guy with incredibly long legs and a really great looking tight butt who plays a mean electric bass. I think I'm in love—well, maybe lust. The drummer is a guy who teaches Ag or something like that at Sul Ross State University here in Alpine."

"You guys and girls just gonna play, or is somebody singing?"

"Singing? What singing? Tonight, I'm the lead guitar and part-time singer, at least in the first set. Actually, tonight we feature local talent besides me—a girl and a guy. You want to come listen?"

"Sorry Charly; I've got horses to feed and the music doesn't do that much for me, no where close to what it does for you. Good luck! Call me when you get back to SA."

She went back to Railroad Blues. I stopped by the Nowatney's Drug Store and retrieved my photos. A quick look showed that the subjects were as dead and as gruesomely displayed as when I shot the pics the first time. It was definitely time to hand this stuff off to the NPS and the Border Patrol. The FBI was heading the investigation, but I still had doubts about Agent Marks.

I dropped one of the three envelopes into a mailer, scribbled Bob Potter's name and his address at Big Bend National Park HQ in Panther Junction, added a short note, and dropped it into the mailbox outside Nowatney's. I intended to give the second set to Captain Juan and head home. The third set was mine. I figured I'd earned it. Stumbling onto those dead guys had cost me several days on my book. It had disrupted my traverse across Big Bend. Frankly I was pissed at everybody, well, everybody except Charly, Susan, and Rusty.

It was late when I arrived in Presidio. The desk clerk at BP District asked for identification. She buzzed me through the security door and informed me that Captain Barrera was out on night patrol. I borrowed an Interoffice Memo envelope, stuck one packet of prints in it; licked the envelop flap and sealed it. I wrote Barrera's name in the "To" column and mine in the place marked "From"; handed it to the clerk. Rusty and I headed back to Los Alamos.

The horses woke us up; and the rain. It was really pounding. A cold wind blew out of the Sierra de Madre in

Mexico, from the southwest. The temperature dropped twenty degrees in about an hour. It probably wouldn't last long. No need to crank up a big fire. I lit the little propane space heater in the living room; loaded my dark roast and pulled on a tee, a flannel shirt, jeans, boots, and my battered black Stetson and hoofed it outside to feed Pepper and Star who seemed pleased to be dry, watered and well fed in their little lean-to. Rusty did his business, ate, and curled up on his pallet in the corner of the living room. It promised to be one of those rare, grey, raw Big Bend days—a good day to have a great breakfast of chorizo y huevos, watch CNN and TWC on my really cool satellite TV, drink strong coffee laced with evaporated milk, and stay and work inside, which is exactly what Rusty and I did. I do believe that he had better naps than I did. It was time to get back to the job at hand, which was working on the book. That little task now included reading the documents Charly had brought from San Antonio. But first, I was drawn to one last look at my photos of the murder scene.

I kicked off the Wellingtons and, sitting at my oak dining-room table, I poured the contents of the drugstore envelope on to the table.

For the first time I realized that there were several items in the packet. The duplicate set of 4x6 pics were there, just as ordered. But so was a note from Nowatney's : "Dear Nowatney's customer: In addition to the prints you've ordered, we have included a separate copy of them on a digital CD, at no cost to you. These photographs can be enhanced by you . . . ." There was a lot of stuff about PC programs and keystrokes and such, all of which I declined to be interested in, at least for the moment. But, what the hell. I shot 'em into my PC, hit "Open" and pulled up the digital pics one at a time. They were even more grotesque than before—five bodies in a sort of row. One had legs together, hands raised like in the old western movies; another was on his side with arms outstretched. Two of the others together made a weird "M" shape. But the blood was everywhere, on the canyon walls, but mostly in the sand. The last guy was a real mess, just like the first time I saw him. He had no face and almost no left arm. The thing he did have was a lot of blood everywhere.

The Hearing Lights that Lisa had insisted on began to blink. At the same time the rain cleared. The sun came out. It was cool, even colder on the north side of the house, but the sky was incredible—that deep turquoise color that I call "Big Bend Blue." Rusty was on the front porch. He looked like he was barking. That meant that the sirens would almost certainly not be operable. So, I pulled on my Wellingtons and stepped out on the front porch.

The white-with-green-stripe Border Patrol Chevy 4x4 Blazer with the two-horse trailer rig was stopped about 200 yards from the house, at the top of the last rise in the road.

This far out in the boonies most folks are not exactly expecting company, and they might not be prepared. So, the polite thing to do is announce oneself from a distance with a couple of beeps on the horn, or flash the lights if it is night. The proper western response is, if you're interested, step out on the porch and wave. That tells the would-be visitor three things: first, you are indeed home; second, you and your significant other are not busy making whoopee, smoking dope, or chasing one another around the couch naked in the living room or something; and third, you're actually sober enough to stand up, open the front door, go outside and wave—all of which means, "Come on; company accepted."

"Rusty, it's Juan! What the hell is he doing out here, all the way from Presidio? Go say hello! Rusty, go!"

At which Rusty hauled ass. If it was Juan, that always meant treats. Rusty dogged the Border Patrol Blazer all the way to the front gate, barking at the driver's door—like that would do any good. And, strangely, every time he did that, sooner or later, the door would open and someone would step out. This time it was his buddy Juan.

"Rusty, here, try some bighorn sheep jerky."
"Lee, sorry about not calling. But I have a chore to do out here anyway and figured if I missed you, I could do my work, leave a note and we'd eventually connect."

Together, we unloaded his Border Patrol issue horse, already saddled. We led him to the lean-to where Pepper and Star waited out of the weather.

"If you have coffee, I have something to lace it with. Black Label work for you?"

"You bet. But what brings you out here, business or pleasure or some of both?"

"Both, Lee. But first let's have that drink, OK? And while we're sitting at the table would you mind if we looked at the photos you took of those dead guys in Mariscal? You know that one of them was my guy, don't you?"

"I really am sorry for your loss, Juan. They all had family. Remember me; I'm the guy who found them."

"I checked with Nowatney's; you had two sets done, right?"

"Yeah, I figured since I was buying them I could order all I wanted. Is that a problem?"

Somehow I already knew that answer.

"Not yet, Lee. Let's just look at the pics. You notice anything strange about them?"

"Juan, there are five dead guys in the damn things; there's about two hundred 7.62 x 39 casings left by more than one killer, or executioner; one guy has no face and no left arm below his bicep. There's blood all over the damn place, and, if that isn't enough, there are no firearms, no tracks of humans or animals except for vultures, no camping equipment, and no identification. Shit, Juan, aside from that sort of thing, oh, and the fact that the scene is in one of the most remote parts of the Lower 48, nothing strange at all about these photographs of five dead guys. Come on, give me a break here!"

"Lee, you looked at these, right, I mean the ones on the disc?"

"Juan, damn right; I paid for them; I get to look at them."

"Lee, you know they're evidence and that they belong to the feds, the investigators?

"Sure they do, but until they come get them and pay for 'em, I'm keeping them. Did you come all this way for these, or for the disc? You could have just called."

"No, amigo. I came to see you and Rusty and to ride down to check on a supposed illegal campground about five miles south. From what I hear it has fire rings, cots, camouflage shading, Igloo coolers. It must be the Hilton of transient camps. You ever see anyone coming through here?"

"Juan, that sounds like one of those "I'm from the Government and I'm here to help you questions. Those folks are just trying to get to jobs in El Norte and send money back home to mama. They don't bother me; I don't bother them. And, for the record, I haven't seen anybody illegal in at least a month. That help? But all the politics aside, I'd like a horseback ride. So would Pepper. Rusty would like the run. Maybe we can take a snack, something to drink. . . ."

"I've got a sixpack of Negra Modelo, some salt and some limes."

"You're a genius. I've got some smoked oysters, avocados and cheese from Garza's, some crackers, and a pocket knife to slice stuff up with."

We stuffed the beers in one of Juan's insulated saddlebags. I parked the food in my saddlebags. We headed south in the sixty degree sunshine with a quartering wind out of the southwest. Pepper hadn't been saddled in a couple of days and was feeling frisky. We rode the first hour in silence; letting the incredible blue sky, rocky terrain, and occasional desert creature keep us and Rusty entertained. I let Rusty roam; it was seldom he got to be that independent and he loved it—the tail wags at about 200 per minute said it all.

"Juan, what is it I don't know?"

"Lee, it's a brutal multiple murder, with international consequences. Best to let the pros handle it; don't you think?"

"You got no argument from me there. I'll give you the photos. All I want is to be left alone and finish up my book on the Southwestern legends of the Ark. You and I have never talked about that have we?"

"No we haven't, amigo, but I don't think I can help you. I really don't know those stories."

"You interested in hearing them?"

"No, Lee, I'm not; sorry. I know you academic types love those stories with no ending, but I deal in real life, crime and death. So thanks, but no thanks. You about ready for a beer and some of those smoked oysters, crackers, and avocados?"

"How'd you know?"

We found an overlook to the west—a place where we could drink Negra Modelo with lime and dine on smoked oysters, some jalapeno flavored jerky, crackers and avocados— and marveled at this incredible Big Bend country. Rusty dined on an MRE entrée "borrowed" from the Border Patrol larder; this one was roast beef and gravy.

"Juan, you gotta quit feeding that dog those MREs. Those things are loaded with salt and preservatives."

"You bet, Lee."

We found the camp. Those guys had chosen well. It was on the east side of a small canyon, tucked out of the prevailing southwest wind and afternoon sun. Most of the camp lay under a row of cottonwoods that flourished near a couple of tinajas that were fed by a small stream and nearby spring. The morning storm runoff had already filled the tinajas. The small spring about a hundred yards north flowed bankfull. The migrant communications system is, I think, far more sophisticated than mere radios, satellite phone links, and such. Not a soul in sight. The rain had washed away any footprints. There were three or four canvas shelter halves lashed to poles, a couple of small fire rings, and one very bright blue Igloo cooler hanging from a homemade tripod. This was not "home away from home." It was a transient camp, and the transients had definitely decamped.

"Juan, where do you think they went? It's like they knew we were coming. How do they do that? You know you'll never stop them all, or even a high percentage."

"Hell, Lee, I'm not naïve enough to believe that we can do that. About all we can do is keep it down to a small stream instead of it becoming a torrent. We find 'em; catch 'em, send 'em back. And as soon as they can collect some seed money, they're back on their trek north. And I don't blame them; we have jobs. They want them, and they're willing. And these guys are really good at what they do. Let's head back."

On the ride back to Los Alamos in the afternoon sun Juan, actually began talking about the murder scene.

"Lee, what about the fifth man?"

"Juan, I'm not a cop; that's your business. But I'll give you my impressions if you want. I don't know—no face, no arm, no uniform. As I remember, I took his fingerprints, at least from the other hand, just like I did the others. Any IDs yet?"

"We identified our guy. It's not public yet, but who're you going to tell, right? He was Agent Rafael Castillo. He came into here from Houston. The Policía de la Frontera guy was Captain Luís Guerro, originally from Boquillas, across the border from Rio Grande Village. I'm pretty sure that Potter has already ID'd the NPS guy as Royce Johnson, but I haven't heard that officially. He was the agent in charge of the eastern end of the national park. The FBI hasn't said anything to me about the TPWD guy. But my guess is that they've already identified him too; they're just not releasing the name.

"The fifth man and the two vaqueros are another story. The unidentified vaqueros are probably easier than the guy with no arm. All the Policía de la Frontera has to do is ask around some of these villages and towns along this stretch of the border. There's not much northern migration from this region. Folks here pretty much stay home. Somebody on one of those large ranches across the Rio Grande will notice some missing wranglers. Trouble is, some of those places are pretty big. Vaqueros come and go. Some are out riding line for weeks. Rancho de Las Tres Estrellas is right across the river. It's 300,000 acres. My bet is that those two fellas are from there. We sent prints and photos to the Federales and Policía de la Frontera. They'll have to figure out that one. Nothing strange, Lee, aside from what you've mentioned, about the fifth man?"

"Nope, not a thing. Although it is sort of odd that he's the only one with a missing arm. But I don't know if some critter hauled it off or one of the killers just took it. None of this makes much sense. Juan, there are five guys. Most of them are law enforcement of one type or another. They are not going to be out here in the wilderness without their weapons. My bet is that more than one guy did the killing. Let's head on back. Tomorrow I have a busy day of writing."

"And I of chasing and hopefully catching bad guys."

Juan stayed for supper, one of those guy meals. I grilled a couple of three-inch rib-eyes. Juan cooked the beans and made the salad. He dug around the back of the BP 4x4 and found something suitable. We broke open a bottle of Shiraz and dined at my oak table. Rusty chewed some pretty expensive steak bones that evening. After dinner we brewed a pot of dark roast. Juan had his black; I laced mine with evaporated milk.

"Juan, get on your jacket and hat. I try not to miss an opportunity to see a Big Bend sunset. Tonight's should be spectacular, what with the front coming through."

He grumbled a bit about the "idiocy of being out in the wind" but humored me anyway. We pulled on jackets and hats; sat on my west porch and watch the sunset between Bofecillos Mountain and Oso Mountain, the highest point in the park. We both felt pretty damn good—good company, good food, good wine and a spectacular sunset.

There are sunsets that will change the way you think about yellow, orange, mauve, purple and grey forever. They will make you thankful you see in Technicolor. And this one was pretty spectacular, even for Big Bend. It happens that way when a front moves through. The wind was still out of the southwest, the weather coming at us out of Mexico. We agreed that it would be a cold, windy night, with a waning quarter moon that would rise about midnight. With our captain chairs reared back on two legs, boots propped on my porch rail, we sat in silence in that cold wind and watched the colors fade to grey.

"Lee, I have to ask you something. You remember that night we met, what, about twenty years ago?"

71

"Amigo, remember me? I'm the guy with the singed hair and eyebrows, second degree burns on my palms and the twenty-four inch long burn scar on my belly. Yes I remember it like it was yesterday. And it wasn't about twenty years; it was twenty years, and three days.

"It was a night like this in October. I was headed north on Texas 170, the river road, between Lajitas and Presidio. It was about ten o'clock, pitch black. I rounded a curve and the mountain in front of me exploded in fire. I skidded to a stop about twenty yards from a burning 4x4. A Border Patrol Chevy had run off the road and landed in a culvert on its side. Flames shot out of the crumpled hood. Thick black smoke billowed from the passenger compartment. I could see an arm waving out the driver's window. I ran down into the culvert. The driver was conscious and alert.

The driver yelled, "I can't get the seatbelt loose. Help me."

I ran back to my truck, grabbed my machete from behind the pickup seat. A few hacks later the driver, Juan, was free of the belt. Good thing, too. The flames spread to the passenger compartment. I used the machete to pry open the door latch and tried to lift the driver door. Jammed; no go there. That's when I burned both palms, second degree burns on both. I leaned over the door sill to drag him out. That's when I picked up the two-foot-long burn scar on my belly. He had burns on both feet and legs; was badly burned over most of his head.

I could walk; he could crawl. Together we crabbed our way back up the hill to my truck. I pulled him up to the bed, screaming all the while. The flesh on both palms was seared medium rare. We lay there in my pickup bed and watched the cruiser burn. He loosely wrapped his scalp, his legs, and my hands in bandages made of torn denim and cotton work shirts. We both took a bunch of Tylenol to dull the pain. It didn't work, but was worth the effort. Neither of us could see a reason so stay. We were closer to Presidio than Lajitas. Besides, there is no medical help in Lajitas anyway. I drove, slowly, using my elbows to turn the steering wheel. Juan mostly moaned and eventually passed out from the pain. Two hours later we were at the Presidio Border Patrol station. I must have looked like death warmed over when I punched the buzzer on the front door with my elbow. We wound up sharing a semiprivate room at Alpine Regional, though it was called something else then. Second degree burns take a while to heal. He couldn't walk without crutches or a cane for almost a year. I couldn't hold a ballpoint pen or a pistol for at least that long. But we both made full recoveries and over the years became close friends. Joined by scar tissue, you might say.

"Would you do it again?"

"What, pull you from the wreck? Sure, it's what you do, right?"

"Yes, I guess so. But I don't know if I could do it."

"Juan, I don't think anybody does until its time. That's my take on it anyway. You know what the American Indians, my people, say don't you?"

"Yeah, Lee, I know. You saved my life. I owe you a life. I've been thinking about that."

"Hell, Juan, you'd do the same thing for me. Forget it. Is there something I need to know?"

"No, Lee There's just a lot of stuff going on. Look, I really enjoyed the day. I do have to admit that those ribeyes made up for those damned smoked oysters that you like so much. Rusty and I enjoyed the evening. But I really have to get back. About those photos . . . ?"

"You really do need them, huh?" The short answer was, yes, he really did need to take those pics back to Presidio and his handlers.

"Juan, just a minute. You load your horse; I'll go get the pics, OK? You can take the prints and the CD back with you."

"Thanks, Lee; I appreciate it."

"No problema amigo."

The digital pics were still showing on the screen. I hadn't really seen the digital version of the photos so I plopped in another CD, pressed "Save to Disc," waited a few seconds while it did its thing, and pressed "Eject." The machine did just that and kicked out the original.

Juan had loaded his horse; he and Rusty waited by the driver's door of his Blazer.

"Here you go, amigo. You really have to get back to the bureaucratic wars tonight? You're welcome to stay."

"I know, but the BP calls."

"OK; later!"

Juan's Blazer and his horse trailer disappeared over the rise about ten p.m., those red taillights winking out over the last rise between us and the road.

I checked my horses, toured the grounds, took a leak on the lee side of the north wall, and turned in. A good day.

CHAPTER 5: LOS ALAMOS SHOOTOUT

The concussion with its accompanying blinding white light disintegrated the bedroom window above my head. Glass sprayed everywhere.

"God damn it, Rusty! What the Hell?"

Thanks to Rusty I was lying on the floor beside the bed with him on top of me. He had pulled me, most of the mattress, and all of the bedclothes out of the line of fire. The roar of bullets and shotgun blasts seemed to be everywhere. I heard the horses screaming in fear and pain.

"Sons of bitches are trying to kill my horses! Rusty, you stay. Stay!"

I rolled out from under him. Lying flat on the floor, I shucked on a pair of jeans that I kept on a chair by the bed. I pulled on my rough-out Wellingtons, scraping my ass on the floor which by now was covered in glass shards. "Shit, glass in my ass." I pulled the 12 gauge, Winchester Model 12 pump out from under the bed. Didn't have to search for shells; it was already loaded with Number 4 buckshot. They weren't after the horses; the bastards were trying to kill me.

"What the hell is going on Rusty?"

Fortunately for me and Rusty, Los Alamos house was built of twelve-inch-thick adobe brick, so it would take a helluva bullet to go through the walls. But sooner or later the gunfire would stop and someone or several someones would come looking for me, aka the Target. My bedroom, now with no window glass, was no place to hide and a good place to die. It was definitely no place to shoot it out with what sounded like multiple gunmen. Time to move and figure out how Rusty and I were going to survive this assault. At a break in the gunfire-- someone was probably shoving a new magazine into his rifle—I reached into the nightstand drawer by the bed and pulled out my .40 caliber Glock, rolled over on my belly, tucked it in the back of my pants and crab-crawled military-style to the hall door, dragging the shotgun behind me. I looked at my watch: 3:45 a.m.

"Rusty, you stay! Don't move!"

Lying flat on the floor I checked out the living room. "Shit!" The front door, at least the bottom half, was still on its hinges and provided some cover, but I sure as hell couldn't go out there. The back door was still closed and looked locked. To me, as deaf as I am, it sounded like all the shots were coming from the north, west, and east sides of the house. At least all the holes I could see were from those directions. That meant that the back or south side of the house was not, at least now, under direct attack. On the other hand, these sumbitches might have placed someone on that side to wait until I stuck my head out. Squeeze off a quick round and the Target, me, is dead. So a quick escape toward the corral was risky and probably not the answer. These guys must have got those bullets for free. My god, there were a lot of them blowing through my house. The night exploded again with the sounds of shattered glass, pings and thuds as their rounds struck and shattered everything in Los Alamos that was not protected by the adobe.

I froze, trying to assess just how much shit I was in. There were a lot of bullets and shotgun pellets ripping through the living room, kitchen, and bedroom, most of which were accompanied by the sound of breaking glass and splintering furniture and doors. One thing was for sure; there were more of them than me. From the way glass and doors disintegrated, it was likely that at least three shooters, maybe more, were doing this. First job for me was to get out of the house and into a position to move if I had too. The only way I could think of was to crawl out the back door. But if somebody was waiting quietly by the cottonwoods in my backyard, I'd be a sitting duck and a dead duck. Ah! The bathroom "dirty clothes drop"; that was it!

The laundry/storeroom out on the porch had been added after the house was built, on the west side of the house, and the state contractor didn't bother to remove the west-facing bathroom window. He or she simply painted over the window panes and let it go at that. Normally the window on that side of the bath stayed shut. But it was still there, hinged on one side. I used it as my dirty clothes drop. It saved trucking around outside to take clothes to the washing machine. Just open the window, drop the dirty stuff directly into the already open washer in the storeroom outside. There were no holes in that window. Maybe no one was shooting through the store room.

It was a tight fit. I stood on the claw-foot tub, pulled myself and the shotgun through the drop window and landed almost head-first on the washing machine. "Whew, Lee, you need to do the wash VERY soon!" I banged my head on something. I fumbled around in the dark; found and put on an old leather work jacket that I kept hanging on a peg in the storeroom. I didn't hear any voices, but they would have had to be standing outside the door screaming in my direction in total silence, anyway, before I heard them. "No guts, no glory, Lee. Besides if you stay here you are definitely dead." Squatting and crouching on my heels I turned the storeroom doorknob and slowly, slowly, cracked the door. And there he was, one of the sumbitches trying to kill me. His arms and shoulders rested on the bed of my truck, actually, TPWD's truck. He was focused on pumping thirty-caliber rounds out of an AK 47 into the kitchen window and door. The muzzle blasts and the steady ping, ping, ping of ejected brass landing in the pickup bed said that the AK was set on semi-auto.

He blasted the kitchen door and window as fast as he could pull the trigger. Now or never! I cracked the door just enough to slide the mouth of the shotgun barrel through.

"Damn, no shot, but I sure as shit can't stay here."

So, maybe aggressive surprise would work better than chicken-shit stealth. I stood, shouldered the pump; kicked the door open with enough force to take it off its hinges and racked a shell into the chamber. The sound of a 12 gauge pump shotgun being racked got his attention. As he turned, the door hit the storeroom wall with a huge "BAM!"

The shooter stood. Bad idea. I shot him with the 12 gauge—three times with Number 4 buck. The tin roof of the carport amplified the sound. It was like I was shooting with a small cannon, and actually I was. I think he was down before the third round hit him. No time to stand still. I had just shot my last three 12 gauge shells, hopefully into the shoulder and head of one of my would-be assassins. Shots still plowed into my house, but not from the west side. Rather than wait, I ran around the back of the truck. The shooter was sprawled on the ground between the truck and my SUV parked on the west side of it. There was blood, flesh and brain matter everywhere. The blood pooled near the left rear tire of the truck. This guy was definitely dead. Most of the right side of his head was gone.

I laid the empty shotgun into the pickup bed. I needed something more than my Glock .40cal. It didn't look like he would be using his AK any longer. I snatched it off the carport dirt, crouched below the door of now-wrecked pickup, racked the bolt, and a live round ejected. Completing the process told me that I had at least one round in the chamber and the balance in the magazine. It was a thirty-round magazine, but I didn't know how many rounds remained. I'd shot AKs before, but it took a couple of seconds to figure out how to eject the magazine. He had two mags lying next to his not-quite-complete head. I stuck one in the rifle, snatched what looked like a satchel of ammo bandoliers lying by his leg and ran in a crouch around the truck to the outside of my SUV on the far west side of the house. It had no windshield and sat like it had at least two flat tires. I felt a little more in charge, now that I was outside the house and had moving room. Peeking over the SUV hood I saw a second guy, the north side shooter. His weapon lay on top of the front adobe fence wall, which he used as a rifle rest. He was shooting from just east of the entrance arch. He aimed at what used to be my front door, which was rapidly being turned into kindling. He stopped firing at the living room and seemed to be looking, searching for something on the west side, my side, of the house. No more firing from his compadre to the west meant that the guy was down or out of ammo, neither a good thing.

"Shit, he's got night goggles, those things the army uses to see in the dark."

And that's when he saw me. In one fluid motion, he shifted his AK around and opened fire. This guy knew what he was doing. The radiators of both trucks exploded and sprayed antifreeze out their grills. No percentage in a frontal assault. Time for a tactical retreat. According to what my younger brother had once told me, the best, most important rule in this kind of combat is to keep moving. Find cover and duck often. He also told me to bring the biggest pistols, rifles, and shotguns you have, all the ammo you have and all your friends and all their pistols, rifles and ammo. He also said that, and this is a quote as near as I can remember: "Never go into a gunfight carrying a pistol the caliber of which starts with a number smaller than the numeral four."

But I had only me, the first killer's AK, with at least two 30-round magazines, and my .40 caliber Glock with 10 rounds in the magazine.

The back of the house seemed free of people trying to kill me. So I swung south toward the corral and shed. Pepper was screaming. In the moonlight I could see blood streaming from the top of his head. Star was down; not moving. An attack around the back of the adobe wall and along the west-facing adobe wall seemed to make the most sense. It was either that or head out crosscountry. But that would mean leaving Rusty and Pepper. Besides, since there were more of them than me, they would have the advantage. Guys in their fifties usually don't run as fast as younger assassins. But whoever these guys were, they probably weren't expecting an aggressive armed shooter. And for sure they didn't know the terrain around Los Alamos as well as I did. My heart was going a good 150 beats a minute and I was making enough adrenaline to power a small city. At the northwestern corner of the front wall I scooted forward on the ground; peered around the corner with my head at ground level.

"Sumbitch!"

There he was, headed in my direction. He probably figured that he too had the cover of the adobe wall. He headed west to find out what the hell was going on with his partner. With his rifle at military port arms he trotted toward the corner where I lay. He was about ten feet away when I stuck the Glock around the corner using my left hand. I aimed at his head and pulled the trigger six times. He opened his mouth and dropped like a rock, but not before getting one round off. I smelled his last breath as his head hit the ground about a foot from my head. His blood sprayed everywhere. My face was covered in it. I hoped that all of it was his. My right hand, holding onto the wall corner about a half inch above my head, felt like somebody had stuck a hot branding iron on it. Blood flooded onto my right cheek and forehead.

"Shit, the son of a bitch shot off my little finger." The next thought: "Maybe they can reattach it." The third thought was: "First I have to live through this *gunfight* and then somebody has to find the damned finger."

Anybody who believes that you can continue your activities oblivious of a gunshot wound to *anyplace* on your body is lying to you—big time. Don't believe it; it simply doesn't happen. I was pumped with adrenaline, and I hurt like hell. Blood streamed into my eyes from a head wound, most likely from something I hit in the laundry/storeroom. My right hand felt like it was on fire. Blood flowed regularly, consistently, out of the place where my little finger on my right hand used to be. Time to retreat. The gunfire had stopped completely, at least for now. In a crouch I ran across the back of the house, peeked around the southeast back corner. Nothing moved; nothing. But hell, whoever it was had a wall to hide behind.

So, what now? Best thing was find a place one guy could defend against whoever was out there and stay put until daybreak. Then I could figure out what the hell to do next. The house seemed the best option now that two of them were down. The back door was shattered, so sliding inside wasn't a problem. First, though, I had to stop the bleeding on my forehead and on my right hand. I found a used bandana stowed in the jacket and wrapped it around my head to slow down the leakage from that wound. I figure that I looked like a biker with a crazoid head wound. There were some rubber bands in my office desk caddy, one adobe wall away from the assault. I scrabbled around in a drawer and used one of them to stanch the flow from the one remaining knuckle, all that remained of my mangled right little finger. I was definitely not a happy camper. My right hand throbbed—BIG TIME. It hurt like hell. I was consoled by the fact that the sumbitch who had done it was now D-E-A-D. Crawling into the bedroom was like sliding over glass, which of course it was, but Rusty was by the bed where I left him.

"Good dog, Rusty. You OK?"

He wasn't. All four paws were bleeding, but it was too dark to attempt to pick glass shards out of him.

"Stay, you stay." And the Hearing Dog Institute training regimen stayed with him. He stayed.

The bedroom door to the living room still hung on its hinges, with lots and lots of bullet holes. The front door lay in splinters. I crept up to the north window, and lifted my head over the sill. That's when I saw him, a third man. He trotted over the north ridge about a hundred yards away. As he reached the ridgetop he turned; took a last look and dropped out of sight. All I could see for sure was the muzzle blast from a half dozen final rounds. I saw a familiar military salute and what looked like a baseball cap on his head. He looked like about six feet tall, but I saw him for only an instant. I responded with two .40cal rounds as a parting gesture. I hoped there were just three shooters, but no reason to take a chance.

"Rusty, you and I are going to stay right here in the living room."

I tipped my heavy oak table on its side and slid it into the southeastern corner. Rusty and I sat there with the adrenaline pumping. Looking at my watch, it was only 4:00 a.m.

"Damn, Rusty! Has this been going on only ten, fifteen minutes? I have to get some help out here. Where the hell is the damn satellite cell phone?"

Sure enough, he didn't know either.

As silence settled in and the adrenaline rush leveled off, I checked Rusty. He had glass splinters in all four feet, but nothing serious. In the dark I pulled what I thought were all of them out of his feet; tore some of Luís's "Southwest motif" curtains in little bandages and wrapped all four feet. Satisfied for now, Rusty curled up on his pallet in the corner and slept.

I ached all over; I had the shakes. I was so wired you could not have forced me to sleep. You could have played music out of my fingertips. But soon, the adrenaline rush cratered and I started shaking for real. I had just killed two people.

"Rusty, holy shit! What's happening here? Why the hell would anyone want to kill me? We are in some real big trouble!"

But I also decided I wasn't going to die crouched behind a heavy oak table in my own living room. If the bastards were after me, I might as well shoot some more.

"Christ, Rusty, what are we in to?"

It was still "dark thirty," a little after four. I checked myself; missing digit, three-inch gash on forehead, lots of blood everywhere, lots of scratches, and a whole bunch of glass shards in my back and chest, mostly picked up from my crawl out of the house. All of them hurt and most still leaked blood. Not to put too fine a point on it; the glass in my ass hurt worst. Most of the glass on my chest I could pick out myself, but it's pretty damn difficult to pick glass shards out of your back and most especially out of your own ass cheeks. However, all things considered, we'd come through this gunfight in pretty good shape. Los Alamos was destroyed, at least all the windows and doors except the ones in back, on the south side.

Things were not going to get better until I got some help in here. It was time to find my seldom-used satellite phone so I could let folks know what had happened here.

"OK, Rusty; let's see if we can find the damn satellite phone. We're going to have to talk to somebody."

We, well, I found it under my bed. And it still worked, but the battery was about out of gas. So, first things first, I stuck it in the pickup charger, running off the battery. The truck's radiator was shot; so was the one in the SUV, so I couldn't crank them up. I don't know shit about modern cars, but it looked like the actual engines were fine. They just needed radiators without bullet holes and tires that didn't have a whole lot of holes in them.

I dialed Luís at Sauceda Ranch HQ; no answer, so I left a message: "Luís, this is Lee. My regular phone is gone; my satellite phone is failing. We have been attacked at Los Alamos. There are two dead guys, neither of which is me. Never mind. I'm wounded; Star is dead. Your TPWD house is really shot up. The pickup needs a new radiator and someone is going to owe the State of Texas a whole bunch of money to repair all this stuff. Call me! "

Next, I called Juan in Presidio, no answer. I left about the same message.

The third call was to Bob Potter at Panther Junction. I got him on the eighth ring.

"Bob, this is Lee. I have a problem." I explained what had happened over the last hour and forty minutes.

"Christ Lee, this is not your week. You OK?"

"You mean aside from being alive? Hell, no, Bob. A bunch of guys tried to kill me; killed my pack mare; shot out the windshield, radiator and tires of my SUV; disabled the TPWD pickup; and shot out most of the Los Alamos windows. I shot at least two of them. A lot of bureaucrats in Austin are gonna be really pissed off. None of the above includes the fact that one of the guys shot off my right little finger. In the plus column, I'm still standing upright breathing on my own and two of the guys that tried to kill me are laying on the ground soaking up the Chihuahuan Desert. So, given all the shit that can happen and that did happen last night, I feel pretty damn lucky. Besides, Rusty is still here and taking care of me. Pepper has only a minor wound. But, amigo, I need some help, like right now."

"Lee, you know that technically the Ranch is not our jurisdiction, but I'm headed that way right now with everything I can muster, including an EMT Sky Flight out of Alpine—I'll call them myself, but it'll take at least two hours. Have you called Lisa yet? You should. Just as soon as this hits the press she will see it. The quickest anybody can get to you, unless Luís or Juan pick up your call, will be two or three hours. You cannot have chosen a more remote place in the Lower 48 to have a gunfight. You are definitely in the middle of nowhere. The EMTs out of Alpine, they can get there quickest. But you know that nothing is quick here; you're pretty much on your own. I'm at least three hours away. You know to stay put and wait. You don't know who else is out there, right?"

"No, Bob, I don't know who else is out there. I have one of their rifles and about 200 rounds of ammo. I have my Glock .40. Yeah, I'll do my best to stay put. I'm going to let the phone charge a few more minutes, then call Lisa."

I checked Rusty again, but there was little to do with his paws until daylight. I couldn't sit still, so I took the AK and did a 360 degree recon around the inside walls and corral. The dead guys were right where they dropped. Rusty, despite his wounds, hung close hobbling along. I needed his senses of hearing and of smell.

"What is the fucking world coming to Rusty? My god, I just shot two guys and I didn't even blink."

My recon revealed that the TV and computer satellite dish were kaput. That first explosion was probably a grenade that knocked the dish off its base. No DSL, no CNN today.

The dead guys were armed to the teeth. I thought about picking up their weapons, but sanity struck, so I left them where they were. The fuzz would appreciate my not really screwing up the crime scene. The pickup truck-guy had a 9mm Berretta and a ten-inch survival knife strapped to his boot. I'd already taken his AK. The second one, the guy I shot with the .40, had a knife, an AK, two grenades, and a Browning 9mm. And he had those night goggles, which I left strapped to his head. They were great for spotting me in the dark, but the lens did not stop a .40cal hollow point. His left eye now had a really big .40cal hole in it—the shortest distance to his brain. He was really dead. There was a second bullet hole through his chin and a third that shattered his left cheekbone.

A quick check on the corral revealed that Star was dead. She'd caught several rounds and probably died pretty quickly-at least that's what I chose to believe. Waiting for the cavalry cooped up in my shot-out living room was out of the question. I treated Pepper's wound with spray antiseptic that was labeled "For Equine Use Only." His wound was a superficial one that had nicked his right ear. Maybe in time we'd all think of it as giving him character. He'd be fine. I put a halter on and led him to the front of the house away from Star's body and tethered him to the hitching post by the front porch. Nobody shot at me, so the bad guys must be gone.

In the bathroom, the mirror and the medicine cabinet were both intact, not even a nick. In the very early morning light, I pulled off the bandana and revealed a really long, ugly three-inch gash across my forehead where I'd hit something in the wash room. Despite the warnings on the label that said "For Equine Use Only," I used the equine spray antiseptic. I used a couple butterfly bandages from my first aid kit to close the edges of the wound on my forehead. Maybe it would help until I got some professional care. I rewrapped my head with another bandana. I now know that as adrenaline drops, pain rises. Or at least it was that way it was with me. I fumbled around in the bathroom medicine cabinet and found a couple of Tylenols and some Percodan left over from a long ago dental surgery.

"What the hell Rusty, one from column A and one from column B." I washed them both down with a drink from the kitchen faucet. I felt better almost immediately.

"Rusty, it is definitely time to get some coffee started; get some help in here and begin figuring out what the hell we have gotten ourselves into."

The stovetop worked, which meant the propane tank had not been punctured. The electric coffeepot was a pile of glass shards and shattered plastic. But I did find a quart pot; poured what I thought was an adequate batch of dark roast into it; added water and lit the burner. In about ten minutes we had cowboy coffee. The ice box, known to most folks as a refrigerator, had more holes than a piece of Swiss cheese. But, amid all the carnage, there was a minor miracle: a can of evaporated milk remained intact. So, aside from my destroyed house, a missing little finger and a dead packhorse, the world was almost complete. I found one cup and a spoon and soon sat my tender, glass-shard-filled ass down on the front porch steps and watched the night fade into dawn over the Sierras. That's when I noticed that every one of my cherished oak rockers was kindling. Only one bench remained.

Almost an hour to the minute later, Rusty perked up and pointed west. I saw the zillion candlepower spotlight first, sweeping left, right and forward into the early dawn. The white Border Patrol chopper with its green stripe arrived first. Juan dropped out of the chopper six feet above ground and ran toward me. The EMT Sky Flight from Alpine was on his tail. I was not alone any longer. A second Border Patrol chopper, this one with six heavily armed agents dropped down before the others' blades stopped turning. They spread out around the house and set up a perimeter. One chopper with one pilot and one agent aboard took off and began a grid search of the area from the sky. Their million-power floodlights illuminated everything within fifty yards.

"Jesus, Lee; you OK?"

"Juan, I'm doing a lot better than the two guys I shot."

"I'll check them. The EMTs here are going to check you out. Let's get these folks to fix you up. You know you're bleeding everywhere. How'd you lose that finger? Never mind; we can talk later. Got any idea who these three guys were?"

"Not a clue, Juan."

The EMTs were good.

"Dr. Phillips, do you know where the rest of the finger is?"

"No. How about we stop the bleeding; suture the damn thing up and pick the glass out of my ass and back. While you're at it, give me some great drugs and you folks can deal with my head wound? OK?"

"Yes, sir, but first tell us where you lost the finger and we'll look." I did; they did, and they didn't find it. They washed the wound, put in some quick stitches, applied some new butterfly bandages, and wrapped my head in a really cool bandage that looked like a bright yellow bandana. I'm going to have some really sexy tick-tack railroad track stitches on my forehead until they plant me in the dirt for the last time.

"Sir, we'll use some bandages and tape to close the finger wound, but you really will need to go to the ER in Alpine to get it treated correctly."

"OK, but how about you do this: Give me a painkiller shot of something in my finger, something that will last a few hours. I really want to stay here for the opening of the investigation. Then, I promise I'll go with you or somebody to Alpine. OK?"

"Yes, sir." The drugs and the fact that they picked some of the glass out of my back and ass, especially my ass, made me feel better immediately.

Luís and Tomás showed up about thirty minutes later with a two-slot horse trailer and a huge veterinarian care kit. Tomás wasn't a licensed vet, but he took care of Pepper and used his magic to pull the remaining glass shards out of Rusty's feet. He even had brought some of Rusty's favorite canned dog food. Afterwards he fitted Rusty with some really great booties. Unfortunately they were pink. I don't think Rusty cared. They were also medicated. Rusty would be fine.

"Sorry, Señor Lee, Star is dead. Pepper has a round hole in his right ear. You had apparently used a spray horse antiseptic . . . ?"

"Thank you Tomás. I also used it on my head wound too. I hope that was OK?"

"You don't look like a horse, but no problema, jefe."

"Lee, before I called Tomás I did a 911 call to TPWD HQ in Austin. They'll have an incident command guy here as soon as possible, but they also switched me to the Texas Rangers. So, those guys are on their way out of El Paso, along with probably most of the law enforcement that State Parks has west of the Pecos."

"Juan, let me borrow your satellite phone; I need to call Lisa. She's gonna be really pissed if she hears about this from somebody else, like CNN."

Lisa answered on the eighth ring.

"Lisa, this is Lee. Yeah, I know it's early. Yes, I'm fine, standing upright and breathing on my own."

"Lee, I didn't expect to hear from you today. What's going on?"

"Lisa, I got attacked; Los Alamos got attacked last night. I'm fine—well, I have nine and a half fingers instead of ten. But aside from that . . . ."

"Lee stop! What do you mean? What?"

I relayed the entire event.

"Lisa! I'm fine; Rusty is fine."

"Lee, remember me, your wife. Words like 'attacked' and 'nine and a half fingers' get wives really upset. What the hell is going on? What have you gotten yourself into?"

So I told her. I think I included all the details.

"My God! You actually killed two people? That's horrible! Do you have help? Did they find the other part of the finger? Did you call the cops? Did you call Susan?"

"Lisa. Here are the answers, hopefully in order of being asked: yes I did; yes it is horrible; yes to the people part and I've already had the shakes about that and will probably have a lot more of them. No to the finger part. Yes to the cops and no to Susan. But as soon as you hang up I'll call her; I promise."

"Lee, I'm coming out there today. See you later."

"Lisa, please don't!"

. "You're fucking kidding, right? Shut up; call Susan. I'll see you soon. I love you. You're crazy! You can't stay out there!"

The second call was to Susan. An aide answered on the second ring. She transferred the call.

"Susan, it's Lee."

"Lee, it's early in the a.m., right? We're in Houston about to load the charter to fly back to New Orleans. What now?"

"Susan, that's not fair; thinking that every time I call you it's a tragedy."

"Lee, every time you call me it *is* a crisis, maybe even a tragedy. The only issue is what level crisis or tragedy."

I relayed the story. She asked a few pointed questions, like: "Your finger OK?"

"No, Susan. Most of it is gone and no one has been able to find what I'm now calling the detached digit"

"You talked to the cops?"

"No, well only to report it to Luís, Juan, Bob Potter and the Border Patrol chopper folks. And I called the EMT folks."

"Don't talk any more. Who is in charge of the investigation?"

"Susan, the attack happened in the middle of the night, about 4:00 a.m. The varieties of fuzz, cops, Texas Rangers, FBI, and county mounties have just begun to arrive."

"Lee, I've been writing while you've been talking. My staff already knows the coordinates of this place. Big Bend Ranch is a state park sprawling across two counties. Brewster County LE and Presidio County LE will fight for jurisdiction. TPWD Park Police and state law enforcement will ultimately be in charge, well maybe unless they turn it over to the Texas Rangers. But then you're on the border so the Border Patrol will want a piece of it.

"Everybody else will try to get involved, but that isn't your problem. Here is what you do: You shut up. Even better, you get on the EMT chopper and get to the ER in Alpine. From what you say, you've got glass splinters all over you, an amputated finger and a scalp wound. If they ask you to confirm the two bodies, you can do that, and you can give them your narrative about what you recall about the attack. Later, if necessary, we can change it if we have to. After all, you're wounded, probably in shock. But you will answer no other questions, submit to no interrogations. Got it? After identifying the bodies and recalling the attack as you remember it, you will get on that EMT chopper and have them haul you and Rusty to Alpine. If you tell them anything more than, 'I'm Lee Phillips and I want my lawyer' I will personally kick your ass across Texas. My staff says two, maybe two and a half hours to the airstrip at the ranch, about the same to Alpine. Where are you going to be?"

"I don't know. Right now I'd like to stay here for the beginning of the investigation, but that may be the drugs talking. Call this number when you're one hour into the flight. I'll know then. Are you OK with that?"

"Yes. My staff has talked with Lisa. We'll pick her up in Austin. She'll be with me. You sure do pick some remote places to get hurt in."

"Yes, ma'am."

I clicked END on the phone; gave it back to Juan.

My front yard and the road back to Sauceda Ranch began looking like a law enforcement helicopter sales lot. The Texas Rangers and the FBI arrived about 7:00 a.m. The FBI showed up in three commandeered BP Blazers. Bob and his people showed up a bit later.

"Bob, you must have called everybody in the free world. Who is in charge?"

"Lee, this is a major cluster fuck. We don't know who is in charge. It's TPWD land; the shooters were using federally prohibited weapons; you've killed two people. So the Brewster County or Presidio County sheriff's offices will be involved—nobody knows exactly where the county line is. We have dead people and wounded people on a state reservation in a home invasion incident along a very sensitive international border. You called the NPS folks, the Border Patrol folks, and the State Parks folks. So it was bound to get messy. I wish you had just called me, and maybe I could have managed it a little. But too late for that now."

"Bob; I just shot TWO people! You gotta admit that this is a little bit out of my line of work. I've been a hunter, a shooter, and marksman most of my life, but dammit it, I'm a historian working on an academic project. I find some bodies and now people are trying to kill me! I get shot; I kill two men in less than three minutes, for the simple reason that they're trying to kill me. I've got enough adrenaline coursing through my system to leap tall buildings at a single bound.

"I can do office wars, bureaucratic wars, meeting wars, even curriculum wars. I'm pretty damn good at it. Real wars are

90

something else, most particularly if they involve people shooting at me and me shooting back and killing them. What the hell is going on in this world? None of this makes sense. I'll have a railroad-tracks scar on my forehead, less than a full compliment of fingers and I'm really pissed off. And, Bob, you're a great guy, but your coffee sucks. You want some real coffee, go in the kitchen and get some. Aah! Sorry, the stove and the kitchen is off limits. Isn't it? Yellow tape and all."

"Yes it is. Are you up to answering some questions?"

"Sorry man. I can't. My lawyer told me to respond to that and all other queries from the fuzz with this: 'My name is Lee Phillips and I want my lawyer.' I've already told you more than she instructed me to say, but nothing you didn't know from my emergency phone call. She did say that I could identify the bodies and relate the story one time only. But she instructed me to answer absolutely no questions. So, if you want to set storytime up, I'd be happy to oblige."

"I'll go tell the others; save everybody some time."

We both smiled and he said: "Let me get you some good FBI coffee. The last can I saw was labeled: 'Sealed in June 1945.' We're gonna be here a while. The EMTs want to take you to Alpine. You going?"

"No. Well, I'm not going right now. But if you guys want anything useful out of me you're going to have to do it soon."

"I thought so. Want any breakfast; my staff and the feds have set up a canteen, complete with eggs, bacon, pork chops, steak, biscuits, chorizo, tortillas, salsa, toast and cream gravy. You interested, last time? I think they even have something good for you like orange juice."

"No thanks. I'm so wired that you could play music through my fingertips, well, nine and a half of them. I want to check on my horse and my dog. Finally, I want to sit in one of the chairs in my back yard and think a few minutes while I wait for you law enforcement types to make up your collective minds. Then maybe I'll take me a short nap. You OK, with that, Bob?"

"Sure, just stay out of the house. Do not cross the yellow tape anywhere. They get testy about that. OK?"

"You bet. See you in a few minutes."

I woke with Rusty licking my left and uninjured hand. The right one throbbed like a sumbitch. It had been only ten minutes and I was beginning to feel every glass shard and stitch. My right hand hurt like hell. The drugs had worn off. I was in no shape to stay out here. It was time to ID these guys; tell my tale and get on that EMT chopper to Alpine.

CHAPTER 6: DECISIONS

When I awoke the Texas Rangers were in charge. I guess I should've felt better, like all was right with the world. But I didn't. They were finger printing the corpse, the one I could see from the backyard and the one I had mentally labeled the pickup truck dead guy. Bob escorted Rusty and me to the crime scene.

"Lee, let me introduce you."

"Not necessary; we met at Castolon."

"Shut up Lee. Ranger Hays, this is Dr. Lee Phillips, until recently this was his home. His hearing is pretty crappy. This is his hearing dog Rusty. Rusty will stay beside Dr. Phillips at all times. Rusty's job is to be Dr. Phillips' ears and to protect him. He is very good at both. He is particularly attuned to changes in voice levels and tones. If he growls at you, I suggest you be very quiet. Don't make any sudden movements and wait until Dr. Phillips tells you what to do next. And, since Dr. Phillips doesn't hear well; you must look directly at him when speaking to him. Do not cover your mouth when you speak. He speech reads in three languages, but his hearing is really pretty pathetic. If he is not looking at you and you wish to speak with him or ask a question it is a good idea to tap his left arm or shoulder. I will stay and assist if you wish."

"Yes, thank you Captain Potter. Dr. Phillips, your attorney and your wife will be landing at the Ranch air strip in a private charter jet in about forty-five minutes. The Border Patrol choppers will pick them up and bring them here. We would really appreciate it if you can you stay a while longer for their arrival. And, maybe you can ID these guys. If you can, we'll take your statement and cut you loose. You OK with that? Can I get you a teeny little more painkiller?"

This sounded good to me. If I stuck it out for a couple more hours, maybe this would all soon fade into a dull, ugly memory.

"Sure, let's do it and get it over with."

We walked to the carport. An agent pulled back the black body sheet. I recoiled at what I'd done.

"Do you know this man,. Phillips?"

"Can't tell; I'm sorry, but this guy doesn't have a face. Before we go any further in this process, I'd like to ask some questions, OK?"

"Sure, ask away."

"You guys check for IDs? Check for any identifying marks; all that stuff?"

"Sir, I apologize. You've met me, but I don't think you've met my associate, Ranger Captain Jesus Fuentes. We're both out of the El Paso office. Because this is state property and a state park, the Texas Rangers will be in charge of the investigation. We'll be assisted by local law enforcement and TPWD law enforcement. And, you know just how close to the international border this crime scene is. So the Border Patrol will be involved. Do you understand so far?"

"Thank you. As you know my lawyer has given me permission to attempt to identify the bodies and tell you guys the narrative. But she told me I'd be singing soprano if I answered any other questions without her present. You guys cool with that?"

"Yes, sir. Here's where we are. We've thoroughly examined the two dead men, at least a field exam for identification. We've thoroughly examined their backpacks. We have found no billfolds or IDs. That should not be a surprise. Let me turn him."

"You know him, ever seen him anywhere?"

"No. Sorry."

The second guy was lying sort of where I left him. He looked different in the daytime. The goggles were still in place. No identification possible there, either. But I don't think I'll ever forget that face and that shattered lens as he hit the ground a foot in front of me and breathed that last sigh into my bloody face.

94

I recounted the events of last night. They abided by the rules and didn't ask questions about the actual shootings. But, as they talked it became clear that the night-vision goggles, its right eyepiece shattered by one of my .40cal rounds was a particular object of fascination.

"Dr. Phillips, can you tell us how you chose to shoot this guy in the eye?"

"Boys, I hurt like hell. I'm going to visit the EMTs. Better living through chemistry—well, through drugs, right? I don't think I can answer any questions. I will tell you that I did not choose to shoot this guy anywhere. I was asleep when Rusty dragged my naked ass onto the floor. Anything else until my attorney gets here? No, didn't think so."

They were very firm in insisting that I stay behind the yellow tape. They filmed the pock-marked walls of Los Alamos, inside and out. They filmed the zillions of glass shards, window frame pieces and shot up furniture. I was ravenous and ate three pretty good FBI egg-and-bacon tacos with some fiery salsa verde, washed down with really bad FBI coffee, no cream or evaporated milk. The caffeine hit and Ranger Fuentes informed me that Susan's plane had landed at the Ranch airstrip and the BP choppers were bringing her and Lisa. They would land shortly. Ranger Hays strongly suggested that the EMTs take another look at the finger and reported that no one had found the lost digit. The EMTs did their magic; gave me an antibiotic injection and another one to dull the pain, not that it much mattered. I felt like someone had beat me with a ball-peen hammer from head to toe, and then he cut off my finger. I felt like shit. But, I was at least upright when Susan, Lisa and the two Dereks landed about a hundred yards north of the Los Alamos compound, where they were fetched by the Border Patrol Blazers.

"Lee, you look awful. Are you alright?"

"Lisa! Guys, give us a minute, OK?"

As they backed off I got a really big hug and a sloppy wet kiss, then: "Lee, what happened to you? You look like shit! I knew that you shouldn't be out here all by yourself; I knew it!

You're too old for these crazy adventures. I thought Rusty could hear stuff for you; did he? You're too old for this cowboy, frontier stuff. You should be at the ER in Alpine. Did they keep you from going?"

"No, Lisa, I'm fine. It was my choice to stay here. Tell you what, let's get me, you and Susan together. We can talk, then I'll chat with the fuzz. OK?"

"OK, but then we're going to the hospital."

We talked, husband and wife stuff. She was really concerned, glad I was still alive. She, Rusty, and I had a family reunion of sorts. Like me, she didn't think much of those pink doggie booties. We commiserated over Star's death; walked out to the corral where Pepper was munching on oats and high-protein feed, his right ear looking really silly with a large white bandage that Tomás had installed. Thankfully, somebody had moved Star's carcass. I didn't ask how.

Susan joined us at the corral. We sat in my canvas festival chairs under the cottonwoods in my backyard. These were the only chairs at Los Alamos still in one piece. I laid it out for the both of them, beginning with my arrival back at Los Alamos a little over two days ago. I even incorporated some of the visit with Charly. As I told it, the tale began sounding pretty damn improbable to me, too. How can that much stuff—bad stuff— happen to one person in so short a time? Susan stopped me a few times, so did Lisa. They asked clarifying questions and then shut up and listened. Susan spoke first.

"Lee, this doesn't make any sense. Why target you? You didn't shoot anybody—well, until last night. But that was self-defense, pure and simple. Hell, your house looks like somebody poured about a thousand rounds through it. You're a lucky guy. Those foot-thick adobe walls and Rusty kept you alive, just long enough for you to get out and make some response. But now the fuzz really needs some answers. Are you up for that?"

"Yeah, I guess."

"Lee, this is really serious. We have two dead people that you shot. The law enforcement types will squabble over jurisdiction, but more than likely the Texas Rangers will guide the investigation. One of your dead guys mostly has no head; the other took three .40cal bullets through the throat, eye and forehead. That is pretty damned good shooting. There are people out there who wonder how you could do that. There are people who also wonder why you shot them both in the head and not the torso. I know the answer and you do too. But you'll have to explain that. And you're going to have to explain it sooner rather than later. Answer the question that is asked. Don't elaborate unless asked. If I think a question should not be answered I will say so. You will not answer it, right?"

"Yes."

"You OK with this?"

"Susan, I killed two people last night in a gunfight. I don't play a musical instrument; I don't fix cars and I don't do gunfights. I do history, nonfiction articles on academic subjects. I'm working on a folklore book. I retired from semipro large-caliber pistol and military large bore rifle competition a long time ago. Now, my residence, simple as it is, is destroyed. I've lost a pinkie finger. I didn't use it for much, but I've had it a long time. I can't even do the Hook'em Horns sign anymore. My dog is wounded; my packhorse is dead; and my riding horse has a sexy but, to him, not-much-fun hole in his right ear. On the other hand, both my wife and my favorite attorney have seen fit to visit. Also on the plus side, I do have a really sexy railroad-track scar across my forehead. That alone is a conversation starter in any bar in the western hemisphere, as in: 'Well, sailor, how did you get that sexy scar?'"

"Lee, get serious, please!"

"Sorry, Lisa. But I'm really happy to be alive. I have a huge amount of adrenaline pumping through my body, along with some pretty neat painkillers. I'll probably feel like crap in about two hours. But for now, I'm ready to talk to the cops. Susan?"

"Lee, I've seen the bodies. They've moved them to that second EMT truck over there. They're wrapped in what is usually known as 'freezer wrap.' It's a procedure that uses a multi-layered, chemically impregnated cloth wrap that mimics refrigeration. It keeps bodies almost at freezing temperature without actually having a freezer unit to do the job. Done correctly, it lasts about three days. It helps out the Medical Examiner. Isn't the twenty-first century something? They're going to ask you again to identify them. Are you up for that?"

"Susan, I already gave that a shot. No sale; I don't know these guys from Adam. But, what the hell, bring 'em on."

And about then a shadow, literally and figuratively fell on our conversation.

"Dr. Phillips, Ms. DeMarco, Ms. Steele; I've already met Dr. Phillips, but not you ladies. I'm Texas Ranger Captain Hays, Jack Hays. This is my associate, Ranger Jesus Fuentes. Dr. Phillips already knows this, but you ladies do not. This is state land and since the local law enforcement has called us in, we are responsible for the investigation of this incident. Dr. Phillips, now that your attorney has arrived, we really do need to ask some questions. You OK with that?"

"You bet Captain; let's do it. I'll be happy to answer your questions. With any luck we can get to the bottom of this really soon, as in now."

"Sorry, sir; I don't think so, but we can get you headed back to Alpine and a fully equipped ER. We have murder or violent death victims scattered all across west Texas—nine of them to be exact—and you, Dr. Phillips, are involved in all of them. Got anything to say about that?"

"Ranger Hays, my client will be happy to answer specific questions. If you have some questions please begin now. Please look at him directly when speaking. Dr. Phillips does not hear well. And he is not a spring chicken, if you get my drift. He did not exactly have a restful and peaceful night and early morning. After your questions, we will insist that he go to the ER in Alpine, whether he wants to or not. And we will leave you to your investigation. As you can imagine, this day has been just a little bit tiring."

"Dr. Phillips, before we take a statement we'd like you to make a second attempt to identify the two dead men. You've had time to think about it; you think you could give it a second try?"

"Yes, let's get it over with."

He pulled down the sheets covering the bodies.

"Ever seen either of these men before last night?"

"No. Never."

"Got any idea who might be behind this?"

"No, I don't."

We sat under a dining fly on camp chairs next to their chopper and did the interview. The camp table nearby had a digital recorder and space for a live-person note taker.

"Dr. Phillips, would you care to summarize the events of last night? The more specifics you can include the quicker we can get this done. I realize that much of this will be a blur, but we would appreciate clarity. I'd like to include the two sheriffs, Border Patrol Captain Juan Barrera whom you know, and NPS law enforcement represented by Captain Potter. Are those arrangements agreeable? Oh, and we'd like to record it."

"Ranger Hayes, as Dr. Phillips's attorney I will advise him to answer or not answer. So, he will wait for my hand signal. I'm sure that will be agreeable to you. And my staff will likewise record the interview; I'm sure you don't have any problems with that."

"Ma'am, we'd rather you not do that."

"Not a problem, sir. This interview is over; let's go Lee, Lisa. Now!"

"OK, OK; it's just not the way we usually do things."

"I'm sure not. Are we ready to proceed? Let's do it."

So, we had two digital recorders, two stenographers, a whole bunch of cops, me, Rusty, Lisa and Susan. Ranger Hays asked that I outline the last twenty-four hours. Juan verified our activities of yesterday and our evening together.

"Captain Hays, before we go further, you mentioned that most of this would be a blur. Sir, nothing could be further from the truth. Everything from the time Rusty dragged my naked ass out of bed until you police types arrived is crystal clear. It is seared in my memory forever. I've never been in a gunfight;

I've never killed anybody, in anger, or otherwise. And I hope I never have to do that again. Do you understand me?"

"Yes, sir."

Hays asked, and I answered and together we covered the "Solitario Shootout," which was what they were calling the activities of last night. We covered the time frame, my reactions and the two self-defense homicides. He asked about the cloud cover, wanted to know how bright the waning moonlight was, all the usual details of a homicide investigation. The questions went on for over an hour. Finally, Susan called a halt.

"Rangers, gentlemen, we have been over this stuff at least three times. The bottom line is that my client was viciously and brutally attacked. His home was destroyed, his hearing dog wounded, his packhorse killed, and he himself suffered two wounds. The only thing we can charge my client with is self defense. Are we clear on that?"

"Ma'am, I'd like to ask two more questions: First, Dr. Phillips, why did you shoot the first guy in the head?"

"'Cause that's all that stuck up over the pickup truck bed. The son of a bitch was trying to kill me. I wasn't ready to die. I had little time to pick and choose my shot. I slammed open the door and pumped three rounds into the SOB. Number 4 buckshot is not particularly selective. But it is effective. My problem was that I had only three rounds in my 12 gauge pump—a mistake I'll not make again."

"Why did you shoot him three times?"

"Because that's all I had and he dropped out of sight anyway."

"Dr. Phillips, did you shoot him again after he was down?"

"I told you. I had only three rounds in the shotgun. There was blood and tissue all over what was left of my SUV and even I could tell that I'd hit him. All I did was lay my shotgun in the pickup bed; grab his rifle; found some other magazines in his vest and scooted."

"Dr. Phillips, are you a marksman?"

"A long time ago I was a member of a pretty fair Austin City Gun Club pistol and large-bore military rifle target shooting team. I have not been involved in that sport for over ten years. I do practice regularly, though not frequently, with my .45 caliber Colt 1911, my .40 caliber Glock, and my M1 Garand. I shoot trap, skeet, and five-stand socially, with one or more of my three shotguns. Yes, I have a concealed carry permit issued by the State of Texas. And, no I don't hunt. Not hungry enough.

"Thank you, sir. Tell me about the second dead shooter. Why did you shoot him in the head? I don't want you, Ms. DeMarco, or Ms. Steele to take this the wrong way, but we have a bunch of dead people with either no head, partial head, or a head with multiple large-caliber bullet holes in them. You have to admit that this many bodies with similar lethal wounds is a little unusual. And, furthermore, we don't have this many homicides in Brewster and Presidio counties in five years. And all these are linked to one person—you, Dr. Phillips. So, getting some answers to these and other questions is essential. Wouldn't you agree? The Chief Ranger in Austin will be on my butt like ugly on an ape if I don't ask them. So I'd really appreciate an answer."

"Lee, answer."

"Captain Hays, the answer is really simple. When I checked the first guy after I shot him I saw that he was wearing a flak jacket. The professional set-up—shooters, three sides, semi-auto fire—told me that these people knew what they were doing. So, I figured, rightly it turns out, that the second guy had on body armor as well. But his face was visible and he was not wearing a helmet. So, I took my shots of opportunity and got lucky. He got me though! I think I hit him three times."

"How many rounds?"

"Six. Yeah, I know that's not a great percentage, but he was moving pretty fast and I was lying on the ground with only my left hand and part of my face stuck around that corner."

"Lee."

"Yeah, Bob."

"When did you know it was three guys?"

"I don't know it was three guys now. All I know is that's how many I saw. Was it—three?"

"Lee, we don't know."

"Dr. Phillips, the two teams of scent dogs have just landed. We've brought them in from Midland and the prison at Pecos. First, we're going to try tracking the third guy you saw. We'll start on the east side of your house. We found tracks there that are not yours. Which reminds me, we'll need your Wellingtons as evidence. They have blood on them and their bloody prints lead from the first dead guy to the front of your SUV. That, of course, matches your story. We'll send an agent into the house to pick up something for you to wear to Alpine. And we have your Glock and the shotgun. I understand you prefer receipts; I'll write one for you. We'll create a grid. We'll do a systematic search out about a mile. Is your dog a scent dog?"

"Sorry, Captain; Rusty does a lot of things, but tracking humans beside me and his buddy Lisa is a little out of his line of work."

"Sir, I know you're headed for the ER in Alpine. We might have additional questions later. Would you be available?"

"Lee, I'll answer that. Ranger Hays, my client will be receiving emergency treatment. He has given you his best recollection of what happened last night. I'm sure you can understand how traumatic an event this was. Now he would like to remove his personal items from inside the house, have Luís and Tomás take them someplace for safekeeping, and get his glass-filled butt on that EMT chopper for Alpine. I think any additional questions will have to wait until he has received proper medical treatment. And, frankly, I am advising him, and you, that all future sessions be cleared through my office or a local Texas attorney that we will engage. Are we clear?"

"Yes ma'am. I would like to have Dr. Phillips sign his statement as soon as we can have one prepared. Is that agreeable with you?"

"Yes. Ranger Hays, but this is how I would like to do that. We've both been recording this interview and we both have stenographers present. I will use my digital copy as my primary reference and you will use yours. We'll both have transcripts done and Dr. Phillips, you, me, and the two stenographers will sign them as the official statements. Any additional interviews must be cleared through his attorneys. Fair enough? Can we agree that this interview is over?"

They both in turn signed off orally, naming those in attendance, the time, place, and date. I signed; they signed. And, finally the interview was over. They allowed the Ranch crew to collect my personal belongings—books, notes for my book, computers, extra Levis, shirts, and my black Stetson, now adorned with two bullet holes. Lisa, Rusty, and I boarded the EMT chopper. Susan and her staff would supervise the collection of my stuff and make sure it all was secured.

"Lisa, we'll see you in Alpine in a few hours. Lee, you get stitched up. This will all blow over, but you know that you can't come back here to Los Alamos until this thing is settled and the guys who attacked you are behind bars. You'll just be a sitting duck."

I faded. The last thing I remember was Rusty licking my face as they strapped me on the gurney face-down and loaded Rusty, Lisa and me into the chopper.

The ER docs at Alpine Regional Hospital were smooth. The biggest problem was not the head wound or even my finger. They left the head wound stitches in place; opened, cleaned, and properly amputated the finger, tucking and stitching a flap of skin over the wound. They shot it and me full of pain killers and antibiotics. It would take some time for it to heal. The result was only a nub of a little finger, not quite to the first knuckle.

The glass shards were the real challenge.

I lay nude, face down on the ER operating table. My back and butt oozed blood from about fifty wounds. The ER interns or residents, three of them, used tweezers and little forceps to pick glass shards out of my back and backside.

"Sir," one of the three young interns working on my back asked, "Were you crawling around in this stuff on your back? There must be fifty of these little bastards. We'll get as many as we can, but some will just have to work themselves out as time passes. You'll be pleased; I think we have all the ones that were in your butt cheeks. We've stitched about a half dozen, but most of these entry wounds on your back will close by themselves. We'd like to shoot you full of antibiotics and keep you a couple of days to be sure you don't have any infection. Your back and backside is going to look a little weird for a time, like someone shot you with birdshot."

"Doc, first of all, you look young enough to be one of my children. Second of all; it would not be a good idea to laugh, smirk or even think about laughing at this point, would it?"

"No, sir; I wouldn't think about laughing, but you really must admit that this is a strange part of your body to have all these wounds, right?"

"Yeah, I suppose so. Stitch me up; lather me with antibiotic ointment or whatever it is you're doing. I really would like to get some sleep. It's been a rough day."

The Brewster County Sheriff's Department posted a cruiser in the hospital entryway; the city stationed an Alpine police officer in the hall outside the room. Lisa and Rusty stayed with me in my room. Rusty curled up in his usual position, which was between me and the door. The private room had a great view of the Davis Mountains to the north and west. Later, Lisa told me that I slept for a full twenty-four hours. She, the cops, and the hospital administration fended off reporters and the media people. Eventually she just turned off the room phone and silenced her cell. My phone, along with its amplifier, was probably with my stuff, or still lying on a shard-covered floor at Los Alamos. I really didn't need it anyway. Before returning to New Orleans Susan or her staff prepared a statement for the hospital to release, and that was the official story. The release referred all questions to the Texas Rangers. Soon, their "We don't comment on ongoing investigations" did the trick, at least for now. The media got the point and quit asking. The Alpine cops were reluctant to allow visitors, but on the third day Bob Potter stopped by. Lisa was out doing errands; she had taken Rusty with her. He was getting pretty crazy cooped up in a hospital. Besides, everybody—nurses, orderlies and docs—all wanted to feed him. It wasn't good for his waistline. The uniformed cop let Bob through because he was a cop.

"Lee, feel like company?"

"Come on in, Bob. I'm at that stage in convalescence where everything in this place is an irritant—the people, the food, the noise, even the drugs, everything. And this is a really nice hospital. Everyone has been competent, gracious and caring. But I am real pissed off. My sabbatical is shot, not to mention my horses, and me. I've lost a finger. My backside looks like I have the pox. The cops have custody of my pistols and shotguns. And I really want get out of here and hunt down the SOBs who did this and whack 'em myself. Tell me, what did you cop types find out? How many? Where did my third shooter go? He couldn't just disappear into thin air. What did the dogs find? The only real positives to this experience are that I am still kicking and at about 7:45 every morning I have this incredible view of the very first rays of the sun reflecting off the silver domes of the observatories at Mt. Locke. You know how far that is from here? Never mind; it is really good to see you. What have you got? And I apologize for running my mouth."

"First, Lee, thanks for mailing the disc and pics of the Mariscal murder scene to me. The package came the next day, the day before the Solitario Shootout. It's the damnedest thing, Lee."

He gave me the whole nine yards. The dogs tracked the shooter for about a mile out north of Los Alamos. Then the scent just stopped in the middle of this flat rocky rise. Nothing, no tire tracks, no horse tracks, no nothing. The Border Patrol and the other cops did a 360 degree search, twenty, fifty and one hundred yards out. The three NPS guys said it was like this shooter had dropped off the planet. They did a quadrant search on the ground with dogs and state troopers. They did a helicopter quadrant search with the same result. Nothing, it was like this guy got beamed up by the Enterprise spaceship.

"Lee, the investigation is at a dead stop and a dead end. The Rangers don't have an ID on the two guys you shot. Their fingerprints are in absolutely nobody's database. We, that is, the Rangers, sent them to Homeland Security, Interpol, the Mexican border states, the Federales in Mexico City, and friendly agencies in Canada, the Caribbean, and South America. It's a bit early to expect a response, but nobody I'm talking to expects a positive outcome. Some of us think these guys are contract killers. If so, you're in a lot of shit, huh? And you might consider getting your butt out of Big Bend. That should make you feel great. I'm sure you and Lisa and your friends like me and Juan would like to know what it is you've done, or what you know, that makes you a guy with a big bull's eye on his shirt. It should also make you happy that the Alpine PD and the sheriff's office have pulled officers off regular duty to babysit you. I'm sure they can't wait until you get your ass back to anywhere but here. You're a major liability for them. Nobody wants you getting shot and dying on their watch, including me by the way.

"The good thing for you is that half of this case was open and shut. It goes in the books as self-defense. Juan and I were in that discussion yesterday afternoon with Captain Hays; Colonel Ned Maples, Chief of Law Enforcement for Parks and Wildlife, the sheriffs of Brewster and Presidio counties and their chief prosecutors. Did you know they found over 200 shell casings? They've closed that part of the investigation. They're still working on the attempted murder part. I don't think they have a clue as to what to do next.

"I did have another conversation with Luís and Juan after you were cleared. Want to hear about it? I think its good news for you. In fact it was Juan who suggested it."

"Wait, Bob. Let's don't fast forward on me too quickly here. So the official reading is self defense—no shit, Sherlock! Good. At least I don't have to worry about a Grand Jury, an indictment, or something equally stupid. Does that mean that they will continue to press the attempted murder investigation? And please, let me finish. Do I get my Glock and my shotgun back?"

"Lee, here is how it will go: The Texas Rangers, the FBI, the Border Patrol, and La Policía de la Frontera have established a joint borderlands task force to continue and coordinate the investigation of the two crimes. They believe that there is a strong likelihood that the two incidents are linked. They're not even sure that you're the link; well, at least some of them aren't sure. I'm in the 'you're the primary link' column. Does any of this surprise you?"

"Bob, I think I'm on the edge of a TMI overload—you know, Too Much Information. I'm really pleased that you folks are really going to continue the investigation of the two crimes. But we have not two murder scenes, but three, don't we? Remember the two vaqueros? Are you guys linking them to the others? Never mind; we can talk about that later. It's been a really bad week. I sidetracked you. Tell me the really good news. I like good news. Good news is almost as much fun as watching a sunrise at Castolon over Mule Ears Peaks, or the sun setting through Santa Elena over the Rio Grande."

"That is part of the good news Lee, part of the really good news. Yes, you do get your weapons back. But, and it is a big but, if you accept what I'm about to offer there will be some really strict rules about carrying firearms in public."

It was really pretty damned revolutionary, a non-park staffer living in a park home. Bob and the NPS offered me, Rusty, and Lisa a living space at Castolon. It was a vacant ranger's quarters. They wanted me to pay the utilities. It was mine until I completed the book. Maria and Carlito would remain in the complex. He didn't say it, but I knew that they were there at least partially to watch over me. To make sure I didn't get into too much trouble, they would station a new NPS cop at Castolon. Her name was Rachael Jackson. Her last post was Grand Canyon. She requested the transfer. Her family was from the borderlands.

"Lee, she doesn't look like a Jackson stereotype. She's Hispanic and is about as dark as you are. She's the replacement for the guy killed at Mariscal. She's bilingual and really sharp. In addition, the Border Patrol swings by Castolon regularly, either in 4x4s or by chopper. As you know, we even have a shared chopper landing pad at Castolon—us, the Border Patrol and La Frontera.

The way Bob described it was perfect: "This house has two bedrooms and two baths. The living room windows face the canyon. The second bedroom can be used as an office. The windows of both bedrooms face east. The house is adobe, just like Los Alamos. The front porch comes with benches but not rockers. It faces Santa Elena. It is remote, but it's not isolated like Los Alamos. Lisa is not going to agree to you being in a place like Los Alamos anyway. And frankly I think it would be really stupid. This house is set apart from the other buildings of the compound and has a small corral and shed for Pepper. It, like Los Alamos, is partially furnished—well, kinda early NPS Depression Style. It has a propane stove and a propane fridge. It doesn't have satellite or DSL, but if you want to pay for it, you can put it in. What do you say? Your personal stuff—books, computer, backyard chairs, that monstrously heavy oak dining table and the few pots, pans and dishes that weren't destroyed by gunfire—are in storage at The Ranch, at Sauceda Headquarters.

"Luís, his crew, and my staff can deliver it anywhere in the Big Bend you want with twenty-four hours' notice. You and Lisa talk about it and let us know. You have that goofy, 'I'm getting sleepy look.' But I need to tell you this before I go: I'm really glad you're still alive. The planet would be poorer without you on it. Next time I'd like to talk more about your book. You any closer to proving that the Ark is really here? We'll talk about that another day. You take care; let us know, right?"

"Thanks, Bob. Lisa and I will talk about it when she gets back. I think they're going to let me go tomorrow."

#

It was a VERY LONG discussion. At first Lisa wasn't really keen on the idea of staying in Big Bend at all. She felt much safer in Austin. She thought that I could complete the book and be safe in our condo overlooking Lady Bird Lake. At least there were cops to call—cops who didn't have to drive fifty

108

or a hundred miles to help you. The last week or so had not been the best in her life, either. We discussed the pros and cons of staying and leaving. My argument was that I had a book to complete. Second, now after being targeted and shot at I really wanted to stay and help find the bastards who tried to kill me. And most important, I wanted to find out why. The formal investigation was going nowhere. Maybe an amateur approach couldn't hurt. And the reality was that Castolon was much safer than Los Alamos. Bob promised to keep an eye on me; Juan too. We called Bob that night and took him up on his offer. He told us both that he and the Ranch park staff would bring our furniture from Sauceda.

They released me the next day. The red dots on my back and ass were healing fine. Lisa could replace as necessary the little pink polka-dotted band aids scattered across my back and butt. I didn't think much of the color, but the young intern reminded me, "Who's gonna know?" I covered my railroad-track forehead stitches with a camo biker bandana. It had some sort of smart-ass slogan on the front, "Better Lucky than Smart." That sounded good to me. One of the interns bought it at the Harley repair shop on the other side of the Union Pacific tracks from Railroad Blues. The docs rewrapped my finger; strapped my entire hand in a metal protective brace, and I was good to go. Fortunately Lisa picked up a new pair of Wellingtons for me so I didn't have to walk out of the hospital barefooted. My good ones, the ones I'd spent two years breaking in, were now living in a Texas Ranger evidence locker somewhere.

Docs, nurses, and hospital administrators in general are all agreed on maybe one thing. Regardless of how you rolled into the facility, if you survive and are discharged alive, you will exit in a wheelchair. That chair will be pushed by someone old enough to be your grandson or granddaughter. No exceptions! Well not quite. I rebelled and told them: "I don't care what the rules are, I'm walking out of this place. Get out of the way." And they did, and I did.

As Lisa and I walked out the front door of Alpine Regional, Luís handed me the keys to an "almost new" TPWD pickup. Colonel Ned Maples, Chief of Law Enforcement at TPWD, stood beside Luís. Maples apologized profusely. He reminded us that all the agencies were doing their best to find the shooters. He also noted that after all I was still the first Writer in Residence at Big Bend Ranch State Park. It was an important program for the agency, this link between TPWD and the academic community. He hoped that the loan of a newer 4x4 Chevy crew cab pickup would be seen as both an apology for the "unfortunate incident at Solitario" and as a gesture of TPWD's goodwill. He hoped that even though I'd be living at Castolon I would still consider myself the first state park's writer in residence. I didn't see the rumble at Solitario as an unfortunate incident. I saw it as a professional assassination attempt. And the horrible thing about the whole mess is that I didn't know why I was a target. But I assured him that I still considered myself the Writer in Residence at the Ranch, and that I did not hold TPWD in any way responsible. And, that I intended to move back into the Los Alamos residence when it was restored.

Lisa and I thanked the colonel. Rusty got treats from Luís and Tomás. Luís said they'd meet us at Castolon with our furniture. We piled the few things we brought to the hospital in the spacious crew cab. Rusty curled up on the back seat. We stopped at Garza's Super Mercado and loaded up on groceries. I detoured by the Alpine PD; thanked them for posting an officer outside my door and retrieved my Glock and 12 gauge pump. Sure enough, no bullets or shells; those had disappeared. No apology for that, either. But I was done with those guys. On the way out of town we stopped at Triple A—Alpine Arms and Ammo. I picked up some ammo for the pistol and the shotgun. My photo had been in the Alpine *Avalanche* and was posted on the front door. This was a notoriety that I could have done without. You'd have thought I was a celebrity.

"Look who's here boys. It's the guy who shot the killers over at the Ranch. You're the guy from Solitario, aren't you? You're the shooter that killed two of the guys trying to kill you. Congratulations! Good job! How does it feel? What are you going to do now?"

"Look, it feels great to be alive. I'm incredibly lucky. Other than that, sorry guys, I'm not talking. That is over. My wife and I'd like to get back to the park. What do I owe you for the shells and cartridges?"

As we walked out the ammo store Lisa said, "You know I haven't asked until now, but how do you feel?"

"I feel like shit. You know I've seen my share of dead bodies, relatives who died of various diseases, more than my share of highway accident victims. But I've never made a dead body myself. And it sucks. I have all these questions swirling around in my head. It'll take a while to sort 'em out. So far I haven't been dreaming about it and that's a plus. But you know, I wonder. Someplace since a few days ago there's a family, maybe a wife or girlfriend wondering when her man will be coming through the door. And everybody, no matter who they are, has a mother. I just wonder, that's all. Then I remember. If they'd shot me instead of me shooting them, you would be the one wearing black. And I guess that helps."

Lisa and I walked to the truck. I handed her the keys, climbed into the 4x4 Chevy and headed southeast to the national park and Castolon. Five minutes later I kicked the seat back and slept.

Alpine is at almost 5,000 feet altitude. Castolon, on the Rio Grande at the mouth of Santa Elena Canyon is more like 1,300 feet. If you travel south on Texas 118, Alpine's rolling greenish brown gentle hills gradually give way to a more arid landscape. The live oaks, Ashe junipers, and sage grasses of Alpine gradually disappear. I awoke at the desert development of Terlingua Ranch, northwest of Study Butte. The terrain there was covered in yucca, creosote bushes, agave, lechuguilla, ocotillo, and tumbleweed. Texas 118 is not the most well-traveled of highways. Lisa, Rusty and I may have met five cars between Alpine and Study Butte, a distance of about ninety miles. Castolon is further, 130 miles from Alpine. One thing I have always liked about the way Lisa drives is that trips are generally quick. This was no exception. She and I had been down this road many times, the most memorable being one cold October night more than a few years back.

"Lisa, remember that time late at night when we stopped at the then-closed Maverick Junction Ranger Station rest area and made love under a full moon on the warm hood of your VW Rabbit? Aah! Outdoor sex; tough to beat. We could hang around Study Butte until it gets dark and. . . ."

"Lee, it's daylight. You're oozing. You have a couple dozen holes in your back. You gotta admit that's not very romantic. The NPS ranger at Maverick is expecting us, and there's a Border Patrol 4x4 standing by to escort us to Castolon. How about we postpone that fantasy until we get settled at Castolon? OK?"

The gravel road from Maverick, past Luna's Jacal and the Terlingua Abajo turnoff was as rough as ever and we ate the Border Patrol's dust for miles. But it was good to be back in a place where I could wake up in the morning and watch the sun rise over some of the most incredible landscape in North America. The last time I'd seen Castolon, the fuzz was hustling my ass into a helicopter and flying me to the hospital in Alpine. Hard to believe it was just a couple of weeks ago.

Bob Potter, Maria Gomez, Luís, Tomás and someone dressed in an NPS LE uniform that I assumed to be Rachael Jackson were waiting at the Castolon Store. The Border Patrol Blazer turned back to Maverick. There was the usual assortment of tourists, but not as many as when I first rode into Castolon to report finding those five bodies.

Luís, Tomás and the Castolon NPS staff had put my books, computers, and even a mostly undamaged chest of drawers in the house. My furniture and the NPS furniture might best be described as an eclectic decorative style. I had this sneaky suspicion that *Southern Living* would not be coming by to photograph our décor. But the décor did include my now famous heavy oak dining table, my queen-size bed and my night stand, the same one I used to store the Glock at Los Alamos. We put the firearms on the bed; piled the groceries on the table; opened some Negra Modelos, cut some lime slices, and everybody adjourned to the benches on the front porch, the side that faced Santa Elena. Good friends, good beer, and a great afternoon in Big Bend. Lisa and I were moved in. She was committed to staying at least two weeks.

Everybody except Bob Potter said their good-byes after about forty-five minutes. Carlito came over. He'd just arrived from school and wanted to play with Rusty and Pepper. He knew how to ride, so he and Bob saddled Pepper. I gave Rusty the "off the clock" signal and Carlito took off with him running around the horse in those crazy circles of his, barking like crazy. He didn't have much opportunity to do that when he was with me. If I needed somebody to listen for me, Lisa could do that. It was just the three of us sitting on benches on our front porch.

"OK everybody, I need to play NPS law enforcement for a few minutes. Lee you can keep the weapons in the house. You have a carry permit, but it is not valid in the National Park. As you know, we strictly prohibit firearms, unless they are carried by commissioned officers. I thought about making you one, but my supervisor said something like: 'Are you nuts?' So don't carry it outside. I know you will anyway, but please don't do it where I'll have to do something like confiscate it. I suggest that you stay in close contact with Ranger Jackson. I strongly recommend that until that hand heals completely you do not go on one of those solo journeys of yours.

"And if you do, tell somebody where you're going and when you'll come back. And while we're visiting that little issue, when you do what I just told you not to do, where will you put that information? I also suggest that you get that satellite phone back and install DSL. You do not need to be isolated. One last thing: Ranger Hays is probably going to come visit. I think he has some more questions. Do you guys have any questions? Now, where do you put the information?"

"Bob, inside the front door there is a boot rack. On the far end away from the door there will be a pair of very highly shined black Lucchese gentleman's boots with a bootjack stuck in one. The note will be in that one. OK? I suggest that if neither of us is here and you wish to leave a note, put it in that boot. Got it?"

After Bob left, I crashed for two hours. That night Lisa and I organized the house. We set up my library and office in the second bedroom and connected the components of the computer. Computers are a really useful tool, but they have all those damn wires.

"Try it, Lee; you're dying to get back to your book. I'm going to bed."

The little prompt showed a disc already inserted in the computer's drive. Click. And there they were, the digital pics of the murder scene near Mariscal Mountain. These were the last photos I looked at before the attack at Solitario. But it was way too late; I was way too tired; and it hurt way too much to view that charnel house. That would have to wait. I ejected it. I found the flash drive Charly had left me, plugged it in, and opened the first of the documents she had copied. Two minutes later I was hooked. This was powerful stuff. Even the first three or four documents would stand the academic world on its collective ear.

"Rusty, my God. Charly was right." Thump, thump.

I scrolled and scanned, skimming through the photocopies of the originals and concentrating on the transcriptions. And it hit me. These documents were blockbuster stuff. If this was true it would change theology in the Western world, the Eastern one too. These fragile parchment documents had the potential of rearranging political alliances in the New World and the Middle East, and would alter relationships between Judaism and Christianity. If the Ark really was in the New World, in northern Mexico, and could be found, whoever possessed it would achieve enormous power. The permutations were world-shattering. If these documents were real, if they were what they seemed to be, the New World was going to become a newer world. It would take years to sort this out.

About midnight Lisa, wearing an old flannel shirt, stumbled into the room.

"Come to bed Lee. This will wait."

"Lisa, this is really incredible stuff. Come look."

"Do me a favor; I don't want to see it or talk about it until you're better. Deal?"

"OK, deal."

In a few minutes my drugs had worn off. My amputated finger had what the docs call "ghost pain." I hurt all over. I swallowed a couple of pills. I shut down the flash and hung it around my neck by the leather lanyard Charly had provided. I was asleep by the time my head hit my four pillows. Rusty took up his usual position, between us and the bedroom door. Lisa and I spent the next four days settling in. For me the days were fine. The nights were, well, a nightmare. The second night I woke up yelling something like: "I'll get you bastards." The third night Lisa found me sitting on the porch wrapped in a serape looking at the stars.

"Lee, what the hell are you doing; it's three in the morning."

"Lisa, I can't get it out of my head, those dead guys. Somewhere there are families in grief. You know, I don't think I'm ever going to get over this."

"Yes, you will; it will take time, just like the doctor said. It will take time, but you will. Just try not to let it make you crazier than you already are."

#

We laughed, we talked about what she called "life after the book." We watched Carlito play with Rusty and ride Pepper. We took long walks to the mouth of the canyon. Daily, Lisa changed my goofy-looking little polka-dotted patches-noting that although my backside would never win any beauty awards, at least it was not oozing any longer.

CHAPTER 7: RETURN

"Rusty, stop it! Stop licking my face."

But he licked, then he pulled, and finally I sat up in bed. Lisa was already gone. It was almost daylight. Rusty pulled, and pushed and pulled and corralled and herded me to the back porch. The little packing rate table held a pot of coffee and two cups. And next to it, oh my! Lisa lying cocooned in a buffalo robe on the porch facing Mule Ears. She flipped back the robe and all she wore was my battered black Stetson, and only my black Stetson, strategically placed.

"Well, cowboy, forgot what to do with this?" As she fanned the hat.

"The coffee or the . . . er . . . hat?"

"Both. Come on in before everything . . . er . . . ah . . . gets smaller. Giddy up cowboy!"

And I did; well, we both did. With both of us naked in the forty-degree dawn, the buffalo-skin robe Lisa was sprawled on sure felt good wrapped around two people who enjoyed rubbing their bodies together. We made love, then watched the sun rise over Mule Ear and sipped coffee out of only slightly cracked mugs. I fell back asleep. It was ten when I woke. Lisa was gone. So was the hat. Rusty was curled on the foot of the robe. I pulled on jeans, and a flannel shirt, poured myself another cup of dark roast laced with evaporated milk and found her sitting on the front porch, reading.

"Lee, your feet must be cold; it's only sixty degrees out here. Go put on those nice rough-out Wellingtons I bought."

"I enjoyed the wakeup. If every American man and woman woke up like that every morning, this would be a much more mellow country to live in. And my feet are fine. You said you want to know what I found at Mariscal, but only when I was better. I am. Come inside; I'll show you. Some of these photos are pretty gruesome. Stop when you want."

116

It was not a pretty picture. I'd photographed them from left to right, the uniformed guys first. There they were, sprawled in that peculiar layout, blood all over them, the sand and the canyon walls. The last shot on the disk was one of the guy with no arm. I pressed what I thought was the "Scan" or "Pan" key so Lisa could see the full scene and all the dead, not just this one guy. But it was no big surprise that the image that emerged was a detail, not a scan. I had pressed the "Zoom" key instead. I use computers and frequently have need of graphics programs. But I'm not really adept at manipulating graphic images. I'm always pressing the wrong key and I did it again. But this time . . . . And, there it was!

"My God, Lisa; there it is!"

"There what is Lee?"

And indeed, there it was: the Star of David with the numeral "7" centered in it, written in the Spanish style with the little crossbar about two-thirds the way up the vertical. The photo framed the dead man's upper arm, well really his lower armpit, complete with other wounds and marks. And there was the mark, the star and 7.

"My God, Lisa; we're in a lot of fucking trouble."

"Lee, it's just a tattoo, a very small tattoo of the number 7 in the center of what looks like the Star of David. It's on a guy's armpit for God's sake. What is the big deal?"

"Let me take you through it."

And I did. I began with finding the five dead guys, reporting that to the authorities, and the rest of it, Charly's research.

"Believe me. We, or rather Charly and I, and now you are involved in something really big, a New World mystery that is at least 500 years old. And I think it has something to do with those guys trying to kill me at Los Alamos."

"I don't get it."

So I laid it out. The borderlands legends have it that Marrano Jews in Spain smuggled the Ark to the New World in the latter part of the 1500s. The story is that it had been kept for almost a thousand years in a hiding place in Granada, which turned out to be the last Moorish kingdom on the Iberian peninsula. The particulars of the journey from Jerusalem to Iberia, both Roman provinces at the time of the move, have been lost to us. No one knows for sure, but many believe that after its arrival in Iberia, the Ark was kept and guarded by a small militaristic cloistered order of monks in a remote monastery outside the citadel of Granada. The lore said that for generations only the Prior, the leader of the monastery, knew just what they were guarding. Ferdinand and Isabella conquered Granada in 1492. That same year they sent Columbus to the New World and cranked up their Inquisition to ferret out nonbelievers. It became imperative to find a safer hiding place for the sacred object.

For almost a thousand years, seven families had watched over the holiest object in Judaism. It was, and remains, the foundation of that religion's theology and the foundation of Christianity and Islam as well. The seven families were charged with keeping the Ark safe and protecting it from all those who would use it for evil purposes.

The leadership of the Seven, as they called themselves, believed that Nueva España offered the safest hiding place. According to the lore, sometime in the 1530s or 1540s the Ark arrived in the New World. At least one member of the Seven accompanied it at all times. It was safe for a time in an Indian village outside Veracruz, then as now Mexico's largest port on the Gulf of Mexico. But then the Spanish authorities in the New World cranked up their own version of the Inquisition. After one of the family members was burned at the stake in Mexico City, the Seven determined to move it out of the reach of the king's New World inquisitors.

Frontiers are fluid places. People come and go. No one asks origins, asks your business, who or what brought you there. So, the Ark apparently wound up in Santa Fe or somewhere close. There are those who still believe that the Seven hid it for a time in a small chapel later known as Chimayo, about forty miles north of present day Santa Fe. The truth is, no one knows. After the Pueblo Revolt of the 1680 it wound up in a safer place.

The documents Charly found, if they are authentic, indicate that it was hidden someplace either in or close to Presidio San Vicente. At the time it was an important waystop on the main Indian, military, and commercial trails from what is now Texas into Mexico. The Spaniards built Presidio San Vicente to stop Apache raids into what we now know as Mexico. San Vicente, or at least its ruins are less than fifty miles to the east of where we are right now. This diary and letters describe some very peculiar writing on the side of one of the crates. They also describe some peculiar rites and ceremonies related to the largest crate. One of the sisters copied the writing from the side of the crate. That leads us to now.

"Lisa, you want to read Charly's digital copies of the original documents and transcriptions?"

"No. What I want to know is what you're going to do next. And that includes these nightmares you have even night. Let's talk about that stuff. Then I'll read Charly's stuff. OK?"

"Lisa, it really doesn't matter if you read Charly's documents. The bottom line is that, as far as they know, you've seen everything I've seen. We can't run from this. They'll find us wherever we are—here, Austin, Colorado, Mexico or wherever. The worst part of it is; I don't know who 'they' is. I also don't even know why they want me, you and eventually Charly—dead. That would be a good place to start, don't you think?"

"So what do you want to do? You've gotta get some help, but I've been married to you a long time. Maybe the way to address that issue is not therapy in the traditional sense, but something else. So, talk to me, Lee."

"Here is the situation as I see it, Lisa. I find some dead guys. I report it. For my efforts, I barely avoid a night in the Alpine jail. I learn some really interesting stuff from a visit with my friend Juan. I am attacked by three guys with lots of guns and bullets, but I survive. Now I learn that all of this might just be part of a 500-year quest by some very bad people. Worse, I'm caught up in it. I'm a historian. I research and puzzle out stuff. That is what I do. But that is history. This is blood. This is the sound of shattered and ended lives.

"Lisa, I killed two people the other night. I did it without thinking. I was running on 200-proof adrenaline. You know what the scariest part was?"

"No."

"I didn't blink once. I just ran, hid, ducked and crawled and I shot one guy three times in the head with a shotgun. A shotgun for god's sake, Lisa! I shot the second guy three times in the head at point blank range from a prone position with my left hand, and only one eye peering around that adobe fence post. He died inches from my face; I smelled his last breath."

"Lee, you're left-handed."

"Yes, usually. But I've always shot right-handed, just like my father taught me. Until a few days ago I was willing to let this whole thing die—the interrogations, the possible jail time. But, shit, Lisa, those bastards tried to kill me. And they'll try to kill you. And they'll try to kill Charly. I got off lucky—just a set of scars across my forehead, a whole bunch of little dimples on my back and ass. And I lost a part of a finger. What do I want to do? I am going to figure this sumbitching puzzle out and I'm going to find those bastards that did this and end it. Lisa, these crimes are related; we, mainly you and me, have to figure it out. There's one more thing. I'm comfortable in this country. I've traveled over most of it too many times to count. I know how to travel and live in this environment. I would rather fight it out here than anywhere else. But you need to be OK with that, 'cause you're involved up to your blond head."

"Let me see Charly's stuff. Leave me alone. This is going to take a while. I'll come get you when I'm finished."

Lisa read; I puttered and rearranged the kitchen a bit, then put on my brand new Wellington rough-outs, and Rusty and I walked over to the store. The Castolon General Store was not exactly school supply central. But it did carry the basics—some for the kids in the park, but mostly for the Mexican kids who lived across the river.

I had a project to work on and all my office supplies were at Los Alamos. I bought some note cards, a pack of 3x5 and three packs of 4x6 ones. Some had lines; some didn't. I bought the last of the Big Chief Tablets and three composition books with those speckled covers. The store did stock thumbtacks; I bought all Maria had, four cards of them. I bought two blue ink ballpoint pens and a box of yellow no. 2 pencils with erasers and a little Big Bend National Park souvenir pencil sharpener. Maria didn't sell Magic Markers but she loaned me three—green, blue and red.

It was time to go to work. The first job was to figure out what I knew. I organized what I knew, what I surmised, and what I didn't know onto those cards, muttering to myself and Rusty as I went.

At one point I heard an irritated shout that sounded like: "Christ Lee, can't you do that without talking to yourself? You're really lucky to have Rusty. He doesn't mind it. You know it drives most people crazy as loons, including me, your incredibly tolerant wife."

I caught about every third word, but I did understand the tone. "Yeah, OK. What'd she say Rusty?" Thump, thump.

I appropriated one wall of the ranger cabin's dining room. Lisa continued to read Charly's material. I began scribbling on index cards, one fact on each one and first laying it on the oak table. As I accumulated a string of data, I stuck those cards on the wall with thumb tacks. I used green, red, and blue magic markers to color code the index cards: green for what I knew for sure; blue for what I surmised; and red for everything else. The idea was to lay out in a logical order the entire series of events since I discovered the bodies. I'd used this system before when working on academic projects. Here it served to lay out the chronology and establish visual relationships between time, events, people, and actions. After about two hours Lisa came in. She had that glazed look in her eyes, probably the same look that I had when Charly sprang this material on me a few days ago.

Together we reviewed the digital photos of the dead guys, including the closeup of the guy with no arm. Together we enlarged it. There was the tattoo, the same six-pointed star with the numeral "7" in the center. We compared the two, the one from Charly's notes and the other from the dead guy's armpit. They were identical. The immensity of the story was slowly dawning on her.

"Lee, I am really scared. I need to think about this some more. And we need to talk."

"Yeah, me too. But right this minute I want to lay these cards out on this table, organize them and use those thumbtacks to place them on the wall."

"I'm going to visit with Maria and use the store phone to order the installation of your DSL service and a new satellite phone. Back in a bit."

By five or so I had about half a wall covered in cards. There were a lot of red corners. But the patterns and relationships, if there were any, eluded me.

It was almost sunset when Lisa returned. By then I was cross-eyed. I'd run out of ways to look at the cards. When she said that we were invited for dinner at Maria and Carlito's house I jumped at it. Ranger Jackson joined us. The tourists were gone, headed back to comfortable hotel rooms in The Basin, Lajitas, Marfa or Marathon. We sat on the porch of the Castolon Store, watched the sunset through and over Santa Elena. We grownups enjoyed a couple of glasses of red wine. I taught Carlito how to play Frisbee with Rusty. During dinner Lisa and Maria ganged up on me.

"Lee, Maria and I have discussed your determination to stay here at Castolon or at Los Alamos to finish this. We both believe that it is insane; we both know that you're determined to do it in spite of what we say. I've lived with you long enough to know that all my protests will, in the end be useless. So, given that all of us are affected by your decision, we, that is, Maria proposes the following. Your turn Maria."

"Señor Lee, tomorrow is Saturday. I would like to see where all this started. Carlito would too. Let's take the pickup and do a weekend camping trip to Talley and Mariscal. Monday is a teacher in-service day. Carlito doesn't have to be back in school until Tuesday. The trip would do us all good. Is that agreeable to you Lisa?"

"Yes. Lee, you have to admit, this has been a tough couple of weeks. It is getting better, but I for one would like to get out of here. I'm not wild about going to Mariscal, but I'm willing. The catch for me is that I will not agree to this trip unless we have law enforcement escort. Maria has help tomorrow and Sunday in the store and Castolon is closed on Monday. What do you say? Rachael, can you come?"

Rachael was on duty. She couldn't go. My right hand was still in its protective metal brace. Lisa and Maria were right; none of us should go without protection. We called Bob Potter at Panther Junction. He was crazy enough to say "Yes, if I can bring my daughter." We all decided to leave at the semi-civilized hour of seven in the morning. Potter would bring his 4x4; I had mine. If I tired, we'd just come home.

#

First stop was Talley. We lunched on the grassy slope along the Rio Grande. Lisa brought fried chicken. My favorite are legs, "walking chicken" as my father called it. Maria provided a cold soup, a salad, pan dulce for dessert, and a few Shiner beers. As we were spreading the picnic blanket, Bob threw a tin of smoked oysters and a packet of saltine crackers in the center of our picnic cloth.

"Your reputation has preceded you, Lee."

"Where did you hear about my smoked oyster fetish?"

"Juan told me."

"My man, you are a prince. Anybody want to share these?"

Only Carlito was brave enough to accept the challenge.

Behind "Boys" and "Girls" pickups, we all changed into swim suits and swam, frolicked and splashed in the Rio Grande. For a time I hoped that all of my family and friends relaxed a bit, for this brief time. I tried not to think that somebody, or several somebodies, somewhere out there was gunning for me, Lisa and probably the rest of us too. It was time to return to the site of the first murders. Carlito climbed in the cab with Lisa and me. He had about a zillion questions about what we were going to see. I explained as best I could, but no amount of sugar-coating could disguise the fact that we were going to a murder scene, a place where five men had died violent, brutal deaths.

"Carlito, if you don't want to see this, you can stay in the truck."

"No, Señor Lee, I want to see too."

The recent rains had washed some of the blood from the walls. Rusty was agitated; he kept tugging on my pants leg, pulling me away from the scene. For him the smell of death remained. I sat down with him, put his head in my hands, and had him look at me while I quietly explained what we were going to do. He thump, thumped. I put his service dog collar and leash on. We did the tour while I described the scene for my wife and friends. About halfway through the litany Maria asked: "Señor Lee, Captain Potter, where did they come from?"

"Who?"

"The men who did this terrible thing: where did they come from? How did they get here?"

Bob and I looked at each other. It was like someone had hit our collective thumbs with a hammer, a look of total surprise and amazement.

Bob spoke first. "Maria, I think you have asked the question that all the local law enforcement staff has missed. We've been asking why and who. We really should be asking the other questions. If we figure out those answers, we'll know who and why. If not, we'll have a better idea about the questions. Then we can figure out the path we should be headed down. Thank you."

We didn't stay long in what the locals on both sides of the border were now calling "Bloody Canyon." We camped at the mine. Well, we really camped at Fresno Camp, an NPS site about a mile or so east of the main Mariscal Mine complex. *Fresno* means ash tree in Spanish, and there were actually a few of them at the campground. The nearby spring and the recent rains had made everything green, except the ash trees. It was autumn and they were losing their leaves. The campground was covered with yellow, red, orange and brown leaves. We cooked out using my propane stove. I baked a Marie Callender apple pie using my really cool portable oven. My father-in-law had given it to me about three years before. It was worth every dime he spent on it. And, using split logs from Panther Junction, Bob and his daughter cranked up a real campfire. After dinner, we roasted marshmallows on coat hangers thoughtfully provided by Bob and the NPS. Rusty thought the world of his toasted marshmallows; he licked and smacked for at least ten minutes. Mine were the perfect blend of char and squishy white puffy spun sugar. If you've never had roasted marshmallows and a good Shiraz while sitting in camp chairs around a campfire in Big Bend National Park, your life has been a waste. You need to get out more. You have not lived.

The next morning, Ranger Bob, "General Potter" to most of us, gave us our marching orders: "Stay on the marked trails; do not go near open holes in the ground. Take a buddy. Everybody clear?" All nodded "Yes" and proceeded to do what they wanted. We split up; I had Carlito and Rusty. Lisa decided to spend the morning with Maria, some girl thing. Bob was off someplace hiking with his daughter.

Carlito wanted to know where we found the vaquero's horse. He, Rusty, and I took my pickup to the mine site, parked, and walked to the hole. It was still marked with yellow tape and three NPS signs warning people to stay back. We stopped at the tape and I explained how we found the horse. Carlito stepped toward the shaft. Rusty grabbed his pants leg and tugged. Carlito pulled away and down he went, sliding down the side of the hole. I grabbed at him, caught his belt and we both slid *into* the hole. It wasn't a long drop, but it was an eternity for Carlito and me. We hit the bottom, actually heavy timbers braced across the mine shaft to seal it. They stopped our fall. We looked at each other, stunned speechless. I grabbed Carlito and gave him the tightest hug he probably ever had. Both of us had that dazed, surprised look on our faces. We had multiple scratches, and torn pants and shirts. I could tell that the stitches in my back had separated. Damn.

"How do you feel, kid?"

"I was afraid, Señor Lee. I thought I was dropping into the mine."

"Well you were. But the timbers stopped our fall. Fifteen or twenty feet is not bad. But I don't think I would want to fall 500 feet. So. . . everything is in working order, no broken bones, nothing more than a bunch of scratches?

"Lee, I have lots of scratches. My nose is bleeding and my head really hurts. And Mama is not going to like it that my good jeans and shirt are torn. . . . Rusty grabbed me. Why did he do that?"

"Carlito, I think Rusty could feel the ground better than you or me. He was trying to get us away from the danger of the hole the best way he knew how."

"He's barking Lee."

"Rusty, go find Lisa. Go, now"!" I hollered up at Rusty. Nothing to do now but wait. Here let me see if I can get that bloody nose squared away."

"He's still barking Lee, but I can barely hear him now. Does that mean that he'll get Lisa and they'll come find us soon?"

While we waited I tore up part of my shirt and used some of our canteen water to clear off most of the dirt on Carlito's face. He had a lot of scratches.

"You know man, it looks like you've been in a fight with sixteen cats and you lost. Nothing really serious, though. General Potter has a big first aid kit. Once you're out of here we can get you cleaned up pretty quickly."

I pulled my small MagLite out of my right pants leg cargo pocket, and took a closer look at the large bump on his head. I shined the light in his eyes, one at a time. Both pupils were fine. That's when the flashlight beam passed over some round objects on a wooden platform tucked under an overhang carved out of the rock. We had nothing to do but wait, so I told Carlito to sit tight and went to investigate. There were eight oblong metal cylinders lying on their side in one long row. Each was about two feet long. They had rounded bases and long skinny necks with some sort of metal stopper. Brushing the dust off one revealed the stencil "Mariscal Mine" and the letters "Hg." I tried moving one. "Good Lord this thing is heavy. This is mercury, a lot of mercury." Lying on the floor nearby was a pack frame. It had almost no dust on it. "Well, I'll be damned. It's the vaquero's pack frame. What the hell is going on?" That's when I noticed four more indentations the size of the flasks.

"Lee, Carlito; you guys OK?" It was a relief to hear Bob Potter's voice. "I'm dropping a rope down. It has a rescue sling attached. Put Carlito in it and we'll pull him up with the truck winch."

We fumbled and stumbled, what with my majorly restricted hand. But eventually Carlito and I rigged the sling correctly. Then it was a simple matter. Potter winched us both out of there. I brought up the pack frame. By the time my head cleared the pit Maria and Lisa were working on Carlito's face, arms and back. The bump was ugly bloody purple and was the size of a jumbo chicken egg.

Bob unhooked me from the sling. He got on the satellite phone and in thirty minutes the Border Patrol command chopper landed about fifty yards away, just north of the old superintendent's quarters. Juan stepped out. He unrolled a tarp and attached all four corners under the belly of the chopper. Last, he threw in what looked like a large sponge. He trotted toward us with his own first aid kit. Five minutes later Carlito and Maria were in Juan's chopper headed toward Study Butte and the emergency care clinic.

"Bob, what do they call that kind of chopper?"

"It's a 'WhisperJet.' It is really quiet. I bet you didn't hear it until Juan landed? They make great surveillance choppers. Unfortunately, it can carry only four fully equipped agents. What's with the pack frame? Where did you get that?"

"Picked it up in the pit. I think it was the one we didn't find when we discovered the vaquero bodies. I'll take it back to Castolon with me."

Lisa swabbed my cuts and scratches. We packed up and headed home. By the time we reached Castolon, Maria and Carlito were already there, sitting on the Castolon store porch talking with tourists. Apparently you get five-star service at the emergency clinic when you arrive by Border Patrol chopper. Carlito looked like someone had dragged him through a cactus patch. But he had that big grin and said he was ready to go again. He and I agreed that we'd wait until his scratches and my hand healed before we did another adventure. And next time we'd go on horseback.

The next couple of days seemed almost normal; nobody fell into an open mine pit, nobody got shot at. It was almost like my discovery of the Mariscal dead, the Solitario Shootout had never occurred. I worked on making sense of my wall of index cards. Lisa supervised the installation of the DSL, and I got my new satellite phone. One day, after Carlito saddled Pepper, I went for a horseback ride. Carlito was back in school. One evening as Lisa and I puzzled over some index cards, Maria knocked, bringing our mail. She noticed the cards, so we explained what we were doing.

"Do you mind if I look?"

She started at the beginning and got as far as my photos of the dead guys. Pointing to the enlargement of the fifth guy, she asked "What's this?"

"Please sit down, Señor Lee. Lisa, please come to the kitchen with me; I must show you something." They returned a few minutes later. Lisa was death-white pale.

"Lee, you're not going to believe this. Maria has a tattoo just like the guy in the photo and just like the markings Charly described. It's in the very same place. She has something to tell us."

"Señor Lee, Lisa, I am from one of the seven families. We have protected the object for almost 500 years. For generations the guardians have carried out their sacred duty. With only one or two exceptions, all those men and now, women, chosen as guardians have fulfilled their duty. All of us have been sworn to secrecy. How did you find this out?"

So, Lisa and I explained what we knew, including the material that Charly had given me.

"I'm surprised that there are women involved."

"That is recent change, only in this generation."

"Do you meet, discuss strategy, talk about how to do what you do?"

"We have codes; now they are by phone and computer. I know the ones in North America. Since 1948 there has always been one in Israel. I'm almost certain that the fifth man you found was that person. We must find a replacement."

"You can't tell me who the others are?"

"No."

"You can't tell me where it is kept."

"Señor Lee, I myself am not absolutely certain of the site. In the past it has always required three to provide certain parts of the directions, the coordinates or whatever you use. I have part; two others have other parts. That is all I can say. I hope you do not use what I've told you. I trust you and Lisa. That is why I've told you this much."

"Maria, I have about a zillion questions. Believe me, that what you tell me and Lisa will stay in this room. Neither of us will divulge any of what you tell us tonight or any other time. Please consider answering my questions."

"Señor Lee, I cannot. By telling you that I actually know them, I have already compromised the Seven, the Guardians. They could be in danger. I cannot talk about this any longer. Please understand."

"Yes, Maria. Thank you for trusting us."

The silence after she left was deafening. Lisa and I simply sat in our living room and looked at the wall with the cards. I could not believe what I'd just heard.

"It has to be true, Lisa. People don't make up stuff like that. No novelist could devise a stranger tale. The bottom line here is that we are very, very close to the biggest story of the last 2000 years. And the other bottom line is that we cannot, under any circumstances reveal any of it to anyone."

"That's right, Lee. But remember that we also have the puzzle on the wall. Somebody has tried to kill you once. I hoped that you and I can figure it out before he or they try again. In my heart I really believe that you and I should pack it up and go back to our condo on Town Lake in Austin. You can complete your book and your sabbatical without people shooting automatic weapons through your bedroom windows. And I'll feel just a tad bit safer in the city than out here, out in the open."

"I don't like running away from things, you know that."

"It's not a disgrace if you stay alive to solve the puzzle and get these people behind bars. You'll at least think about it?"

"Yes, I'll think about it."

"I'm going to bed. Tomorrow, Carlito's school is hosting one of those 'Career Days.' He asked me to talk about being a counselor in a battered women's shelter. How do you tell kids about that? I think I'll talk about ways of knowing abuse when you see it, even if you're a kid. And, I think we'll talk about what you do about it when it happens to you or someone you care about. It's a ninety minute ride to Marathon. We'll leave about six. See you in the morning or when we get back. Wish me luck."

"Luck."

"Smartass."

#

The next thing I remember was Rusty barking in my ear and tugging on my leg. Lisa was screaming my name from somewhere outside. I pulled on the Wellingtons and followed Rusty. He tore across the compound toward the sound. There was Lisa on Maria's front porch yelling and waving. I ran across the compound, totally nude except for my boots, and bounded up on the porch. Lisa yelled, "They're in there. Maria's on the floor by the door. What do we do?" I picked up one of Maria's porch benches; threw it through the window beside the door. Lisa crawled in the shattered window and unlocked the door.

130

Together we dragged Maria outside into the compound. Jackson came running up, shouting "Where is Carlito?" She bolted inside and in fifteen seconds staggered out with Carlito in her arms. Both Maria and Carlito were unconscious. We carried them to the store porch, away from the house. Jackson took Carlito, I took Maria, and we began CPR. Carlito responded in about two minutes. The CPR wasn't really working on Maria.

"Jackson, Maria keeps a small bottle of oxygen in the store in case one of the tourists needs a hit. It's inside her office, by the desk. Go."

By the time she returned, Maria was breathing on her own, shallow and ragged. A couple of hits from the oxygen bottle perked her up enough so that she was able to give me a once over and ask me, "Señor Lee, where are your clothes? You're naked!" And indeed I was—cold, too.

"She's right, Lee. Go get dressed. Jackson'll call for help."

Jackson did just that. She called her boss Bob Potter first, then the EMTs out of Alpine. She also grabbed some clothing, blankets, and camping gear from inside the store and used it to wrap Carlito and Maria. When I returned, clothed this time, Jackson and I discussed our situation. She figured that the two were victims of gas poisoning. Sure enough we checked the propane tank and turned off the valve. Jackson gingerly opened doors and windows. The rising south breeze would soon clear out the propane. After ten minutes Jackson entered the house. She checked the pilot lights. None were burning of course, but all were in the 'ON' position. That had probably saved their lives.

By now, the EMTs from Alpine knew the way to Castolon. Jackson's radio crackled. She let us know that Potter and the Border Patrol were both headed in our direction. The south end of the national park was fast becoming a regular destination. Lisa and I thought Carlito and Maria might need watching after, so Lisa packed a few things and was ready to go when the EMTs landed. Carlito was responding well, but not Maria.

They loaded both of them on the chopper. About all Potter, Juan Barrera, Jackson and I could do was wave when the EMT chopper took off.

CHAPTER 8: BREAKTHROUGH

"Rusty, what?"

He stood on the bed, well really my chest, barking and pulling at the covers, his muzzle about two inches from my nose. Even with only one eye open I could see the "phone is ringing" light blinking like it was signaling the end of the world—10,000 watts of blink, blink, blink.

"OK, OK, Rusty, I'll answer the damn thing." I did.

"Lee, I'm leaving Alpine. I'm going to San Antonio with Carlito and Maria on the Air Ambulance. Maria's not responding to the treatment. They think the poison center at Brooke Army General can help. See you soon; I'll call when we have news. Take care. I love you. Be careful."

Click.

Since I was now wide awake, I took up puzzling over the cards and the events since Mariscal and since the "compound" incident of yesterday. In the late afternoon Rusty, and I sat on the porch watching the afternoon sun slide toward the mouth of Santa Elena Canyon. Park Ranger Rachael Jackson walked across the compound, kicking up size-9 dust devils with every step. She wasn't wearing the uniform, and no sidearm.

"Jackson, what's the deal? No pistola. Taking time off?"

"Off duty. I've got two really great steaks, two inch rib eyes. And no one to eat them with. You interested? I'll even grill 'em to your specs; as long as it's not too weird."

"Come right in. Ms. Phillips didn't raise no idiots for children. What can I get you? I think we have something of everything. Maybe a glass of wine?"

"Whatcha got?"

"I got both colors, red and white, and a variety of vintages, types, prices and flavors in each. What's your pleasure?"

Do you have any Australian Shiraz or some Hill Country Claret? A lot of those go good with steaks. Where's the charcoal and the lighter? Ah, never mind, I'll find it."

I popped the cork; she lit the fire. I made the salad. We let the coals burn down while we sat and looked at what we all call the Santa Elena afterglow. It was sort of like you might describe good sex, afterglow and all. And in a way it was. Watching the sunset and the gathering darkness over Santa Elena was almost better than sex. And the nice thing about it was that you got to do it every day. Well, every day that you were at Castolon. Every day was mostly not like sex unless you were some studly 30 year old, which I definitely was not. But the Santa Elena afterglow was always different and always the same, like good sex with a great partner.

Jackson and I talked; she grilled. Mine medium rare; she liked hers rare. We cooked them with a dry mustard rub, salt, white pepper, Worcestershire sauce and lime juice—a recipe that I'd found in a barbecue cookbook. We ate on my oak table in the living room and exchanged personal info. I told her about me and Lisa meeting, our collective careers, our two sons who were now out of school and on their own.

"So, Jackson, you're gonna hate this question: How did a nice girl like you get to be in a place like this?"

"I've heard that before, Lee. My family is from here, several generations. But we moved to Colorado when I was a kid. I grew up in Boulder. Then there was the usual—divorce, theirs; marriage, mine; divorce, mine. I decided to go to college and become a cop. But I loved the outdoors and got on with NPS. I got lucky enough to put in for this job."

"Jackson, let me show you something Lisa and I are working on. Maybe you can help."

I scooched the blank cards out of the way, which prompted the question: "So what is all this stuff?"

I pulled back the sheet and showed her the puzzle matrix and explained how it worked, red, green, blue and so forth.

"You know you can do this on a laptop. I'll go get mine if you want."

"Yeah, you can, and yes I can. I even have a laptop that can handle it. But there's a certain comfort in doing it this way. The whole thing builds in its own time and sequence. Besides, I don't have to look at one of those damn screens and those blinking cursors."

"OK, how about we try the cards on the events of last night. I think I'll start with: 'I came out of the door and what did I see but a naked man headed straight for me. I'm really not going to say that. But you, totally nude except for the boots, were bending over an almost nude woman, kissing her on the lips—heavily, lots of tongue. I could probably actually put that to music, or at least poetry. You'd be a celeb at Railroad Blues."

"Don't even think about it. Not kissing—CPR. You knew that instantly, right?"

"Of course, but I'm thinking what a great story it will make at the NPS Law Enforcement Association meetings for about the next ten years. And of course I'll have to fill in some of the, uh, intimate details, you know. Fortunately for you, as the story grows, so do you. What do you think?"

"Jackson, don't go down that road. I know where you live. I will come and find you. You can believe it!"

"Just kidding. But you absolutely have to admit that was a pretty interesting scene. How about we try your 'card trick' for real on my case? Are you game?"

"Go for it, but I get to deal with the 'naked man' part, OK?"

So we went through it. The lights were out when Lisa walked over to the house, expecting to take Carlito to school. Lisa, Jackson and I dragged Maria and Carlito out of the house. Both of them were suffering from probable propane poisoning. Later we, that is Jackson, discovered that all the pilots were out. That prompted a discussion.

"So how do all the pilots in one house go out at the same time, Lee?"

"There's only one way that I know. Somebody cut the sumbitch off. Right?"

"OK, so let's assume that's what happened. Then after the pilots flame out, someone cut the gas back on, right?"

"Yep, and you know what, that's what saved their lives. Had even one of the pilots been on, the supply of gas in the

135

house would have triggered the Big Bang! And bye-bye. Bye-bye house; adios, Maria and Carlito."

"Yes, Lee, but then the next questions: who, and why? And those are the biggies, right?"

"Yes. OK, we need to figure two things first—access and motive."

So we talked access first; and eliminating illegals, a few had access but no motive that we knew of. We both knew that Maria fed the hungry whenever they showed up at her back door, as long as it was not in broad daylight. We talked about who else might have access. Eventually we eliminated tourists—no motive that we knew. That left only the "official" visitors.

"OK, Jackson, who would be in that category?"

"I think I'm about two jumps ahead of you. There are only three possibilities. There's La Frontera; they landed two choppers that afternoon. They were here ten, maybe fifteen minutes. That was before dark and normally Maria would cook later in the evening. So at least for now I'm going to rule them out."

Both of us scribbled on green, blue and red cards. In a half hour we each had a handful. We decided that the only possibilities for bad guys were NPS and the Border Patrol. Jackson wanted to tack the new cards on a new string, start a new crime. After some discussion we agreed that we wouldn't do that just now. We would use the sequence that was already started, especially since we did not have a clue as to how all this shit might be connected.

We both put new cards on the wall, all of them relating to Jackson's "Propane Poisoning" case. There were lots of green cards, a whole bunch of reds and some blue surmises. And it was the surmises that freaked out both Jackson and me. We did not plow too far down that row. She had early duty and split around midnight. I saw her walk from our cabin to hers, her figure and shadow splitting the cold silver moonlight at every step of the way across the compound. She flashed her porch lights twice as per our signal. I turned back to the puzzle.

If a third of these surmises were accurate, Jackson and I had an attempted murder on our hands. And again we didn't know who. And we didn't know why. But, given the way the cards fell, we might just be closing in on the who.

And, after a while, there it was, spelled out in the cards. The only possibility for the poisoning was an official person—La Frontera, NPS, or BP. That narrowed it down from millions to less than a dozen. And the scary part? Jackson, Maria and Carlito, and I knew every one of them. What are the characteristics of someone who will intentionally attempt to murder a professional associate, a friend, or acquaintance? What is the common thread? That is what my index card system was designed to reveal. And as far as I could figure, there was only one. If they wanted to target me, they could have sabotaged the propane tank at our cabin. But they didn't. Maria and Carlito were the targets, well probably Maria only. But why? She wasn't involved in the first five deaths. At least I didn't think so. She wasn't involved in the Solitario Shootout. At least I didn't think so. So, what was left?

I don't dream often but when I do, most of them are pleasant. Well, except for the recent nightmares about the killings and the shootout. I really don't dream about sounds; that doesn't compute very well. My dreams are more about idyllic or pastoral scenes, vistas, canyons with incredible colors, roaring surf or waterfalls. My dreams include deserts where the dreamer can see for a thousand miles. Color combinations that make you think you're doing some incredible dope, or colors that will make you change the way you think about light forever. They focus on places that will imprint your mind for a million daybreaks. And, what are dreams without great sex—you know the kind, where you spend an eternity removing some filmy nothing of a garment from your intended partner, every move revealing another curve, another hollow, another bit of soft creamy flesh, all of it incredibly better and more sensual than the act itself. And every second is a pleasurable eternity, that sort of stuff. If my dreams are not about sex, they focus on colors. Colors are the essence of life; blue and green are my two favorites. But red, orange, yellow, and about a million shades and tones of mauve, purple, purple tinged with orange, yellow and red, all those get my attention. And colors are about the only thing that rivals great sex or vistas—colors. Colors are sex, believe it.

I sat bolt upright in bed; looked at my watch; it was about three a.m.

"Son of a bitch!"

To nobody in particular.

"He saluted me! He saluted me! Can't be, Rusty; can't be! Why the hell?"

I shucked on some jeans and pulled on a desert sand-colored sweatshirt that read "I'm From Downtown Study Butte." I cranked up some coffee and trotted barefoot across the compound. Within the compound we had phone service that could reach across the ocean and the mountains, but we couldn't call across the dirt and rock parking area. Go figure. I pounded on her door.

"Jackson, come on! I have it! Get your ass out of bed! Don't fear; this time I have clothes on; no dangling dongs. It's thirty-five degrees out here. My feet are freezing; I'm going back to the house. Follow me; I have the best coffee west of New Orleans and great, semi-cracked cups to drink it out of. Come on! You're gonna get to be a hero, well, heroine. Move your butt."

And she did.

In three minutes she was at my door. She even had most of a uniform on. This time she wore her duty belt complete with a .40cal Smith and Wesson auto and three magazines. She carried a short barreled Mossberg 12 gauge pump with a pistol grip and a stock and what looked like an eight round magazine. She had a bandolier of 12 gauge number 4 Buck shells slung across one shoulder.

"Damn, Jackson. I feel safer already; lots of firepower, that. What the hell, good idea."

I poured each of us both a large mug of dark roast. She drank hers black; I put about three dollops of evaporated milk in mine.

"Goddammit Doc, this better be good! I don't run too well on three hours sleep. What is it?"

I pulled back the sheet covering the cards and ran it down for her. "Jackson, Maria is the link, not me. At least that is what I think. The Seven Guardians are involved up to their collective six-pointed stars. I don't know how, but they are the core. Something is going on here, much bigger than the two of us. And, given what we talked about last night, we have only three real suspects for your attempted murder of the night before last. You know that, right?"

"Yeah, Lee; I do. But I figured only two—Bob Potter and Juan Barrera. Are those your two as well?"

"Yes."

"And the third?"

"You. You, Jackson. What's your maiden name?"

"Arredondo, why?"

"You know why. I thought something like that. You know the first time I ran into that surname?

"No."

"A few days ago in some correspondence I was given concerning sisters in this area about 400 years ago. One of them, well actually her husband, was involved in guarding something with the symbol "7" surrounded by the Star of David. His name was Arredondo too. Any relation?"

"Yes."

"How long has your family been here? Never mind, I don't want you to answer that right now. OK? Thanks."

"Lee, you want to puzzle through this some more?"

"Not really. But here are my red cards for the wall. First, if it is Bob Potter, why would he be involved? OK? Next, if it is Juan Barrera; why would he be involved? Right?"

"Yeah."

"If it is Officer Jackson, why would she be involved?"

"You're right, Lee. So, given those red cards, what next?"

139

"Road trip. I'm going to San Antonio as early as I can get out of here. I'm going to talk with Maria—and Charly. I'll keep you posted."

"Who's Charly?"

"Old friend; I'll tell you later."

"You don't fully trust me, do you?"

"Jackson, here is my definition of the word *trust.* If I'm in really deep shit, who would I call to meet me on a dangerous street corner in some foreign city with a passport, $1000 in small bills, and a loaded handgun? And you know what; there are damn few people in that list. And, I'm sorry. Right now; you're not there. You could be—maybe, but not now. But in the future, who knows?

"Here is who I trust: Lisa, Rusty, Charly, Susan and me, in that order only. 'Course Rusty doesn't have access to ATMs. That's all. Period, the end. Do you have it? I hope that list changes because I want to trust you. Now that I've waked your ass up, told you my theory and pumped you full of caffeine, Rusty and I are going back to bed. Tomorrow will be here far too soon. Rusty and I are headed for San Antonio in that really cool Chevy crew cab 4x4. I'll call you."

"You didn't tell me all of it, did you?"

"No, sorry. Not yet. Maybe after I get back from SA."

#

I called Bob before we left. He suggested that Rusty and I stop for coffee and breakfast at Panther Junction. Bob's wife Mary Lou grew up in Chihuahua. Her kind of breakfast—eggs over easy, grits, biscuits, bacon AND sausage, and blackberry jam with the seeds left in—will cut the trail for you on a long road trip. Rusty got a double helping of sausage and two biscuits with butter slathered on top. He was the happiest camper in the room. Mary asked about Lisa, Maria and Carlito. She suggested that she, Bob, and their kids would be pleased to have Carlito stay with them until Maria recovered. All of those kids attended the same school in Marathon. Her invitation sounded good to

140

me. I told her I'd pass it along. On the way out Bob asked me to stop by the LDS warehouse in San Antonio and pick up some staples for him and his fellow Mormons in Big Bend. He gave me the list; I said sure, no problem.

Driving north out of the park from Panther to Marathon at the crack of dawn, the brightest light on the horizon is the Border Patrol inspection station about fifty miles north of Panther. There must be 9,000,000 watts or lumens or whatever. It's like having an entirely separate sunrise, this one out of the north. You can see the lights for at least twenty miles. Any illegal who has an I.Q. above single digits will avoid the place like the plague. Usually I put Rusty in a harness and a very short leash. Those BP guys use dogs to sniff for dope and explosives. Rusty doesn't think highly of other dogs sniffing around "his" car. Normally state vehicles get a cursory once-over and a "Sir, you have a good day. Be careful." This time, no exception.

Marathon, Texas, population a little over 400, is absolutely, positively dead at 6:00 a.m. Even the restaurant at the Gage Hotel is still closed. U.S. 90 east to San Antonio is a long, lonesome highway, 406 miles from Panther Junction to downtown SA. Interstate 10, further north, has taken most of the big truck traffic and most of the Highway Patrol. Occasionally a semi will blow by you on U.S. 90 doing 80-85 mph, going up hill. But the road is mostly empty except for the local ranchers pulling cattle trailers, Union Pacific Railroad track inspectors trolling for rail misalignment, and the occasional RVer pulling a Saturn or Jeep. Along Hwy 90 the towns of Dryden and Sanderson are dying, former oil and ranching market towns that now sport empty buildings, abandoned gas stations, boarded up storefronts, almost no traffic, and that "I once was prosperous, but soon will be gone, look."

The stretch U.S. 90 between Langtry, Comstock and Del Rio has a storied past that has been embellished in song, history and film. Langtry is best known as the home of Judge Roy Bean, whose unrequited desire for Lillie Langtry, the accomplished actress at the 1890s, was legendary. It is less well known as the location of one of the most important

141

anthropological finds in North America, numerous American Indian burials dated to about 1000 to 1500 years ago. Just east of Langtry where the Pecos River joins the Rio Grande, I made a pit stop at Seminole Canyon State Park, location of some of the most astounding pictographs in North America. The staff provides excellent interpretive tours, but all Rusty and I wanted was a bathroom and a place to stretch our legs. Comstock, another 30 miles to the east is best known for having absolutely NO radio reception. The country is so desolate that there's not even a border crossing between Comstock and Mexico.

Del Rio, the county seat of Val Verde County, is different. So is Ciudad Acuña, its Mexican counterpart across the river. Both have the usual border amenities—bars, pretty good Mexican restaurants, whores, more bars, cheap liquor on the Mexican side in the tourist mercados, and an abundance of cut-rate second-hand clothing stores in Del Rio. Recently, Del Rio has become one of the major border crossing points in South Texas.

The town was once also the home to radio station XERA or XERF, 500,000 watts of clear channel radio broadcasting power. Actually the transmission tower was out near Comstock. Some say that Wolfman Jack, whom many consider to be one of the founders of Rock 'n' Roll in the 1950s, got his start here on one of these outlaw Mexican stations.

In those days, late at night on the road anywhere between the North Pole and Tierra Del Fuego, you could hear Rock 'n' Roll, Country Western, and all sorts of evangelists and programs proclaiming that for one dollar you could buy an autographed photograph of Jesus Christ. They didn't tell you that "Jesus Christ" was actually Jesús Cristos, a drummer in a Del Rio salsa band. They did promise to throw in the prayer cloth for free: "You pay just postage and handling."

You could also hear advertisements from a "Dr. Brinkley" in Del Rio who would implant "goat glands" in guys—to enhance their "marital pleasure." It was one of those phrases that you did not ask your mother to explain. Eventually, lawsuits from disgruntled patients shut down Dr. Brinkley. Wolfman moved to LA. Legend has it that the U.S. Air Force's Strategic Air Command's B-52 bombers routinely listened to XERF, Del Rio, Texas, and used it as a homing beacon. Eventually the feds and the Mexican government shut XERF down. Too bad, the world should always have a venue like that. It keeps the rest of us honest.

During the Cold War, Del Rio was famous for something else. I remember a university colleague telling me stories about pulling over at a rest stop outside Del Rio near Laughlin AFB, eating a bologna sandwich while watching U-2 spy planes take off on training missions. All the while of course the U.S. Air Force denied that the airplane existed.

"Rusty, the world is a poorer place without XERF."

Thump, thump.

It's a long drive from Castolon to San Antonio. Lisa and I had friends in the King William Historic District in downtown San Antonio. Rusty and I stayed with them that first night away from Big Bend. I called Charly; set an appointment for 2:00 p.m. the following day. I called Lisa. She and Carlito were at our condo on Lady Bird Lake in Austin. I figured I'd be done in SA in early evening and would be in Austin tomorrow for dinner.

Maria was in Room 913 at Brooke Army General Hospital.

"Maria, you look good! When do they think you'll be going home?"

"Señor Lee, it is so good of you to come. Gracias! Hola Rusty." Thump, thump.

"De nada, Maria. I understand that Carlito is with Lisa in Austin. He wishes to go home to Castolon? Es verdad?"

"Sí, Señor Lee. Carlito wishes to go home to go to school. I will be well soon; I will take him home."

The two of us chatted. We negotiated Carlito's return to West Texas. We settled the issue of Carlito going back to the national park and living for a time with Bob and Mary Lou.

"Señor Lee, I have been having a dream, a bad dream. I do not wish to offend you in any way, but I must ask you this question: The morning of the accident, I keep seeing this image, this picture in my head. I have seen you naked, bending over me, kissing me. Tell me that such a thing is not true. You have a wife; you should not be doing these things."

"Your dream is correct. It is absolutely correct, Maria; but I was not kissing you. I was giving you CPR. I was trying to save your life. Officer Jackson did the very same thing with Carlito. But she was dressed. And yes for a time I was out there in the compound nude. I ran outside when Lisa and Rusty called me. I can tell you, it was very cold. I sleep without any clothes. Rusty dragged me out of bed and I ran across the compound without any clothes on. It was important to get you and Carlito out of your house quickly. I hope you forgive me."

"Señor Lee, it was a little bit enjoyable, a naked man bending over me. And now I know much more about you, much more than I did."

"I was afraid of that. When you return to your work, talk with Officer Jackson. She will be very, very happy to tell you some other stories about me. But I came from Castolon yesterday to ask you some questions about the Seven Guardians."

I briefly explained parts of my theory that the Seven were probably involved in the killing of the five men in Mariscal. They were somehow related to both my and Maria's attempted murders. She couldn't believe it. We talked for almost two hours.

"Maria I must know. You must tell me what you know that can help me figure this out. I do not want you to violate your oath, your family's historical charge and trust. But give me something I can work with to keep you, Carlito, Lisa, and myself alive and safe. Por favor, por favor!"

And she did.

"Señor Lee, go back to the mine. I am sworn to secrecy. If I tell you, I am damned to eternity. But do this: Look at the maps. Look at the buildings. That is all I am saying. Thank you for caring for Carlito. I will be well soon. Soon you, Señora Lisa, Officer Jackson, Carlito, and I will grill the best cabrito ever, at Castolon."

"Vaya con Dios, Señora."

"Y usted, Señor."

I attempted to cancel with Charly.

"Lee, you absolutely, positively must come see me. We have much to discuss. I have much more to tell you. Don't go back to Big Bend until after we meet."

"Por qué?"

"You absolutely must meet me. I have information that will change your life, and maybe save it. Got a suit?"

"No. Why would I need a suit?"

"Got a sports coat, slacks, any shoes besides those damn Wellingtons? Even those Luccheses are better."

"No to all of that."

"Lee, they pay you more than $1.98 an hour at the university. I know you have a credit card. Shop! Get the stuff. Meet me at my office downtown at 2 p.m."

"OK, but this better be good. I don't need a tie? Right?"

"Forget the fucking tie, Lee. Show up with the other stuff. It will make a better impression."

"Who am I meeting?"

"I'll tell you when you get here."

Four hours later I rang the bell.

"When is the last time you shopped Lee?"

"I don't remember. Lisa usually takes care of that stuff. Do I look presentable?"

"Absolutely. Blue blazer, khaki slacks, real leather belt, cordovan Lucchese boots with a walking heel, even a white cotton button-down shirt. You clean up pretty good as the cowboys would say. Let's go."

"Whoa, whoa, chica. Just who are we meeting?"

"Oh, yeah. We have an audience with the Archbishop, Archbishop Diego Sanchez. It is a rare event. He does not often grant meetings with infidels like you and me, particularly you.

"Charly, I'm not an infidel. I'm a Druid, Reformed. We're the ones who don't paint ourselves blue. . . . All kidding aside, I'm actually a baptized member of the Episcopal Church. Will that do? How 'bout you?"

"Unchurched, Lee; you know that. Let's go. I think you will be amazed."

The three of us piled into Charly's SUV. Thankfully, she drove. Navigating downtown SA is a little above my skill set. The Archbishop's residence, a modest three-bedroom home tucked in the rear of the secluded grounds of San Fernando Cathedral in downtown San Antonio, was filled with antiques from Europe and the New World.

"I am honored you have agreed to meet with me, Dr. Phillips. Do you mind if I offer Rusty a treat?"

"Don't know why not. Everybody else feeds him. It's a wonder he's not the size of a whale. Please, your Holiness; call me Lee. Forgive me, but I don't normally hang out with priests of any stripe. What exactly do I call you, you know, when we're talking?"

Rusty munched while we talked.

"I'm a simple priest Lee; Padre or Father will do. Is that alright with you?"

"You bet. You have some pretty nice sticks of furniture. That's some pretty incredible Revere Ware, late 1700s. And the armoire, Mallard of New Orleans, yes? The Navajo rug, late 1890s, yes? I recognize some of the other pieces and some of the art. I didn't realize the priest business paid so well."

"It doesn't. We have very kind and gracious parishioners. You are very knowledgeable. Do you collect?"

"No, Padre, I'm afraid not; too expensive for a mere professor's salary. But the small painting? I've seen the structure before, well, maybe a drawing of it. It's the Presidio de San Vicente, isn't it?"

"A good eye, Lee. Unfortunately, we do not know the artist. But it was probably painted in the middle eighteenth century by a self-taught mestizo, a mixed race person who lived somewhere along the Rio Grande. That is something that you are familiar with, no?"

"The art, or the concept?"

"The concept; I understand that you are a Norte Americano mestizo of a certain type. Es verdad?"

"Charly, you spill the beans or what? Yes Padre, that's true. Should I ask how you know?"

"Lee, please don't. No, Lee, Charly did not tell me. I know these things from other sources. Please be seated. Coffee with evaporated milk, yes? We have much to discuss and you have places to go. Am I correct?"

"Yes, Padre."

"You know San Vicente, yes?"

"Padre, I've been there twice. Not much left now. But I'm sure you know that it was a very busy place in the late seventeenth and early eighteenth century."

"Yes. But tell me of the events since you discovered the five dead men in the canyon. Please."

So, I did. In more excruciating detail than I related it since the very first day. But now there were more days to—Los Alamos and the so-called Solitario Shootout, the fall into the shaft, the attempted murder of Carlito and Maria. And in telling, things began to jell. Some of them were impossible to believe.

"And that's it, Padre. End of the line. What do you think? You think I'm nuts?"

"No. I suspect that you have inferences, your blue cards, that you have not passed on to me. He pulled a calling card out of his jacket pocket, clicked his black pen and wrote something on the back. He handed it to me. It was a scribbled phone number with a Houston area code.

"Lee, I think you should call this gentleman in Houston. You might already know him, Rabbi Ray Koen? He and I have been clerical associates for years. Our families have known one another for generations. Do you understand what I'm telling you?"

"Yes, Padre; I think so. Thank you."

"Then, this is Rabbi Koen's number. I strongly urge you to call him as soon as possible. Will you do that?"

"Yes, Padre. But first I really must get to Austin. As a favor, will you visit with Maria Gomez over at Brooke Army General. I am sure she'd appreciate it. And if she tells you a story about a naked man kissing her, don't believe it."

"That is good to know Lee. When you come back I will be honored to hear your confession."

"Gracias Padre, but how do you know I'll be coming back and that I'll need a confession?"

"You will, Lee. If you do not, you are not the person I think you are. By the way, in the National Park Service do you know an Officer Arredondo, Rachael Arredondo?"

"Padre, I know an Officer Rachael Jackson. Her maiden name, she tells me, was Arredondo. Would she be the person?"

"I'm certain of it. Please tell her that I asked about her and that I'm doing well. I'm sorrowful for the end of her marriage. I pray that things will turn out well for her. Vaya con Dios, Lee. Adios Rusty."

"Ms. Burnside, it is a pleasure to visit with you, as always. Vaya Con Dios."

"And you also, Padre."

Sitting in her car, Charly and I did a brief recap. I agreed to call Rabbi Koen, but only after I answered a couple of other questions about Mariscal.

Rusty and I got back in our Chevy 4x4 and I drove to Austin. On the way north I stopped at Academy Sporting Goods and bought some replacement stuff for the camping gear I'd lost in the shootout. Most of my equipment had bullet holes or glass shards in it. I bought a new tent, pots and pans, lanterns, ground cloths and a couple of sleeping bags to replace those that I left on the bodies or were destroyed in the shootout. I saved my receipts. The government might actually, at some time in the dim future, have some desire to reimburse me. I wanted to check out the mine shaft again, so I picked up some rope and rappelling equipment, several sets.

Next on my list was to take Maria's advice and look at the maps of the mine. She believed that they would tell me what I needed to know about the location of the Ark.

I spent two days at the University of Texas at Austin searching databases for old surveys and maps of the Mariscal Mine. It is amazing what a gazillion dollars in hardware and search engine software can do for your research. It won't

148

eliminate the effort, but those electronic tools will sure help you focus your search. By the afternoon of the second day I had what I needed. I had found two 1920s surveys done by the precursor of Texas Parks and Wildlife. And there were several references to three photo collections: one in Alpine, a second in San Antonio, and a third at the General Land Office near the State Capitol.

Normally I'd ask Charly to look into these photo collections, but she was working on the other aspects of the Ark project. Long story short, it sort of all fell together. Two of the photo collections were available online. I'd research the Museum of the Big Bend in Alpine on the way back to Castolon. At Texas Parks and Wildlife Headquarters in Austin, in their curatorial collection, I found two 1930s preliminary Civilian Conservation Corps surveys and maps that plotted the mine.

I pulled up the online photo collections at the State of Texas General Land Office and the Institute of Texan Cultures in San Antonio in turn. I plugged in my search parameters, quickly scanned the photos and in minutes the departmental printer was spitting out my choices, all nicely digitally printed. Taken together, these maps, surveys and photos gave me my baseline. A quick email exchange with Bob Potter confirmed that he had a 1988 aerial survey and a more recent GPS survey and map overlay of the mine. Time to get back and get out to Mariscal Mine. Nothing beats being there.

The last evening in Austin, Lisa, Carlito and I shopped for Carlito. We bought school stuff; shopped for some outdoor wear for me and Lisa. She needed winter clothes. I'd finagled a two month extension on my sabbatical from the University, so I'd need some cold weather things as well. The weather in Big Bend ranged between seventy-five degrees in the day and freezing at night. And when a cold front blew through it could be downright miserable, freezing rain, snow, forty mile an hour winds. At 5:00 a.m. the next morning I opened my storage locker in the condo basement. From my gun safe I extracted my M1 Garand and about 200 rounds of ammo held in eight round clips. World War II ended over fifty years ago, but the .30–06 semi-auto M1 worked for me.

Most of my pistols were in the custody of the Texas Rangers or the FBI. I stuck my small, five shot hammerless .38 Special in a belt holster that fit in the small of my back. Years back when I actually carried a concealed weapon, this pistol was my favorite. Almost as an afterthought, I shoved my reproduction .45 single action Colt Peacemaker, fifty rounds and a Western-style gun belt and holster in a brown paper bag. I stowed pistols, belts and holsters under the driver's seat for the 480 mile drive to Castolon. I put the M1 in its carrying case on the floorboard under the back seat of the pickup.

Carlito, Rusty and I drove back to San Antonio. We loaded Bob's LDS warehouse staples and headed west. Carlito was long overdue to return to school. He and I talked about school stuff and even skirted some of the events of the last few days. We arrived in Panther Junction at sunset. I got Carlito settled in with the Potter kids. Everybody ate dinner. Bob and I unloaded the staples. Then he, Rusty and I walked over to his office. Together Bob and I reviewed maps and NPS surveys of Mariscal. I picked out copies of what I needed. Bob printed copies for me.

"Lee, is this stuff for your book?"

"Bob, this stuff is background material for the book. But I'd rather you keep the fact that I have this stuff between just you and me, OK?"

"Sure, Lee, no problem. I do have to make a note in my official log though. You know that, right?"

"But that's not public, at least not for now. Right? I need just a little time to work this out."

"Not a problem. Call if I can help. By the way, Jackson says she's making progress on the propane thing at Maria's place. She's pretty closed mouth about it. Do you know what she's up to?"

"Bob, I've been gone for almost a week. She reports to you, right? No I don't. Rusty and I are headed to Castolon."

I hit the road. By afterglow time at Santa Elena, I was sitting on my porch drinking a Negra Modelo with lime. Rusty was curled on his cedar shavings pillow bagging zzz's.

CHAPTER 9: CLARITY

At 5:30, in the pre-dawn dark at Castolon, Rusty and I went for what I call a Run-Walk. Run a short distance; walk a long distance. Jackson passed us on the way back to the cabin. Rusty and I offered her breakfast. She said yes. Huevos a la Mexicana con tocino y tortillas de maize makes a pretty good start on the day. If you couple it with grapefruit juice and Community Dark Roast Coffee, you have a winner. Us Southern boys will eat eggs, bacon and any kind of bread, even corn tortillas, though biscuits for breakfast are the preferred fare. We ate on my east-facing porch; watched the sunrise over Mule Ear. Rusty loved breakfasts like this—more eggs, more bacon, more fat, more leftovers. He hated my usual breakfast—soy protein powder, blueberries and some sort of juice, usually grapefruit. After breakfast and over coffee Jackson, Rusty and I sat around my oak table in the living room and pondered the cards tacked to the wall.

"Lee, it is either Bob or Juan. What do you think?"

"I think this: The Archbishop, His Holiness Diego Sanchez of San Antonio, tells me that his family has known your family for generations. He emphasized the plural. He asked me to tell you that he is sorrowful that your marriage has ended. He also asked me to tell you that he asked about you. Finally, he wishes you well in your new career, Officer Arredondo. That's what I think right now. I also think that I now have two, not three, blue cards for the attempted murder of Maria and Carlito. It's pretty tough to beat an archbishop as a 'vouch for.' So you're off my would-be-murderer shit list. I might even ask you to meet me on a dangerous street corner in some foreign city with money and a pistol. Congratulations."

"If you do, I'll be there."

"I know. Jackson, I need to tell you something. Remember the night I woke you up about three in the morning?

I told you only part of the story, only part of what got me so wired and pumped."

"So, what didn't you tell me that night?"

"He saluted me."

"Who saluted you? When did he do it? Where did he do it?"

"I'll answer in reverse. The 'where' is, or was, Los Alamos. The 'when' was the night of the Solitario Shootout. The 'who' is a blue card: Captain Juan Barrera."

"Lee, don't joke around. You're kidding, right? The reason you would suspicion that is exactly what? Has Captain Barrera ever saluted you before, or since?"

"No, and that's the problem. He has never saluted me, ever, ever. I don't think he's saluted anybody since he left the Marine Corps after his second tour in Vietnam. But it's a body movement type. Jackson, I saved the guy's life. He and I spent a month in a semi-private hospital room together. We spent a year in rehab together. We've hunted and fished together. We ran Santa Elena Canyon in canoes and kayaks when the Rio Grande had water in it. We've hiked huge parts of this Big Bend country together. We've pissed in the Rio Grande together. We even closed our share of bars in Alpine, Boquillas del Carmen, and Ojinaga together.

"You know the story. He and I were both burned pretty damned badly in that car wreck, him worse than me. For God's sake, he didn't walk without a crutch for six months and without a cane for a year. My left hand still doesn't have the grip of my right. And the right doesn't have the strength that it had before that October night on Texas 170 outside Presidio. Christ, Jackson, I was the best man at his wedding to Maria, Mary. Lisa and I are godparents to their children. It doesn't get much more intimate than that. I've done everything except sleep with his wife."

"But now?"

"But now, I don't know. I really cannot believe that my friend Juan Barrera would do such a thing."

153

"Lee, did the man on the ridgeline, the man who saluted you, did he fire a shot at you at all from the ridge?"

"No, he didn't. I shot at him though."

"If he did that, if he and his business partners or his political partners attacked you at Los Alamos, do you think either he or one of them could have turned off, then turned on, the propane at Maria's house to keep you from knowing what you know now?"

"Well, two of them, some of those associates, are really dead. I took care of that little chore. But, yes, I do. If he had done that at Los Alamos, he would be capable of the propane job."

"That's an attempted double murder, Lee. That's a pretty terrible thing to say about a friend, an intimate, isn't it? What that implies is that you really don't know this person."

"Yeah. It's kinda hard to take. That's even scarier than the nightmares I have about shooting that guy in the eye. Surely it's not true. Where did I miss it?"

"Can't help you there right this minute, Lee. I'm late for work. See you later."

"Shit, Jackson. Thanks. Never mind. Come by for a drink after catching the bad guys all day."

"I'll take you up on that. Bye, Rusty." Thump, thump.

I packed a lunch, my usual—smoked oysters, crackers, two Negra Modelos and a fresh lime. I saddled Pepper. He, Rusty and I rode to the mouth of the canyon and to the Terlingua Abajo cemetery. Rusty and I dined amid the decaying headstones of the little Mexican cemetery. It was a great morning. I had a lot to think about, what with Juan and all. I rode into the compound at Castolon about three in the afternoon. As Pepper climbed the rise into the compound I saw the vehicles, two of them. One was a dark green Ford Crown Vic with three antennas—how do you get more conspicuous out here? The other was a white Border Patrol 4x4 Chevy with that slash of green stripe on the side.

"Pepper, Rusty, this is the fuzz. You guys be nice." Thump, thump.

154

And the Fuzz it was, our old buddies Special FBI Agent Carl Marks, with the "C" and the "k" as opposed to the "K" and the "x". His buddy, Texas Ranger Captain Jack Hays was with him. Two law enforcement agencies, no good can come of it. There they were, lounging on my front porch, boots propped on my railing; my captain's chairs kicked back on two back legs.

"Doctor Phillips, we have good news."

"Guys, how would I know that?"

"'Cause we brought your .40 caliber Glock and your shotgun back."

"Far Out! I'll get us some coffee or a soft drink since you're on duty. What's your pleasure gentlemen?"

"Oh, we can come in and get it. Save you the trip."

"I don't think so, fellas, not unless you have a warrant. You don't, do you?"

"No, Lee, we don't."

"Sorry boys. I like both of you and I'll feed and water you, but you're not getting through the front or back door unless you have a search warrant. What do you want to drink?"

Marks wanted a Coke. Hays thought he'd like some coffee, black.

"Not to belabor a point, Captain Hays, but did you have a great-grandfather or great-great-grandfather named Captain Jack 'Coffee' Hays? He was a Texas Ranger during the Texas Revolution and the Republic period. Killed lots of bad guys, then defined as anybody who was not white. And I'm not holding that against him. He was a helluva lawman."

"Sure did; how did you know?"

"I'm a historian, Captain, remember? That's what historians do. We remember that detailed shit; drives my wife Lisa crazy, my remembering that 'old' stuff."

We sat, drank, and talked. Well, they talked. They explained why the investigation was moving so slowly. Captain Hays had talked with Susan Steele and had cleared four pages of questions. He even offered to give me time to call her. I said, "No." He asked; I answered.

"This sucker is at a dead end, isn't it, Captain?"

"Yes, sir, it is. It is at an absolute dead end. Neither we nor the FBI know where to go from here. Do you have any suggestions?"

"Ranger, after visiting the site one of my friends mentioned the following: "Where did they come from?" I think that would possibly be a place to start. Figure out where they started from and what they wanted, the dead guys and their accomplices, friends and associates who are presumably still alive. That might even get you a handle on motive. Was it lust for flesh? Lust for power? Lust for money? Was it some sort of crazy theological or ideological lust? Was it a combination of some or all of the above? Were they just plain crazy, or do they have a larger political goal?"

"We'll incorporate those questions into our investigations, Dr. Phillips. Is that OK with you? Besides we did say that we brought good news. Want to hear it?"

"You mean about my guns, yes?"

"Yeah, we brought them back. The state and federal governments are returning the firearms that you used at Los Alamos. And the really good news, we are dropping all investigations of you. Clearly it was a matter of self-defense. We'd like a receipt."

"Touché, gentlemen."

Marks took the lead in the Q & A. Hays taped questions and presumably typed my answers into his trusty laptop.

"Dr. Phillips, the battery on this thing is fading. I sure could use an outlet. Maybe we can set up inside."

"Hays, you're the luckiest guy on the planet. I see you have a cord. There's an outlet right there next to your boot on that support post. Will that do?"

"Yes, thank you."

"Look guys, you are not getting inside the house without a warrant. We already covered that. Hang it up; ain't gonna happen. My people have been having problems in trusting 'the government' for over two hundred years. We have had a lot of "not very good" experiences with what my grandfather called "The Law." And right this minute, I've got two of them sitting on my front porch with that "We're from the Government and we're here to help you" look in their eyes. How do you think I'm gonna respond? I like you guys, well, you Hays because of your ancestor. You Marks, I don't know. But don't expect that I'll cut either of you a lot of slack. You're both good with that, right? I will answer your questions; I will be cooperative as I can. But this is business, not love. It's not even sex. Are we cool?

"You didn't bring my weapons back as a favor. You brought them back because I have a high-powered, bad-ass attorney in New Orleans who is a member of the Texas Bar and who will stay on your butt until you do the legal, correct thing. Right? Don't answer."

"We have a few more questions. Ms. Steele has reviewed them. You OK with that? The first is about the five dead guys."

So we went through it for about the millionth time. They knew the IDs of the four guys on the left. Their questions centered on what they were now calling, "the fifth man."

"Lee, Dr. Phillips, I am required to ask you these questions according to a very specific protocol. So during this portion of our visit I'll be addressing you as Dr. Phillips. Please do not take offense. We'll begin with my stating the date and location of this interview. You'll then state your name, your full legal address and the location and the time of this interview. I hope that is OK?"

"No problema, Agent Marks. But I still like Hays best, just kidding. Let's do it."

"Are you able to identify the fifth man?"

"Marks, we been down this road before. The guy's got no head. Well, he has no face. He has only one arm. Did you folks ever find the other one? I suspect not, or you wouldn't be asking me these questions. The short answer is 'no'."

"Did you notice anything unusual about him?"

"You mean except that he was dead, that he didn't have a left arm below his bicep, and that the buzzards had had a pretty good feast on what remained of his head? Hell no, nothing."

I knew it was coming; the enlargement. There it was; The Star of David and the 7 with the cross bar about two-thirds up on the vertical.

"What about this?"

"What do you mean?"

"Have you ever seen it before, Dr. Phillips?"

"Yes, yes I have. But I'm not really prepared to talk about that."

"Dr. Phillips, this is really important. We would prefer your cooperation. But if you wish, we will provide a subpoena, which we have in the car, and we'll haul you're ass before a federal grand jury in Midland to answer these questions."

"Well, guys, if you put it that way . . . . Yes I have. Sit back guys and I'll tell you a story."

And I did. I began with the thesis of my book, which by now was about as boring as dirt, at least to me. But I covered it all for them. I related Charly's visit, the information in the letters in the archives in San Antonio, the Star of David with the 7. I even gave them some of the family names—some, not all.

"Dr. Phillips, would this dead guy have been a member of one of the seven families? What do you think?"

"I don't know, Marks. I don't have any more idea about his ID than you do. I really don't know. I don't know what their rules were, or are. All I know is that about 500 years ago seven families were charged with guarding and caring for the holiest symbol in Judaism and Christianity as it made its way to the New World. It appears that they took their charge seriously. They've done a pretty damned good job of it since. I guess. You don't seem to have a clue. Neither do I. That should tell us something, huh? Do other members have the tattoo; you pick it. I'm not a cop. What do you have next?"

Marks flashed a photo of one of the flasks on his laptop screen.

"Have you ever seen one of these, Dr. Phillips.?"

"Sure, you bet. You see them all around the Big Bend. It's a mercury flask. They were used to transport refined mercury from the mines at either Terlingua or Mariscal to the railroad, usually at Marathon. You can tell by the symbol on the side—Hg. Hg is the periodic table symbol for Mercury. Your photograph should tell where it was mined and refined. Does it?"

He hit the Zoom button.

"Yes it does. This one says 'Mariscal Mine'."

"So why are you asking me?"

"Dr. Phillips, our agents picked this one up in San Antonio. Well, actually we found it in the back of an illegally parked pickup down the street from the Alamo behind the Crockett Hotel. The next photo shows that this flask remains sealed. After we confiscated this flask we sent it to our lab in San Antonio. It is full of refined mercury. That have any significance for you?"

"Sorry guys. Well, the Alamo obviously has significance. The flask, no."

"You have any idea what the price of mercury is, by the ounce?

"Not a clue. But I'm sure you do; tell me."

"Industrial grade mercury, not laboratory mercury goes for about $200 an ounce. That means that a seventy-six pound flask is worth what, about $240,000. That's a fair piece of change. Wouldn't you agree?"

"You bet. More then the three of us make in a year, combined. I'd say that a flask of that poison is worth a lot of dinero. But you still have to find a buyer, right? You can't just walk into your favorite corner mercury shop."

"And there's the rub, Dr. Phillips. If the legal market supports $200 per ounce, what do you think the illegal market would be?"

"Guys, I'm an academic. I'm writing a book about the legends of the Ark of the Covenant in the borderlands. I don't know what the legal or illegal market for refined mercury is. Although I am beginning to think I ought to hunt up some of the stuff find a buyer and retire."

"Mercury is a poison, Dr. Phillips. In rivers and bays it will kill fish. Fish that eat it are poisonous to people. If you put it in water, it will kill you. This is dangerous stuff. Let's say, Dr. Phillips, just for argument, that you wanted to poison the water supply of a place, say the City of Austin, or the University of Texas at Austin, the State Capitol complex, or the Alamo. What do you think a flask of mercury would be worth to you: $200,000, $400,000, a million? What if you had a bunch of these flasks and you strategically placed them in Galveston Bay? What do you think would be the effect on the oyster industry, the fishing industry?"

"Don't know. Look guys I'm not in that business"

"We think this flask came from where you found the bodies. What do you think?"

"Guys, I found five dead bodies. I did not find any flasks or anything that would tell me about flasks. Got it? I think I've run out answers. I think you boys have run out of questions that I can answer. Any more questions, call Susan, OK? Thanks for returning my firearms. I wish I could help you out. You boys have a safe trip home."

We shook hands. I watched them get back in their car and 4x4 and head north toward Panther Junction. I waved; Rusty thumped.

"Come on Rusty, we got stuff to do and places to go."

But first I had a call or two to make. I called Luís Galvan over at the Ranch. He could probably help me solve my problem.

"Luís, I'm going horseback camping, back to Mariscal. Now that Star is no longer among the living I need a pack animal. I know that is not something the Ranch specializes in. But, got any ideas?"

"Lee, you can't go back there. Does Lisa know you're going? That's crazy. Am I talking with the same guy whose house was shot up? Who was wounded? Come on, Lee. Another trip is an invitation to be murdered."

"Luís, thanks for the concern. I really appreciate your views. But I'm going back whether you know of a pack animal or not. Can you help me out? Do you know of a pack animal in the area that I can buy or borrow?"

160

And he did. Seems like he knew a guy in Shafter, the ghost town just north of Presidio, who had a pack mule, sixteen hands high, a tall animal. The mule was for sale—$500.

"Luís, that's a bunch of money for a mule."

"Jefe, you will love this mule. He is not only a pack mule; he is a riding mule. He will treat you better than a woman, no offense to Lisa. His name is Ace. He is six years. He is brown with black ears and a black, very short mane. His tail is black too. I have seen him; he is a good mule. He will carry what you wish. Do you want him?"

"What the hell. Why not? You want cash or a credit card, or is my word good enough for your seller? Hey, I thought mules came with girl names."

"Yes, jefe, but this one is so big, so tall; she is a he. Cash or credit card will do fine."

"OK, but I want a pack saddle frame and a riding saddle included in the price, and I want him delivered here in Castolon."

"No problema, jefe."

Luís made some calls; did the deal. Tomás was coming our way anyway, returning with the dos caballos trailer.

"When were you planning to go camping?"

I gave no answer to that question. But eventually the mule Ace arrived in the BBR double horse trailer. It was very late. I paid Tomás. And my God he was big; not Tomás, the mule!

"Christ, Tomás, where the hell did they find a mule like this? He's huge!"

"Sí, Señor Lee. This mule came from the state of Mississippi. I think that is where you are from, sí? He is six years old. I picked him out myself."

"Tomás, I did not come from Mississippi. I came from Tennessee—like many good Texans."

"But they are near, yes?"

"Yes."

Tomás, Rusty and I put Ace in the corral with Pepper. They nuzzled one another. Pepper kicked a couple of times; Ace kicked a couple of times. We left. They either would, or wouldn't figure it out.

I was trying to make sense of several levels of maps, grids and surveys when Jackson knocked on the front door. She carried an uncooked 'Pizza Supreme.' This one included ham and pineapple, black olives, onions, garlic, green peppers and assorted spices. She also had an uncorked bottle of Becker Hill Country Vineyards Claret.

"You mind?"

"Nope, not as long as you help me on this puzzle, this whodunit. Be my guest."

Jackson cranked up the oven, set the timer and watched the pizza as it browned. I fooled with the puzzle. Actually, I attempted to make sense of the maps, overlays, numerous surveys and such. Finally, I simply called her: "Lets see if we can't get this baby squared away."

Eventually, one pizza and an entire bottle of claret later, we did. Well, we narrowed the possibilities down to two or three. The maps done in the 1920s and mid–1930s, when there was still hope that Big Bend would be a Texas state park, matched almost perfectly with the surveys done later. The most recent ones, done by NPS with GPS mapping technology, showed some anomalies. Neither Jackson nor I could tell anything unusual using the aerial photos. But I had enough info to be in business.

"Shit, Lee, I can't go with you tomorrow. Bob can't arrange NPS law enforcement cover this part of the park on short notice."

"Rachael, listen to me, please. I do not want 'cover.' I don't want an escort. I am not going to live the rest of my life in some sort of damn cocoon, wrapped in cotton balls with 'cover.' It ain't gonna happen. You ever hear of a book called Moby Dick? I thought so. Someone once asked the author, Herman Melville, what he wanted out of life, or maybe it was a line from one of his novels. Hell, could have been another nineteenth century author as far as my failing memory allows. Here is a paraphrase or maybe a direct quote of what he replied: 'I want to sail tumultuous seas and land on barbarous shores.' Jackson, I am not going to die in a cocoon; got it? Good."

Not to be deterred: "Captain Potter is not going to like it. Neither is Juan. Your wife cannot be in favor of this adventure, this camping trip. Lee, not too long ago we, rather, you, decided that you and I had two primary suspects in the Propane Attempt, or whatever the hell we're calling it now. Right?"

"Yeah, we did, Potter and Barrera. You're right. But I think we've gone about as far as we can in thinking about this thing—using green, blue and red cards and sticking them on a wall. Talking, discussing, meeting—none of that will do the trick. None of that will solve the puzzle. We gotta put boots in the dirt at Mariscal. And those boots have to be mine."

"Yes, but can't we do it in a safer way; a way that doesn't risk your life?"

"You don't get it, Rachael. If it's a sure thing, if I have NPS, FBI, Texas Ranger or Border Patrol cover, there is no way the folks will come after me, particularly if our prime suspects are already 'official.' Right? And if I'm a target anyway and anywhere, then I might as well make a good faith effort to solve what might just be the most important puzzle of the last 2000 years. Don't you think? Well, Jackson? Come on."

"OK, OK, OK. But we absolutely must have a 'Plan B.' If not, then I'm going to tell Potter. He and the Rangers will stop you, even if we have to put you in protective custody. Got it?"

"Yes, I have a 'Plan B.' I'll roll it out to you tomorrow at Johnson Ranch. Is that OK with you?"

"Yeah, but Lee, I really don't . . . ."

"Done. Wanna go meet my new mule, Ace?"

"I thought mules had girl names . . . ."

"Don't go there, OK?"

A clear indication that an evening has not gone well is that one, some or all parties begin talking to mules. The really scary part is that sometimes mules talk back. Even scarier is that sometimes they begin to make sense.

"Oh, hell, Lee; why not?"

Our evening had gone far enough.

163

Four a.m. in late October in West Texas Big Bend country
is really dark and cold. Daybreak is but a distant hope. Jackson
and I loaded the pickup and the trailer with all the horse and
mule stuff—saddles, packsaddles, camping gear, clothes and
such. We loaded Pepper and Ace into the trailer last. They had
apparently decided to become buddies, at least for now.
Jackson, Rusty and I pulled out of Castolon about 4:30. I'd
planned a week-long trip to the canyon and the mine. We
unloaded at Johnson Ranch at seven. It was getting light, but
true dawn was at least three hours away. Jackson, unlike most
NPS staff, actually knew how to saddle and load a pack animal.
Ace seemed grateful; well, he didn't bite or kick either Jackson
or me. And he didn't kick Rusty. I packed and loaded. And
last, I strapped one rifle scabbard onto my riding saddle on
Pepper and another onto the packsaddle on Ace. I shoved the
shotgun into the scabbard on Pepper and dropped the M1 into the
packsaddle scabbard.

"What's this about?"

"It's a shotgun and an M1 Garand. I've also loaded about
200 rounds of full-metal-jacket .30–06 ammo, along with about
50 rounds of 12 gauge number 4 buckshot. I also will carry,
courtesy of our federal and state governments, my .40 caliber
Glock and about 100 rounds of hollow point ammo for it. I have
a state issued carry permit for the .40cal. It seems that they now
believe that the shootout at Los Alamos was actually self-
defense. Du-uh, what do you know?"

"Lee, an M1 is an automatic weapon. You can't take that
into the park."

"It's not an automatic weapon. It's a semi-auto. Let it go,
OK? Arrest me later. You're the one worried about me being
'covered' and being safe. With this much firepower I'll either be
very safe or very dead, but if they want to kill my ass they'll
have to beat me to death with a rifle, shotgun or pistol that
doesn't have any bullets or shells left in it.

"By the way, if something happens to me Rusty will be in touch. He is Plan B; listen to him, pay attention to him. Think of him as Lassie from the '50s TV series. OK? Besides, you have my itinerary—the canyon where I found the five dead guys and the mine. I'll spend much of the week at the mine. If you don't hear or see either Rusty or me after five days, get your butt in gear and get to the mine. Bring all your friends, all their friends, and everybody's guns, bullets and shells. Kill everybody that doesn't look like me, Rusty, Pepper or Ace. By then I'll need everything you can muster. Got it? See you soon, or not. I'll be OK. Go."

"OK. I love you. Be careful."

She secured the stuff on the trailer and loaded up.

"Lee, do you want me to tell Bob or Juan what you're up to?"

"No, absolutely, not."

"OK, be careful. Watch him Rusty!" Thump, thump.

Late October is not the same as early October in the Big Bend. First, the Rio Grande is really, really cold. That water coming out of mountains in New Mexico feels like barely thawed ice. Second, sunrise is later; sunset is earlier. The nights are longer. I spent the first night at Talley. About 2:00 a.m. I woke thinking about "I love you." Oh, shit; I don't think I'm ready for this. I know I can't handle it. I don't have the inclination or the interest or the moral fiber to deal with that. Besides there was that "for better or for worse thing." So, I figured I'd deal with the "I love you" the next time Rachael and I met. Even after coming to that resolution I still didn't sleep worth shit.

Next day I spent a long four hours hunkered down at the murder site, or at least the site where I found the bodies, looking, feeling, looking some more. The two days between Johnson Ranch and Mariscal Mine were a good breaking in period for Pepper, Rusty, Ace and me. I decided not to camp at the official Fresno Campground. Instead, the animals and I pitched camp right outside the concrete and stone mine owner's home that overlooked most of the Mariscal Mine complex. It was about one hundred yards from where we found the dead horse—where Carlito had fallen, where I'd snapped the pics of the eight flasks. It was about 200 yards from where we found the bodies of the two shotgunned vaqueros. The yellow "Do Not Cross" tape still flew around the mine shaft. It was still hooked to temporary steel posts left by the NPS cops and the FBI. Tomorrow I'd lay out the maps and surveys, set up a search grid, and begin crossing off the possibilities.

Almost dusk, that second night, Rusty and Ace heard the chopper. I'd started a cook fire with logs that Bob had left from the earlier trip. Tonight was steak and what remained of the salad stuff I'd brought from Castolon. Rusty nudged then pulled; then barked, then barked again. Ace made that awful "hee-haw" sound that mules do. I'd never heard of a "hearing mule" before. But Ace had possibilities. I saw the chopper as it over flew our camp, coming from southwest to northeast—that distinctive white-with-green-stripe Border Patrol color. The pilot did a 360 and headed due north for a landing. I trotted out to meet the pilot. Sure enough, it was Juan. He dropped out of the pilot's seat; pulled the rolling protective tarp across under the chopper, hooked it, and walked toward me. We saluted one another. Then the obligatory abrazo, that masculine hug Hispanic males do if they really care about one another.

It was nonstop questions: "Qué pasa, amigo? What the hell are you doing out here in this country? There are a lot of people who want you dead. You got a death wish or what? Does Lisa know you're here? You could'a called. What are you up to?"

"Juan, you want to shut up a second? God Damn! You're worse than Jackson or my wife, for God's sake. You're some sort of motor mouth tonight. You here for the night, or do you have to go save the world from the infidels and fly someplace else?"

"Actually, I can't stay. But I heard that you were out here so I thought I'd stop by to visit. Maybe see if you were still alive. And you sure look alive to me. Got any coffee? I gotta get back to Presidio but I have time for a cup. I'll stop by another day when we can spend more time. You know it's gonna be in the 30s tonight."

"Yeah, but we'll be alright."

In the gathering dusk we sipped our coffee and walked to the roped off mine shaft.

"How did they get him out of there?"

"Get who out?"

"The dead horse. When Carlito and I fell into the shaft, the horse was gone. How did you guys get the dead horse out of the hole?"

"Bob went down. He rigged a sling. We used two winches on two 4x4s and pulled the animal out. One of the NPS guys pulled him about a mile west. I suspect that there's nothing left now but a few bones. Why?"

"Just curious."

"I gotta go, Lee. I'll check you later, tomorrow or the day after."

"Juan you be careful in that little bitty chopper. It's awful dark out here."

"Don't worry, man. This baby, courtesy of the U.S. taxpayers, is loaded with all sorts of infrared, ground hugging navigation systems. I can fly it blindfolded if I punch in the coordinates of where I am and where I want to go. Take care."

And, poof, he was gone in a whisper of helio-blade "shush, shush, shush." He waved as he swung the chopper toward Presidio. I waved back.

With only the light of a zillion stars, I sipped my after dinner coffee laced with Jameson's Irish Whisky. Rusty curled up on the north side of the dying embers. The wind was out of Mexico, out of the south. The animals were secure. I'd run a picket rope from my small two person tent to a boulder about ten feet south of the fire. Ace and Pepper were close by, both wearing their NPS–issued horse blankets. We were a cozy group. Most people don't believe it, but even stars can cast a shadow, especially when there is absolutely no other available or ambient light. The square black holes that defined the windows of the manager's house looked like cave openings, weird but oddly comforting. Something Juan said gave me pause.

"Bob went down, Juan said." Bob went down. Why? Well, Bob was a small guy. He had that semi-pro cyclist frame—five–ten, about 160 pounds, two percent body fat, way smaller and about ten years younger than me. Lean and mean he called it. So it would have been logical for him to volunteer to go down. He was the lightest in weight. He knew how to rig a sling. Besides it was his park. OK, all that was fine.

But why didn't he report finding the flasks? Maybe he didn't see them. Maybe they were covered. Covered with what? I didn't remember seeing any covering on them when I dropped in, well fell in. No, that doesn't make sense. There had to be another explanation. The problem was, I didn't have a clue. But fortunately, as Scarlett O'Hara said in that last line of _Gone With the Wind_, "Tomorrow is another day." How true Scarlett, how true. I slept the sleep of the just, or at least the sleep of the well-guarded and well-armed.

In New Mexico they call it "Turquoise Sky." I call it that in Big Bend. It's that deep, bright blue that I've seen only in three places: looking down from the deck of a sailboat into the 600-feet-deep waters of the Gulf of Mexico, in northern New Mexico, and in Big Bend. Every time it happens I say a prayer to the Great Spirit for allowing me to see in Technicolor.

I had my maps, surveys, and GPS readings spread on my sleeping bag by 8:00 a.m. Ace hee-hawed. By now I'd christened him the "hearing mule." I didn't even bother to put him on the picket line. He roamed free with just a halter. I saw the dust plume in the south a good ten minutes before I heard the truck and the grind of the shifting gears.

And then, "Sumbitch, Rusty, Ace, look who's here. It's Officer Jackson. Go, Rusty. Ace, you stay."

Weird, saying "Stay" to a mule. But damned if he didn't.

"Jackson, what the hell are you doing here? I thought we agreed on five days?"

"Yes, can't help it. I think I can help. I ran some more cards last night on your living room wall. We can talk about them now or later today. Whatcha got? I figured the more boots in the dirt, the better."

"OK, but now that you're here, what the hell is Plan B?"

"Maria's back. She's a little weak, but she has help. Rusty knows her. Besides, I'm Plan B."

"Anybody know you're here besides Maria?"

"No."

"Not Juan, not Bob, not nobody?"

"No, Lee. Not a soul, OK? You don't trust anybody, do you?"

"Well, damn few, and we've covered those, right?"

I laid out all the charts. We spent eight hours checking coordinates, reviewing surveys, hiking, walking, squinting at building corners, taking compass readings. We reviewed, looked at and measured buildings and distances. Nothing, nothing, nothing! We were two really frustrated human beings. It was 5:00 p.m.; the time of long shadows and shallow weak light, even in Big Bend in late October.

"Lee, wait. Got your flashlight? Come on; I have a hunch."

"Jackson, hunches, smunches! We've been all over this ground today."

"Come with me; bring the 1930 mine HQ survey and the 1997 GPS survey. Please Lee, just do it. Humor me, OK?"

And in ten minutes, there it was. Jackson, Rusty ,and I walked up hill to the western side of the mine superintendent's house. Plain as day, there it was. A small addition on the western side of the house, built of identical materials as the rest of the structure. It was about 8 x 8, no doors and no windows.

"Wha'dya think, Jackson?"

"I think we'd better go eat; get a good night's rest. We can tackle this in the morning. Congratulations! I think you and I may have figured out the greatest puzzle in Christendom, Islam and Judaism! If we're right, you know what's in there? Right?"

Together we roasted Cornish game hens, aluminum foil wrapped corn-on-the-cob. Rachel created a salad. And we were in business. We'd eaten, had coffee. It was about time to turn in, when . . . .

"Lee, there's something I have to show you."

"What, Rachael?"

She stood, turned her left side to me, and began unbuttoning her duty blouse.

"Whoa, Jackson! What the hell are you doing? Damn, you're curvy and all, but you know that I don't . . . and I just can't . . . ."

"Shut up and look! Guys like looking at good looking chicks with great tits, right? And I have them. Pay attention; look at the fucking tattoo.

She completed the job; pulled the sleeve off her left shoulder, dropped the blouse completely and raised her left arm. I have to admit that Jackson, Rachael, was really attractive— *really* attractive. She was almost nude from the waist up, wearing only this frilly, tan, see-through lace front-closure bra that barely covered her very hard, dark chocolate nipples. Forty-degree temps and no clothes will tend to promote erect nipples. I think my mouth dropped about a foot.

"Jackson, I . . . ."

"Shut up, stand up and look. What do you see?"

"Holy Shit!"

"If you're looking at the tattoo and not my really great tits, you might also appropriately say something like: 'You're one of the Seven, aren't you?' To which I'd reply, 'Yes, I am.'"

"You're one of the Seven aren't you?"

"Yes I am. Where do we go from here?"

"I think we found it, don't you?"

"Yeah, Lee; I think we have. I'll still ask the same question. Where do we go from here?"

"I don't know; I really don't know. Can you stay around for daylight tomorrow? If you do, I do ask that you put your clothes back on. My God, Jackson! What do we do now; what now? I have some other questions concerning the Seven. Can you answer them?"

"Like what?"

"Like who among the Seven knows the full location of the holy object? You're either a helluva actress or you didn't know. You didn't know, did you?"

"No, neither Maria nor I knew the full coordinates."

"The dead guy, do you think he knew?"

"Maybe he knew. I don't know. My guess would be yes; he was one of the senior members. But since I've never actually seen any of them except Maria, I don't know. Listen to me. Here is how it works as far as I know. The three senior members of the Seven know the exact location. Those three do not live in the same city, county, state or even country. They are charged with passing on that information to the junior members as they reach the age of seventy. Then they, the old ones select their own replacements. At all times the remaining four know only parts of the location. It has been this way for a thousand years, mainly because the ancestors, the early guardians, did not trust either themselves or their heirs fully. I'm sure you can understand that, given how precarious life could be 500 or a 1,000 years ago, it was important to have some sort of fail safe way to keep the knowledge secure."

"It's really quite simple; it's called deduction. Each of the four junior members of the Seven has a "piece of the puzzle" if you want to think of it in those terms. If something happened to all of the senior members the junior members would possess sufficient information to find the Ark."

"You and I got lucky. The original guardians and eight or ten generations of the Seven did not reckon on GPS, sophisticated computers, or that primitive red, blue and green card game you play on your living room wall. Regardless, we're going to have a helluva tomorrow.

"Lee, you're in luck. I have a couple of bottles of red in the truck. I think we should sit, look at the superintendent's house, drink and talk about our problem and what we're going to do about it. If not that; why don't we all punt and take this up early in the a.m.? Wha'dya think?"

"Rachael, I could sure use a couple of glasses of wine. But I don't think it would stop there, either the drinking or the other. Instead, I'll help you pitch your tent. We'll both have clear heads and a lot more sleep if we hang on to those two bottles of red. That OK with you? We can do them later."

"You have a deal. I'll see you in the morning. Say, does that mule actually watch you and follow you around all the time? You don't even tether him like you do Pepper. I've never seen a mule do that; you?"

"Nope, never. First time for everything, huh? Mañana."

CHAPTER 10: FINDERS KEEPERS?

"You know Lee; I thought this morning would be a piece of cake. We'd wake up. Get some great coffee, wolf down a couple of breakfast tacos, and go to work. We found it. At least we're pretty sure we have. So, we get some hammers, crowbars, and such out of my truck, open the building, rip open the room where the Ark should be and confirm our conjectures. Is that about where you were? Or maybe you're still there?"

"It's where I was; not where I am. I don't know, Rachael. I really don't. Let's say we do just what you said. But let me put it in slightly different terms. After coffee and breakfast we get the tools and tackle this job. Here is what some others might think: These two people, one a federal employee, the other a long-term state employee, desecrate, attack and enter a registered national landmark, a sealed building on a federal reservation posted with signs saying things like "Keep Out" and "destroying federal property is a violation punishable by fines and jail terms," that sort of stuff. None of that includes the niggling detail that you, Officer Jackson, are clearly violating the oath you took as a commissioned NPS police officer. Stuff that ought to give you pause."

"But Lee . . . ."

"Wait, please; let me finish. So let's assume that we do all the things both of us just mentioned. And let's assume that Mariscal Mine does not become Grand Central Station and no tourists arrive to ask what we're doing. And no jefes like Bob Potter or Juan Barrera or other feds show up and slap the cuffs on us. And let's assume that the Ark is actually in there. Once we've opened the room, this Pandora's Box, just what are we supposed to do with this thing? We can't exactly take it home and park it on the library shelf of the Brewster County library.

"This may be the most important religious icon ever. If either one of us owned the certified bones of Jesus Christ, that would pale in comparison. This thing is the foundation, the cornerstone, the bedrock of Western Civilization. Are we just gonna board it back up and pretend that we did not do what we just did? I don't think so! Got any ideas?"

"Yes, I do. Here's what I suggest. First, let's eat our chorizo y huevos tacos. We'll feed the animals. Then we take our after-breakfast dark roast and amble over to the house with Rusty and that mule of yours. This time, we'll critically analyze the structure and plan how we will do this desecration, as you so aptly put it. I also have a suggestion about what happens after we actually find the Ark. That's the problem we really need to confront, right?"

"Yeah, tell me."

"They've been asking you to come back to Los Alamos, right?"

"Yes they have. Luís has been after me for a week, well, maybe two. The problem of course is Lisa, Charly, Bob Potter and both my kids. Lisa is adamant that I not go back to such a remote place, at least not until the folks who attempted to kill me are caught. And in some ways I agree with her. But what's your point?"

"Let's load it in my pickup or the dos caballos trailer. We'll haul it back to Los Alamos. Got any idea where to put it?"

"Jackson, does anybody have any idea how big this thing is? Like is it two by two feet; six by eight? Does it weigh twenty pounds or two hundred? Makes a big difference, don't you think?"

"You bet; only one way to find out, huh?"

"OK, so I suggest the following plan. You load up; take all your stuff, tent, everything. You get back to Castolon or wherever and pick up shoring timbers. Most of that stuff has been stored outside anyway. It will be weathered and will blend in. Load that, nails, come-alongs, any gas or battery operated saws or other equipment you think we might need. Your patrol truck can re-charge most 8 to 24 volt battery-powered tools, right?"

"Yes."

174

"You come back tomorrow. We do the deed. You cool with that plan?"

"Lee, should I tell Maria, Bob, or Juan?"

"No, don't. I have some reasons, and we'll talk about that when you get back. OK?"

"I want to check the cards again. You don't have a problem do you?"

"Knock yourself out. While you're poking through the house there, pick up some frozen ribeyes sitting in the freezer on the back porch. Pick two; bring some canned ranch beans and some canned biscuits. We can have a, and you're gonna hate this, 'last supper' before we open the room."

"You're right, trite. Cute, but trite."

"OK, OK. Go! But not until we figure out what we need."

So we poured our coffee and ambled over to the building; figured out what tools we might need. Jackson loaded up and split. We agreed that tomorrow or the next day would be soon enough for her return.

I had some time. I saddled Pepper, loaded a light bundle in the packsaddle on Ace. I tried it without a lead rope; Ace was fine. He followed along like a puppy. Rusty, me, Pepper and Ace trekked back to the river. I unsaddled Pepper and Ace; they drank. Rusty drank and swam. I took a bath in the prick-shrinking icy Rio Grande. We dined—the horse and mule on the local grass; Rusty on a real treat, canned dog food. I pulled out my next to last can of smoked oysters, my last stack of saltine crackers and enjoyed fine dining with two Negra Modelos and lime. It was a glorious afternoon. The temperature was in the 80s. I river washed my clothes, flung them on the packsaddle to dry, and rode naked back to my Mariscal Mine campsite. Well, naked except for my hat and riding boots. Some would say that such attire would make for an interesting tan line.

Back at camp, I dressed in my now dry river washed clothes. The "Police Line" yellow tape fluttered from those crude stakes that circled the mine shaft. I'd planned to go back down in the shaft tomorrow morning.

"What the hell, Rusty. May as well do it now."

In the fading sun, I rigged two rappelling lines into the shaft where the horse had died, where Carlito and I had fallen. I sent down two gallons of water and enough Meals Ready to Eat to keep me alive for about five days. Nothing down there to shoot at, so I left the weapons in the truck. I figured that if something happened I could survive in relative comfort until somebody came along.

It was a short drop. Standing on the heavy blocking timbers I clicked on my eight-cell flashlight. Sure enough, they were still there. All eight flasks lay in that almost perfect row along the hollowed-out rock shelf. The indentations of the missing four flasks reminded me that someone, or several someones, had already removed a bunch of them. Someone had stenciled "Hg," the periodic table abbreviation for Mercury, on each of the flasks. All had that mine cap and seal, imprinted "MM." In addition, each had a wax seal, an embedded serial number that looked like a combination serial number and date stamp. Each wax seal had another stamped "MM." I rotated each one. "Mariscal Mine" was stenciled on opposite sides of the flask, one stencil on each hemisphere. Each was seventy-six pounds of pure poison or industrial metal, depending on your point of view. I rotated the last one on the right, the one closest to the shaft opening and there it was. It looked like a ballpoint pen that had been run over by a semi; except it wasn't. One end glowed a soft orange; it pulsed, about one beat every five seconds. Nothing else, just that soft, barely blinking glow. Someone had duct taped it to the side of the flask about halfway down. I sat on the dirt floor and began puzzling this thing out my usual way, muttering to myself.

"Well I'll be damned," to nobody in particular. "This has got to be a sensor or a transmitter. Or maybe it's both. Wonder what the hell it's transmitting? Who is receiving? Holy Shit! I'll bet this little thing is a motion sensor. Juan's visits are not just coincidence. Somehow he's involved in this. Oops, I think maybe I've stumbled into a sting operation. That's it. That has to be it!"

I'd been down there about twenty minutes when Rusty began barking topside. Ace began that crazy hee-haw that even I could hear. Flipping the flask back over, I rappelled back up out of the shaft in time to see the Border Patrol chopper blades flutter to a slow hiss. Juan pulled off his flight helmet, dismounted and waved. As always, he pulled the protective cloth across under the chopper and snapped it in place. He reached back in the chopper and held up a bottle as he walked toward me.

"Sun's below the yardarm someplace amigo. Got time for a drink? I can stay the night this time. Whatcha got to eat?"

"Juan, I didn't expect you for another day or two. Got nothing but MREs, but have a good selection. What is that?"

"It's a pretty fair Chianti. I've dined on MREs and sipped on this many a time. What have you been up to today?"

I brought him up to date, including my recent trip down the shaft.

"What do you mean, eight flasks of refined mercury from this mine? Are you sure? How do you know that the flasks contain mercury? They could be empty."

"Juan, I know the difference between a full flask and empty one for God's sake. Gimme a break. You wanna go look? Here, I'll belay the rope. I even worked out a pulley and counterweight system. It'll make the return trip easier. Here, use my light."

Ten minutes later he was back topside, complete with a serious frown.

"Lee, let me get on the horn. There's something I need to do. This clarifies a bunch of stuff. I'll be right back. Meanwhile, you get that vino open. Even Chianti ought to breathe."

He wasn't gone three minutes. When he returned his face was ashen, completely drained of any coloring.

"Juan, you look like death warmed over, like you've seen a ghost. What's going down man? Tell me."

"I can't Lee, just some tough decisions. I really gotta go. I can't stay the night. I will have a glass of that fine Chianti with you. I see you brought firewood. Crank us up a fire, jefe. You remember how to do fire, right? I do. You ever think about that night?"

"No, almost never. When I get my annual physical, they always ask if I have pulling or tightness across my belly. The answer is always, "Yes I do." Always have, at least since it finally healed about a year after the accident. But, you know how that works. You stay active, work out when necessary. The activity keeps the scar tissue as flexible as possible. The medical response is always, 'Well you tell us if it gets any worse.' I always promise that I will. So far it hasn't."

"I think about it all the time. You know, my legs are a mass of scar tissue and skin grafts. You want to see?"

"Shit no, Juan. Remember me? I was in the next bed. I saw 'em and smelled them when they had scabs and ooze. I sure as hell don't need to see them now. You look like shit right now, like you lost your best friend or your mother. It's not anything like that, right? Anything I can help with?"

"You going to be out here long, Lee? Maybe I can get back out."

"I'm going to be moving around. Here a couple more days; then around the north side of Mariscal Mountain. I'll camp at a site called Rooney's Place. You ever been there?"

"No, not that I know of. What's there?"

"Nothing now, houses all crumbled into mounds. It's just flatland, some of it grown up in huge cottonwoods. It's a pleasant place to camp on the river. I hear it's a place illegals can cross without getting their knees wet. I'm supposed to pick up a guide there. Luís made the arrangements last week. So, if the guide shows up, he'll take me downriver to San Vicente Crossing. I have an entry permit. We'll cross over. I've been to the ruins at the Presidio de San Vicente, but it was a long time ago. I want to take some photos and look at a couple of abandoned cemeteries. Besides, you can find me if you want to, using that cute little chopper of yours with all that electronic gadgetry. With any luck, this trip will wrap up the research on my book."

"That's a myth Lee. All the electronic gadgetry in the world doesn't substitute for eyeballing the ground and following the tracks. Be careful my friend. Vaya con Dios. I gotta go. Sorry I can't stay for the fire."

Rusty and Ace heard the "shush, shush, shush" of that little chopper about daybreak. Rusty tugged on my sleeping bag. Well, he really tugged on my sleeping bag covered right foot. Ace hee-hawed. I crawled out of the warm bag and . . . sumbitch, there was Juan. He had a huge coffee thermos in one hand and another slung over his shoulder. His smile said, "Breakfast."

"What the hell brings you out so early?"

"I got your favorite coffee, Community Dark Roast, laced with evaporated milk. Its the color of you, just like you like it. I have my own black coffee thermos. And, most important; you don't have to cook. I have two chorizo y huevos tacos for you, two for me, and two bacon and egg tacos for Rusty. Sorry to surprise you. I tried to call. Aren't you carrying your satellite phone?"

"Yes, but one of the pleasant things about this place and about what I do is that I don't have to turn it on very often. You know, it has all those features. But I don't need the news. I don't need the weather; for that I can just look around. It's over there hanging on the tent pole. Like yours, mine has a little emergency beacon. I programmed mine to blink only when Lisa calls. Rusty watches for the little light and gets my attention when it blinks. Enough talk about phones. I'm hungry; let's eat."

I built a small fire in my cooking ring. We sat on saddle blankets around my campfire circle, drank good coffee and dined on pretty fair tacos, spicy but not fiery. It looked to be one of those perfect blue sky Big Bend days. If we'd stood on the summit of Mariscal Mountain we could have seen for fifty miles into Mexico and all the way to Santa Elena Canyon.

"Lee, I have a proposition for you. I'm involved in something that I can't tell you very much about, but I do need your help. You've been in the shaft. What did you see?"

179

"I saw eight flasks, just like you did last night. They're full, presumably with refined mercury. At one time there were twelve flasks. Someone has removed four of them. At least there are four more indentations. That's what I saw."

"Lee, does anybody else know about these things? I mean, have you told anybody else about them? Did Carlito see them when he fell into the shaft?"

"The answer to both is no. I haven't told anybody but you. Carlito was in too much pain and was too afraid to notice much about his surroundings. All he remembers is his fall and his scratches and bruises."

Juan laid out the scope of a sting operation. There were multiple agencies involved. The FBI was leading the investigation. The Border Patrol, Texas Parks and Wildlife law enforcement and the Texas Rangers all were involved. Even La Policía de la Frontera had a piece of it. In fact, according to Juan, that agency brought it to the Border Patrol's attention.

"Lee, you saw the two dead Mexican vaqueros. These two guys worked for that huge ranch across the river, Las Tres Estrellas. They knew this land better than you, me, or Potter. Free range cattle don't pay much attention to international borders. They're just looking for good grass. These vaqueros were over here a couple times a month picking up strays. La Policía and my agents all knew these men. According to what I understand from La Policía they're the ones who found the cache of flasks, totally by accident.

"It seems that two prize bull calves belonging to the ranch fell into that circular depression that marks the mine shaft. It was fenced, but part of the fence was down. Calves can't read the 'Do Not Enter' signs. The flooring, with its covering of sand and dirt, collapsed under their weight. I'm sure you can figure the rest of it. Vaqueros go down; they pull up the bull calves. They see the flasks. Everybody around here knows what the flasks are. These guys may have been illiterate, but they knew these things were worth a lot of money."

"Juan, aside from their killer or killers, I may have been the last person to see those guys alive. They were leading a packhorse with four of those heavy canvas bags. You know, the ones in the historic photos of Mariscal Mine. The bags used to transport the mercury flasks to Marathon and the railroad. The bags I saw were empty. Those guys were headed here to pick up their flasks. That's why they directed me south. They knew there was no water in those tinajas."

"That's right. They still looked like vaqueros, but when you saw them they were contrabandos—smugglers. So, can I take you away from your research? I could use the help, on both ends of the trip. It won't take long, couple of hours at the most. You can even leave Rusty here. He can mind the horse and that weird mule of yours."

The plan was: We'd load four flasks on the chopper and take them to a landing strip at Black Gap where we'd drop them. Someone else in either the Rangers or the FBI would monitor them. Eventually the bad guys would show up. The good guys would capture them. Juan didn't want to talk about the good guys or the bad guys or the details of the stakeout.

I agreed and we loaded four, the four farthest from the mouth of the mine. I tethered the animals to the picket line, left Rusty in charge of them. We planned to be gone only about two hours, just long enough to fly to the northern end of Black Gap, unload the flasks and come right back. Not a big deal. I'd be back before noon.

Black Gap Wildlife Management Area is about 40,000 acres of some of the most remote high desert rangeland in the world. Texas Parks and Wildlife maintains it as a pristine habitat for antelope and bighorn sheep. The HQ is down south, near the hamlet of La Linda. There are three hunting lodges, a few primitive roads leading to a dozen or so primitive campgrounds and three or four bladed, dirt airstrips. The total staff is five. But one of them had ended up dead in that little canyon; now there were four.

We landed at the airstrip farthest north. TPWD had used a bulldozer to clear the cactus, ocotillo, creosote bushes, and other vegetation out of the way. They'd made an approximately 3000 foot packed dirt runway. There was nothing else except a listless wind sock and a small metal 10 x 12 storage shed on the north end of the strip.

"Give me a hand Lee. We'll unload these flasks and put them in the shed. Then we'll get back in the chopper and get out of here. OK?"

Juan opened the door to the shed. The smell of dried blood was awesome. Something else—something was rotting in there!

"Juan! What the . . . ?"

And he turned and pulled the pistol on me.

"I'm sorry Lee; we gotta do this. You know what this is, right?"

"The five guys' packs; all their gear is here, isn't it? There's something else. I know the odor of dried blood. I also know what rotting flesh smells like. Is the fifth man's arm here too? Christ, that's barbaric! You were there, weren't you? You killed them? What the hell Juan? What is going on here? You don't want to be doing this!"

"Lee, you got any idea what I do? What I put up with? What I make a year?"

"I have an idea of what you do, and maybe a little idea of what you put up with and what you make. You're probably knocking down about 90K a year, plus a car, a house and this chopper to fly around in. You have a great family in Mary Lou and the kids. You're a pillar of the community. People look up to you and respect you. Your family's been here for generations. Is all that enough for all the risks you take? Probably not. But remember me? I'm the guy that pulled you out of that burning truck! Whatever it is you're into, I'll help you work it out. I know an amazingly successful lawyer. Susan can help you get through this. Come on!"

"Too late, Lee. Look, we gotta unload the flasks, or rather you do. I'll keep you covered while you do it. I am really sorry. You know about the other, the other, don't you? The tattoos?"

"Yeah, I do. Is that why you tried to kill me that night at Los Alamos? You were the third man, weren't you? You were the guy at the top of the ridge, the guy who saluted me and didn't fire back, right?"

"Yes, I was. I didn't want to shoot you myself. I just couldn't do it."

"But you set my ass up. Dammit, that's the same thing, Juan! It's the same thing as pulling the fucking trigger yourself."

"I didn't see it that way."

"Who were the other two guys? I want to know the names of the men I killed. Juan, the second one; I smelled his last breath! You owe me that."

"They were contract hitters out of Houston. I don't even know their real names."

"How much was the job worth? How much was my life worth to you and your business associates? You can tell me that. You tried to have me killed. For how much loot? Tell me."

"Lee, it was $100,000."

"That's a lot of money for a one-time hit. But probably less than a percent of what this whole caper is going to net you and your buddies, right?"

"You got an idea what refined mercury is worth on the strategic industrial metals market?"

"Not until two weeks ago, Juan, until I fell into a mine shaft and found eight seventy-six pound flasks of refined mercury from the Mariscal Mine. I didn't have a clue. But I understand that the legal market is about $200 a refined ounce. That about right?"

"Yes. But do you know what the smuggler's market, the black market price per ounce?"

"No, should I?"

"I'll tell you, $1,000 an ounce. You can do the math. The net is about twelve mil. There are six of us. Well there were six; there are three now. I can live pretty damn good on four million deposited in an offshore bank. Come on, Lee, unload the damn flasks and stack them along that wall."

Unloading and stacking took less than ten minutes, but I was sweating and wondering what was going to happen next. He had the pistol. He could shoot me and leave my body someplace on Black Gap. It would take years for anybody to stumble across the bones.

"Turn around; I absolutely must cuff you."

He locked the shed. He put me in the passenger seat, wrists cuffed behind my back. On the flight back he quizzed me about the tattoo.

"Hell Juan, until somebody shot up Los Alamos I didn't even know that the damn tattoo existed. I discovered it by accident, after I'd relocated to Castolon. I hit the zoom button after I got out of the hospital in Alpine. You guys acted too fast!"

That wasn't exactly true, but it worked. I didn't admit that I knew about the guardians and the Seven in any other context. Not wanting to get in any deeper, I decided not to ask about the "Propane Event." My biggest problem was that I was handcuffed, flying in a helicopter with a guy who had a lot to lose. But he was still a friend of mine.

"What next?"

"We're going go back to Mariscal. You will help me load the last four flasks. They're worth a million each. Lee, I am not going to kill you. As your people say, I owe you a life. But I need forty-eight hours. Will you give me your word on that? I think you will, but just so you're not tempted I'm gonna leave you in the shaft. I saw the food and water there. We'll take the horse and mule off the picket line. Pepper and that crazy mule will be OK. Rusty can go for help or somebody will come by. If you agree to that, when we land I'll take the cuffs off. Whatcha say?"

"All right; done deal. But tell me about the sensor. It's a motion detector right? That's why you seemed to show up around Mariscal Mountain just in the nick of time. Somebody trips the motion detector or the radio frequency and bingo, you're on your way. No problem getting there. You have that chopper assigned to you 24/7. Right?"

He did not answer. We landed, cut the horse and mule loose. I fed them the last of the oats. I gave Rusty two double handfuls of dry food. Juan took off the cuffs. I rappelled down into the shaft, roped the flasks. Juan pulled them up one by one and loaded them on the chopper. I did use my boot on the sensor that was taped to the final flask. Its little orange light winked out after the second heel strike.

"I gotta go Lee. I'm really sorry about all this. Mostly I'm sorry about how this must hurt you and destroy our friendship. You'll give me the forty-eight hours?"

"Juan, about last night. You talked to someone on the radio right? He told you to kill me, yes? Well?"

"Yes, Lee he did. I told him that if I did that, it would complicate things. Things would get out of control."

"That's why the ashen, crumpled face. It wasn't that you had a death. It was that our friendship was dead and this really was the end. Right?"

"You said that according to your people's rules, I owed you a life. I've given it. Somebody will come along. You know that. You'll give me the forty-eight hours and we're even. OK?"

"Yeah, get out of here."

I waited about thirty minutes, then called Rusty.

"Rusty, you go, you go find Jackson. Find Jackson, go NOW!"

I waited fifteen minutes and called his name again. Nothing. Hopefully that meant that he was headed back to Castolon. Ace answered though, that grating hee-haw, hee-haw. Nothing for me to do but sit. Well, there was one thing. I did a thorough search with my flashlight. Sure enough there was a second sensor. I thought about stomping it too, but not now. Juan needed to know that I was still here, for a while. So I watched its little orange light pulse on/off, on/off. It was mesmerizing in a way. I took out my pocket notebook and scribbled notes that might be useful later. With any luck, Rusty would bring help soon. If not tonight, then by tomorrow afternoon or evening. Muttering helps focus my attention, so I muttered while doing my survival-supply inventory.

"OK, genius, we're in one fine fucking pickle here. Next time somebody tells you to get out of Dodge or Big Bend, pay attention and do it, dummy! On the other hand, let's see. We have one flashlight. It's probably good for about ten hours of continuous operation. Just before leaving, Juan tossed down two saddle blankets. I have my jacket, black hat, and gloves. I won't freeze. I've got two gallons of water and MREs to make it though at least a week. Somebody will come along by then, surely."

About midnight, Ace broke out in that incessant, totally irritating sound of his. It continued for a good ten minutes, until. . . . Then the sound of a pickup horn blast, long, short, long short. I could see headlight beams. Then the sound of Rusty's bark, which meant, given my crapped-out hearing, he was standing right on the ledge.

"Good dog, Rusty. Good dog."

"Lee, where the hell are you? You in the mine shaft?"

I think she was standing right at the edge yelling at the top of her lungs. Even I could hear that. And a sweet sound it was! I yelled back.

"Get a rope and get me out of here. I've had all the fun a guy can have alone in a mine shaft. You know Jackson, this bears out one of my life rules."

"And would that be guy-in-the-mine?"

"It's better to be lucky than smart, or lucky rather than rich. In this case it's better to be lucky and know someone with a great rope, rather than lucky and know someone who doesn't have one. I'm through talking. You got a rope? Get my butt out of here."

Juan had taken the rappelling ropes and equipment. Jackson threw down an old greasy parachute strap that she used as a tow chain. We rigged a basket on my end for the water and supplies. I put the sensor in my pocket and tied myself in a fireman's rescue sling. She hooked me to the pickup trailer hitch, put it in gear, and just drove me and my survival gear out of the shaft. Something else I could strike off my list of stuff to do: don't need to spend the night in another mine shaft. I ruined a good jacket, pair of jeans, and work shirt, but otherwise I was fine and happy to be standing upright on the ground and not under it.

"Christ, Rusty runs faster than even I suspected."

"I met him at Johnson Ranch. His tongue was hanging out, but he was hauling ass. I think he recognized my truck. He piled in; we turned on the afterburner and here we are. Are you OK?"

I relayed the story but cut it short. I was ravenous. One of the great things about MREs is that they come with "heat sticks." At least that's what I call them. A heat stick is this chemical tube. You break it and it can heat your MRE to what is an almost acceptable temperature for fine dining. Well, maybe not exactly fine dining, how about survival dining? Jackson chose Swiss steak with veggies. I chose beef stew with "vegetable medley." Those guys who write those menu descriptions really ought to get some sort of advertising prize. Or alternatively, they should all be shot at dawn. Regardless, it was palatable chow.

"You're not going to give him forty-eight hours are you? He's a criminal; he murdered four, five, or maybe seven people if you count the vaqueros. He attempted to murder you. Goddamn Lee, you can't do that!"

"Yes, I can; yes I will. And you will, too. Besides you and I have some really important work to do. Don't you think?"

"You don't mean we're still going through with that, do you?"

"Absolutely. Think a second, OK? If we report this now, half the law enforcement in Texas will be here in a heartbeat. And, because of what's on my wall in Castolon, and what the two of us and Maria know, they will figure it out. So, how about let's get to work at daybreak. You have the tools and the timbers in the truck. Before we attack that issue, I'd like to talk through some ideas about this 'Mercury Caper', as I've begun calling it. You game?"

"I brought some more sticks of firewood. How about we crank up a good campfire? I'll break open a bottle of that Red I have stowed in my truck. We can sit on saddle blankets around a friendly fire and we can puzzle this thing for a while. Will that do?"

"You bet. Let's do it."

I ran a picket line, put Pepper and Ace on it. Jackson had thoughtfully brought more oats for Pepper and Ace. Ace was raucously grateful. Pepper was happy to have his horse blanket again. He nibbled an apple and swished his black and white tail. As for Ace, I'm pretty sure I'll never be associated with another animal with a worse sounding voice. On the other hand, he is entertaining. If he didn't weigh 1100 pounds and stand over six feet, he'd make a great indoor pet.

I pulled out my pocket notebook. I'd scribbled several pages of notes.

"Jackson, who did he radio? When he came back to the camp he was ashen. He looked horrified, like he'd seen his children hacked into little pieces in front of his eyes by some psychopath. Who do you think he talked to on the chopper radio? Got any ideas? Or, to paraphrase the Vichy cop in the movie *Casablanca*: Who are the usual suspects?"

"OK. At Castolon I sat in your living room and stared at those damned multicolored cards for hours. Here's what I came to. For me, there are three people who could be ringleaders in this thing. And by the term 'this thing' I mean only the mercury smuggling. I'm not including the Ark. You understand that?"

"Yes, but do you think they might be mixed? Or maybe some of the players in one are players in the other?"

"Lee, I know you're not a mechanic. But I like to use the automobile carburetor analogy. I don't have the first idea about how to dismantle or put back together a car or pickup. But I figure that if I can dismantle or put together a carburetor, piece by piece, I can eventually work up to the entire vehicle. That make sense?"

"For the record Jackson, nobody uses carburetors anymore."

"Lee, you're being a smartass. Shut up and listen. What I'm trying to do is tackle this very large and complex problem in a small, incremental way. Then, maybe we can tackle the larger part of it."

"Got it. Do it."

"The three people I came up with, using that sophisticated card system of yours are the following: Captain Juan Barrera, Ms. Maria Gomez, and Captain Robert Potter. Juan's a given. That leaves two. Of course I'm not considering either the FBI's Agent Marks or the Texas Rangers' Captain Jack Hays.

"I thought about Comandante Felipe de Lara Oconor. He is the jefe of all Policía de la Frontera in the Mexican state of Coahuila. He lives in Ciudad Acuña. The de Lara's and the Barreras go back a long way in this country. I suspect the two people are related. He, like Captain Barrera, has his own chopper. That gives him great flexibility. And you know, as the comandante, he wields a lot of power in northern Mexico. He has almost none north of the border. And the market for the mercury is in the United States, Europe, and China. Mexico is not a player. I think we can rule him out.

"My next choice was Maria Gomez. We know she is a member of the Seven. She has informed you about certain things. Without her information, we would not have found the Ark. Her family has been in Big Bend for generations. The problem is, I don't think she has access to a radio."

"Jackson, do you think the 'Propane Incident' was staged? You don't think Maria would risk the life of her son, do you? That's plain crazy. Clearly, she loves him more than life itself. I'm not buying."

"OK, jefe; maybe not. Guess what? That leaves your other good buddy, Captain Bob Potter. I am convinced that he is involved in this thing in some way. Granted ,he is not Hispanic. But, just in case, I ran his bio on the NPS website. He was born in Utah. He's a Mormon in good standing, several generations long. I'll bet that is a surprise? He has access to people and information outside Big Bend. Not only through NPS, but he can access a worldwide Church of Jesus Christ of Latter Day Saints network. He could find a market for this mercury. He has 24/7 access to numerous radio channels. He doesn't have a chopper 24/7, but he has access. He's been in Big Bend for over fifteen years. And Lee, you may not want to believe this. Bob Potter, the Mormon, would love to deliver the Ark to the Temple in Salt Lake City or to the Mormon community in Mexico. Take it to the bank; you can believe it."

"Jackson! Mormons killing others for gain? I have a hard time getting my head around that."

"You're a historian Lee. Did you ever hear of the Mountain Meadows Massacre? Mormons slaughtered a whole bunch of men, women and children just to keep them out of Utah. Mormon history is as bloody as that of Islam, Christianity, or the early Israelites. Get real. The Mormons gained an entire empire through a series of massacres. They're no better or worse than anybody else. Case closed."

"OK. You think Bob could do this for money? I think no. You think he and Juan have discussed transferring the Ark from Jewish custody to LDS custody, for a huge sum of money? I don't know, but why not? I can see Juan, and Maria for that matter, expediting the sale of the Ark to the LDS church. That makes sense to me, well a little bit of sense. Let me put it this way: that sort of thing makes more sense than selling it to total strangers, or selling it to the Palestinians or Saudis. But there are a couple other options here, right? There's a very small but very powerful country called Israel that might want to have the Ark returned to its rightful place. That would NOT be Northern Mexico, Salt Lake City, or the Texas borderlands. It would be Jerusalem the capital of the Jewish state, would it not?"

"Here's the real question, Lee. Juan has found the flasks. Does he want to keep them? My answer is no; he wants to sell them. We've found the Ark. If we have, others will eventually figure it out. Who gets to keep it? I say we do; others say no, most emphatically."

"Morning is coming awfully early, Jackson. We have a full day ahead of us. But I think I see a return trip to San Antonio and another to Houston. There are some people in both places who might be interested in helping us. Let's go to bed.

You have our tents and sleeping gear someplace in that truck, right?"

"Same place we packed 'em, Lee. The storage box behind the cab, along with your sleeping bag, pad, my bag and pad, and all the rest of the camp stuff."

In ten minutes we had the two tents set up, pads in place and sleeping bags rolled out. We banked the fire. The temp had dropped to the mid-30s. I crawled in my bag. Rusty took up his usual place at my feet on his own pad. I was asleep in less than two minutes.

CHAPTER 11: THE FACE OF GOD

Jackson and I slept in. Well, Rusty and I did. Well, maybe just me. I woke to the pungent smells of coffee brewing and bacon frying and the crackle of an early morning campfire. While lying there listening and smelling the delicious camp odors, I realized I'd had not a single nightmare; no gunfire, no dead bodies, attempted murders. That bit of revelry was broken by . . . .

"Come and get it or I'll throw it out! Rusty, drag his ass out of that tent."

The cry of the old range cooks will sure as hell get your attention. It sure got my butt out of bed. Remembering that there was a lady in camp, I shucked on my work jeans inside my tent; pulled on my Wellingtons and flannel shirt. My jacket was a little worse for wear, what with having been dragged over about fifty feet of rock and scrub. But it sure did feel warm when I zipped it up and popped out of my tent. Rusty beat me to the warmth of the fire. His entire body wiggled and wagged in anticipation of bacon, eggs and pancakes soaked in real butter and syrup.

If I'd had a tail, I would have wagged it too. About the best I could do was to give our "chef du jour" a thank you for starting the fire and pour myself some camp coffee into one of my enameled light blue speckled tin cups. Jackson was dressed in her fatigue uniform and bundled up against the early morning cold. It felt like about twenty-five degrees. She'd put feed bags on Ace and Pepper. They'd slept with their horse blankets securely strapped on. That campfire sure did feel good. If I had to get out of a warm sleeping bag, this was almost the best way to do it.

Jackson, Rusty, and I savored that trail breakfast. I ate three eggs over easy with at least four strips of bacon. I drowned my three pancakes in butter and syrup. My two cups of dark roast laced with evaporated milk kicked in. I felt like Paul

Bunyan. I felt like leaping tall buildings at a single bound. I felt strong enough to cut down tall trees with a single axe blow. I would have relished the idea of saving damsels in distress. I was even prepared to find the Ark of the Covenant.

"You know Jackson, if I ate like this all the time I'd weigh 300 pounds."

"Me, too. But today, both of us will need every carb and all the protein in this breakfast. Are you ready to do a recon? We can figure out how to attack this thing. I'll drop the trailer. We'll take the pickup to the site. It has all the tools in it and an air compressor. No sense in dragging essential tools things back and forth."

So that's what we did. The mine superintendent's house overlooked everything except the main refinery or smelter. It was what some architects might call "composite" construction. Part of it was frame; part was adobe. The final additions were concrete. The window panes and frames had long since given way to the weather and vandals. Years ago NPS had installed interpretive signage and placed heavy six-gauge wire screening over all windows and doors downstairs. The upstairs windows were boarded up.

"Hell, Jackson, it'll take bolt cutters to get inside. This is six-gauge steel. Each strand is about three-eighths inch in diameter. We'll need some *serious* bolt cutters. I think we want to go in through the second room on the left. Don't you? That opening looks like it is sealed with 4x6 bolted planks. That your read on it?"

"My man, you are in luck. You know somebody with bolt cutters that will free a hobbled Harley in about two minutes. Let me show you."

She walked back to the truck , and pressed the start button on a Honda air compressor. It hummed as she walked back with some air-drive bolt cutters. These were actually bolt cutters on steroids.

"Christ Jackson, that tool looks like what I've seen described as the "Jaws of Life." It'll cut through just about anything. What do you use this thing for?"

"Anything I want. I often free hobbled Harleys. I've cut people out of wrecked cars and pickups. I cut wrongfully attached tow chains. I can even pop the occasional locked security gate, that sort of thing. Stand back and learn, gringo. Watch one of the miracles of twentieth century technology, the wonders of the portable air compressor."

Two minutes later, the wire was off the front door of the former superintendent's home. Jackson and I walked in without raising a bead of sweat. The first part was by far the easiest. Even the air-drive circular saw failed to cut through the second set of doors. The timbers, pressure soaked in creosote-like railroad ties, stymied all our blades.

"I'll be right back Lee."

Even I can hear the ugly roar of a chain saw. Jackson returned with it already running. She handed me a pair of protective glasses; motioned me back and engaged the chain blade. It took about ten minutes to rip through those six inch planks. We saved most of the door, the better to reuse it when we packed up.

Fifty years earlier NPS construction crews sealed the windows of the second room on the left. From the outside the façade looked like stucco. Inside, the construction crew hadn't bothered to make their concrete block filler look like the original house structure.

"Jackson, you into archeology?"

"No, why?"

"Look at this stuff. Archeologists would call this a midden. We call it a trash dump. The NPS crew that worked on weather proofing and securing the mine area in 1964 must have camped in this house, or maybe even this room. Look, cigarette butts. These are Marlboros; these are Winstons. This one is a Kool. Here's the Playmate centerfold from a June 1964 Playboy. Wha'dya think? Don't answer that. It's pretty tame by pay-per-view and internet porn standards. This corner over here must have been the 'designated garbage can.' Look, crumpled cigarette packs, pork-and-bean cans, Vienna sausage. Hey, here's a Spam can! Look, Jackson: my favorite camp food—

smoked oysters. These were some really classy guys. This whole room is a time warp."

She gave me that 'you gotta be kidding me, look.

"How do you know they were just guys?"

"Jackson, listen—1964. A whole 'nother planet, remember? This was before Women's Lib, before bra burning, before equal-opportunity legislation. Trust me, they were just guys, a long-ago time warp."

"Lee, we have another 'time warp' thing to deal with. You ready? Let's do it."

This one was a simple door. But there were two other not-so-simple doors behind it. The last one, the third, was steel. I was thinking: How the hell did they get this thing up here? Jackson, ever the pragmatic, went back to the truck and trundled in an acetylene torch. She fired it up, pulled down her visor, and in about an hour she tapped the thing with her five pound maul. It wiggled.

"Lee, I think it is ready to fall. Are we ready?"

"No, not really. Can we stop just a minute?"

"Sure."

"Jackson, are you a religious person? Do you pray?"

"I was raised Catholic, but now I think I'm what is considered lapsed. So, no, not really to either question. Why?"

"Me neither, but do you mind my offering something?"

"No, have at it."

"Would you hold my hands?"

She did, with Rusty between us.

"I want to ask the blessings of the Great Spirit and the Godheads of all that is holy in the universe to bless this enterprise and to forgive what we are about to do. Amen."

"Amen."

"OK. Hit it!"

She gave it one whack with that five pound short-handle maul. The steel door shuddered. She pushed it with one hand and it toppled back into the darkness. We turned to one another, mouths open. Now what? Now what? If what we thought was in there was really in there, we were soon to be in the presence of the Holy of Holies. I looked up. On the door frame to my right was a Mezuzah.

"Jackson, you know what a Mezuzah is, right?"

"Yes, why?"

"Look up. There's one right there on the top of the doorframe. Look do you mind? I have a King James version in my gear. I'd like to read the chapters in Deuteronomy out loud before entering the room. Is that OK?"

"Sure, go get it. I'll wait."

So I did. I came back with my small cordovan bound King James version and read Deuteronomy 6:4-9 and 11:13-21. The key message is the belief in one God and only one God, and that people will honor that and teach that to their children. And finally, they will post that message on the doorposts of their homes. Which is exactly what a Mezuzah does.

"You ready?"

"Yes. I guess. After you, officer."

We clicked on our flashlights and entered the room. I've been in a lot of closed-up spaces, but this one smelled like it was 3000 years old. It wasn't, of course, but it had that "old air" smell. You could taste it. An early twentieth-century British archeologist called it "the smell of history." Unfortunately, he later died of pulmonary disease. So maybe he was not exactly correct.

Our lights flickered from side to side, up and down, finally settling on the largest crate in the center of the room. It sat on a slightly raised rock platform, in the dead center of the space. There were two other, smaller crates, one on either side. All three were of weathered, stained and hand-hewn wood. All had the six-pointed Star of David scrawled on each side. The largest crate had the star and the numeral "7", with the cross hatch about two-thirds up the vertical. That symbol was on each of the visible sides. And there was something else. It was written in Hebrew. I don't read Hebrew. Jackson did.

"It says Exodus 20, Lee. You know what that is, right?"

"Yeah, it's the Ten Commandments, the Mosaic Law. My God, this is really it, isn't it?"

"Yes, I think so. What do we do now?"

"I think we follow our plan. We can't leave it here, right?"

"No, let's see if we can move it."

It was surprisingly light; couldn't have weighed more than 150 pounds. The crate even came with crude handles on each side. We picked it up, snaked it out the room, through the next room, out the door and lifted it onto the truck. The last two smaller crates weighed no more than twenty pounds each. We each carried one and put them in the truck. Jackson had even brought several pieces of heavy foam for the crates to rest on. We strapped them down and covered everything with a NPS tarp.

The hardest part of the entire venture was rebuilding what we had destroyed. We couldn't rebuild the metal door. But using the planks Jackson brought, we rebuilt the other doors. We stained them to look almost like the originals. By the time we left, the stain had dried. It was difficult to tell any difference. We brushed our tracks out of all the rooms. Jackson had even brought six-gauge wire steel mesh. We replaced the stuff we sawed through. We rolled the cut materials into a tight cylinder and shoved all of it into the truck.

"We gotta get out of here, you know that. Right, Lee?"

"Yeah, we do."

I pulled the motion sensor from my pocket and explained to Jackson what it did. She suggested, and I agreed: "Decommission it with a boot heel. Drop it in the shaft. Juan will wonder, but he won't be back, not here. He'll think you just got pissed off and stomped on it."

Done deal. We broke camp; loaded the animals, and in an hour we were out of there, headed toward Talley, Johnson Ranch, and Castolon. Jackson drove; we talked mainly about what we should do next. We agreed that we couldn't keep the Ark in the pickup. We couldn't keep it anywhere in Castolon.

"Jackson, Luís has asked me to come back to Los Alamos. He says the house is rebuilt. TPWD would like me to continue my Writer in Residence thing."

"Lee, this is not exactly the kind of thing you park in your living room with a tablecloth draped over it. You can't exactly stick it in your laundry room. First of all, there's not enough space. Second, about the third person in there would ask questions. Questions like: "Why do you have this crate with these strange Hebrew scribblings in your laundry room? Got any ideas?"

"Yes, but first let's get to Castolon. We don't talk about this to Maria. We should talk with her about the flasks and about Juan. I need to make some calls to Lisa, Charly and Captain Hays. By the way, you got any idea where Juan might have gone with those last four flasks and that white and green BP chopper?"

"I wish. If I did, I could get about three promotions. When do you want to review the material I found and tacked to your living room wall?"

"We'll say howdy to Maria and Carlito. Then I'm outa gas. I gotta have some sleep. I'll shower and hit the rack. I hope you do the same thing. See you in the morning."

"Christ Lee, what do we do about the Ark?"

"It's covered with a tarp, right? We'll unload the animals, feed, curry, and water them. They'll be happy in the corral behind my house. Who knows what's in the back of the pickup besides me and you? Nobody! Park the damn truck by the corral. Ace will wake the dead if someone messes with the truck. So will Rusty. You have a whole bunch of guns; I have a whole bunch of guns. We and the Ark will be OK."

And we were.

#

"Rusty, where the hell is my campfire breakfast? Ah, you don't cook."

I called Lisa about 6:30 a.m.

"Lee, I've been worried sick. Your satellite phone is out of service. Where the hell have you been? I've been calling for about three days. I called Maria; she didn't have a clue. I called

198

Luís; same. I called Bob; he thought you were at Castolon working on your book. I tried Juan. His phone doesn't work, either. I thought you were dead."

"I'm not, Lisa. It's really good to hear from you, too. Rusty wants to say Hello! I have a new pack mule. His name is Ace. He follows me around like Rusty does. He 'barks' with an awful 'hee-haw.' It's loud enough to wake the dead and for me to hear, well, sorta. I think I'll adopt him into the family. Unfortunately he's too big to sleep at the foot of our bed.

"Speaking of which, I sure would like to have your hot body next to mine, well, maybe we'd best wait on that idea. I am planning a trip back to San Antonio and Austin day after tomorrow. We can chat then. I have a lot of stuff that I can't talk about on this phone or in email. FYI, Juan's phone will be out of service for a while; I'll explain when I see you. I love you."

"Lee, what happened to your satellite phone? I thought it blinked and Rusty would come get you?"

"It had a malfunction, Lisa. You know how the Big Bend is. I've been fine. I found the material I need to complete the book."

"You haven't been doing anything stupid, have you?"

"Lisa, how you gonna define 'stupid'? I'm sorry. I know I've been out of touch. I know you worry. But I'm fine. I have good news about my research, which is that I think it's done. We can talk more about it when I get to Austin in three or four days. I'm going to Alpine tomorrow. I'll pick up a replacement satellite phone when I'm there. The first call I make will be to you."

"OK. I'll talk to you when you get to Austin."

"Love you; see you soon. You'll hear from me tomorrow."

My second call was to FBI Special Agent Carl Marks.

"Agent Marks with the 'k', not the 'x', this is Lee Phillips. Got a minute or two?"

"Sure. What's up?"

"Marks, let me back up. Is your phone secure? Mine isn't."

"Yes, Dr. Phillips, my phone is secure. I thought your satellite phone was secure."

"It had a Size 9 Wellington work boot heel malfunction. Understand?"

"How you want to handle this?"

"Remember that flask issue we discussed? I have more information on that. I think maybe I should meet with you guys as soon as possible. Can you and Captain Hays get down to Castolon this afternoon?"

"My administrative assistant is arranging a chopper as we speak. We'll see you in two, well, maybe three hours. I don't need a warrant, do I?"

"No, Marks. I think we're on the same side in this. See you in three."

I walked over to Jackson's cabin. I found her sitting on the Castolon Store porch with Maria.

"Con permiso, Maria. Jackson, the forty-eight hours are up. I called the FBI. Agent Marks, Captain Hays and lord only knows who else will be here in about three hours. I think it will be a very good idea for you to be on duty—anyplace but here. I'll call Bob in an hour or so, after you've split.

"They will interview me about the flasks. I've also talked with Lisa; I'll be driving to San Antonio and Austin in about three days. I want both of you to know that. Maria, you should be aware that Juan Barrera will very soon become an official fugitive from justice. Every law enforcement agency in Canada, the U.S. and Mexico will be searching for him and that chopper of his. There's nothing I need to know, is there?"

"No, Lee, nothing."

"Maria, can Carlito look after Pepper and Ace? I'll be happy to pay him."

"Sí, Lee; Carlito will be pleased to care for your animals. Do you wish him to care for Rusty as well?"

"No, Rusty goes with me."

Jackson and I loaded the three crates into my TPWD pickup. We strapped them down and covered everything with a tarp. I parked it under my carport.

"Rusty, the best place to hide something is in plain sight." Thump, thump.

Jackson changed into her Class A duty uniform and headed toward Panther to return the tools she'd borrowed. She waved and tapped her horn twice as she headed out.

The fuzz arrived at 10:00 a.m., almost three hours to the minute. There were two choppers. Marks and Hays hopped out as the first one landed. I'd covered the card wall with a curtain. I invited them in. We sat on my back porch, drank coffee while I gave them my statement.

"You mean it's been almost forty-eight hours since he placed you in that hole to die?"

"Marks, I had water for a week, food for a week, blankets and a jacket. I was OK. Juan knew I'd send Rusty for help. Besides, I gave him my word."

"Christ, Dr. Phillips, your word! Since when did that trump catching a criminal who admitted to you that he'd killed at least four men? Since when?"

"Since forever. Marks, you don't get it. Twenty years ago I saved his life. According to my people, he owed me a life. Juan knew that; he always respected that. He kept his piece of the bargain. I gave him my word. Don't you get it? God damn it! I gave the man my word. Look, he could have shot me, shoved my dead ass out of that chopper somewhere over Black Gap. They'd never have found the bones. The coyotes and vultures would be feasting on my corpse today. Or, he could have set that chopper down somewhere on the north side of that 40,000 acres; shoved my handcuffed ass out of that chopper and waved goodbye. I might have made it out, but who knows. Instead, I'm here to give you this statement. You want to ask me what Juan said about his accomplices? Or do you already know that answer?"

"OK, what did he say?"

"He said that originally he had six associates; now he has three. That should narrow the search, don't you think?"

"It either narrows it or makes it almost impossible. That is probably the reason the three, or two or one, killed the guys that you found. You agree?"

"I'm not a cop, Marks. But if I were going to start an entire new life in some foreign country, I'd want the biggest pile of Ben Franklins that I could find. In this world, a large mound of $100 bills go a long way toward making you happy."

"You think they have off-shore accounts?"

"Marks, look; if I had millions of dollars in 'ill-gotten gains,' or the prospect of same, I'd look for the most favorable offshore banking country I could find. But I'd probably want one that wasn't too far away. The Caymans, Panama, some of the other postage stamp countries in the Caribbean might fit the bill. On the other hand, maybe they'd want some place far away. There are a few places in Southeast Asia, several in Eastern Europe and more than one or two in Africa. Personally, I don't have a clue what the chosen country is. But I'll bet you that Captain Juan Barrera and his two associates do. What about you?"

"I think you're right."

"But guys, those are not the critical questions, at least I can't see them being the critical questions. To me the critical question is 'Who', as in who do you sell this stuff to? How do you maximize your revenue? And the real biggie: How does one go about finding that person, or those persons, who will buy this sort of thing. You gotta admit, fencing twelve flasks of a strategic metal is not exactly like going down to your corner pawn shop and unloading the family silver you just swiped. This is what some would call a real 'niche market.' Don't you think?

"Let's say you weren't going to sell this stuff on the legal market. That you would find an different kind of buyer. I think that is exactly what the two vaqueros intended to do. Look what it got them. Let's say you wanted to sell this stuff to a terrorist or a criminal gang who had plans to use this industrial poison to further some screwy or weird political ends. What kind of person would you look for? Where would you do that? And frankly, I don't have a fucking clue. But I bet you boys in the FBI, the Texas Rangers and the Homeland Security nerds, I bet you folks can focus in on some suspects in San Antonio, Austin or Houston pretty damn quick."

"Lee, you think Juan and his buddies whacked the Mexican cowboys?"

"I do, but that's not proof, is it. And I'll tell you, Juan never mentioned it to me, even in passing. So your guess is as good as mine. I have a question for you fellows. If you flew out of Mariscal in a BP chopper loaded with four flasks of refined mercury, where would you fly to? And the multi-million-dollar question: Where the hell is the mercury and where the hell is Juan and the government chopper?"

"It's not a big chopper, but it still is a chopper. It's not like you just take it to the 'Helicopter Hideout' joint. It still has a footprint. My bet is that it's still out here in Big Bend someplace. What about you guys?"

"I think we're about done here, don't you Captain Hays?"

"Yes, I think so. Thank you for being so forthcoming, Dr. Phillips."

"You boys want to go to Mariscal? Or you want to bitch and moan about this some more? If you don't want to take a chopper ride, I'd like to show you my new mule, Ace. You want to see him?"

Captain Hays spoke up for the first time: "Marks, I'll get on the horn to Colonel Maples at TPWD Law Enforcement. We'll get the coordinates of that strip on the north end of Black Gap. You want me to see if I can get somebody from the Wildlife Management Area at Black Gap to meet us there?"

"Shit no, Hays. For all I know, they're all in it. Tell the agents in the other chopper we're leaving in ten."

"Lee, you ready?"

"Let me get my jacket. You know we gotta take Rusty?"

"Yeah, no sweat; bring him. Sometime he makes more sense than any human being I deal with, including you."

"Marks, I've found that to be true as well. Let's go."

The two chopper pilots set those borrowed Border Patrol choppers down at the mine. As the blades slowed, they dismounted, reached under their choppers and pulled the 'drop cloth' across under the machine and hooked it. It finally hit me.

"Marks, that's how he did it. Look, did you guys search for marks, traces at the first murder site, hydraulic fluid, oil leaks, that sort of thing?"

"Yeah."

"And you didn't find anything, right. It was like the killers disappeared into thin air."

"Yes, Dr. Phillips. We didn't find a trace of anything."

We talked with the pilots. Yes they all used the same system, the exact same technique. It was environmentally sensitive. It left no trace for the bad guys or the illegals to notice.

"You're right, Dr. Phillips. That's how he did it. I'll be damned! It was right in front of our eyes all the time."

We didn't stay long at Mariscal. They sent three younger guys into the shaft. Sure enough all they found was the crushed sensor. They photographed the scene. They electronically swept the shaft just in case there were other sensors or transmitters— nothing. Two or three of them mumbled that if the civilian, meaning me, had not crushed it, they could have figured out the frequency, blah, blah, blah. By that time I was really not paying too much attention. Two men, a Ranger and an FBI Agent stayed behind to complete their site investigation. One of the choppers would pick them up on the way back.

"When we get to Black Gap Dr. Phillips, you and Rusty stay in the chopper. Do Not; repeat, Do Not attempt to help out, unless we specifically ask. You got that?"

"You bet Marks. You guys do your thing. I do hope that nothing happens to the chopper driver. It's a long walk to the La Linda road."

Nobody laughed. We landed. Those cops boiled out of those choppers like they were assaulting Iwo Jima. I think everybody, except me, was disappointed that nobody shot at them on their way out of the choppers and into the shed. There was nothing and nobody there. Marks eventually waved me over to the shed.

"Everything like it was when you left?"

"No, it isn't. The four seventy-six pound mercury flasks are gone. I unloaded them from the BP chopper and stood them on end right there, just to the right of the door. Like I told you; that's when Juan cuffed me. Aside from that, everything is the same—he same smell of dried blood, the same stench of decaying flesh, the flies. I suspect that you'll find a decaying or desiccated arm somewhere in that pile of camping gear. Anything else?"

I had Rusty on a tight leash. He kept pulling away. An agitated seventy-pound Shepherd is not really easy to handle. Rusty wanted out of that place; it was hard to hold him. Blood and dead people don't compute too well with him.

"Guys, my dog is really freaking out. I'm going back outside and upwind, OK?"

"Sure. We'll get a pilot to take you back to Castolon. If we need you, can you leave a number?"

"You bet. Good luck folks."

It was definitely time to go .The fuzz would do their job. The chopper pilot took Rusty and me back to Castolon. He dropped us off at the chopper pad just north of the compound. He waved; I waved.

"Jackson, what are you doing back here?"

"Maria called, said you and the fuzz were gone. Bob asked me to check out some hikers at Terlingua Abaja. How'd it go with Marks and Hays?"

"Not a problem. They were really pissed about the forty-eight hour delay. Just like you were. Tough shit, Sherlock."

Before heading out to Alpine, Jackson and I really needed to figure out a way to hide the Ark and the other two smaller crates. The small ones were 2x2x2. If I'd wanted, I could keep them in my pantry. The Ark was another thing. It was three feet tall, three feet wide and about four feet long. I proposed hiding all of them at Los Alamos.

"How about we just put them in the horse shed. We'll cover them with hay bales . . . . No that won't work."

Over a two-hour period we ran through dozens of ideas. We took a break.

Almost at sunset the school bus dropped Carlito off. He wanted to ride Pepper and exercise Ace. I told him to let Ace run free. See what happened.

Maria, Jackson, and I sat on my porch, sipped our favorite adult beverages and watched the sun fall into Santa Elena. Jackson and I dined with Maria and Carlito. Tonight was chicken- fried steak, French fries and salad. After dinner Jackson and I came back to my oak table and worried at our problem for two or three more hours. About 10:00 p.m. Jackson abruptly said: "I'll be right back; I've got an idea."

Ten minutes later she strode through the door with a tape measure in her hand.

"I've got it! They're doing construction work at Los Alamos. Here's the plan. We stop in Alpine at Big Bend Contract Supply. We buy a 'Site Lock Box', you know, one of those huge steel boxes, usually painted yellow or red, the ones contractors use to securely hold their tools. We have one here at the maintenance shed. The Ark and the other crates will fit in it; I've just measured it. We'll put them inside, on cushions like they're riding on now. We'll take it to Los Alamos. On the way we'll stop by Sauceda. You'll tell Luís that you want to rebuild some of your own furniture and this storage box will keep your tools separate from those belonging to the contractors.

We'll stencil your name on it and bolt it to the concrete slab in the carport. All of these boxes come with four serious locking points. We'll get some serious locks. Besides nobody, but nobody messes with someone else's locked storage box, particularly if it is yours. You are considered to be a very dangerous man in this country. They call you "El Pistolero Supremo"! To put it in street vernacular where you grew up: You're the "Baddest of the Bad"! Whatcha think?"

"The notoriety sucks. It is horrible to me that people think of me that way. I'm not a 'Pistolero.' I'm not a killer. I'm just a guy who shot in self-defense and got very lucky and who is thankful to be alive. I have nightmares about that shoot-out almost every night, at least that's what Lisa tells me. Lot's of busy nights. But the notoriety; it could be useful for now."

"Lee, I didn't want to tell you. I heard you in the other tent that night at the mine. You woke me. You were shouting obscenities at several someones. I thought I'd heard about every kind of profanity in the very fertile English language, but I think I learned a few new, and potentially, useful terms that eventually I'll put to use."

"I'm sorry; I didn't know. The next morning I didn't remember any of that."

"It's OK. But you know that Lisa is right; you're gonna eventually have to deal with this shit. You will, right?"

"Yeah. Meanwhile, back to our problem at hand; I think you're a genius. It's time to quit. Do they really call me those things? You know I take no pride in what I did that night. I know we really should look at the new cards on the wall. But honestly, I don't have it in me. How 'bout we tackle that when we come back from Los Alamos? Here's a glass of claret. Let's go look at what we have in the truck? You up for that? Pepper and Ace will enjoy the company."

We pulled back the tarp. There they were. Together we read the words we'd first seen in that little room at Mariscal Mine.

"It's pretty incredible don't you think Jackson?"

We sat on my back porch, wrapped in work jackets and serapes. We drank cold red wine in silence. In the weak starlight, we looked at the crate holding the Ark of the Covenant. Somehow it seemed right at home in the bed of my TPWD 4x4 crew cab pickup.

"Jackson, I've been in lots of churches in lots of places on most of the continents. This is about as close to an authentic religious experience as it gets."

"Yes, but you know they can't stay in a site job box very long, even if it will be safe at Los Alamos for right now."

"Yeah. I'm going to San Antonio day after tomorrow; then to Austin to see Lisa for a couple of days. Then I think I have some work to do in Houston. You need to get back to work. Bob is a great boss, but he'd probably like to have a full time Law Enforcement Ranger. You know, somebody to take care of the tourists."

"He did give me permission to go with you tomorrow to Los Alamos."

That's when Maria walked around the corner of the cabin wearing a serape and carrying a flashlight.

"I know you did not wish to tell me. But I knew it was here. I could feel it. I too would wish to sit with you. Is that agreeable?"

"Maria, I only attempted to protect you. Yes the Ark is here, in the truck. Please join us. Rachael, please get our guest a glass of wine."

Maria walked to the pickup, circled the truck. She put out her hands and laid them on the Ark.

"It is like electricity, is it not?"

"Yes, it is. Join us please, Señora."

"Lee, Rachael; can you tell me how you did it?"

So Rachael did, including bolt cutters, the cutting torch and the chain saw.

"What do you intend?"

"Maria, it will be better for all if we do not tell you, es verdad?"

"Yes, that is true. But the holy object will be safe, yes?"

"Yes. And the senior members of the Seven will consult with you and the others of the group. I have no desire to be a part of this or of that decision. You must believe me, Maria."

"Sí, Señor Lee. I know."

"Gracias, Señora."

So we sat. And in the eastern sky about midnight there was a shooting star.

Jackson was the first to break the silence: "You know meteors are a portent for momentous events."

We left at five. It's a three hour-drive from Castolon to Alpine. We reviewed what Jackson surmised and what we both guessed. As we rolled into Big Bend Contractors Supply, we were in agreement about four things. First, we'd eliminated Maria, mainly because of the propane incident. Both of us believed there were too many uncontrolled variables for her to have staged it. Second, Juan was the ringleader of the group that intended to sell the mercury. Third, the second and so far unknown person probably worked at Black Gap Wildlife Management Area. Third, we could not agree on the third person. She believed that Bob Potter was somehow involved. I had a number of problems with that. But she made a good case. So, we left it undecided.

We bought a bright yellow, heavy gauge steel, job site box; used a can of black spray paint to scrawl my name and "El Pistolero Supremo" on the top and front. I picked up four combination locks that looked serious enough to deter anyone. Five miles into Big Bend Ranch we stopped and transferred the Ark and the two other crates to the job box.

Luís was pleased that we were coming to see the reconstruction his contractors had accomplished at Los Alamos. Indeed, they had worked miracles. They'd buried Star; towed away my shot-up SUV and the state's pickup. They'd swept out the shattered furniture and the broken glass. Most of the interior and exterior pockmarked walls were filled and painted. We watched them pull out the scarred floors and reinstall new planking. All the windows were in, complete with a newer version of "Southwest motif curtains." The stove and my fridge had been replaced. It was a grand reconstruction. Of course it could never be the same. The shotgun pellets and the AK–47 bullets had forever ended that pastoral idyll.

"It should be ready in two weeks Lee. We hope you will complete the last two months of your residency here. Is that possible?"

"It's beautiful, Luís. I'm amazed. It was pretty damn shot up. Your men have worked a miracle. You bet, I'll be back. I intend to rebuild most of the furniture and leave it for the next writer. I'm having some lumber sent to Sauceda. I have this box with tools in it. I'll be bringing my other things in about ten days. This will be safe here, right?"

"You bet, Lee."

The crew helped us set it down. They used a Ramset to bolt it into the concrete pad outside the kitchen door under the carport. Jackson, Rusty and I loaded up and were headed out when a plasterer walked up to my side of the truck. He handed me a sealed brown envelope. In Spanish he said that the man had given him this letter. He was not to say anything to anyone but El Doctor Lee. I thanked him.

"Let's go, Jackson."

"What is it?"

I tore open the envelope.

"It's a note from Juan. It says, 'I'll contact Charly in three days. We must talk.' Shit Jackson, maybe he wants to give up, to turn himself in to me."

"You are too trusting to have lived this long. He'll kill you this time. He doesn't owe you a life. Call the cops, the FBI, the Texas Rangers. Don't do something stupid. Let them catch him."

"I'll think about." And I did, all the way back to Castolon.

CHAPTER 12: ROAD TRIP

"I'm going to meet him."

It was 5:00 a.m. Jackson and I sat at my oak table having our morning coffee. We laid out the new cards. Many of them pointed to Juan, no surprise there. Some, deduction cards, or surmises we called them, pointed to Potter. Not because we had any strong evidence. We just didn't have any information that excluded him and had plenty that gave him opportunity.

"I knew you would. But I'll go along with this insanity only if you and I call Agent Marks and Ranger Captain Hays before you leave. If you don't, I will. Not to do it is crazy, Lee! Lisa and your kids would never forgive me if I didn't insist on it. And I insist that we share all the information we have with both the FBI and the Rangers. Are you OK with that too?"

It was time. The consequences for not involving law enforcement were too great. I agreed to meet them in San Antonio. I chose a busy restaurant in El Mercado in San Antonio's busy tourist district. After begging them not to come looking like cops, they agreed.

"Lee, can't you tell me what you know over the phone?"

"Absolutely not, Marks. I'll see you in San Antonio day after tomorrow at one-thirty in El Mercado."

Charly owned a restored three-bedroom one story stucco Spanish Revival cottage in the King William Historic District, a neighborhood of exquisitely restored Victorian homes just south of downtown. It was within walking distance of San Antonio's fabulous River Walk. It was also within walking distance of some of San Antonio's finest hole-in-the-wall Mexican restaurants. Her home had a setback gated entrance and was surrounded by a very pleasant, well-designed and formidable six-foot high steel-rod-reinforced concrete wall finished to look like stucco. I punched the entrance code; the steel gates opened and I drove my TPWD pickup inside.

"Cool, huh Rusty?"

His tail was going ninety miles a minute. He knew where we were. Charly was always good for a treat.

The place was jam packed with books, maps, guides and dictionaries. There were three or four very large library tables overflowing with documents, translations and Xerox copies of stuff. In what she called her "Research Center" located in a windowless room in the center of the house, Charly had three very large servers capable of handling and processing huge amounts of data.

"I haven't seen you since you updated your computer search-and-process capacity. But Christ, Charly, you've got enough memory in this room to warehouse, sort and store most of the Library of Congress .That stuff must have cost a mint. I know I pay well, but it sure won't cover that. You must have a new and very affluent client, yes?"

"Yes, Lee; several. But let's not go down that road, OK? Let's sit outside, watch the birds and listen to my new waterfalls. You can tell me the news from Big Bend. By the way, I got the strangest phone call this afternoon from an Agent Carl Marks, FBI. He said that you had information for the both of us. We chatted just a minute or two. I think he is expecting your call. Funny thing; as you know, I sweep my electronics every ten minutes for viruses and bugs. Guess what your agent left behind? A cute little tap. Got any ideas?"

"Sure, it's the FBI Charly. What do you expect? I'll be meeting them and the Rangers tomorrow at El Mercado. I'll tell you the story in a minute. What about the tap? Did you remove it?"

"Lee, of course not. That just makes them crazy. I just diverted it to one of my programs that provides 'almost useful' information. They still believe they're getting new information and I am relieved of the concern that they will try another tap, at least for a week or two."

We sat in the back yard surrounded by burbling waterfalls, the better to mask conversation, and I brought Charly up to date. Rusty thumped his tail on the Saltillo tile and nibbled on treats.

"Lee, you know you're going to have to quit using that antiquated cards-on-the-wall system stuff? You can do the same stuff with a simple laptop."

"Yes, I know. Ranger Jackson told me that too. And eventually I will come into the twenty-first century with that stuff. But not until after this little thing is solved."

"I have some news for you. I've been doing some additional genealogical research using those cute servers and some pretty sophisticated search engines that are newly available. These search engines have some nifty features. You plug in the name or names you want, give them some geographic parameters and some beginning and ending dates and guess what? You get some pretty good, very well-organized info back. Want to see? I've got the spread sheets inside."

"Later, give me the summary."

She summarized. She had plugged in the names of all those people I'd given her. Then she added all the names that seemed associated with the stuff she'd already located for me in the Bexar Archives. Then she dropped in the names of the survivors of the Gutierrez-Magee Expedition of 1813. The dates were 1675 to present. The geographic boundaries were all the Texas counties from Webb County (Laredo) to El Paso County, New Mexican Counties from the border up through Santa Fe along the Rio Grande, and the Mexican states of Coahuila and Chihuahua.

"So, Charly, you got a raft of new data."

"No, just a little. The following families, as we suspected, are related, and those relations go back to the retreat out of New Mexico in 1680—Carbajal, De Sosa, Barrera, Gomez, Gutierrez, Oconor, Arredondo, Galvan. There are more; I just can't pull them up out of my overloaded feeble brain."

"Yes, we knew all that."

"But you didn't know this. Your Captain Bob Potter is a fifth generation Mormon. His people went to Utah in the first wave in 1842, with Brigham Young and that crowd. His family fled to Chihuahua in the 1870s when the U.S. government and the church leadership began moves to outlaw polygamy. They returned fifty years later. And, yes your friend Bob was born in Utah, but he married a woman from Chihuahua. Her family had fled at the same time of Bob's but they didn't return. What do you think?"

"Can't be Charly. Bob's wife is as fair-complexioned as you are. She's not Mexican. Besides her family name is Barkerwood, Bakerfield, Baker or some such."

"It's Bakerfield. And what you mean is that she's not Indio. And she's not; she's Spanish but she is also Mormon. That community never let go of their U.S. heritage. My research indicates that they have always maintained that their point of view would be vindicated. She probably speaks English better than you do. Her mother's family name is De S Carbajal—De Sosa Carvahal. That name ring a bell? She's related to two of the major families who were originally chosen as guardians."

"Oh my God! That's it. Bob wants the Ark. If you and I pieced this thing together then he did too. He had access, even more than I did. He's the third man! I gotta call Jackson. Got a secure phone I can use?"

I called, no answer. Maria and Carlito were away on a field trip. It would have to wait.

"Come on, Lee; I'm hungry. We can walk and talk."

Charly, Rusty and I walked a few blocks north to a small place called "La Comida del Mar." It was owned by a diminutive Mexican lady that everybody seemed to address as Mamacita Luisa. On the way, I explained my problem with Juan's requested meeting. Specifically, I needed a safe place that we could meet. And, frankly, I needed one that would halfway satisfy my need for security, Juan's need for security ,and that would offer the FBI a chance of catching Juan, thus bringing most of this caper to a close.

"The Alamo, Lee, meet him at the Alamo. There's a very large live oak in the Plaza close to the Cenotaph. Meet him there. I suggest you wait on the benches facing the chapel itself, not those facing the street. It is very, very public. He won't try anything there. You'll feel safe, so will he. That might give our fuzz a chance to nab him. What do you think?"

"Great idea. I'll call Marks; tell him our place. Juan may not like it, but he really can't protest too much. After all, the last time we were together he left me in a mine shaft."

And in a few minutes the deed was done.

"Marks, you can't go around tapping the phones of my friends. Take it off now or the meeting is off. Do it now, while we're on this line."

He either did it or they got extraordinarily better at it in a very big hurry. Charly continued her regular electronic sweeps. As I was about to hang up, Marks said: "After we end this call, go to the front yard. Lying inside the entrance gate will be a package. In it are two phones. One is black, the other is silver. Use the black one to confirm our meeting tomorrow. After you use it, drop it in a trash can somewhere. Put the silver one in your pocket. When Juan shows up at the Alamo, put your hand in your pocket and squeeze the sides of it—twice. It will make the call automatically. That's all you have to do. OK?"

I agreed. Charly went to the yard and picked up the package. The phones were as described. She and I spent three hours reviewing new information on the "Legends of the Ark in the New World" book. By now that seemed a little superfluous. But I was determined to write it anyway.

Juan called Charly at midnight. I proposed the place. He initially didn't like it. Although he was calling from what was probably a throwaway cell phone, he didn't want to stay on line long. We set the time for 3:30 tomorrow afternoon at the Alamo.

I called Marks the next morning; confirmed my meeting with him and Juan. As instructed, I dumped the black phone in a trash barrel. When I met Marks and Hays at El Mercado, it was almost like old home week.

"Marks, Hays; we're gonna have to stop meeting like this. Someone is bound to suspect us eventually."

Neither thought the comment at all humorous. Our meeting was cordial and short. I brought them up to date on what I knew about the mercury. They had some pointed questions about my deductions. They could not see how Potter could be involved, or what his motive might be. And, given that

I didn't tell them about the Mormon connection, there was no need. We agreed to disagree. I suggested that meanwhile they press their search for the chopper. I believed that it was still hidden in Big Bend. They thought Juan had flown it to someplace out of the area. I suggested a satellite search with the footprint of the chopper programmed into the search data base. They had zero interest in that approach. It was horribly costly and they didn't think it would work. Justifiably, they were most interested in knowing who bought the mercury and how it would be used.

"OK, guys; I'll ask. I presume that the cute little silver phone is actually also a recorder/transmitter. Please don't answer. I want to know where Juan's chopper is too. I'll do my best."

"Lee, you do the interview with Juan that works for you. If you can get that information, great. If not, we don't want you to do anything stupid like try to apprehend him yourself. This guy is wanted on multiple murder warrants. We'll have a bunch of folks there. If he tries to grab you or cuff you, fight him. More than likely he won't try to shoot you. We'll be close. If the conversation is getting dicey, take your sunglasses off, raise them to the top of your head. We'll move in. Got it?"

"Guys, this is beginning to sound like a 1960s spy movie."

"Believe us, it isn't. This guy is dangerous. Also believe it, we want him alive. We really need to know where that mercury is."

Alamo Plaza in the middle of the day in the middle of the week is always busy. And on this warm late October afternoon the place was jammed. There were two bus loads of German tourists, one bus with French speakers and two busses of seventh graders from the nearby town of Castroville, along with the usual assortment of families, young honeymooners, street people, bongo drummers, and mothers with strollers. It was the perfect place for a meeting of two people who did not wish to be alone with one another, or could not afford to be alone with one another.

At 3:15, Rusty and I took our appointed seats on the concrete benches surrounding the massive live oak. Rusty saw him before I did. His tail wagged and he pawed my leg furiously.

"Mind if I give him a treat? How are you? Look, Lee, I'm no good at this, but I wanted to see you one more time."

"In order: no, give him a treat. And, I'm as fine as a person can be whose longtime friend has betrayed him and has turned into someone that I don't recognize. Other than that I'm OK. You going somewhere? Tell me, how did it get started?"

"How else? I needed the money. Lee, I have terminal cancer, liver disease. I hoped to get a bundle for the family, especially for the kids' college education. The offshore accounts are already set up. If you're wired, these accounts are not traceable, even by the FBI. It was supposed to be a simple deal. We were just going to get those flasks out of there, sell them, and split the money. The flasks were abandoned; there was a market for them. I found the contact; well he actually found me. It was such a simple deal."

Juan related the story to me in detail. How the two vaqueros looking for strays found two bull calves in the mine shaft. They went down, saw the flasks. Everybody knew what they were. They recruited a friend in La Policía de la Frontera.

"He contacted me because I had the contacts on both sides of the border. I brought in the NPS and TPWD people. I brought in the local BP agent. So altogether there were eight, including the vaqueros. The comandante, the vaqueros and I figured out how to get the flasks out. It was simplicity itself. Nobody suspects vaqueros in that area. Dozens of them cross back and forth every week looking for cattle. The vaqueros pulled the flasks out of the sealed mine; packed them over to the place where you found the bodies. Either my chopper or the Policía de La Frontera chopper would take the flasks to the shed where I took you at the north end of Black Gap. The buyer would send a plane to that strip and get the mercury back to Austin, San Antonio or Houston. None of us knew exactly where, or cared. The local NPS and TPWD agents served as look outs. We figured out that it would take only a short time, maybe a month, to get all of them out of there."

"Didn't work out quite that way, did it? What went wrong?"

"I made a deal with a buyer in San Antonio. Turns out he was a middleman. The true buyer contacted me. Turns out, he was a member of the Seven. We established a bond. He found a buyer who would offer more, much more. After we sold the first six flasks at an inflated price, he and I met the other four at the Tinajas Canyon site. The comandante and the other three wanted a new split."

"Juan, we've been calling this guy the 'fifth man'. What was his name?"

"Jose Carvajal Barrera. He was a distant cousin of mine. But he was no friend of mine. When the group revolted and threw down on us, Jose and I shot back in self defense. You found them; it was a real mess. After they were all down, Jose turned to me and said something like, 'I'll just get it all.' He shot at me. I had a 12 gauge and shot him twice at very close range. I bundled the money up, picked up all their gear, his severed arm, and hauled my ass out of there. The next day I met the vaqueros who were attempting to haul out two more flasks. One of them was related to the comandante. They fired; I fired. They died. I think that's about the time you stumbled into this."

"Yeah, I think so. I really wish those bastards had not taken my water north of Mariscal."

"I never thought it would turn out like this. I just wanted to leave Maria and the kids a nest egg."

"What about me Juan. I just stumbled into the damn thing?"

"My partners, all of them wanted you dead. They thought you were too big a risk. We know how that turned out don't we?"

"Juan, I have to know. Who bought the mercury?"
"I don't know."
"What are they going to do with it?"

"I'm not exactly sure. But I overheard something that indicates that they might put in the water supply of the University of Texas at Austin, maybe with a timed bomb. There was something about a ransom. Mercury in that water supply would cause a serious disruption in Austin. That's about all I know. You know where it is, don't you Lee?"

"Know where what is?"

"The Ark, Lee; you know where it is, don't you?"

"I have a pretty good idea."

"Are you gonna do something about it?"

"Juan, should I? Right now, I'm not interested in doing anything about it. Not until something else happens."

"I don't owe you a life any more, you know that, right?"

"Yes, I saved yours; you did not take mine when you could have. We're even. Turn yourself in, Juan. Save Maria the heart ache of a trial. You know they'll eventually find and capture you."

"Maybe, maybe not, Lee. Listen, I know I betrayed our friendship. I am really sorry I did it. Maybe I wouldn't do it again. But I can't fix that. I do ask that you forgive me someday. Will you at least agree to work on that?"

"Yeah. I wish there was a way we could go back, but there isn't. We both know this is not going to turn out well. There's nothing I can do about that right now. But I have two questions for you. The first is, where did you hide the chopper?"

He smiled that quirky smile of his.

"Can't tell you."

"What about the names of your accomplices?"

"Not a chance, Lee. Good-bye. Thanks for pulling me out of that burning truck. I'll always love you."

"Bye, Juan; same here. Vaya con Dios."

"I'm going, Lee; don't try to follow, please."

I raised my sunglasses to the top of my head.

"Wouldn't think of it. Good-bye Juan."

Two agents darted out of the Long Barracks about thirty feet away. Two more came from around the corner of the Alamo Cenataph. I saw a fifth man running toward Juan from the shuttle bus stop about thirty yards down Alamo. Juan may have been ill, but he had his escape route planned. He sprinted across Alamo Street into a crowd of German tourists, plowed through the throngs waiting to buy tickets to the IMAX theater and disappeared down the stairway into the River Walk. The FBI guys were a very poor second. Rusty and I waited by the live oak. Ten minutes later Captain Hays trotted up.

"We lost him. You got any idea where he might have gone?"

"Hays, you guys heard the conversation. You have as much idea as I do. Look, I've done everything I could to get the information from my friend. I tried to get him to surrender. I think he has something else to do. But I don't know what that might be. I think I'm done with this project. You guys want to talk some more, you better call my attorney. Got that?"

"I think we're good, at least for now. Can I have the silver phone?"

Rusty and I walked a couple of blocks, caught the southbound Alamo Street-King William shuttle, and in fifteen minutes I knocked on Charly's gate. She had her look of mild amusement; the one that said without saying, "Didn't catch him huh?"

"Nope. I think he wanted to get away more than they wanted to catch him. I have a feeling he has something else to do. What about you?"

"Come on Rusty; bring your really dense buddy there. Let's go to the back yard. He and I will have a beer. You can have this beef rib bone."

Standing in her kitchen, she popped the tops on some Negra Modelo longnecks, stuck slices of lime in the mouth of each and turned.

"Lee, you don't get it; he's going for the Ark. I'll bet you the cost of next month's utility bill. He and his remaining partners, or partner will go back to Big Bend and go find the Ark. He knows its position about as well as you did, right? Also, does anybody believe that all twelve of those flasks have been located and secured? Marks told you that they'd found one.

And that one was found only on a fluke. Are you headed back to the wilderness?"

"Yes, after I see Lisa. I'd also like to visit with your buddy the Archbishop one more time before completing this road trip. Can you get me in this afternoon or tomorrow morning?"

She retreated inside to make the calls and returned in ten minutes, with a smile lighting up her face.

"You are so lucky to know me. Tonight is out. I did talk with his appointments secretary. The Archbishop will be pleased to grant you an audience tomorrow at 8:00 a.m., if you can come to the cathedral. He celebrates Mass at seven. His secretary suggested that if his Holiness saw you in the congregation he would be very pleased. You think you can do that.?"

"Do I have to wear a tie?"

"No, Lee, it's early morning mass. Just show up in your traveling clothes. Oh, he also said to drive that truck of yours around the south side of the church. Park in the space marked 'Space Reserved for Archbishop.' You're one of the favored few."

I was packed and loaded at six. Charly reviewed the newfound research for me; gave me a sheaf of papers and three disks. She also handed me her latest statement. She stopped at the front door.

"Lee, you're dealing with people who have a lot more at stake than academic tenure. These people have killed a half-dozen men. Their payoff, if it includes the Ark, is in the billions. You understand that, right?"

"Yes I do. I'll be careful."

"Do this for me. Listen and follow the advice of the Archbishop. He is extraordinarily streetwise, especially for a priest. He also knows people you would not be able to contact. He will almost certainly suggest that you meet with certain people in Houston and Galveston. Do it. And one last thing: Do you remember those mountain men from the early 1800s?"

"Yes, Charly, I do. In fact when I was a little kid I wanted to be just like them."

"They had a saying: 'Keep your eyes on the skyline and your nose in the wind.' I know you've heard it. Do it, please. I'm not walking you to the truck. Good-byes suck. Be careful on the road my friend."

And with those happy thoughts swirling in my head, Rusty and I went to Mass. We sat on the second row, at the center aisle. Fortunately for us, mid-week early morning Mass is noted for both its very small number of congregants and for its merciful brevity. Given my particular involvement in a number of precarious adventures at the moment, I thought that Communion might not be a bad thing. Rusty and I both participated. I think it may have been a first for him. I'm certain that it was a first for the Archbishop.

As the service ended, an acolyte approached. She nodded to the door on the right side of the altar and whispered: "Ten minutes, sir."

The Archbishop stood as I entered his small, sparsely furnished study.

"Lee, please join me for a cup of dark roast, yours laced with evaporated milk. Is it permissible to offer Rusty a treat?"

"Father, why not. I've decided that if there is a heaven and if people get to join dogs there, you will be in Rusty's version, especially if your hand holds a treat. Thank you for meeting me."

"I must ask. Have you found it?"

"Yes sir, I have. And I admit that being in the presence of the Ark is a transforming experience. Touching the crate that protects it is electrifying. You can ask my associates."

"Is it safe?"

"Yes Father it is. Father, as I remember my scripture, Jesus was a carpenter. Correct?"

"Yes, Our Savior was such."

"Well, as we speak and for the next several weeks the Ark is being guarded, unknowingly to them ,but guarded just the same, by about fifteen carpenters. Nothing will happen to it there. It is safe."

"Have you opened the crate?"

"No sir. I can't do that. If such a thing happens, it is the duty of the Seven Guardians, not me."

"Lee, my son, do you have any recommendations? Where do you think we should secure it? Should we leave it in the New World? Should we return it to Israel? Should we care for it in the Vatican? I know that the 'End Time' Jews and Christian sects as well as some Moslem groups would wish it returned to Israel or someplace in the Middle East. Do you have an opinion?"

"No sir. I'm not part of the Seven. From what I know, most of which comes from the magnificent research of our mutual friend Charly, they are the Guardians of the Ark. They should make those decisions. But since you asked me, I suggest that the Seven do that in a face to face meeting. As you know, there is at least one vacancy in their number. It is soon to be perhaps more. I believe that a decision of this magnitude should be made by a full complement. Don't you, Father? Do you have any recommendations?"

"Yes, I recommend that you call and visit a certain gentleman in Houston. If you like I'll make the introductory phone call now."

"Who is he?"

"I believe I mentioned him to you before. His name is Rabbi Ray Koen. He is currently the chief rabbi at Temple Beth Israel in Houston. Would you let me find out when he can see you?"

"Of course, Father. But remember I absolutely must go visit my wife Lisa in Austin first. If I don't, she will kill me way before these other people who are already standing in line."

I heard only half of the conversation.

"Ray, this is Diego. And how is Sara? Wonderful! Ray I have Dr. Lee Phillips in my study here at the cathedral. Yes, the same one I spoke of before. He has agreed to visit with you at your convenience. However, he must spend the next two days with his wife in Austin. Yes, I know services are Friday night and Saturday. Yes, Sunday will be fine. At the temple? Yes. I am sure he can find it. Yes, I am certain he will be pleased to meet with the other gentleman. Bless you and your family also. Vaya con Dios, Ray."

And the deal was done. We chatted a few more minutes. I thanked him for the loan of his parking space. Rusty and I headed for Austin and for a long-anticipated conjugal visit with my blond wife.

#

"Rusty, brought the world traveler home, huh? Hey, do I know you, gringo? Oh, I got it. You're the guy who likes cowboy hats and daybreak sex. Come on in cowboy. I see you brought the hat. You know, Lee, I thought that by marrying an academic I'd be hanging out with somebody who had a nice safe, clean and intellectual career. Boy was I wrong. But I tell you; this thing of ours is never dull. I love you. Interested in a glass of wine and looking at Town Lake from the balcony? Or interested in something else? Show me the hand that the guy shot. It looks OK to me. But you're right; no more 'Hook 'Em Horns' signing for you. If you catch the guy who shot your finger off, sue him."

"He's dead Lisa. I shot him in the eye. Sorry, I shouldn't have said that. How about booze and chat first. We'll figure out the rest of the day and evening later. That OK?"

It took a full two hours to get her up to speed, and another hour for her to get me caught up on what she was up to. Lisa is a very intense listener and is very adept with questions. By six I felt like somebody had been beating on me with a hammer.

"Lisa, let's go for a walk or ride bikes around the lake. Then we can come back, eat and rub up against one another."

And we did. Between the walk and rubbing up against one another, a few friends joined us on the balcony. I got caught up on the goings on in Austin, where as Raoul Duke once said, "When the going gets weird, the weird turn pro." About eleven we opened the glass doors from the bedroom to the balcony, lit a dozen candles, popped the cork on a bottle of very, very dry champagne. The late October Texas full moon provided sufficient illumination for me to revel in those delicious lips, rosy nipples, and soft thighs.

I slept until ten the next morning. Rusty woke me, licking my nose.

"Lee, I thought you were headed for Houston. Time's awasting cowboy. Move your skinny butt."

That led to a redo, but not on the balcony. But I can testify that half-dressed sex is incredible! So much left to the imagination! It was enough to wean a man off hanging out in isolated Big Bend without a wife. But not quite. I spent the day and another night in Austin. Rusty and I left at eight the next morning. Getting laid regularly will get more than your mind squared away. Unfortunately, that last nooky put me in Houston at the rush hour which in Houston is 24/7. Saturday and Sunday are no exception.

Temple Beth Israel is on the near southwest side, on Old Spanish Trail. On Sunday the parking lot was empty except for two cars. I opened the door nearest the cars. A very large young man dressed in a very black suit, wearing a yarmulke, and sporting a very large bulge under his left breast pocket stopped me. He was very polite. He asked my business. I told him. He talked into a cell phone earpiece. He then informed me that if I chose to see the rabbi he must frisk me. I saved him the trouble and handed him my Glock .40cal.

"You're expected, Dr. Phillips; down the hall to the left. Third door on the right. My associate will greet you and Rusty."

"What the hell? We have security and armed guards in synagogues these days? What is the world coming to?"

"Sir, there've been two death threats on the rabbi's life in the past six weeks. I apologize for the inconvenience. But it is necessary."

"Holy shit! Excuse me; I apologize if I've offended you."

He said something in Hebrew which I didn't understand, but took to mean 'No problem.'"

That's when it snapped to me. He was expecting me, but he was also expecting Rusty.

"Rusty, the world gets weirder and weirder!"

I'd done a little research too. But first I had to get by the second bodyguard. He was only a little larger and much more heavily armed than the other. I could see the distinct outline of an Uzi machine gun under his coat. After the obligatory pat-down, he ushered me into the Rabbi's office.

"Dr. Phillips, Rusty; welcome. I apologize for the security situation. It is onerous and at times humiliating. Is it permitted to offer Rusty a treat?"

"Of course, Rabbi; everybody else in Texas feeds him. You should too. It is good to meet you. But all of you are going to have to share the expense of sending him to the fat dog spa."

"Please call me Ray. May I call you Lee?"

We agreed on names. We covered the do you know, I know him/her; been there done that in about three minutes. He got down to business.

"You know that Diego is one of the Seven Guardians?"

"I didn't know it, but I suspected it. You recommended him right?"

"Yes Lee, he is the first 'wholly Christian' person to be a member of the Guardians in over one thousand years. However, his family is of the Seven. Did you know that? Do you know what that means?"

"Ray, I knew some time ago that the Archbishop's family name is directly related to the original seven families. I believe it is actually his mother's family name, Arredondo. They go back to the seventeenth century and perhaps before."

"It's before, Lee. The Arredondos came with the Ark from Spain. But let's not get into genealogy. Is the Ark safe?"

"I think you know the answer to that. I'm sure you've discussed all that with the Archbishop. I'm sure he has explained to you my opinions about what should happen next. Yes?"

"Yes, but not quite next. I'd like you to meet someone. But we must go to Galveston. Are you game?"

"Sure. Rusty and I always love a road trip. I'd feel better if we took my truck."

"I'd feel better if we took my armored Lincoln and we'll let my bodyguards drive. The three of us, me, you and Rusty can sit in the back and talk."

"Given the way you put that, I will feel much better if we take your armored Lincoln and we let your bodyguards drive. What the hell is the world coming to? Who wants to whack you? You're a religious man, yes?"

"I'm also outspoken. There are those who do not appreciate that. I've been targeted. Are you interested in knowing anything about the guy we'll be meeting? Never mind. His name is Levi Goldman. He represents a government favorably disposed to the advancement of Jewish interests internationally. You understand?"

We met at one of those strip mall storefront offices about 45th Street and Seawall. We were early. The rabbi, dressed in jeans and a Hawaiian shirt, and I, dressed in jeans, sandals and a T-shirt, took a walk on the beach. We sat on a granite rock on the Galveston beach. We pulled off our shoes and relaxed. It had been a while since I'd squeezed Gulf of Mexico sand between my toes on Galveston Island. Rusty frolicked in the surf, chasing sea gulls. It was a great place to talk, better than trickling waterfalls in San Antonio.

Goldman showed up about thirty minutes late.

Koen did the introductions.

"I'll leave you two gentlemen to discuss your business. I really must visit with a colleague at Temple B'nai Israel. Mr. Goldman, please call me when you gentlemen are about to conclude your business."

"Dr. Phillips, thank you for meeting me. Do you have any idea what you've become embroiled in?"

"I'm pretty sure not. But I am convinced that it is larger than twelve flasks of mercury. But before we continue I need to know exactly who you represent."

"Certainly, Dr. Phillips. Here is my passport and my identification card. Here is another, and another, and, oh yes, one more."

I looked at them. I had a fistful of passports and identity cards. Every name and country and occupation was different. I looked up; he smiled.

"Please, for our purposes my name is Levi Goldman. I think you know the government I represent. I am here to discuss not the flasks, but the other object, the Ark. Do you have it?"

"Here? No, I don't have it here. And to save us some time, I do know where it is. It is safe, absolutely and completely safe. And, I am not going to make the decision about who will receive custody. Nor will I make any decision concerning its future whereabouts. Are we clear on that? That is the job of the Seven."

"Sir, my government wishes to make the case for not returning the Ark to the Middle East, at least not overtly. We believe that to do so would set the region on a course so destructive that neither you nor I can conceive of its fallout. And I mean that last term literally. As you know there are those on all sides of the current unpleasantness who would wish to control the Ark and use it for their own purposes."

"Yes I realize that. I also know that the ultimate realization of the Return, if you will, is that the Ark will be returned to its rightful place in the Temple on the Mount. I'm not Jewish, but I can understand that certain political 'imperatives' might stand in the way of such a public return."

"It's an old struggle, Dr. Phillips. The return of the Ark is not going to solve it. Nor will it stop it. Do you know the identity of the fifth man you found?"

"Yes. His name was Jose Carbajal Barrera. Juan told me about him. But that's about all I know about him. Well, that, and he was missing most of a face and all of an arm below his bicep when I found him in that little box canyon south of Mariscal Mine. And that he had a very small, but very important tattoo."

"OK, here is the short version. Jose Carbajal Barrera was actually born in Eagle Pass, Texas. He is a distant cousin of your Juan Barrera. In 1948 his parents emigrated to the new state of Israel. They were ardent Zionists and they were very conservative. Young Jose grew up in a community of zealots who believed that when the Ark returned to the Temple Mount, Israel would reign supreme over the Middle East. His father was one of the Guardians, and at his deathbed in 1967 named young Jose as his replacement. The other members of the Seven ratified that decision without ever meeting young Jose. For some time our records and information indicated that this Jose C. Barrera was unstable and unpredictable. So for us he was a security risk. However, he did make an excellent informant. When he left Israel two years ago we continued to monitor his activities. We were not surprised when he and your Juan Barrera connected. After all, they were cousins. And we were not surprised when he and Juan Barrera decided on the present course of action."

"You weren't? I sure as hell was. I've known Juan Barrera for twenty years. I'm sure you know the story. I have been on a constant 'surprise trail' since I found those dead guys splattered all over that canyon. I've been threatened with jail, had my finger shot off, had my pack horse killed, my home destroyed. Shit, Goldman, I can't ever go back to the life I had before these events! And right now I have some serious SOBs dedicated to terminating my 'Standing Upright on the Planet, Breathing on my Own' privileges. So my question to you, Mr. Representative of Unstated Foreign Government, is where do we take it from here, *and* just what can you and your government do to help me?"

"Lee, Dr. Phillips; here are two cell phones. Both are encrypted; both are satellite. I imagine that you have only one associate. One phone is for you, the other is for him or her."

"Goldman, Big Bend is not satellite nirvana. Cell phones don't work and satellites work maybe sometimes."

"Lee, these will work. We, that unnamed government, have three satellites totally dedicated to receiving calls from these two and from three others. I'll tell you this; one of those three is tucked in Rabbi Koen's suit pocket. You call; we'll be there. Or, to put it a way you Americans understand, "Operators Are Standing By." By the way, in the interest of full and open discussion, we have been and are continuing to cooperate with both Agent Carl Marks and Ranger Captain Hays. We've found them to be above reproach.

"I do suggest that you work with the rabbi and with Marks and Hays to deal with this in some final way. You cannot be one of the two people who know where the Ark is located. Eventually someone will force either you or the other person to tell them. It will not be pretty. And believe me, you will tell them what they wish to know. Do you understand?"

"Yes, that I do believe. Well, I think I have work to do both with the rabbi and back at the ranch. I will count on the support."

"De nada, amigo."

"I really must get back to Castolon. I think we both have phones that will work. I'll be in touch. If you don't hear from me, you'll hear from an NPS officer named Rachael Jackson. Her maiden name was Arredondo."

CHAPTER 13: BLACK GAP GUNFIGHT

Castolon was a welcome respite. I actually worked on the "Legends" book for a day, then put it aside. It didn't seem relevant. Rusty and I took a day trip to Los Alamos. The guys were working furiously on the exterior. The job box sat under the carport, exactly where we left it with sturdy combination locks securely attached. Next day, Rusty and I took Pepper and Ace on a two day camping trip east toward Mule Ear. We dawdled and piddled. Lisa calls it "putzing." Long ago I figured out what I like about the desert. It is quiet. There are no people, people who beeble, talking nonsense, people who after about two minutes sound like a bird cage full of Zebra finches. Well, that's not fair. The finches make more sense. The days were clear, a welcoming warm. The nights were cold, little wind, not harsh. The dawns were filled with a hundred colors of pink, then orange shades that were quickly transformed into incredibly blue sky. Those clear, fall, turquoise blue skies were balanced by millions of stars draped across the night sky.

The world was almost perfect, except for the missing mercury flasks. Then there was the question: What to do with the Ark? Jackson and I would be forced to make that decision pretty damn quick.

The sixth day back, Jackson and I sat at the oak table working on the cards. Except now we pretty much had it figured. Shortly after ten in the morning the phone rang. It was Marks.

"Lee, you marked those flasks with some sort of code didn't you?"

"Yeah, I did. I put my initials and the month and year on the bottom. Then I smudged it with my finger."

"Could you identify your own marks?"

"Sure. Why?"

"We think we know where they are, over at Black Gap somewhere. We want you to go with us, to help identify these specific canisters. Bring Jackson, too, if she's around. But you can't carry your pistol."

"No sale Marks. It'll never happen. If you change your mind, you let me know. Otherwise you can ID those babies by yourself."

"We really do need you, Lee."

"I don't care; I'm not going in there unarmed. Call me when you get back."

"OK Lee, you win. We'll deputize you as a Federal Marshal for a specified time period. You OK with that?"

"Do I get a badge?"

"No, Lee; no damn badge."

"Shoot! Man, I am real disappointed! OK, I'll do it. But I'm telling you, my grandfather Samuel Adolphus Phillips, who died when I was six, is spinning in his grave right about now. He didn't have no truck with what he called 'the Yankee Law.' And if he was still alive I'd have to do an awful lot of explaining. When are you guys coming?"

"We're leaving Alpine at four in the morning. We'll pick you and Jackson up about six. You'll have some of that great coffee, right? And would it be asking too much for Maria to do about a dozen huevos y chorizo tacos?"

"It's not a problem Marks. But those tacos, those babies, especially at that hour, will cost you and your guys three bucks each. OK? No checks, no credit cards. Cash only, small bills."

"Lee, why don't you just stick a gun to my head? Hell, yes we'll pay. See you mañana."

"Marks, how many choppers? How many agents?"

"Just one chopper. There will be two FBI, two Rangers, Rusty, you and Jackson. That's six, well six and a half. Both of the FBI agents are armed with M16 semi-autos and 9mil Berettas. The Rangers have .40 caliber Glocks just like yours. Well, they have the large-frame edition. They also carry 12 gauge pumps. It should be enough firepower. Our agents tell us that the bad guys are long gone. I'm comfortable with that."

"Marks, you're crazy. I wouldn't go into that country blind with less than three choppers crammed full of guys packing full auto weapons, pistols, knives, grenades, garrote wires, night sticks, everything. But Jackson and I are in, if you deputize me and her. And I am carrying my Glock and my M1 with as much ammo as I can stuff in my pockets."

"Christ Lee, you can't do that. You're a civilian! This may be Texas, but, dammit, you can't go carrying an automatic weapon around a state park as a civilian. Can't let you do it."

"First, it's not an automatic weapon; it's a semiautomatic weapon. And second, if it don't go, I don't go. End of story. Oh, and it's not a state park; it's a Wildlife Management Area."

Jackson piped up: "If Lee doesn't go, I don't think I can participate in this adventure."

"OK, but don't use it unless I say so. Got it?"

"You bet."

#

It was still almost pitch black when the chopper arrived around six the next morning. Marks first words were, "Let's eat, everybody."

Everybody ate $3.00 tacos on Maria's front porch. They washed them down with my incredible dark roast coffee. Everybody strapped on bullet proof Kevlar vests. They offered me a helmet. I've always thought the new, and one must assume safer, helmets used by the police and armed forces look vaguely like those "coal scuttle" helmets worn by the German army in World War II. I declined. I stuck with my battered black felt Stetson. Before we took off, I handed Jackson the second "friendly government" phone.

Then we were off to catch the bad guys, or at least find the flasks. The first stop was the shed where Juan had forced me to unload a bunch of flasks. To nobody's surprise we found nothing. Then we landed at a remote hunting camp on the far northeastern edge of the refuge. It had a small dirt airstrip and a 20'x 20' shed. Nothing there, either.

"Marks, Hays; you guys ought to try the La Linda sector maintenance compound. It's closest to the border. It also has the longest airstrip and a huge metal storage shed. I was there once. As I remember it is about 150 feet long and about 60 feet deep. It's divided into three large bays. Think of each of them as a really roomy garage without a garage door. The shed might be roomy enough to hide a chopper and a couple of trucks. Come on; give me a break. When we find the stuff you can pretend I'm a hero."

I think I was the only one to find that at all humorous. Jackson gave me a look like, "How about you just shut up?" Which I did.

I don't know what war movies these guys had watched. They sure didn't watch the same ones I did. Everybody knows, you pick your target; you come straight at it; you land hot, no circling. Everybody boils out of the chopper guns blazing. You kill everything and everybody standing. The theory is: Let God sort 'em out. You count their dead; chop off the assorted souvenir ears, fingers, and so forth. Well, maybe the Rangers and the FBI couldn't do that; but they sure could in the war movies. Then you choose and collect your war booty. Then you leave. End of story. Next?

Marks didn't do any of that. He had the chopper circle twice. That gave plenty of warning to the bad guys if any were around. He did have the chopper land at the end of the building, rather than at the center. That gave a bit of cover. We hit the ground hard. The agents and Rangers sprinted for cover at the end of the metal storage shed. I hunkered down under the chopper body. Rusty lay on the chopper floor.

While the rotors were still turning a burst of automatic weapons fire shattered the windshield. The pilot's head exploded. So much for bulletproof vests. I watched his fingers twitch on the stick as his blood ran down his arm and pooled on the floor of the chopper. We lost an FBI agent in the first ten seconds, cut down by a burst of automatic weapons fire from a window on our end. Given the full auto fire pouring out of that building we were in deep doodoo. We were outgunned every way you can think of. I figured four guys blasting away.

"Rusty, come. Go!" Five fist clenches meant he was to haul ass for fifty yards. I pointed my arm away from the shed and Rusty took off. The chopper was not the safest place to be. Hearing was not going to be my problem for the next few minutes. I grabbed the M1 from under the peanut gallery seats in the chopper; ducked behind the aft end away from the shed; fired three clips of eight rounds each into the side of the shed, about waist high, from front to back. An M-1 makes a weird "Piiing" when it ejects the spent clip. After the third "Piing" the shooting from inside stopped. The agents looked at me like I had a magic stick.

"Guys, it's only an M1. This one happens to be about sixty years old. But a .30–06 jacketed bullet will go through a tin shed like Sherman through Georgia. It will permanently stop just about anything it comes in contact with."

"Holy shit, Lee; you shouldn't have done that."

"Marks, even with no badge I'm an official, certified Federal Marshal, right?"

"Yeah, but . . . ."

"No buts. It's either real or it's not. Which is it, El Jefe Federale?"

"It's real."

"Cool. Now, we gonna talk or we gonna shoot? Do we figure out a way inside this puppy or wait for them to make the next move?"

"We gotta take 'em out, don't you think?"

"Yes, sir."

Marks, Hays, and the other Ranger went through the side door. Jackson and I rounded the front of the shed and there was the dead guy, well, the almost dead guy. He was dressed in a Class A TPWD Law Enforcement uniform, brass, duty belt, shined shoes and everything. Unfortunately for him he had left his Kevlar vest at home. He had three very big holes. Two were in his chest; the third was in his gut. Blood was everywhere, soaking into the La Linda dust. Bloody foam bubbled from his lips; his breath was shallow and ragged. He died as Jackson leaned over him to hear his whispers.

This bay of the shed was empty. Well, empty except for the dead guy.

"What next, Marks?"

Hays saw the white flag first.

"I think they want to surrender."

Jackson shouted: "Not a chance Hays. These guys have nothing to lose. They're up to something. Trust me."

"OK, men, watch out."

Marks shouted: "Guys inside the shed, throw your weapons out; come out with your hands up. When you come out of the shed twenty feet, turn to your left and stop with your hands above your head. Do not move. I repeat, do not move. This is FBI Special Agent Marks. Dip the flag three times if you understand and agree to comply with these orders."

The flag dipped three times. There was silence. Then: "Wait a minute; we're talking" from inside the shed.

Even an almost deaf guy can hear the unmuffled roar of a chopper, and that is what happened about two minutes later. The green and white BP chopper cranked and accelerated. And there it was, charging through the far opening of the shed. It wasn't rising; it aimed straight at us. We were the ones standing in front of the shed, mouths open. A man ran towards the chopper from the middle bay. Someone, probably Marks or Jackson, cut him down. Everyone in the chopper fired at all of us with full auto weapons. Bullets bounced and pinged everywhere. All of us were fully involved in those maneuvers called "ducking and crawling." Some would call it "Ducking and Puckering." From our point of view it looked and sounded like both the pilot and the passenger and were firing at the unlucky stiffs on the ground. A Ranger yelled: "I'm hit!"

Jackson, Marks, and I crab-crawled our way to the almost-safety of the second bay filled with tractors, a bushhog and assorted ranch equipment. All of us dropped to the ground and hugged Mother Earth as bullets bounced off the farm equipment steel.

Hays grabbed the wounded Ranger and dragged him into the relative safety of the second bay.

The pilot revved the turbine engine, and the machine leaped into the air about twenty feet and accelerated around the corner of the shed, toward where our chopper sat. All of us ran outside, weapons ready. We were just in time to see the BP chopper hook one skid under our chopper's main rotor and snap it off like kindling.

The detached rotor blade pinwheeled toward us. It was not a pretty sight. Everybody ran like hell. That damn rotor bounced all over, whipping and twisting. Huddled against the side of the shed I saw the BP chopper turn. The passenger fired a final "your their heads down" burst. Then the damn chopper rotated. The pilot saluted and was gone, headed west. Call this inning for the bad guys.

"Juan, you son of a bitch!" I screamed.

We were in a lot of trouble. We had two dead, plus one Ranger with a leg wound that was seeping blood regardless of what Hays did to control it. Marks and Jackson did a quick recon.

"Lee, come look at these flasks. Let's see if these were some of the ones you saw in the shaft."

And they were, but there were only four. They found one in San Antonio, purely by accident. These four came with a heavy price—two of our guys dead, two of theirs. My mental addition/subtraction said that seven of these things were out there someplace, each containing seventy-six pounds of poison. The good guys had been able to capture less than half of the missing flasks. We were not exactly ahead of the game here. Crouching in the dirt, I identified these as some I had marked back at the Mariscal Mine shaft.

Marks used his satellite phone to call the El Paso office of the FBI. According to him; "They would get right on it."

He then called the Border Patrol check station about thirty miles north of Panther Junction. They were short staffed, but promised to send help as soon as possible. They figured they could make it in about ten hours. First they'd have to get a chopper from El Paso, blah, blah, blah.

237

While I fooled around eyeballing the flasks, Jackson attempted to get us some help. We didn't have any cars, trucks, or choppers. We had water, no food. We had a wounded guy who needed medical attention pronto. And we were pretty close to being in the center of nowhere.

Jackson fished her new "friendly government" satellite phone that Goldman had given me from her pants pocket. There were several numbers taped to the back. She dialed the one at the top.

"I need the number for the Policía de la Frontera HQ in Ciudad Acuña, across the Rio Grande from Del Rio. Can you give me that number?"

That kind of priority can get you pretty much anything you want pretty damn quick.

"Jackson, most phones won't dial Mexican numbers."

"Lee, you want to hear it ring? Shut up. Get a pencil out just in case we need to take notes or something."

"La oficina del Comandante Felipe de Lara Oconor."

"Felipe, cómo está? Con permiso, I have some friends here who only speak English. I'll speak English if that is agreeable?"

She explained our situation—one wounded, no food, some water. She talked with Felipe about the renegade BP chopper; asked him to call his U.S. counterpart in El Paso or Del Rio. In about five minutes, according to Jackson, help was on the way.

Marks was impressed; so was Hays. I sure as hell was too.

Marks found his voice first: "OK, Jackson, what next? You can't tell me that they'll just hop in some 4x4s, cross the closed and guarded international border at the La Linda Bridge and get here inside of six hours."

"No, Marks, they can't; well, they could. But they're not. First they don't have anything at La Linda that can help us. Just a few lightly armed infantry troops guarding their side of the bridge. Second, just dealing with the bureaucracy on our side would take longer than six to eight hours. So, they're flying in. Oconor should be here in three hours or so with two choppers."

"Bullshit, Jackson. You can't get permission for the armed forces of one nation to bring two military choppers full of armed soldiers across this international border in two weeks, let alone two hours."

"Wake up, Marks. This is Big Bend, not Washington, DC or El Paso. Who said anything about getting permission? They'll just follow the river on the Mexican side until they get to a suitable crossing place, a place where our radar or satellites don't pick them up. They'll cross; they'll be here when the comandante said. His family has been in this country for 400 years. He knows it like you know your backyard. Now, let's see if we can't keep our guy alive until they get here."

Hays made his man as comfortable as possible. Jackson, Marks and I did a thorough search and inventory of the site. There was a chemical toilet in a curtained off area of the shed, a 200-gallon tank of drinking water and 10 fifty-five gallon barrels of fuel for the turbine engine of the chopper. Ten more empties lay out behind the shed. These guys had been flying missions to someplace other than Castolon and Marathon.

Marks broke the silence: "Shit, we're in a world of hurt. No wonder we can't locate these bastards in Texas or the U.S. They're flying this stuff to someplace in Mexico. Got any ideas Jackson?"

"No, sir. I can't imagine where."

"Lee, got any ideas?"

"Only one. Let's assume that our boys want to sell this stuff to the highest bidder. And that those people want to get it where it'll do them the most good. That of course means the most damage, right?

"Flying into Mexico is stupid. Mexican radar is not quite as sophisticated as ours, but it is good. They will pick you up within a few miles south of the border. The closest places would be inland at least one hundred miles. And then you're no place useful to you. You're going the wrong way. So, to me that leaves three directions. There's north. But Juan only had clout in the border area. Besides you'd have to fly all the way to

239

Pecos, Midland or some town on U.S. 90 for it to be useful. You'd attract too much attention.

"My choices would be either El Paso, Del Rio, or Laredo. If you take the flasks to El Paso, to me that means you're headed to the west coast with them. Remember me, these guys were my friends. I never heard of either of them mentioning friends or associates on the west coast. On the other hand, they never contacted me about high jacking twelve flasks of mercury either. I sure can't claim infallibility. So my money is on either Del Rio or Laredo. Juan has connections all along the border. He can make up some story that other Border Patrol agents would accept. Marks, you got any idea what the range of that chopper is? You guys use something similar, right?"

Marks thought a few seconds. "Yeah, It will do about 500 miles on a full load of fuel. You could do the Del Rio round-trip on one tank of gas. But you may be right, Lee. Del Rio might not be the place. You could fly that trip on a fill-up here. But even then you'd be flying on fumes the last fifty miles coming back here unless you had a re-supply at the drop off point. What do you think about that idea Lee?"

"You're right Marks, Jackson. It's a simpler trip but why bother. Laredo gets you a lot more than Del Rio. If I were these guys I'd want to get this stuff out of this barren, sparsely populated country. I'd want it surrounded by commerce, semi tractor trailers, airplanes, people going and coming. My vote is Laredo. Ship this stuff in a semi up I-35, the main line of Mid-America. You could run this stuff all the way to Canada and never change interstate numbers. You could move this stuff anywhere you want once you get it to Laredo.

"But here's the trick. You can't simply land this BP chopper in downtown Laredo and say, 'I got contraband, come buy!' Where, close to Laredo, does the BP have the most emergency strips or chopper landing pads? Which direction from Laredo?"

Hays chimed in: "North and northwest. It is very remote, but you would still need some sort of road access."

Jackson added her nickel's worth: "Lee is making sense Marks. The amount of money the buyers are paying, I think Laredo is the spot. The closer these guys get this stuff to their buyers the better their selling price is going to be. Hays, don't you guys have a Ranger unit in Laredo. They ought to have some pretty solid contacts there, on both sides of the border?"

"Yeah we do, but I can't really call them from here. As soon as we can get our butts to some semblance of civilization I can begin to get some answers. Jackson, can I borrow that phone for this?"

"I'm sorry Hays; I think it's out of gas."

Almost four hours from the minute Jackson called Oconor, the two Mexican Policía de La Frontera choppers popped over the southeastern horizon. Rusty heard them before any of us saw them, for good reason. They were running black, no lights on until they got within a half mile of the shed. Then it was like being in a strobe light show. Literally five million candlepower of hot bright light swept the area. They circled twice.

In English and Spanish through very loud, very loud speakers a voice said very clearly: "This is the Mexican Frontier Police. Step out in the open. Face the helicopter. Put your weapons on the ground. Do not, repeat, do not move until instructed to do so."

"Everybody do it," said Marks. "Now."

And everybody did. Oconor landed the choppers. Identified himself, and motioned the paramedics to the wounded man. He greeted his distant cousin Rachael Arredondo Jackson. He too gave his regrets about the end of her marriage. He carried greetings from their cousin Diego Sanchez. Only then did he apologize for the rudeness of requiring the FBI and the Texas Rangers to lay down their arms.

"Although I did enjoy it, at least for a moment," he said.

After retrieving his weapons, Hays broke the shocked silence. Comandante, I think this is a very rare event, a Texas Ranger surrendering even temporarily his weapons to a Mexican officer. That aside, I really need to get my man to a doctor and a real ER. Can you help us out with that?"

"Ranger Hays, I've contacted the Border Patrol inspection station between Panther Junction and Marathon. I told them of your need. They have informed me that an EMS chopper out of Alpine will meet my helicopters at that station. Your man will be in the ER in Alpine Regional in about two hours after we take off. I do have a small problem. We will need fuel at the inspection station or we cannot return home. Do you have any ideas how to deal with this problem."

We all laughed, even the wounded guy.

Jackson piped up, "Sorry Felipe, please let me show you. We have barrels and barrels of fuel. Enjoy! Believe me, you have no worries about fuel. Can you fly us to Alpine?"

"Sorry, amigos. The BP station north of Panther is as far north as we go. I'm probably breaking about three hundred rules of my government right now, just being here. I could be court-martialed. I could serve twenty years in a Mexican Army prison. Believe me, neither you nor I want to do that. That doesn't count the international incident that would explode if the Mexican army "invaded" Alpine. I can get your man to that station. We'll land before the EMS chopper gets there. My professional friends at BP will ensure that this remains private. I'm sure you understand? I'm sure your associates in the government of the United States can find you a ride. Es verdad?"

Marks' curiosity could not be contained: "Please pardon this question, Comandante, but your English is impeccable. Where did you learn to speak it? You grew up in northern Mexico, yes?"

"Well, yes and no. As for my English, my family has been bilingual for over 300 years. And, of course, four years at one of the finest universities in the United States did not hurt."

I couldn't resist: "And when did you graduate from the University of Texas, Comandante?"

There was this silence, then a little laugh, a chuckle.

"Sorry, Dr. Phillips; wrong university, although a great one. I did the Law Enforcement program at Texas A&M—Gig 'Em Aggies!"

"Touché Comandante! Hook-em." I held up my now Longhorn/shorthorn salute.

"Sorry about your wound, sir. But I hear you gave a good account of yourself."

Marks chimed in: "Well, he also nailed one of the smugglers, terrorists or whatever with that antique weapon of his. Can we load these two dead guys into one of your choppers as well? I think we have body bags, or we can improvise. We'd like to get them to a lab. Besides, the critters out here might like them as much as those in that little canyon where Dr. Phillips found the five bodies. Let's saddle up; get our guy to the inspection station. By the way, can you take us back to Del Rio with you? It's the closest place we have an FBI Field Office. We have some fugitives who we just might catch if we can get to Ciudad Acuña or Del Rio tonight. We can begin making phone calls."

Felipe agreed, reluctantly, "I can get you to Acuña."

It was a short hop to the BP inspection station north of Panther on U.S. 385. Their Kleig lights lit up the central part of Brewster County—literally one hundred lumens of light. Their lights threw a shadow for ten miles. No circling this time. Oconor landed hot; we pulled out our wounded guy out. Hays stayed with him. Marks, Jackson and I collected some sandwiches and Cokes offered by the BP guys. Rusty and I took a leak in the lee of the lead chopper. Oconor trotted over to his counterpart; they both saluted and we were gone in less than two minutes, no running lights. This little exchange looks like something these guys had done before. Next stop, Del Rio.

Felipe called ahead. Three Mexican Army camo Suburbans met us at the chopper pad south of town. He offered to put us up at the base. We declined, preferring to be transported to the border.

"Carl, Lee, Rachael; it's midnight. Border traffic is slow at this hour in Del Rio. Have you folks looked in a mirror? I'm telling you, the way you look, both La Policía de la Frontera and the U.S. Border Patrol will think twice about admitting, particularly since you're carrying some pretty serious ordinance.

It is a serious felony in both countries to do that. Stay overnight here. Eat, take a bath; sleep. I'll even find someone to bring Rusty dinner. If you need a phone, we'll furnish that. OK? I'll personally escort you across the border tomorrow. Tonight you can make your calls and arrange transportation."

Rachael and I used our special phones to contact the folks back in Castolon. We even allowed Marks to make one or two. However, we did not allow him to access the three numbers on the backs of our phones.

"This is the best reception I've ever heard on the border. Where the hell did you guys get these?"

In chorus, Jackson and I: "Don't ask Carl, please. Think of them as a friendly loan from an ally."

"Shit, I wish I had allies like that."

The Mexican Army has their version of Reveille. Like on American bases the Mexican bugle-call wake-up is a recording. It happens at 4:30 a.m. Felipe met us for breakfast at 5:00. Rusty was apparently the first dog in Mexican Army history allowed in the dining hall. The four of us dined with the officer corps. Comandante Oconor introduced us around.

Someone, probably Felipe, had told them about my hearing deficiency. They all talked loudly. Rusty has this quizzical look when people speak loudly to me. He cannot tell if they are friends or bad guys. It freaks him out. I politely asked the young officers to please look at me. Please talk slowly in a normal volume, in either English or Spanish. All were excellent students at speaking to deaf people-excruciatingly so. But I was a minor characters in this tableau. Rusty was the center of their attention. About twenty soldiers told me that he was the very first dog they'd seen in any Mexican Army dining hall. They fed him; they petted him; they fed him again. He and I would need a very strict diet when this caper ended.

Seemingly by magic, toilet articles and clean and appropriate clothes appeared in our rooms at dawn. We no longer looked like derelicts or down-and-out drug dealers. Equally magically, three camo Chevy Suburbans appeared, driven by immaculately turned-out Mexican Army sergeants. It is amazing what connections will do. We, the four of us seated in the middle Suburban, breezed across the border into Del Rio, Texas. Everybody we saw saluted. No one even glanced in the cargo bed of the Suburbans, loaded with serious firepower. At the U.S. Border Patrol inspection station on the U.S. side we changed the camo Suburbans for three very black Suburbans with very dark windows. A Border Patrol agent transferred the luggage and the firearms.

Marks informed the BP sergeant and the Del Rio Police Department Captain who greeted us to take us to the Del Rio FBI office located in the U.S. Federal Building in downtown as fast as possible. Ten minutes later we all ordered coffee and Marks was ordering electronic GPS maps of the area around Laredo. He put the BP Captain of the Laredo office, and the FBI Agent in Charge of the Laredo office on the speaker phone. In an hour, we had isolated five possible landing sites. The BP captain volunteered that he'd heard from Captain Barrera by radio only three days ago. It was something about a secret mission, need to know only. Barrera was his senior. He agreed to keep it hush-hush.

The Texas Rangers loaned us one of their choppers to supplement the one Marks borrowed from the Laredo PD. We found the site on the third try. It was the classic ranch landing strip. This one was set in a slight bowl, a slight depression that protected it from the prying eyes of U.S. and Mexican radar. It had the obligatory wind sock stuck on a twenty-foot- tall metal pole that was bolted to a 10x10 metal shed.

No circling this time. The two choppers landed thirty yards from the shed. Everybody except me and Rusty boiled out of those choppers, probably a repeat of Black Gap. They immediately took cover. Marks used one of those screeching FBI bullhorns. He called for those inside, if there were any inside, to come out with their hands up. No sounds and no movement. They waited two minutes, then at his signal they charged. Someone produced a set of bolt cutters and in about thirty seconds they were inside.

"Lee, come on over; leave the M1."

Sure enough, there they were—two flasks.

"Can you ID these?"

Indeed I could and indeed I did. But my crucial identification was upstaged by Jackson calling from outside. She pulled a tarp back and there sat five 55-gallon drums of chopper turbine engine fuel.

"You think that's scary. Let me show you this."

We followed her around to the back of the shed. Five empties lay on their side.

Marks spoke first: "What now, boys and girls, what next? Jackson, any ideas?"

"When we find the truck attached to the tires that made those tracks outside, we'll find the last five of these things—maybe. But I don't think we'll find any of them close to here. Whoever has the last five has at least fifteen hours head start. Those things are headed up I-35."

"Lee?"

"I think Jackson's right. I also think this: If the black market value of that stuff is $500 an ounce, and it is probably more, then the street value of those five flasks is about $3,000,000. That is a helluva lot of money. The FBI or Homeland Security might find those last five. But you gotta admit that you boys, the FBI and the Rangers are batting barely over .500. And when it comes to this kind of toxic metal, that is not good. I also think you won't find them in this county, or maybe even this state. But the other problem is that our guys have flown the coop. We know they have about 500 miles range on their chopper. But I have no better idea than any of you where they're headed. And I'm tired. I think I've had all the fun I can have being a Temporary Deputy Special Agent or Marshal, or whatever. I'll be leaving the Law Enforcement to you people. You folks are the professionals at this. I think it's time for this amateur to bow out and for you pros to go to work unencumbered. Now if somebody can get me and Rusty to a plane or chopper that can get us back to Big Bend, I'll be a happy camper. Jackson, you coming?"

"Thanks for including me, Agent Marks. But I need to get back to my park, too."

It took a full eight hours, but by dusk we were home.

CHAPTER 14: REDEMPTION

"Señor Lee, it is difficult to believe that it was only about a month ago you rode into the compound to report finding the dead men."

"A lot has happened since then Maria."

Maria, Jackson, and I sat on my porch. We drank hot chocolate laced with peppermint schnapps and watched the fading sun.

"You know ladies, I've probably seen five hundred of these sunsets. I'm in awe; I'm stunned every time. Just when I believe that it is impossible to invent a new shade of orange, yellow or mauve, there it is. I'm telling you; if there is a Heaven it is a place where dogs go and sunrises and sunsets are."

The cool October evenings had given way to cold November evenings. When the radiant heat fell below the horizon at Santa Elena it got cold, quick. While we were away adventuring with the Border Patrol and the FBI, Carlito had built a third wall on the simple shed for Pepper and Ace. He had taken on the responsibility of caring for the animals. Each evening he checked their water, added bedding and, if it was supposed to be below freezing, bundled them into their horse blankets. Before catching the school bus in the morning he removed their blankets, fed them, and turned them loose in the small corral.

He had not returned from a short ride on Ace. Saddle mules were rare in this part of the world. Carlito was enthralled. We saw him at a trot coming up the Santa Elena Road with Rusty leading the way.

"Maria, after you two have dinner and after Carlito goes to bed, would you join Jackson and me in my living room? We have some thinking to do and some decisions to make about the final disposition."

"Sí, Señor Lee. We must talk. We cannot leave the Ark where it is. The carpenters will be finished soon and the job box will become very obvious. I'll come about nine."

Maria arrived as promised. We sat in front of the wall of index cards and discussed possible courses of action. Mostly we made lists—well, card lists of possibilities.

Suddenly Jackson said: "Look everybody, we can't be sure our decisions are implemented until Juan and Bob are out of the picture. Either of you heard anything from Agent Marks or Ranger Captain Hays?"

Neither of us had.

"So, if the FBI or the Rangers don't capture them what do you think Juan and Potter will do? Maria, you've known them longer than almost anyone else."

"No, Señor Lee has known them longer. But I think they will come for the Ark. Will they not? Don't you agree Señor Lee?"

"Yes I do. We found seven flasks. That leaves five unaccounted for. Both of them need much more money than those five will bring. Yes, I think they will come for the Ark. Juan knows pretty damn well where it was, and maybe even where it is. I borrowed maps from Bob. So he probably has a fair idea as well. What to do? I recommend that until the Rangers or the feds catch them, no one of us or Carlito is ever alone in the compound. I also recommend that everybody be armed, especially at night. If everybody is OK with that, how about tomorrow we tackle the logistics of getting the Seven together. They're the ones who should make the decisions about the Ark. Everybody OK with that idea?"

"Señor Lee, can we discuss this issue in two days? I wish to ask you to accompany me to a parents' meeting at the Marathon High School tomorrow evening. Rachael will be here with Carlito. We will return before ten. They will be safe."

I protested. I recommended that they come with us to the meeting. But everybody's mind was already made up. Maria, Rusty and I left about three. We met the school bus when we turned north on U.S. 385 to Marathon. We waved; all the kids waved.

The meeting seemed to last forever. Since I knew a little something about curriculum, Maria had asked me to address some of the parents' concerns about changing the history textbook for the seventh and eleventh grades. I did. But I don't think my talk changed a single mind. There was much discussion and no consensus reached.

It was after ten when we headed back to Castolon.

As we turned the last corner and pulled up the grade into the compound we both noticed that all the lights were out, every single one.

"Maria, don't you usually leave the store porch lights on?"

"Oh, no! Señor Lee, stop at my house now!"

The front door was ajar. No Carlito.

"Maybe he's at Jackson's house?"

Her door was also ajar. We ran to my house and there it was—a note on a legal-size piece of paper tacked to the card wall. It was in Juan's handwriting: "You've spoiled it all. We have Rachael and Carlito. We'll exchange them for the Ark. Bring it to Los Alamos day after tomorrow. Tell no one, no one at all. Come alone."

It was signed Juan Barrera and Bob Potter. Maria was horrified, beside herself. It took several hours to calm her down enough for her to stop crying and blaming me, Rachael and the Seven for this. Eventually we agreed that we really did not have many choices. We agreed that she would remain at Castolon. I would obey the instructions and go to Los Alamos. I attempted to sleep on Maria's couch, but mostly stared at the ceiling. Nobody got any sleep that night.

By dawn I was packed. Maria and I loaded my oak table, my bed, desk, side table and chairs including three porch rockers into the pickup. I hitched up the dos caballos trailer and loaded Pepper, Ace and all their gear. We loaded the back seat of the cab with pots and pans, knives and forks, clothes and such. I tossed in two 20-pound bags of oats and horse feed. I stuck the M1 and my 12 gauge pump in the back seat and slid my .40

caliber Glock under the driver's seat. Maria handed me a thermos of my favorite dark roast already blended with evaporated milk. In a separate brown bag were two huevos y chorizo tacos for breakfast and four carne guisada tacos for lunch—two for me and two for Rusty. After that I was on my own.

"Maria, you'll need a pistol. Do you have one?"

"No, Lee I don't."

In Jackson's house we found her large frame .40 caliber Glock with four spare 12 round magazines. Jackson even had a little .380 Smith & Wesson automatic. We found about twenty rounds for it, and a clip-on holster. Maria knew how to shoot.

"Maria, remember the rule: 'Shoot 'til it clicks.' OK?"

"Sí, Señor Lee. But the better rule is: 'Shoot 'til he is dead.' No?"

"Yup. I'd be happy for you to watch my back."

I kissed her cheek and hugged her tight. She held me tightly and wished that God would protect me. I got into the truck and sat there putting on the seatbelt. I turned, mostly expecting Maria to be crying for her kidnapped son. Instead she had a look of grim determination as she practiced inserting the ammo clip into Jackson's Glock. Rusty and I headed west, along the Maverick Road to Study Butte, Lajitas and The Ranch. The pickup strained up the ten-percent grades on Texas 170 between Lajitas and Presidio. The extra ton of supplies and horses really tested that TPWD engine. But by noon we honked our presence at Sauceda Ranch HQ. Luís trotted out to meet us.

"Lee, cómo está? Stay for lunch, sí?"

We agreed to meet later at Los Alamos.

By three in the afternoon, Luís and his crew of three were working to move me into Los Alamos.

"Lee, you have very little furniture."

"Yeah, but that's why I have my power tools in that very large yellow tool box. You received the lumber that I ordered, yes? Luís, you and the TPWD contractors have done an incredible job. The compound is beautiful. I do regret not having been here when the cottonwood leaves turned golden. But that could not be helped."

I thanked Luís, Tomás and crew. They returned to Sauceda HQ. At dusk Rusty, Pepper, Ace and I were alone at Los Alamos, for the first time since the shootings—and the killings. To prepare for tomorrow I wrapped a chain around the job box; hooked it to the pickup trailer hitch and dragged it outside the adobe fence to a spot near the front gate.

Los Alamos sunsets were not as dramatic as those at Santa Elena. After my dinner of grilled steak, baked potato, and salad, all shared with Rusty, I sat under the cottonwoods in the backyard and mourned the loss of friends and friendship. Bob, Juan and I had shared many a sunset, many a fifth of Jack Daniels' Black Label, and many a beer in this place. It was almost sacred to me. Those moments of friendship and comradeship were now sullied by the events of the last few days. The memories were tainted. Those men that I'd shared good times with were not the same ones who kidnapped Jackson and Carlito. The kidnappers were men with broken souls.

Rusty and I spent an uneasy evening. At 11:00 p.m., my "friendly government" phone rang. It was Maria.

"Señor Lee; do you have any news?"

"No, Maria, I don't. It is dark; it's cold; the wind is out of the north. I will call them tomorrow morning. Then I'll call you to bring you up to speed. Is that OK?"

"Señor Lee, please don't try to call after 8:00 a.m. The phones here are not working well. I will probably not be able to answer or call you back. OK?"

"OK Maria. I'll do my best to free Carlito. I'm sure he is fine. If I can get through, I will leave a message on your phone."

It was a restless night. I cranked up a fire in the fire place; slept under a pile of blankets. Before sleep I wrapped the animals in their horse blankets. Rusty slept on the floor beside the bed. At dawn when I checked the thermometer it registered twenty-five degrees. The wind picked up out of the north, accompanied by light snow. This one promised to be a miserable day.

The Los Alamos phone rang about 2:00 p.m.

"Yeah."

"Stay put; we're on our way. You haven't called anyone about this, have you?"

"Nope, Juan, I can read. I read the ransom note. But want our people back. We're ready to negotiate. OK?"

"Lee, you don't understand. There will be no negotiation. These are not requests; these are demands. They are requirements to keep your people alive. They are requirements for their return. Do you understand that?"

"OK, Juan. Tell me what you want."

"We want the Ark. Where is it? Can you get it to us? We have Jackson. We're sure she helped you hide it."

"She did. But I've moved it to a new location. Only Pepper, Ace and Rusty know the exact location."

"OK; we'll land the chopper out of sight."

"About where you landed the night you and your hired killers tried to kill me, right?"

"Lee, I'm sorry about that, but yes. Bob will escort Carlito to you. You show Bob the Ark and Carlito is free."

"Juan, you're not listening. You can land and do whatever. But until Carlito is over the first rise west, headed toward Sauceda HQ on Pepper or Ace, you don't get a word out of me, or a hand signal. Are we clear about that?"

"OK, OK; we'll be there in thirty minutes. You OK with that?"

"Yeah, come on. Wait! I want to hear Jackson's voice, and Carlito's voice. And I want that right now—right now! Do it!"

"No, Lee!"

"Tough shit, guys. You're never gonna see the Ark. Your great-great grandchildren are never gonna see it. The Big Bend is a huge place. I moved it. Get real. Do what I ask, OK? I'll give it to you, but I want my friend and Maria's son free. That don't happen, Bob; the nut fringe of LDS Church is never gonna see this thing—ever, ever, ever. And you're never gonna see a fucking dime. You sumbitches are gonna have to find a new

253

planet to live on. If you kill me, my kids will come after you. If you kill them, their kids will come after you. You crazy S.O.B.s are going to have to carry on without it. Good luck!"

"Lee, this is Bob. You gotta understand; this is theology, not politics or money. I wouldn't do it otherwise."

"Bob, we've had this conversation. And I thought I was the only one on serious drugs. Turns out you are on some sort of 'crazoid' dope or have a serious fucked up thinking process. You want to march backward, back to the middle nineteenth century. You want to have five or six wives. You want four of them to be teenagers. Even Brigham Young couldn't buy that any longer. The true church in Salt Lake outlawed polygamy over a hundred years ago. Sorry, amigo; no sale. Ain't gonna happen. I gotta give you the Ark in exchange for Carlito and Jackson. But I don't have to love you any more. And I think you're bound to Hell on the Devil's Tricycle. Put Jackson and Carlito on; I want to hear their voices, right now!"

Bob did. I told Jackson and Carlito to hang loose; we'd all be safe very soon.

"Lee, this is Juan. Keep your promise, OK? Nobody has to die tonight. We'll land where I said. Bob will escort Carlito to you. You'll be unarmed. Once Carlito is mounted and on his way you'll show us the Ark. We'll release Jackson. We'll go our way; you and Jackson will go yours. Is that acceptable?"

"Yup, it is Juan. Let's do it."

As promised, Rusty and Ace heard the chopper. Carlito and Bob walked south over the rise.

"Señor Lee!"

"Carlito, walk slowly to me. Then, when Señor Bob and I signal, you must mount Ace and ride at a trot toward Sauceda HQ. Can you do that?"

"Yes, Señor Lee."

"Is that OK, Bob?"

"Yes."

"Do it Carlito."

In twenty seconds he was headed toward the rise to the west, toward Sauceda.

254

"Where is it Lee?"

"Here."

"Here, where?"

"It is in the box."

"It is in this yellow job box?"

"It's a job, Bob. A big one I gotta admit, but yeah, it's here in this box."

"You mean the holy object has been here all along in a yellow job box?"

"Well, not exactly, not all along if you mean for the last 500 years. But it has been here since I put it here."

"Shut up, Lee. Open it! Put it on the ground in front of me. Open it."

"I'll put it in front of you, Bob. I'm not qualified to open it, and I won't."

"OK; put it on the ground in front of me. No funny business; I'll kill you if I have to. Got it?"

"You bet. But when do I get Jackson?"

"When we lift off with the Ark."

"Done deal!"

I turned the combinations; opened the four locks on the job box and raised the lid. I turned to Bob.

"What next jefe?"

"Lift 'em out. Put 'em on the ground in front of me."

"I can lift the two small boxes. But it will take both of us to lift the Ark out."

In three minutes all three crates were on the ground about ten feet in front of the job box.

"Lee, back away. He yelled into his cell phone: "I've got it Juan, bring the chopper!"

"I want Rachael."

"She's in the chopper; you'll get her."

The BP chopper popped over the north horizon. It started to settle about fifty feet away to pick up Bob and the Ark. Bob rigged a sling to pick up the Ark and load it onto the chopper.

Rusty ran over me, knocked me down. Then, even I heard it, the sound of the second chopper.

Juan pulled the green-striped BP chopper back into the air, firing an M16 one handed at me as he did. Rusty and I ducked. I threw myself toward cover behind the job box, not nearly quickly enough. I felt something tear at my left shoe. As I fell I saw the second chopper, Juan's real target, clear the house out of the south roof by inches. It dipped, touched the ground about seventy feet from us. Bob stooped to pick up the Ark and turned back north, headed for the rise and Juan's chopper. The second chopper popped back into the air and swerved to the right. Juan continued to fire. The pilot shoved a pistol out the window and shot back. It was a La Policía de la Frontera unit.

A figure, it was Maria, dropped to the ground about fifty feet from me, Bob, the Ark and the job box. She rolled, came up to the classic target pistol kneeling position. She cradled the large-frame Glock .40cal pistol in the palm of her left hand. I saw the flashes, then heard the sound, that flat blat, blat, blat that a .40 caliber Glock makes. Bob tumbled and rolled over, clawing at his pistol. Maria ran toward him; kicked his pistol and M16 away.

"Señor Lee, your leg." She dragged me completely behind the job box as Juan continued to fire.

"Where is Carlito?"

"He's safe Maria. He is riding Ace, headed back to Sauceda. He'll be OK."

"Where is your pistol?"

"Other side of the fence to the right."

"Stay here; I'll get it for you."

She sprinted to the fence, turned, bent over, picked up my pistol that I'd hidden before Bob and Juan arrived and tossed it to me. A bullet had ripped open my shoe, tearing at my left ankle which now sported a long red, oozing groove on the outside.

Two shots pinged off the job box. I risked a peek. Bob was about fifty feet away, sitting, holding the Ark on his lap. His chest was covered in blood. Using his backup pistol he fired again. Maria shot him twice. He fell over backward, still clutching the Ark.

Juan flew low over the north horizon; Felipe came out of the west higher. When I thought they'd collide, Felipe turned south. Juan, sensing a collision turned hard to the east. His rotor blade clipped the far corner of the ruined satellite dish support. His chopper cart wheeled into the ground hitting the dish support and the outside corner of the adobe fence. The engine screamed at 10,000 rpms until, overloaded, it simply blew up and sputtered to a stop. Gray smoke blossomed out of the aft engine compartment and seeped into the shattered cockpit.

"Rachael's in there!"

Maria and I ran toward the wreck lying on its left side. Together we pried open the passenger door.

"Here, I'm in the back. They handcuffed me. Quick, get me out!"

We got Rachael on her feet. I reached behind her with my pocket knife and cut the plastic cable tie cuffs. Her arms freed, she practically sprinted out of the smoking cockpit.

"Rachael, is Juan alive?"

"I don't know."

"Go, go; you and Maria go. This thing is gonna burn!"

I climbed back on the wreck. The fire licked at the cabin from below and aft, feeding on the pool of kerosene turbine fuel puddled on the ground under the cockpit.

"Juan, Juan; can you hear me?"

"Lee; I'm trapped. I can't get out. Help me!"

I dropped down into the cockpit, one foot on the ruined dash, the other on the passenger seat lower armrest. I could see him. Blood oozed from a massive wound in his chest. One of the chopper blades had fractured, hit the ground in front of the chopper, bent almost double and boomeranged back through the windshield into the cockpit. The broken end impaled Juan, passing all the way through him. There was no way I could help. The look of horror on my face was telegraphed to Juan as the flames rose around his feet.

"Juan, I can't get you out."

"Lee, don't let me burn. For God's sake, don't let me burn alive. Do something!"

The flames flared around us both.

"Juan, I can't get you out. The chopper blade is all the way through you. Even if I pulled it out, you'd die within minutes I'm sorry."

I pulled myself up toward the passenger door. The flames boomed around the two of us. My left pant leg smoldered. There was a second flare and the flames shot out of the chopper through the passenger door, completely engulfing me and Juan. They seared the left side of my face. Juan screamed as the fire ate at this feet and legs.

"For God's sake Lee, shoot me. Please shoot me. You owe me!"

"Juan, I can't; I can't do that. But—here!"

I cocked the Glock, dropped back down into the chopper, fished around for Juan's right hand and placed the pistol in it. I maneuvered his finger onto the trigger. His eyes met mine. He nodded and gripped the pistol. For an instant the barrel shifted toward me. He mouthed: "Thank you. Go. Please go!"

His and my clothes were on fire. I clambered out of the passenger door. Several hands and arms pulled me out of the death chamber and threw me on the ground. Someone rolled me over in the dust to put out the flames. I heard him scream. Then I heard the shot, then another. Then nothing except the giant whoosh of the engulfing flames. Then nothing at all.

"Señor Lee, are you OK?"

"Is Juan . . . ?"

"It was a good thing you did for him, Señor Lee. Yes, he is dead by his own hand. It is better than burning alive in the helicopter."

"Maria, it is the worst thing I've ever done. How long have I . . . ?"

Felipe's face filled my vision. Rusty licked my right hand. I rubbed his nose and he lay down at my feet.

Felipe spoke first: "Only minutes Lee. We pulled you out of Juan's chopper. I must admit that you look more than a little strange. You have no hair or eyebrows on the left side of your head. But aside from that, you're fine. Well, you have almost

258

no clothing, but I understand that such a state is not unknown to you. One palm has first-degree burns. The left side of your face will look like a topographical map of Big Bend for a while, with all those creases and valleys as a result of the burns. They appear to be first degree only. You'll hurt like hell for a few days, but antibiotics and ointment should help you heal. You're wrapped in blankets. Your legs, arms and body are fine, well aside from the facial stuff."

"Carlito, he didn't see all this did he?"

"Lee, this is Rachael. No he didn't. Remember, you sent him to Sauceda. Maria will take your truck and follow him. That mule of yours is fast and doesn't require 4WD. But she might actually catch them before they get to Sauceda. When she does, she will stay at Sauceda with him. She won't bring him back here."

"Lee, this is Felipe. I do not wish to intrude, but we have business, immediate business to discuss. I am dreadfully sorry about your friend Juan. I grieve with you and for you. He was a friend to me as well. Our families were related. But before I go back to Acuña, I must tell you three things.

"First, someone must report this incident to the proper authorities. I think that someone must be either you or Officer Jackson. Second, neither my helicopter nor I are licensed in the United States. We have not been cleared by the Border Patrol or Homeland Security. I really must go. Please do not mention me in your communications. And you and the Seven must make a decision very quickly. I might be able to help, but perhaps not. Third, someone must convene a meeting of the Seven Guardians. That must be you."

"Felipe," I whispered, "I can't do that; I'm not Jewish. I'm not Catholic. I'm not a member. Rachael, what is the tradition? Who is permitted to call a full meeting of the Guardians?"

"According to tradition the eldest must call a face-to-face meeting. And that call must be supported by at least two members. Rabbi Koen is the eldest; we must contact him. And Lee, you will not be invited. You understand."

I croaked a weak, "Yes."

"I must go."

Felipe saluted. About all I could do was nod and croak a whispered thank you. I hurt like hell. Jackson rubbed burn ointment from the La Policía chopper's first-aid kit on my face, left hand and lips. She muttered something smart-ass about my looking like the Invisible Man in the movie, with all the gauze wrapped around my head and hand. My throat was on fire; my lips felt like some sadist had stuck a thousand hot needles in them. Pulling Jackson close with one hand I croaked, "Call Hays; number is on my cell on the oak table."

Rusty licked my hand. He stretched out between my legs with his massive paws on my chest; his wet black nose about two inches from mine. He did what dogs do when someone is in pain. He licked my face with that long, slurpy, wet shepherd tongue of his. Something at least was right with the world. So much for antibiotic ointment.

CHAPTER 15: LA LINDA CROSSING

"Ranger Hays, this is Officer Rachael Jackson, NPS Big Bend. What I have to say is very sensitive. I'm calling on behalf of Lee Phillips. Please find a secure phone and call this number. It is really, really important."

"What is it Jackson?"

"Please find the secure phone; call me back ASAP. I'll wait for your call."

Five minutes later he called. It shouldn't have taken that long to find a secure phone. I figured that he was arranging to record the conversation. She held a tablet and I scribbled my observation with my unburned right hand. The left one hurt like hell.

Rachael put our phone on speaker so I could hear. I couldn't hear it anyway, but Rachael repeated Hays' end of the conversation. Rachael told him the story, most of it anyway. She described the incident including the deaths of Juan Barrera and Bob Potter. She made no attempt to tell the entire thing, just hit the high points. She noted that there was a complicating situation that she could not discuss on the phone. She indicated that it was internationally sensitive and must be addressed quickly and discretely.

Her last lines were, "That's pretty much it Hays. We can stay here and secure the area until help arrives. But Lee should be seen by a doctor. How soon can you get here?"

"Ask Lee if he has any objection to Marks being involved?"

Rachael relayed the query. I shook my head no and pulled Rachael close. I whispered and Rachael relayed my croaks into the cell.

"Hays, no problem with Marks. But I don't think you want dozens of Rangers and FBI tramping around Los Alamos. Try to handle this with as few guys as possible . . . ."

261

My voice totally collapsed. I'd probably inhaled way too many fumes from burning turbine fuel. Hays promised to be at the Ranch in two, maybe three hours. He'd bring a four man forensics team and an EMT to treat my burns. He also promised to bring a counselor for Carlito and Maria whom he would drop off at Sauceda on the way in. He promised to call when the team was within thirty minutes of the Ranch airstrip. Jackson shot some painkiller into my arm and I took a nap—unfortunately a short nap. She shook me awake, turned my face so I could read her lips and told me that they, Ranger Hays and Agent Marks, had a question that only I could answer. They wanted more information on the "internationally sensitive issue." They understood that I couldn't tell them, but they asked for some comparison.

I croaked into the phone, "OK guys, think of the Middle East blowing up. It's that big. I can give you one number. Call it; he'll only answer it one time and will not talk for more than a minute. Ready for the number?"

They called back in less than five minutes.

"Here's the plan Lee. We called your man. You're right. We called Colonel Maples in Austin at TPWD law enforcement. We've told him that we've discovered some highly toxic materials that if not handled properly can escape into the atmosphere and poison the entire southern end of Presidio and Brewster counties. We've established a joint incident task force—TPWD, BP, Texas Rangers, FBI, and the Policía de la Frontera. I'm the point of contact. Maples agreed that our HazMat expertise is more extensive than his. Besides, we've convinced him that this incident is more a national problem than a state park problem. He is sending a team to clear the park. We'll seal it off. TPWD cops and Border Patrol officers will patrol the perimeters; our guys will be the only ones allowed inside. You guys sit tight. Stay off the phone."

#

Jackson helped me back to the house, to the living room where I would be safe and out of the elements.

Then she cobbled together a quick plan to secure transportation and bring Maria up to speed. She saddled Pepper; rode back to Sauceda and borrowed Luís and three men, along with four vehicles. She'd convinced Luís to leave three vehicles at the landing strip and return to Sauceda. Carlito and Maria would stay at Sauceda.

She used my truck to return to Los Alamos. She retrieved her duty weapons from the front porch where Maria had dropped them. Jackson put a chain on the job box and used the truck to drag it back to its usual position.

It was no trick to get me to lie down. I was in exactly the same place she left me when she returned. She sat on the front porch steps in the evening gloaming to wait for the arrival of the Rangers and the FBI. Rusty and I napped for about an hour. Rachael removed the Ark from the now-dead Bob Potter's lap. She put it and the two other boxes back in the job box and snaked it back under the carport. Finally, she took a cottonwood branch and wiped out all the tread and skid marks.

The plane came in low out of the west over Los Alamos. The pilot flicked on the landing lights and clicked them off. Twenty minutes later Jackson and Rusty heard the whine of the four-wheel-drive Suburbans and crew-cab pickups as they pulled up that last rise to Los Alamos. They stopped close to the front yard and kicked all the headlights on high-beam. The team secured the area. Marks came in the door.

"Jesus, Lee; what a mess. This place looks like a war zone. These guys must have wanted that thing awfully bad. Where is it?"

My throat, or vocal chords, were majorly fucked up. I motioned for my tablet and pencil and wrote, "Good to see you too, Marks. The guy who answered, he told you how sensitive this is?"

"Your handwriting looks like you flunked second grade. Where is it?"

"I did, and it's not far."

"I don't like this very much Lee, but I can live with it. Meanwhile let's get my EMT guy to give you some antibiotics and wrap those burns. You sure look like shit, no eyebrows and all. I bet your wife will be tickled when you get back to a safe and sane life in Austin."

I scribbled and asked Marks to call Lisa, explain the best he could and help her make arrangements to get to the Ranch or to Big Bend. After being reassured that I was indeed alive and not in totally awful shape she was not so much hysterical as really pissed. And, most importantly, she said that the FBI had offered to make arrangements to fly her to Big Bend.

Marks asked us to walk him and Hays through it, so we did. They asked questions; we answered them. Well, Rachael answered most of them. The forensics guys did their work quietly and quickly.

The EMT guy was magic. He sprayed some potion in my mouth and throat. He glopped a thick coating of something slick on my lips, all the while muttering, "Damn, where the hell did all this saliva come from? Your skin feels like you've been licked by a pack of wolves."

"Potter's got four holes in him. Who did that?"

"Maria."

"Don't piss off mama bear, huh?"

"Either one of you go close to the chopper after the fire died?"

Neither of us had. There wasn't much left of the chopper. Plastic melts in a turbine fuel fire. Not much left of Juan. Not much left of my pistol either. They found the barrel slide and a puddle of charred plastic clutched in what remained of his right hand.

"That must have been pretty tough, Lee. What a helluva choice to have to make—either shoot this guy who had been your best friend, let him die in the flames, or give him the pistol so he could kill himself. Shit!"

I scribbled, "Yeah, Marks, it was. I'll deal with that later. Can we just get this squared away tonight so this part of the country can get back to normal as quickly as possible? I'm sure you understand that Jackson and I have something else that needs to be taken care of really, really soon. I'll go see a shrink later."

They brought in two more planes that night. The second had heavy equipment on it. They had to cut off the rotor blade to get what was left of Juan out of the burned wreckage. They bundled him and the sawed off chopper blade into a body bag. Then they loaded the burned wreckage of the chopper on a flatbed and hauled it off. There wasn't much to move anyway; just some aluminum struts and internal supports, some charred wiring, the steel seat springs.

The helicopter rotor hub and engine block were the largest and heaviest pieces left after the fire. The forensics team used a block and tackle and hoist to move them. Except for Rusty, nobody slept. I kept running that endless loop of my last interaction with Juan through my head. I don't think I'll ever forget that picture of his face when he nodded and mouthed: "Get out of here."

By dawn the two large planes were headed back to El Paso. Marks, Hays, Jackson, Rusty and I sat on the porch. In my honor they ate smoked oysters with crackers and hot sauce and drank several beers each. I drank some sort of "good for you" thin soup and had two beers. It had been that kind of night.

"What next, Lee?"

"Guys, Jackson and I have one more thing to do. Come here, let me show you something. You earned it. Jackson, can you give me a hand?"

I led them to the carport; dialed the combination locks, and opened the job box.

"There it is men. That is what got those guys killed. Well, their desire to posses it at all costs got them killed. In that box, or in those boxes is the Ark of the Covenant, the one in The Bible. Right there, in my carport in this yellow job box is, arguably, the foundation of Western Civilization, the bedrock for the world's three major religions. It's an humbling experience and an awesome feeling. Maybe if I look at it long enough I'll forget Juan's face in that burning helicopter. But enough of all that. You guys gotta go. Jackson and I, well mainly Jackson, have a bunch of work to do. Thanks for your trust, your professionalism and your help. We'll be in touch."

Hays spoke first: "Thanks Lee; thanks for trusting us. I can't tell you how honored I feel, how in awe of what is there."

"You haven't opened it, have you?"

"No Marks, I don't feel worthy to open it."

"Can I just touch the crates?"

"Sure."

Marks put his hands on the crates.

"I think I've touched the face of God. I'm not a churchgoing man, but there is power in there. Was that how you and Jackson felt?"

Jackson responded: "Yes, it is Holy. It is filled with a Loving Power in every way you can imagine."

"Hays, want to touch too?"

"I can't; I don't feel worthy; I can't."

"Nobody's worthy, Hays; that's not the point. The point is that what is in those crates is the connection between us, the unworthy and the Other. The guys in AA have it said in a way that makes sense to me: It's that Higher Power that stands for everything we're not and everything we should strive to be. And striving is what we do; not perfection. Go ahead, touch."

"I can't."

"OK, cool."

"Folks, we have a plane to catch. Jackson, Rusty, Lee, you folks take care. This has been a life changing night."

"Me too, Marks. Let's hope that the next time we get together it will be someplace else, maybe on a Mexican beach or in an El Paso bar. You boys be careful."

"You too, Lee. I assume that you have a plan for this, the Ark?"

"Yeah, we do. I can't tell you though."

"Please don't. Vaya con Dios, Amigos."

And in two minutes they were just tail lights disappearing over the rise, headed toward the airstrip and that plane to El Paso, and a week's worth of paperwork.

Jackson collapsed on the new sofa that Luís and TPWD provided. I slept ten hours on a cot in my newly redecorated bedroom. Jackson and I just kinda wandered around the grounds the next afternoon. We talked and replayed the events of the past three days over and over. We both slept the sleep of the just.

I woke to the smell of dark roast brewing, bacon frying and rain slicing against the bedroom windows.

"Hey hero, want some wakeup coffee? You look like shit. Boy, am I glad you're alive."

"Lisa, when did you get here?"

"A few hours ago. You know this stuff has got to stop, right? How much more do you need to do out here? You're going to keep on and really get killed. I'm sorry about Juan and Bob. It must be horrible."

"Yeah, it is. I don't know what to think. Except that I think about the 'what ifs'. As in, 'what if I had done something differently?' 'What if I had picked up on the clues earlier?' You know. 'What if Bob hadn't wanted to sell it to the LDS Church?' That sort of thing."

Jackson had cranked up the wood heating stove. There were only a few bullet holes in the front windows. The two of them used duct tape to patch them to keep the wind from whistling through. We ate at my oak table. I looked up from my plate of eggs over medium with bacon and toast. Lisa was smiling.

"What?"

"You know Lee, Rachael, by all rights you both should be dead. I'm smiling because I'm alive, warm, have a husband and a good friend to share my breakfast with and will soon be going back to my regular job. Rachael says its forty out there; wind out of the southwest at about twenty.

"Lisa, Lee, I know that this is not the perfect time for this, but there are calls to make. Since you are not a member of the guardians, I must make those calls. This is the perfect day to make phone calls and decisions. Lee, we can't wait any longer. The eldest and Maria and I must call a meeting of the Seven.

Luís has loaned me a truck. I'm headed back to Castolon. Maria and I will call the eldest. I will recommend that even though you are not members of the Seven, you and Lisa should be allowed to attend. It is the proper thing to do. After all, you found it."

"Jackson, I appreciate it very much, but if it causes problems, please do not have us in attendance. OK?"

"Lee, do you have any suggestions as to where they meet? We can't meet here; too remote; can't meet at Castolon for the same reason. How about Alpine? They'll be having their Alpine Winter Arts Walk Festival in three days. Six new people won't be noticed. That should give us enough time, don't you think?"

Jackson used our "friendly government" phones and in about an hour had the meeting set. The Seven agreed to hold the meeting in three days at three in the afternoon in the board room at the Museum of the Big Bend on the Sul Ross University campus.

"You're not going to haul the Ark to Alpine are you?"

"No, but it will be close."

Jackson left and returned to Castolon to complete the arrangements. Lisa stayed with Rusty and me. The first night was not too bad; at least Lisa said so. I only tried to run out the door to "save my friend" twice. The second night she found Rusty and me on the porch looking at the black smudge that was my friend of twenty years and his chopper.

"Lee, it's twenty degrees; you have to come back in. You'll freeze."

The last night we made love in my old bedroom, drank a bottle of Hill Country Claret and talked about the future—life after now. She extracted a promise that I wouldn't do any more of this crazy stuff without really rigid rules concerning my safety.

"Lee, it makes me mad with worry. I keep thinking that you won't come back."

"I always do."

"Yes, but what happens if you don't?"

"Lisa, that's how life is; some day I won't. I will promise that I will offer you the opportunity, every single time, to come with me, to adventure with me, to live life on the edge. As the writer said, "to sail tumultuous seas and land on barbarous shores." Barbarous shores are getting kinda rare, but I'm gonna keep on trying. OK?"

I slept on an air mattress in front of the fireplace under a goose down quilt for ten hours. I woke with my dog and my incredibly beautiful and caring wife staring at me across the living room. Rusty crossed the room and licked my face—welcome home gringo.

Three days later, at three in the afternoon, the Seven met in the boardroom at the museum. The campus was mostly empty; faculty and staff were attending the Art Walk. In Alpine that festival meant cruising the art galleries, listening to music on four outdoor stages, and a lot of semi-serious eating and drinking.

This was the first time that many of the Seven had met one another. In fact, it was the first meeting of the full Seven in over one hundred years. Rabbi Koen, as was appropriate, chaired the meeting and led the discussion.

"Ladies and gentlemen, this is an historic occasion. First, until recently women were excluded from this group. Such is clearly not the case now. Second, this is the first time that two females recently chosen have initiated a meeting of the Seven Guardians. Thank you, Maria and Rachael, for doing this. Also, this is the first time ever that a non-member and his wife have been allowed to attend our meeting. We thought it appropriate, given that Dr. Phillips was instrumental in recovering the Ark. We have a momentous decision to make. Quite simply it is this: Where shall we secret the Ark now? The New World has served us well. It saved the Ark from almost certain confiscation and perhaps destruction over 500 years ago. But is it appropriate now?"

The discussion continued for three hours. In the end, it was Koen who brought everyone back to the political and religious realities of the day.

"Some time ago, Archbishop Sanchez and I opened conversations with representatives of the State of Israel

269

regarding the disposition of the Ark. Initially I thought that it should be returned to the Middle East. But representatives of that government are reluctant. In their opinion it would be politically and religiously inflammatory. However, they might be interested in "pretending to have the Ark" as a way to keep the other sides guessing. I'm sure that all of you know that, eventually, some inkling of what has transpired over the last few weeks will become public in some fashion. At that point the Israeli government can leak the appropriate information. I proposed a subterfuge. I've spoken with the Israeli representatives; they have developed a plan. And the Archbishop has a proposal. Your Holiness, please."

Archbishop Sanchez outlined a plan.

"There is a small group of cloistered nuns in northern Chihuahua, Mexico, called in English 'The Sisters of Sierra Madre.' I have spoken with their leader. She, and they, have agreed to shelter a certain holy object under the altar of their chapel dedicated to the Virgin of Guadalupe. Of course someone must deliver it. For that we would perhaps rely on our newest member, you, Comandante."

"Certainly, Your Holiness; it is our pleasure."

"As for The 'pretend' Ark that is repatriated, I propose that Officer Jackson and I transport it to Laughlin Air Force Base in Del Rio and turn it over to a Mr. Goldman who will meet us at the gate. I believe that you, Rabbi, and you, Lee, have met and trust this gentleman. Can everyone live with this plan?"

Koen had a reservation.

"I would dearly hope to have a service, a religious and ecumenical service, before the Ark is taken into seclusion again. Would anyone object? Lee, do you think you could find a place to hold such a service, someplace close to Mexico, but also with access to highways and an airstrip?"

"Yes, Rabbi. I think I have the place. We'll hold it at the maintenance shed at the La Linda District HQ of Black Gap Wildlife Management Area. I'm sure that Colonel Maples at TPWD law enforcement will approve it and will provide perimeter security."

"Please make it happen; can we do this tomorrow? Oh, one small problem. We absolutely must have ten believers. As of today, we have the Seven, plus you Dr. Phillips and Ms. De Marco. That leaves one short of the required number."

"Rabbi, I think I can help. I propose inviting Carlito Gomez. He is a man under these rules. And if you don't mind I'd like to invite my research associate Ms. Charly Burnside. She is Jewish and I'm sure would be pleased to be included. What time, Rabbi?"

"Normally we would conduct this service in the morning, but I recommend that we do it at dusk. That way the activities that follow can be cloaked in darkness."

It took a little scrambling, but by dusk the following day all were assembled in the maintenance shed at La Linda HQ, about thirty miles from the international crossing at La Linda, Texas. The Rabbi led the service, at least the first half. The Archbishop led the second half. As we filed out, Koen and Sanchez sat together on the folding chairs we'd brought and talked quietly. Soon they joined the others, their faces beaming.

"Are you ready Lee, Comandante Oconor? Lee, I've arranged for a small plane to take our couriers to Del Rio. They will call us when they are on the ground at Laughlin."

Everyone had an assigned task. Marks and Hays would escort Carlito back to Castolon and would stay with him until Maria returned. Sanchez and Jackson would escort the Ark to Del Rio. The others traveled in different directions. Comandante Felipe Oconor would meet us at the border.

Eight hours later, Lisa and I drove the Camo-colored H2 Humvee with no license plates at about 10 mph across the highest part of the arch on the La Linda Bridge. The crossing had been closed since 9/11, but tonight the Border Patrol and U.S. Customs staff were absent. There were no lights, no flags. Just past the center of the bridge, barely inside Mexican jurisdiction, I touched the brake and the huge SUV creaked to a stop. The Mexican border control gates rose in front of me. There was one sergeant of the Policía de la Frontera dressed in full ceremonial dress uniform, complete with nineteenth century shako hat, white gloves and white ammunition belt. As we approached, he turned and saluted. There is one dim street light above the sentry box. It briefly silhouetted Felipe as he stepped toward me. Then the light went out and anyone on the American side saw only the brake lights of the Humvee.

Felipe opened the door. I climbed down, bringing Rusty with me. Lisa exited the passenger door. Felipe mounted up, shut the door. The brake lights went out as the truck rolled into Mexico. Felipe stopped the truck, rolled down the window.

"Lee."

I shook his extended hand. He made the sign of the cross and rolled up the window.

It was time to go. I turned; shouldered my dispatch/ backpack. Lisa and I headed north across the bridge back to the U.S.

The brake lights of the Humvee popped off and the SUV moved forward to the end of the bridge. The driver clicked on the right blinker. At that signal the plaza lights at the Mexican end of the La Linda Crossing popped on. Two ranks of impeccably uniformed Mexican Army Rangers, sixteen on each side of the highway, dissolved and opened the way as the Humvee reached them. They formed two crisp lines on either side of the Mexican bridge approach and as one, saluted.

"Sergeant de Sosa, what time is it?"

"It is 3:30 a.m., Captain Oconor."

"Thank you Sergeant."

"Sí, mi Capitán."

"Sergeant, dismiss your squad."

"Come Lisa, Rusty, let's go home; they're waiting."

We turned and headed north across La Linda Crossing. The job was done. I reached for Lisa's right hand. Rusty licked my right knuckles. The three, Rabbi Ray Koen from Houston, Charly Burnside from San Antonio and Señora Maria de Sosa Villareal y Gomez from Castolon; waited, facing south toward Mexico. They waited for Lisa, Rusty and I to cross back into the U.S.

"Señora, Rabbi, Charly; I think it's done."

"You mind if I make the phone call Lee?"

"No, Ray; have at it, but cell phones don't work this close to the border."

"This one will; it has a special frequency; it'll work."

The conversation was extraordinarily brief, just one word.

"Go." Click and the connection was broken. Ray pushed two buttons in the center of the keypad simultaneously and tossed the cell phone in the road ahead of us. It hit the ground and flared, leaving nothing but a few ashes.

"Ray, I'm impressed."

"Don't need it any more, Lee. Señora Gomez, Ms. Burnside, it just goes to show that God has long arms. It's been a long day. You guys want a beer? I have some in the truck."

"You bet Ray. Actually Ray, it's been a long month and a half. And it's almost over, finally."

Maria, silent until now, asked: "Lee, who was the driver?"

"One of the Seven, OK?"

"Sí."

"Charly, we wouldn't be here without your work."

"What next, Lee?"

"Its 3:35 a.m., right?"

"Yes."

"You guys want to listen to this? This is the phone that Jackson was carrying. Here, I'll turn it on speakerphone. This was part of the deal."

It was, as they say, loud and clear.

"This is Laughlin Control; clearance to roll IDF."

"This is IDF #1, on our way. Thanks Laughlin."

There was some static and then . . . .

"This is Sinai Control #1. We read you loud and clear Laughlin and IDF #1. IDF #1; Code?"

"Sinai; this is IDF #1. Code is: Yahweh Speaks. Out."

THE END

COMING IN 2010 FROM OCOTILLO PRESS

OcotilloPress©

THE HEAD IN THE LAUNDROMAT

By

W. Phil Hewitt

ANOTHER LEE PHILLIPS THRILLER

There was a guy in the #3 dryer on the front row facing me. Holy Shit! It wasn't a guy; it was a head; a bloody head, a really bloody head. The dryer spun and spun and the head rattled around in there like a nine-pound bowling ball, making that awful 'Thump, thump' sound that I felt and Rusty had heard from the second floor apartment bedroom where Lisa and I slept.

About every third rotation, the dead man's brown staring, but unseeing, eyes locked on mine. They were wide and locked in a horrified unbelieving stare, like the last thing he saw was the axe, the knife or the machete that ended his time on the planet.

Blood flowed across the floor from the Laundromat door to the dryer, a three-foot wide trail from the marina entrance. The bouncing, revolving head oozed crimson. Thick, dark crimson droplets fell from the long black curly unkempt hair and the gaping neck wound. They splattered in a bloody counter-clockwise spiral as the machine turned and the head bounced and turned and bled.

Ten minutes ago I was sound asleep, nude, lying beside my curvy wife with what some would call "early arousal . . . ."

It started with; "Dammit, Rusty! What is it? For God's sake it's not time to go out. It must be three in the morning!"

Usually, when my red German shepherd hearing dog pulled my leg, it was something important. He didn't bark much; wouldn't have helped. My hearing is so pathetic that those are sounds that I barely notice. But he could pull, mightily and without breaking the skin. I've never figured out how he does it. There have been times when he has dragged my naked ass out of the bed and never has he broken the skin.

"OK, OK; I'm coming. I'm coming."

Lisa and I sleep in the nude. Before following Rusty down the outside stairs to wherever the hell he wanted to lead me at the "Bobby Rose's Beer, Bait, Marina, Philosophy and Laundromat," I shucked on my attire du jour—a pair of worn khaki shorts and a faded yellow T-shirt that read on the front, with apologies to Arlo Guthrie: "You can get anything you want (almost) at Bobby Rose's Beer, Bait, Marina, Philosophy and Laundromat, Port Isabel, Texas." It featured a Texas Lone Star at the top, a sailboat outline at the bottom, and a tilted, crushed beer can on both sides.

On the way out of the upstairs apartment overlooking the marina I grabbed my black, eight-cell aluminum flashlight and tucked my hammerless, stainless steel, short-barreled Smith and Wesson .38 special into the right front pocket of my shorts. Lisa didn't stir, not a twitch. Barefooted, I hauled ass down the stairs.

Rusty was way ahead. "Hang on chief; I'm a'coming, I'm a'coming."

By the time I reached the pier level even I could hear it, or rather feel it: Thump, Thump, Thump, coming from the 24/7 "YOU CAN BE A CLEAN SAILOR LAUNDROMAT." It actually said that on the 40 foot by 100 foot, billboard-sized, much larger than life, red, white and blue neon sign that accompanied the million watt "Welcome Home Marina" sign facing north on the Southern, tail-end of the Inter Coastal Waterway. I turned the corner, pulled open the screen door closest to the marina and saw him, or it. And I'm now standing in front of a commercial dryer with a head bouncing around inside.

"Holy Shit, Rusty! It's a dead guy in the dryer." Rusty thumped his tail against my right leg and hung tight.

I screamed: "Lisa, Lisa come quick! Now!"

Lisa too had the foresight to pull on some jeans and a T. Hers, as she popped open the screen door, in a faded teal green, read: "Port Isabel—Gateway to The World."

"Lisa, there's a dead guy—well, a head in the Laundromat. I've gotta stop it."

She looked. She screamed.

"My God Lee, that's horrible. We have to stop the dryer. Can you stop the machine?"

Normally the quickest way to stop a dryer is to open its door. I didn't want to do that— blood everywhere, fingerprints on the door handle and all.

"Lisa, hang on, don't move; don't touch anything."

I sprinted as fast as a fifty-three year old guy with a gimpy knee can sprint to the breaker box located on the Inter Coastal, the marina side of the Laundromat. I pulled the main breaker marked "Laundromat." Everything went dark, even the zillion watt "Welcome Home Sailor" sign. I clicked on the flash and sprinted back to Lisa. The bloody Laundromat head rested in a pool of blood at the bottom of the stainless steel cylinder, eyes locked on mine and Lisa's.

"Lisa, go to the Bait Shop and call 911. The Port Isabel City fuzz will be here, as promised, in no longer than ten minutes. Wait for them in the parking lot. Tell 'em to come find me. No need for you to see anymore of this."

"Lee, my feet, all the blood . . . ."

"Lisa, please go. Go!" She went.

Using the eight-cell MagLite, I found the little opening between the machines and the outside building wall. I squeezed inside and inched my way forward. I pulled the 220v electric plugs on every dryer in the row. I crawled back out, tripped the main breaker back to "On" and clicked on the Laundromat lights. The crime scene was even more grotesque in the harsh lighting of those fluorescents. Whoever had done this had used the head like an incense sensor in a Roman Catholic Mass. He, or maybe she, must have swung it wildly, probably using the hair as a hand-hold. Blood sprays were everywhere, some as high as ten feet above the floor. The stainless steel dryers ricocheted the white fluorescent light over the still sticky, wet bloody spatters. I looked down; my bare footprints were everywhere. So were Rusty's.

"What the Hell, Rusty; couldn't be helped. Cops aren't going to like it though. Heel. Stay close, OK?"

Rusty thump, thumped on my right leg, just like the folks at the San Antonio Hearing Dog Academy had taught him.

Dogs don't mind if you mumble to them. They are really pretty cool about that. According to the studies, our words are mere tones, nuances, soft and large sounds. They all sound pretty much the same to dogs. I talked to Rusty all the time; he wagged his tail; licked whatever part of my body was available. It drove my friends and Lisa crazy! I not only talked to the dog; I talked to myself. But professors can get away with that kind of shit—with a few exceptions, Lisa included.

"C'mon Rusty, Lisa's got the street. Let's backtrack the blood. See what's out there on the dock." Rusty thump, thumped and off we went.

The blood trail led down the marina dock to a sixty foot, steel-hulled shrimper tied up at the "T," the end of the dock. I didn't recall checking her in. The name on the bow was *Nuestra Señora*—Our Lady. Her homeport, stenciled on her cabin, was Puerto Escondido, which I took to be a fishing port on the Mexican gulf coast. I flicked the light to her stern. Sure 'nuff, there it was—the red, white and green flag with that serpent and eagle, the national flag of Mexico.

The blood trail pulled us to the boat's boarding plank. Rusty and I trotted up the plank. *Nuestra Señora* had a serious list, about 20 degrees to port, away from the dock. And she was sitting low in the water. A sixty foot shrimper, empty, will ride with her deck about eight feet above the dock at Bobby Rose's place. *Nuestra*'s deck was almost level with the dock planking.

"Holy shit, Rusty; she's sinking."

The thirty-slip marina was almost full, a combination of shrimp boats, high speed sports fishing trawlers and about eight sailboats. Most were transients, but there were about a dozen live-aboards. It was time to get some help. The Welcome Home Marina has a customer activated emergency siren system. There are about a half dozen big red push-buttons along the dock. I sprinted to the closest one and punched it. The red strobes on the four twelve-foot poles lit up with about a million candlepower each. The 140 decibel siren was almost guaranteed to wake the dead. The sound was something that even I could hear. It was tortuous to Rusty. He yelped and jumped around like someone was hitting him on the head with an eight pound ball-peen hammer. I grabbed him, held his face to mine, yelled and motioned: "Rusty; go. Find Lisa; stay with her. Stay."

He split. Smart dog.

Time to get some help.

"Help, Help! Come on everybody; we've gotta save this boat. Get your asses out of those racks and pump!"

And damned if they didn't. Within two minutes I had all the help a body could want. Roger, a retired diver, former shrimper and live-aboard, and I went aboard and below *La Nuestra*. Fumbling around in the aft hold's chest deep water Roger and I found four sea cocks on the stern of *La Nuestra*. We shut 'em even though we had to duck under the bilge water to do it. We went to the forward hold. Someone wanted this boat under water. Standing up to our chests in seawater we fumbled around, held our breath, dove, found and closed those sea cocks.

Sailors from the marina cranked up four of the emergency pumps on the dock; ran three two-inch hoses to the boat, fore and aft. Soon *La Nuestra* began to rise.

Before going below for the second time I stopped and turned. It was time to clue in the others. Most were talking in speculative clumps near the starboard side of *La Nuestra*.

"OK, everybody, listen up. This boat's not gonna sink, at least not right now. We have a dead guy in the Laundromat. The Port Isabel fuzz will be here pretty damn quick. So, anybody with stuff you don't want the cops to find—dump it or hide it. Then we can use the help monitoring the pumps."

It was assholes and elbows. Marina patrons hustled back to their boats; put their stuff in their secret hidey-holes, or dumped it in the calm, dark waters of Laguna Madre. In a few minutes the waters surrounding the marina were covered in "tea." It looked like the Boston Tea Party redux. They did their thing; we did ours. *Nuestra* rose and settled in the water, riding like a shrimper should.

"Lee, what's that shit all over your face. You look like you've been dunked in pepper."

"So do you Roger. But it doesn't smell like pepper. Doesn't smell at all. But you really should take a shower when you get back home."

"You too, chief. Let's get back to work."

Roger and I searched the below decks, the crew cabin, the galley—nothing. No body, no notes, no nothing, except a lot of soggy stuff, clothes, staples and such. Topsides, we cracked the pilot house door. I looked at my watch—ten minutes had passed. The Port Isabel PD ought to be here by now. I opened the pilot house aft door.

"Oh shit, Roger. There's a body."

The flashing red emergency strobe on the dock punctuated the fact that this body had no head.

"Roger, you shouldn't be here. You go; stay with Lisa. Bring the Fuzz here."

"Yeah, Lee, sure. But who would do this—chop off a man's head?"

"Damned if I know Roger. Please, just go; I'll stay here."

At least he waited until he got on the pier to puke all over his boat shoes. I spilled what was left of a mostly digested, pretty good New York strip with a spinach salad all over my bare feet right there in the cabin. Good God it was awful!

It looked like somebody had worked on this guy with a chain saw. But it was probably just a machete. Well, maybe three machetes. And all of them were jammed into the body front to back. They pinned what was left of this guy to the captain's chair. His wrists were duct taped to the pilot wheel. The pilot house was awash in blood. There was blood on the deck, the bulkheads, the ceiling. It's amazing how much blood there is in the human body, particularly when you start punching holes in the container, beginning with multiple machete thrusts to the torso and ending with decapitation.

To nobody in particular: "My God, this is a slaughter house. Rusty, let's get the Hell out of here."

Someone tapped me on my right shoulder. I turned and looked—nobody. Then looked down. It was Mary Ellen Goode, rather Captain Mary, owner and operator of the sports fishing boat "Compleat Angler" and three others named "Nautilus," "Peaquod" and "The Spray." Captain Mary was about 5′ 2″, fiftyish, hundred twenty pounds. She was round where girls need to be round and not round where they weren't. She had a doctorate in English literature from Cambridge, the one in the U.K., an MBA in international finance from the Wharton School, and an "All Oceans, All Tonnage" captain's ticket from the U.S. Maritime Academy. She was what the barflies affectionately labeled "Someone You Do Not Fuck With." She gave Rusty treats; he loved her. She also ran an incredibly profitable sports fishing business. Her philosophy was: "Get there as fast as you can; fish all day, catch the hell out of them; bring the tourists home as fast as you can." Her boats were incredibly fast; she made a lot of money. Using both hands she turned my head to face her lips and mouthed: "Lee, Rusty's not here. Listen, watch my lips. The sirens; the cops. You want to throw up now or later?"

"I already did that. Look at my feet. Let's do later."

"How long since you called 911?"

"Looks like thirteen minutes; something else must be happening someplace on the island. They're usually pretty damn good at meeting that ten minute deadline."

"Well, Lee, the SOBs are actually here in thirteen. You don't think there's any possibility of opening the bar, do you? I could sure use a drink."

"Roger, Mary. Me too. I'm going to meet them. You stay here. Don't let anybody on the boat. Don't touch nothing, OK? And, no, there is absolutely no chance of opening the bar."

"Damn, too bad. That would actually make this early morning wake-up interesting."

I trotted back toward the Laundromat and the bar. Everybody in the marina was awake, clumped in those odd formations of people speculating, hoping they can find out something, gossiping. I noted several bottles being passed around. Rusty met me about halfway down the dock. He tugged on my shorts, danced backward and headed for his other buddy, Lisa. She waved, just visible around the corner of the Laundromat. She had someone in tow. I stopped and waited.

At about arm's length she stopped; touched my chin and turned it to her face so I couldn't miss her words. She spoke clearly and deliberately, not slowly but with a clear show of purpose. A long time ago she had figured out that yelling definitely did not help.

"Lee, look at me. This is Detective Sergeant Hiram William Durham, Port Isabel PD. He hates the name. Insists we call him Buck. Do you understand?"

I nodded yes. Rusty thumped.

"Lee, can we turn off the goddamned siren?"

I gave the instructions. Lisa hit the "Stop" button at slip 13, and the world was blessedly silent for them, at least for most.

"Mary, thanks. I'm pretty sure the cops can handle it from here."

"Thanks Lee, let me know if I can help. Meanwhile, I'm gonna go kick start my morning. Officer, we're not going to be allowed to leave are we, at least until this crime scene has been cleared?"

"Yes, Ma'am, I'm afraid so."

Lisa said: "Lee, I'm going back to the store. I'm going to make some coffee. You or Rusty call me if you need me, OK? I love you. Please stay out of this if you can."

"Dr. Phillips, take me to the boat. We have people coming who will process the Laundromat. Can you do that?"

"Sergeant, I thought you guys promised ten minutes' response time. I am really disappointed; what the hell happened?"

"Five car, two semi wreck on the Queen Isabella Bridge. That sort of stuff will seriously fuck up your evening. Every body but me is working it—Brownsville PD, our uniforms, Texas Rangers, everybody. Every uniform is there; you're stuck with me. There are three dead from the wreck: two teenagers and an abuelita—a beloved grandmother. Two more are crispy critters from the tanker fire that followed. A tanker filled with 9,000 gallons of High Test will burn, big time. Sometimes the world just sucks."

"Yeah, thanks for telling me. Boat's this way. Let's walk on the left side; lots of blood on the other. Half the marina population has tracked through it, including me and Rusty. Couldn't be helped."

"You guys have majorly fucked up the investigation of this crime. You realize that, right? What did you say your name was? Phillips?"

"Yup, Lee Phillips."

"Your wife said "Doctor." I got it! Sumbitch!. You're that Dr. Lee Phillips; the one from the University in Austin. Shit, I know you! Well, I know of you. You're famous. You're the guy in the newspapers. You were in all the Law Enforcement journals about two, three months back. You're the guy that shotgunned that guy out at that west Texas state park ranch, then shot the other shooter in the eye. Right?"

"Yeah."

"Damn! Never thought I'd meet you. How'd you do it?"

"Got lucky. Look, I really don't like talking about it. They were trying to kill me; I shot 'em. I got lucky and I'm really grateful to be alive. I killed those guys. End of story. Lots of really vivid nights; not a lot of Alpha Wave sleep between then and now. How about we get on with this?"

"You bet. Sorry. Damn, what a night. No, shit; you're the guy. Wait 'til I tell 'em downtown. What a night!"

"Mine or yours?"

"Both, Dr. Phillips."

He asked and I answered, including the obvious: "What the hell is this stuff on the deck?"

"Puke, Roger's. Mine's inside. Started out as a pretty damned good New York strip and salad. And, to answer your next thirty questions, we found nothing else in or on the boat—well, except for the body. But then none of us have scoured the thing. I'd just like to get back to the real world. Do I really have to take you to the pilot house?"

"I really need to know exactly what you and this Roger person saw. Can you do that?"

We did; I did. Nothing left to puke.

"Dr. Phillips, did you or Roger search the cargo holds?"

"No. Look Buck, we were down there, but we were trying to save the boat. We didn't search anything; we just closed the sea cocks. We figured it would be better to wait for the cops for the rest of it. Our thought was that you guys might actually know what you're doing. You'd investigate all that stuff. That'd be right, yeah?"

He gave me that, "you really have not been paying attention to the operation of the real world look." But he was kind enough not to say that I was an absolute, complete and total idiot to my face.

"Take me to the pilot house. You don't mind if I call you Lee do you?"

"No, let's get on with it."

It looked just like it did on my first visit. Buck kicked open the pilothouse door.

"Holy Shit! This is a butcher shop, Dr. Phillips. What the hell happened here? Did you and your people see this?"

I relayed the story, minus most of the details.

"You OK going below?"

"No, I'm not OK. But yep, let's do it. Somebody has to. Rusty, you stay on the dock. Go." And he did.

Shrimpers are not exactly in the running for Best House Keeping Merit Badge. Most boats are manned by men whose sole purpose is to net as many shrimp as possible in the shortest possible time; bring 'em on board, sort 'em according to size, ice them down and get the catch to port as quickly as possible. That's when they get paid. About the only thing they all have in common are those really cool calf-high white rubber boots. Every shrimper on the North American Gulf Coast wears the damned things. They are available at every marine supply house and every discount store on the Texas and North Mexican Gulf Coast. They are the mark of a true shrimper. Frankly, I never understood why they chose white.

Meanwhile, during the trip, they absolutely must eat; they must sleep (at least a little) and they must catch, sort, size and ice the haul. Rudimentary is a very kind description of their accommodations. Matching china, checkered table cloths and paisley curtains are not in the cards.

Below decks was a mess, a jumble of soggy, smelly clothes, boots, rotting food and an odor that would make a garbage dump smell like the ladies' monthly Blue Ribbon garden party. The galley had not been under much water, but it too stank to high heaven. Nothing in the small propane fueled fridge except rotting meat, a six pack of Shiner and soggy vegetables. Opening the cabinets revealed mops, cleaning equipment and, in the back of one, a rifle—an AR-15, fully automatic, the civilian version of the AK-47. It was loaded with a twenty round magazine.

"Well, Lee, why would a shrimper need a rifle like this?"

"Damned if I know, Durham. Can we examine the damn thing top sides. This place reeks!"

"It's Buck; no shit Sherlock. What did you expect? At least there are no more bodies right here. Let's go below. We really gotta inspect the holds. You game?"

"What the hell; why not? But do I get a merit badge, or at least an oak leaf cluster or something for this effort?"

He gave me that goofy "you gotta be shitting me" look, probably reserved for children, mental defectives, and wayward college professors. And I fit a couple of those categories.

"No, but I am going to temporarily deputize you. That way when the judge asks if "appropriate" personnel participated in the find I can say "Yes, your Honor. Raise your right hand." I did. He did.

Using my Mag-Lite and his 12 volt 8 cell aluminum "cop" light we searched the mid-ships hold. Nothing. The aft hold was absolutely empty, except for the bilge water sloshing about two feet deep. The pumps would soon take care of that.

"Ready for the engine room, Lee? You know engines, yes?"

"Buck, I'm a historian. Bobby Rose is the owner. He knows engine rooms. I know what one should look and feel like. I'm not a diesel mechanic; but I'll go."

We searched the engine room. Those two big, mustard yellow Caterpillar Diesels looked like they should to me—to Buck too. We agreed that neither of us saw anything that did not normally belong. A search of the mid-ships added nothing.

"Hang on Lee, I got a call." He listened; I waited.

"Lee, you know anybody named 'Karl Marx,' spelled that way, with the K and the X? Or a Captain Jack "Coffee" Hays? Whoever it is, says it's important."

I smiled; nodded yes.

"Well, yes Agent Marx. You are acquainted with Dr. Phillips? Oh, I see; Marks with a K. Sure 'nuff; I'll turn you over to him. Yes, best wishes to you as well."

"Lee, what the hell is going on?"

"It's not Carl with a "K" and Marks with an "X". You're fucking with me, right?

"Sure Lee; where the hell you been?"

"Don't ask Carl. What's it been, four, maybe five months?"

"I hear we got a dead guy on the Intercoastal; makes it a Federal crime. I thought you and Lisa were on vacation after the Mariscal Canyon thing. What the hell is going on? You attract chaos like flies on cow shit. A guy with no head? Crap!"

I relayed as how Lisa and I were in need of a break and a short vacation. After my Mariscal Canyon adventure I'd had taken Bobby Rose up on his offer to baby sit his marina for a few weeks. Seemed sensible enough; he hadn't had a vacation in a while and he had a cutie in some Mexican coastal town about a hundred miles south of Matamoros. He wanted to spend time on the beach lying naked in a hammock with his honey in some beachside beer joint, getting laid and drinking beer. Lisa and I love the coast. Port Isabel was a no brainer. All had gone wonderfully until the middle of last night.

"Cut to the chase Lee."

"Carl, all I know is that until a few hours ago, I was in my nice secure bed nuzzled close to my very naked, very curvy wife in a semi-tumescent state, fully expecting to have a fantastic wake-up. Instead, Rusty drags my naked ass out of bed. There's a dead head in the #3 dryer. Far too quickly I'm standing on Bobby Rose's Marina dock with steak dinner puke on my toes, a head in the Laundromat, blood splattered all over the marina and the Laundromat, and the rest of the body duct taped to the destroyer wheel of a Mexican shrimper named *La Nuestra*

Señora. Her home port, stenciled on the cabin is Puerto Escondido, Vera Cruz. She was sitting, sinking, at the "T" end of the dock. How the hell do you think I feel? As we speak, I'm standing calf-deep in bilge water in the stinking hold of a formerly sinking shrimper, talking to an FBI agent. Marina customers are really seriously pissed, and I'm gonna be involved in yet another FBI investigation. How do you think I feel?

"And, you'll be happy to know, American capitalism thrives. I already have customers asking for live and dead bait and, most importantly, when we can get the goddamned bar open? What do you think?"

"Too damn bad Lee. Bar's not gonna be open today until I get my crew out of there. I'm sorry but you have to believe that. See you in a bit. I'm bringing Hays. It's his jurisdiction too. Put Durham back on. I need to talk to him."

What he must have said was: "Hold everybody there until we interview them. They can stay on their boats, hang out on the marina dock, send out for food courtesy of the U.S. government, but they have to be sober when we, the Feds and the Texas Rangers get there. Got it Durham?"

Durham passed the instructions on to the residents. To say that nobody was happy was an understatement. Folks were really pissed! Captain Mary was losing serious money, $5,000 a day. The other commercial boats, already in hock up to their ears, were losing money big-time. Everybody was out of luck for that day, including Bobby Rose. The live-aboards and the commercial captains, allowed to return to their boats, were steadily getting more and more stoned. Fortunately for them (not so good for the FBI and the Texas Rangers), most had well-stocked bars on board, so they made the best of it.

Meanwhile, Durham and I went back to the boat search. Only place left to look was the for'd hole. *Nuestra Señora* was down by the bow which meant she still had water there. We popped the for'd hatch, shined the lights and, "Shit, Lee, this one is still almost full."

For ten minutes brown/black water poured out the pump hoses.

"O.K., let's go."

And we did. I dropped down the ladder first, landing up to my knees in lukewarm salt water. I bent down, up to my armpits in this mess, and found it—a seacock that remained open. It took both hands to crank it closed, but almost instantly the water dropped as the pump worked. My light caught a reflection far forward.

"Durham, you might want to take a look at this. Quit worrying about getting your fingernails dirty. However, once you're down here, I do suggest that you not pick your nose or wipe your eyes until after undergoing a serious de-lousing program. This place must house every germ and bacteria known to mankind. But you really should see this."

"What is it?"

"Hey, you're the cop. I'm the other guy. You tell me. Get your ass down here."

I showed him. Stuck as far forward as possible was not one, but two bundles. It looked like they were wrapped black plastic garbage bags and sealed with duct tape. Durham sloshed forward, grabbed one, held it up, took his Leatherman knife and slit the thing from top to bottom. Out popped not one, not two, but four AK-47s. I grabbed one to keep it out of the water. He managed to hold on to the other three. We looked at each other with that "Oh, shit" stare and stood there for about four eternities, which was really only about five seconds.

"Somebody's in a lot of trouble, aren't we Durham?"

"Yes we are, Lee. What the hell? We have a tortured and murdered guy whose identity we don't know. We have a scuttled shrimper, and now we have two bundles of very illegal fully automatic rifles. I think this is a case for the FBI and the Homeland Security pukes. Fortunately, both groups are on their way. How about you? And besides I think we should get our asses out of this place and wait for the pros, who should be arriving shortly.

Made in the USA
Columbia, SC
02 July 2023

19877372R00161